Life,

Unscheduled

OTHER TITLES BY KRISTIN ROCKAWAY

The Wild Woman's Guide to Traveling the World
How to Hack a Heartbreak
She's Faking It

Young Adult

My Epic Spring Break (Up)

Life, Unscheduled

KRISTIN ROCKAWAY

 Montlake

Published by Montlake, Seattle

www.apub.com

Amazon, the Amazon logo, and Montlake are trademarks of Amazon.com, Inc., or its affiliates.

ISBN-13: 9781542027717
ISBN-10: 1542027713

Cover design and illustration by Liz Casal

Printed in the United States of America

For my almost-sisters,
Marci and Jessica

CHAPTER ONE

Parisa's wedding plans were extremely disruptive.

Let me be clear: I was absolutely thrilled for her. Mike was a great guy. Hardworking, intelligent, loving, supportive. He made Parisa radiate joy. If she wanted to have a magnificent celebration to honor their union, then dammit, that was what she deserved. And I would do whatever I could to help make her day as special as possible.

The problem was, I had plans of my own. A meticulously organized schedule, with important meetings and strict deadlines. I had to stick to them. Otherwise, I could kiss my hopes and dreams goodbye.

I wanted it to work—I *tried* to make it work—but in the end, there was no room in my schedule for both her plans and my plans. Inevitably, something important always got shunted aside. Someone was always disappointed.

The first time Parisa's wedding plans disrupted my schedule, I was eating lunch in the company dining hall. That was what they called the cafeteria at Virtuality: the "dining hall." Like we were college students instead of full-time employees. The food was far superior to anything you'd find on an undergraduate meal plan, though. For one thing, our menu was designed by the most recent winner of *Top Chef*. For another, it was free of charge.

On the day in question, I ordered a beef bulgogi bowl. I always ate bulgogi on Wednesdays. The line cook, Dwayne, knew exactly how I liked it—"No green onions for you, Nicole!"—and placed it on my tray with a warm, familiar smile. I took it over to my usual table in the back left corner, where I sat down next to my usual crew, Vimi and Ben. The three of us always ate lunch together. At least, when we didn't have to work through our lunch breaks.

"I can't stay long," Vimi said, between breathless bites of her sandwich. "I've got so much work to do."

"Neither can I. I've got a meeting at one." My mouth went dry at the thought of it. "With Jon."

"Your performance review?" Ben asked, casually scrolling through his phone.

"Yeah."

"You look nervous," Vimi said. "You know there's nothing to worry about, right? You always get a stellar review."

"I know." She was right. In the five years I'd been working here at Virtuality, I'd never received a rating lower than *4: Exceeds Expectations.* The highest rating there was.

I'd also never received a promotion.

Which, to be fair, was largely my fault. My performance was consistently stellar, but that was also true for most of the other five-hundred-odd employees at the company. This was Virtuality, a top-tier tech company specializing in cutting-edge artificial intelligence software. Their interview process was designed to root out the unproductive and unenthusiastic; they only hired the best of the best. So you couldn't just sit around and expect a promotion to fall in your lap. If you wanted one, you had to ask for it. And I'd never asked.

This year, I swore, would be different. This year, I would make my intentions clear. I was ready for growth, for change, for recognition of my accomplishments. It was time to reap the benefits of all my hard work. As soon as I finished this bulgogi bowl, I was going to march confidently into Jon's office and ask for that promotion.

Thing was, I didn't want to admit that to Vimi and Ben. What if Jon told me no? Then I'd be completely embarrassed. Instead, I said, "I've just got a lot on my mind."

"I feel you," Ben said. "I'm juggling four different projects right now."

"Yup." Vimi nodded, chewing frantically. "I've been sleeping at the office. Haven't been home since Sunday."

Such was life at Virtuality. Long hours, tight deadlines, multitasking to the max. We were all stretched thin, all putting in 110 percent of our efforts all the time. Which made me wonder why I deserved a promotion above anybody else. Vimi, Ben, and I were all junior user experience designers with comparable qualifications. Who was to say they weren't worthy of a senior title instead of me?

Popping a chunk of beef in my mouth, I tried to remember the talking points I'd outlined the night before. Nothing excessive, just some highlights from my Virtuality career to make my argument more persuasive. But my phone instantly dinged with a text message, derailing my train of thought.

CAN YOU BELIEVE IT?!?

It was Parisa. I hadn't heard from her in over two weeks, since before she and Mike had taken off on an epic New Year's island-hopping adventure in the South Pacific. They'd decided to leave their phones at home in LA. She called it "extreme digital detox." To me, it sounded like extreme torture.

This text must've meant she was back in the States, but I didn't understand the question. Was she asking if I could believe she'd survived two weeks without an internet connection? If so, the answer was no.

I plucked a thinly sliced radish from the top of my bowl, and the chopsticks made it halfway to my mouth before another message arrived. No words this time, just a photo of her extended left hand, deeply bronzed from the Fijian sun. A diamond ring sparkled on her third finger.

Parisa was engaged.

The radish slipped from my chopsticks and skidded down the front of my clean white shirt.

"Omigod!" I cried out.

"You okay?" Ben asked, his brow furrowed with concern.

"Yeah. I just found out my best friend is getting married."

"That's nice," Vimi said, a tinge of longing in her voice.

I wrote back, OMG congrats!

Thanks! she replied. He proposed on the beach in Bora-Bora. Caught me totally off guard.

Your ring is stunning, I wrote, and it truly was. Bright, clear, and classic, the round solitaire dazzled without being ostentatious. It suited her personality to a T. How do you feel?

Three dots bounced on the screen before disappearing and reappearing again. This went on for a while, as if she was thinking about the right way to answer my question. Finally, the reply: Like I'm about to embark on the adventure of a lifetime.

Considering she'd just returned from a once-in-a-lifetime trip to far-flung islands most people could only dream of visiting, that was quite a bold statement. Her life was one adventure after another. Mine was decidedly not.

But right now, she wrote, I need to sleep. My plane only landed like two hours ago, I just couldn't wait to tell you. We need to catch up once I'm over this jet lag. Dinner Friday?

I swiped over to my calendar app and perused Friday evening's schedule. At six o'clock, I was supposed to attend a live webinar at work. In theory, it was optional, but the whole design team was planning to grab food from the dining hall and gather in the fourth-floor conference room to watch it together. Afterward, we'd hit the office game room for our usual Friday-night tournament.

As I tapped my reply, another message popped up on my screen: And don't even try to tell me you are spending it in the office. You are

27 years old, it's a Friday night, and your BFF just got engaged. LIVE A LITTLE, NICOLE!

My thumbs froze midsentence. Normally, I wouldn't see any problem with my plans for Friday night. I spent most of my waking (and some of my sleeping) hours at the office, but it wasn't always about work. It was also about camaraderie and community. I ate my meals here and hung out with my friends. In a way, Virtuality was like my extended family.

But after all this talk of grand adventures, my Friday-night plans suddenly seemed small and sad. Like I didn't know how to live, even a little.

Friday's good.

Dinner with Parisa wasn't exactly an adventure, but it would at least be a change of scenery. I reconfigured my schedule, deleting the blocks of virtual time labeled *Webinar with the Design Team* and *Game Tournament* and adding *Dinner with Parisa* in their place.

There. That worked out nicely.

"I'm gonna skip out on the webinar this Friday night," I said.

Vimi stopped chewing and slid a sideways glance toward Ben, who squinted at me like he couldn't quite understand what I'd said. "Why?"

The tiniest twinge of discomfort took hold in the pit of my stomach. "I'm gonna have dinner with my friend. To celebrate her engagement."

Ben raised his eyebrows and went back to scrolling through his phone. Vimi swallowed and said, "That's nice."

I could tell they thought this was a terrible idea. And maybe they were right. Maybe I shouldn't be bailing on this webinar. It wasn't required, but I knew how things worked around here. Everyone else on the team would attend, making my absence all the more apparent.

I was about to ask my boss for a promotion. Now wasn't the time to start slacking off.

My smart watch buzzed against my wrist with a reminder for my performance review starting in five minutes. I hopped to my feet and said, "I gotta run."

"Good luck," Vimi said.

"You won't need it," Ben added. "You're golden."

"Thanks, guys."

Leaving my half-empty bulgogi bowl behind, I made my way to Jon's office. With each step I took, I felt the panic rising in my belly. What if I stumbled over my words? What if he laughed me out of the office? What if I wasn't going to get the good review I had been hoping for?

When I arrived at Jon's closed office door, there was a thin layer of sweat on my upper lip, and my heart was pounding like I'd run a marathon. Worrying about these what-ifs was throwing me off my game. The key to success was to stay calm, confident, and focused. I shook my head and took a deep, cleansing breath. *In-two-three-four, out-two-three-four.* Then I slapped on my most self-assured smile and knocked at the door.

"Come in," he called.

"Hi, Jon."

He motioned to the guest chair facing his desk. "Everything okay? You seem out of breath."

"Everything's great," I said, perhaps a bit too forcefully, then pointed to my smart watch. "Just trying to get my steps in whenever I can."

He nodded, my explanation making perfect sense. "I hear you. It's hard to find the time to exercise with everything else we've got going on around here. Have you tried one of those new treadmill desks they hooked up in the gym?"

"Not yet, but I'll definitely check them out soon." Truth was, I hadn't set foot in our state-of-the-art employee gym since I was hired. I had no intention of going now, especially not to try those new treadmill desks. Working out was not my favorite activity, to put it mildly.

"So . . . performance review." He clicked his mouse a few times, eyes scanning his computer monitor before flicking over to my face, then, ever so briefly, down to my chest. I followed his gaze to discover what was so distracting: a withered curl of radish clinging to the third button on my shirt.

Without a word, I plucked it off and flung it into the trash can beside his desk, leaving a streak of brown bulgogi sauce behind on the white fabric. I shifted, crossing my arms across my chest in an awkward attempt to hide the stain, but it was a pointless effort, considering he'd already seen it.

This was off to a bad start. I really wanted to put my best foot forward in this meeting, in every way possible. To appear calm, confident, and focused on the outside, even if my insides were riddled with anxiety and doubt.

Jon dived right into the review. "As usual, you're doing great. The design team benefits immensely from your contributions."

If I wasn't mistaken, this was the same exact thing he'd said to kick off our last performance review. And possibly the one before that.

"We can always depend on you to deliver on time and according to spec."

His praise was annoyingly vague, too. Frankly, it could've applied to anyone at Virtuality, in any department.

"Whether you're working independently or collaboratively, you always perform well under pressure and maintain a positive, can-do attitude."

Jon had been the director of product design for as long as I'd worked here. I wondered how many years he had spent in a junior role like mine, accepting murky, impersonal critiques from his manager, before he'd started to rise through the ranks.

"To wrap things up, your rating this period is a *4: Exceeds Expectations*. Keep up the good work, Nicole."

With a firm nod and a small smile, Jon turned his attention back to his monitor. It was a signal that we were done here, a cue for me to get up and return to my desk. But I wasn't going anywhere.

This year was going to be different.

After a moment of awkward silence, his eyes slid back to focus on me. "Is there something else you wanted to discuss?"

There was a lot I wanted to discuss. Unfortunately, now that I finally had the floor, I couldn't think of a single coherent thing to say. My brain had turned to sludge, all my thoughts jumbled together, none of them making sense. I couldn't remember my intentions or my talking points or why I even wanted this promotion in the first place. I was seized by the urge to hide under a big blanket and hope this problem would somehow work itself out.

Except Jon was starting to look concerned, which meant my window of opportunity was rapidly closing. I employed a few body language tricks to help myself appear more confident—chin up, shoulders back (bulgogi stain be damned!)—and launched into my speech.

"I've been a junior designer at Virtuality for five years now. I consistently go above and beyond my job requirements. I always put in extra hours, and I've never once missed a deadline. Every six months, you give me an excellent performance review, but I've yet to receive a promotion."

My heart raced, the blood swooshing through my ears as I waited for Jon to respond. He didn't say anything, though. He just sat there, staring at me as if I hadn't properly finished my thought.

Leaving no room for ambiguity, I said, "I'd like a promotion."

"Oh." He scratched the back of his neck and frowned down at his keyboard. "It's not that I don't think you deserve it, Nicole, but I can't make that decision myself. Every staffing change is subject to committee approval."

"Right." I'd heard of this practice but didn't know precisely how it worked. The company shrouded the whole process in secrecy, and no one who'd been through it was supposed to share details with their colleagues. The atmosphere at Virtuality was nothing if not highly competitive. "How can I go about pursuing committee approval, then?"

"You'll need to assemble a portfolio. Samples of your work, both for Virtuality and for your own personal projects. Written statements defending your request. Letters of recommendation."

I gripped the arms of the chair to avoid flinching. This sounded frighteningly similar to a college application. And what kinds of personal projects was he talking about? I didn't do anything outside of my work for Virtuality.

"Also," he continued, "you'll need to demonstrate some quantifiable accomplishment, usually by making a significant contribution to a successful, high-profile project."

"Can you assign me to a high-profile project, then?" I asked. "I'd really like the chance to prove myself."

He tapped his index fingers on the desktop as he mulled it over. "We're onboarding a new client—a *big* client—who wants a customized chatbot. I was going to give it to Charles, but if you're really interested, I can try to switch some things around on the project calendar."

Ugh, Charles. If Virtuality were really an extended family, Charles would've been my wicked stepbrother. He'd been hired last year on the design team as a senior user experience designer—a position *I* should've been given. There was no way I'd let him take another opportunity away from me.

"I am really interested," I said. "And I'd love to be involved."

"Are you sure? Management's hoping to get it out the door by June, so it's gonna be a lot of work on a tight timeline."

"I can handle it."

"Okay." He jotted something down on a Post-it, then said, "Let me get your name added to the project team. The kickoff meeting is being held next week."

"Great."

This time, when Jon turned his gaze toward his monitor to dismiss me, I immediately got to my feet, a smile spreading across my face. I'd done what I'd come here to do, and now my stagnant career was in forward motion. In hindsight, all that worry and dread seemed pointless.

As I opened the door, Jon called after me, "You're going to the webinar Friday night, right?"

"Of course." There was no way I could blow it off now. Parisa and I could meet up later in the evening, or maybe for brunch the next day. She'd understand my dilemma. Even though she often gave me a hard time about my workaholic tendencies, she understood how important Virtuality was to me. How closely entwined my sense of self was with my sense of professional accomplishment.

And now, after five years of grinding away and going nowhere, I was finally getting the chance to climb the org chart. These next six months would no doubt be challenging, but I was determined to knock this chatbot project out of the park and convince the committee to give me the promotion I so greatly deserved. All I had to do was work hard, stay focused, and minimize disruptions.

It sounded doable.

Little did I know what Parisa had planned.

CHAPTER TWO

When I told Parisa about my predicament, she suggested we meet for dessert instead of dinner.

There's a place on Beverly I've been wanting to try, she texted. Vespa. It's kind of schmancy, but their dessert menu looks insane.

Sounds good! I replied, my mouth already watering at the thought of a decadent dessert. Parisa knew all the good places to eat in LA, which was great, since I rarely ventured beyond the confines of the dining hall.

The webinar itself went well. I learned a lot of good stuff I could use for the chatbot project, and in the end, I was super glad I hadn't blown it off. It ended shortly after eight o'clock, at which point people started making their way over to the game room. Vimi said, "I've gotta bow out tonight. I'm behind on my work."

"Too bad. They just installed a vintage *Galaga* machine." Ben cracked his knuckles and turned to me. "Looks like it's just you and me, Palmieri. Ready to get your ass handed to you?"

"Actually, I'm not going either. Remember? I'm going out with my friend."

"Oh. I thought that got canceled."

"No, I just moved it so I wouldn't miss the webinar."

He frowned. "So I'm on my own?"

"Sorry. Next Friday, for sure." I patted him on the shoulder, then made a beeline for the door, but my foot had barely crossed the threshold when a familiar voice called, "Nicole?"

Ugh, Charles. I turned to see him striding toward me, wearing a strained smile, like his belt was cinched a little too tight. "How's it going?" he asked.

"Fine." Weird. Charles never asked me how it was going. "What's up?"

"Jon told me he assigned you to the big chatbot project."

Oh. That was what this was about. "Yeah. I'm really excited about it."

"I'll bet." His smile faltered a bit. "It's gonna be a huge undertaking. Lots of work. You feeling ready?"

"Absolutely. I've got a lot of ideas and—"

"Because I was thinking," he interrupted, "if you need some help, I'm available. I told Jon I'd be more than happy to join the project team, too."

And let him steal my thunder? I'd never get a promotion that way. "I think I'll be fine."

"You sure? I wouldn't want you to feel like you're out of your depth."

I clenched my right fist, my fingernails digging into the soft flesh of my palm. Considering I'd been working at Virtuality for five years—four years longer than Charles, by the way—it was more than a little insulting for him to imply this project was beyond my abilities. The truth was, I deserved the role he had right now. I deserved the bigger paycheck, the senior job title. This was my opportunity to prove it.

"Like I said, I think I'll be fine." I glanced at my watch, the universal signal for *Are you done yet?*

"Got somewhere to be?"

"Yeah, actually, I have reservations."

"Well, I won't keep you, then. But if you change your mind, let me know."

"Definitely." As in, *I will definitely not change my mind.*

I walked out of the conference room with my chin up and my shoulders back, leaving all thoughts of Charles and the chatbot behind. Tonight, we were celebrating Parisa's big news, and I wouldn't let work get in the way.

Our reservation was at nine, so I rushed home to change into appropriately kind-of-schmancy attire. After stripping off my jeans and sneakers, I put on a jumpsuit I'd bought nearly a year ago but had yet to actually wear. Using a flat iron, I gave my long brown hair some beachy waves, then topped off my ensemble with chandelier earrings, ballet flats, and my most fashionable pair of glasses—oversize cat eyes with a rose-gold frame. When I looked in the mirror, I couldn't help but smile. It felt good to get all dressed up.

I arrived at the restaurant five minutes early to find Parisa already seated at the bar. She wore a long, flowy, off-the-shoulder dress in a bright-pink tropical print. It was wholly inappropriate for the cool January weather, but by the dreamy look on her face, she was probably still on island time.

A guy stood next to her, chatting her up, as was usually the case whenever Parisa went out in public. She was stunningly gorgeous, with glossy black hair and huge brown eyes. Strapping men turned to puddles of goo in her presence.

Like this guy. He was easily six feet four, burly and broad and wickedly handsome, undoubtedly used to women fawning all over him. Yet he gave Parisa this sweet, overly familiar smile, one that clearly conveyed he was at risk of falling in love.

One glance at that rock on her finger, though, and there was no doubt she was spoken for. It twinkled brightly as she waved in my direction.

"Hi!" She squealed and wrapped her tanned arms around me, then pulled away, eyeing my jumpsuit. "Is this new?"

"Newish."

"I love it. You look amazing."

"So do you. Your tan, your dress, your ring. You're glowing."

"It's been a surreal couple of weeks." Her face flooded with joy, and I couldn't help but hug her again.

"I'm so happy for you."

As I formed the words, a surge of emotion sneaked up on me. This was a major milestone, one of those rare events that signified the beginning of a brand-new chapter of her life. Over the course of our decades-long friendship, we'd experienced quite a few of these at more or less the same time—getting our periods, learning to drive, graduating high school, cashing our first real paychecks—but this one seemed different somehow. More serious. More momentous.

Because this chapter of her life had a coauthor: Mike. And while I'd never speak this out loud, there was a small, sad part of me that felt like I was getting left behind.

Now wasn't the time to dwell on the arid wasteland that was my romantic life, though. It was the time to celebrate. Preferably with one of everything on this reportedly insane dessert menu.

Taking a seat beside Parisa, I turned to hook my purse on the back of the chair only to see that broad, burly, wickedly handsome guy lingering behind me, that same sweet smile on his face.

His gray eyes bounced from Parisa to me and back again. When she caught sight of him, she said, "Oh, I'm so sorry. Brandon, this is my best friend, Nicole. Nicole, this is Brandon. Brandon and I know each other from a long time ago, but it turns out he's the GM here at Vespa now."

"Hi, Nicole." He held out his hand for a shake, and I let his big palm envelop mine. "Pleasure to meet you."

"Likewise." Brandon had a slick undercut and the sharpest jawline I'd ever seen. I wondered how Parisa knew him. I didn't remember her ever mentioning a Brandon before she met Mike.

"Well," he said, dropping my hand, "I'll leave you ladies to it. Congratulations again, Parisa." And with a nod, he retreated into the crowded dining room.

As soon as he was out of earshot, I asked, "Is he an old hookup or something?"

"No. Remember when I worked on *Off the Grid*?"

Parisa was a makeup artist with a growing list of celebrity clients, but she also worked a lot of gigs on the sets of random reality TV shows. Lasting only one season, *Off the Grid* was a cross between *American Ninja Warrior* and *Man vs. Wild,* in which amateur wilderness enthusiasts were dropped in the middle of nowhere to compete against each other in survival challenges, such as building a shelter or foraging for food. The participants obviously had no need for a full face of makeup, but Parisa was responsible for keeping the host looking ruggedly handsome.

"Was Brandon a contestant?" Given his good looks and buff build, that wouldn't have been a surprise.

"He was the winner," she said. "I think he took home a couple hundred grand. I haven't seen him since the reunion show they taped in Vegas, though. I barely recognized him just now. He used to look like a grizzled mountain man, but he's cleaned up nicely."

"Yeah, he's cute."

Her eyebrows shot up. "I can ask him if he's single."

"Please don't embarrass me again." She was forever trying to set me up on dates, which to be fair was something I *did* need help with, but that wasn't what we were here for tonight. "Enough about him. Tell me everything about the proposal."

The dreamy look returned, her deep-brown eyes dancing in the dim light. "Well, we were staying in this beachfront villa in Bora-Bora. Super secluded and private, with an incredible view. We had dinner on our balcony overlooking the water and then went for a walk along the shore. Just as the sun was setting, he got down on one knee and pulled out the ring."

She extended her left hand so I could get a closer look. "It's gorgeous," I said. "Such a perfect style for you."

"And the diamond is ethically sourced! From the Ekati mine in Canada. He knew that was important to me."

"Did you have any idea this was coming?"

15

"Not at all. I was totally shocked." She wiggled her finger and watched the ring sparkle. "It was the best surprise I could ever ask for."

"Good evening, ladies." The bartender appeared, a bottle of champagne in her hands. "This is compliments of Brandon Phelps. He told me you're celebrating a very special occasion tonight?"

Parisa's eyes lit up. "How thoughtful of him!"

Presenting the bottle to us for approval, she asked, "Is this to your liking?"

I had no idea how to judge a bottle of champagne, so I deferred to Parisa, who nodded and said, "It's wonderful, thank you."

The bartender set out two coasters topped with two flutes, then popped the cork and poured. As the bubbles fizzed and settled, Parisa asked, "Can we see a dessert menu, please?"

"Sure." After depositing the bottle in an ice bucket, the bartender placed a small leather-clad folder on the bar before us. "I highly recommend the chocolate-bourbon mousse."

My salivary glands tingled at the very mention of it. "Okay, we're definitely getting that."

"I'll be back to take your order in a minute," she said, then hustled to the other end of the bar to prep an order.

Parisa lifted the bottle from the ice-filled bucket to examine the label. "This is expensive champagne."

"Well, then," I said, raising my glass. "It seems like a toast is in order."

She eyed me sideways. "Don't feel pressured to drink this on my account."

"I don't feel that way at all." Maybe I felt that way a little. But this was a special occasion, and there was an expensive bottle of bubbly, and I wasn't about to let my weird hang-ups about alcohol get in the way of celebrating my best friend's engagement. A few little sips of fizzy French booze wouldn't hurt me. "Just make sure I don't try to dance on the bar."

The concern on her face faded away, and we both laughed, remembering the reason I'd sworn off drinking in the first place. After all this time, I could finally laugh about it.

"I've got you covered." She raised her glass. "Thanks for coming out tonight."

"Of course. I'm so happy for you. Cheers."

We clinked our flutes, and that surge of emotion swelled within me again. My best friend was engaged to be married. She had found someone to spend the rest of her life with. She was in love—which was something I'd never experienced. And at this point, I wasn't sure I ever would.

All of a sudden, my throat felt tight. A generous gulp of champagne loosened it right up.

"This is delicious," Parisa said, and to my surprise, I agreed. It was cool, crisp, the perfect balance of sweet and tart.

She set her glass down in the center of her coaster and cleared her throat. "There's a reason I wanted to hang out tonight. I mean, aside from celebrating. There's something I need to ask you: Will you be my maid of honor?"

"What?"

"My maid of honor." She looked at me as though concerned for my health. "In the wedding."

"Are you serious?"

"I know it's a commitment, so if you don't want to, I understand. But we really want a small, simple wedding, and I—"

"No!" I cut her off instantly. "I mean, yes! Of course I'd love to be your maid of honor. I'm thrilled. Sorry, I just wasn't expecting you to ask me. What about Roxy and Leila?"

She grimaced and took a sip of champagne. "What about them?"

"They're your sisters. I'm assuming they expect you to ask one of them to be your maid of honor. Or even both of them together. Won't they be mad you asked me?"

"They'll be bridesmaids. And I don't really care if they're mad."

"Oh." I cared. When her twin sisters were mad, everyone suffered. I wasn't sure I could deal with their identical sour facial expressions and passive-aggressive commentary for however long this engagement was going to last.

"Anyway," she continued, "I've always felt closer to you than to them. You know that. I love them, but you're the person I trust the most in this world, the one I want to stand by my side through this whole thing."

"I'd be honored." My voice caught on the last word. While it was true I had yet to experience the thrill of a serious romantic relationship, in that moment, I had never felt more special, worthy, or loved.

As I washed down my imminent sobs with a healthy swig of champagne, Parisa consulted the dessert menu to complete our celebratory feast. We settled on three dishes to split—the caramel-apple upside-down cake, the coconut-cream bread pudding, and the chocolate-bourbon mousse—then indulged in sugary goodness as Parisa regaled me with tales of her trip. She'd gone snorkeling in Tahiti, sailing in Fiji. It had been two weeks of straight-up adventure.

"What'd you do for New Year's Eve?" she asked, spooning a heap of custardy bread pudding into her mouth.

"Nothing." That wasn't precisely true. I'd actually worked until ten o'clock, then swung by the dining hall to grab a late dinner before watching a time-delayed recording of the Times Square ball drop in the TV room with Vimi and some people from the engineering team.

"You didn't go out?" When I didn't answer, she said, "Do I need to stage an intervention, Nicole?"

My gaze dropped to my champagne flute, which was still half-full. "For what?"

"Your workaholism is affecting your life negatively in the following ways. Number one—"

"Okay, okay, I get it."

"You have no social life."

"That's not true. It's just that most of my social life overlaps with my work life."

"Yeah, and don't you think there's something strange about that?"

"No. Virtuality is like a family." I took a frustrated gulp of champagne. The bubbles burned the back of my throat.

"Some family. They run you ragged with their ridiculous workload, and they've never even offered you a promotion. They've had you locked into the same position for years."

"For your information, I'm up for a promotion right now."

She smiled widely. "Oh! Well, that's great! So we have two reasons to celebrate tonight! What's your new job title?"

"Well, I haven't been promoted *yet*. There's a whole protocol involved. First, I have to submit a portfolio to this committee . . ." I couldn't bring myself to finish the sentence. Now that I said it out loud, the whole idea of a promotion committee seemed absurd. Who was even on it? Why wasn't Jon's feedback alone sufficient to justify a bump in my pay grade? He was the one who oversaw my efforts, who doled out my assignments, who witnessed the hours I spent toiling away at my desk every day.

Absurd as it seemed, though, I just had to accept it. Virtuality was one of the most prestigious tech companies in the world. Working there was the ambitious career woman's version of attaining the Holy Grail. If I didn't want to play along with their promotion protocol, there'd be plenty of other people who'd be happy to take my place. And I wasn't giving up so easily.

"It's as good as mine," I said.

Parisa shoved a forkful of apple cake into her mouth, then chewed slowly and thoughtfully. After she swallowed, she wiped her mouth with the edge of her napkin and said, "Look. You give that company a lot of your time. Time is your most precious commodity, and you'll never get it back, so . . . I just really hope they do right by you. That's all."

"They will."

I spoke with confidence, punctuating my reply with another large sip of champagne. Because I truly believed they'd do right by me. Besides, I was going to rock this chatbot project so hard there'd be no legitimate reason for the promotion committee to turn me down.

The moment I drained my glass, Brandon appeared behind the bar. "Everything tasting okay, ladies?" His eyes fell on our empty plates, and his lips curled into a smile as he glanced my way. "Looks like you enjoyed the desserts."

Before I knew what was happening, words gushed out of my mouth in a seemingly endless stream of nonsense. "They were amazing. So scrumptious. I could eat, like, three more of them. Particularly that mousse. The bartender was so right about it."

Good Lord. This was why I didn't drink. One glance from a gorgeous guy, and I suddenly had verbal diarrhea.

Fortunately, Parisa jumped in to save me. "Everything was truly fantastic. And thank you so much for this champagne. It's delicious."

"My pleasure." Brandon plucked the bottle from the ice bucket and refilled our flutes. Under no circumstances was I going to drink a second glass of champagne—one was clearly more than enough for me—but it would've been rude to tell him to stop pouring.

Parisa sipped her drink and asked him, "Do you do private events here? I'm looking for a place to host my bridal brunch. Someplace intimate and informal where all the members of the bridal party can meet and get to know each other."

"Yeah, we have a couple of options available. How many people are you expecting?"

"Probably about ten."

Brandon handed her his card and said, "Text me with the date you're looking at, and I'll see what I can do for you."

"Awesome. Thanks so much."

"No problem."

He smiled at Parisa, then at me, and I quickly averted my eyes, staring down at my lap to avoid another episode of mindless blathering. When he walked away, I took off my glasses and wiped them with the corner of my napkin. Somehow, they'd gotten fogged up.

"I'm totally gonna ask him if he's single," Parisa said.

"Don't. Please. I'm embarrassed enough as it is." I put my glasses back on and asked, "So, who else is going to be in your bridal party?"

"Roxy and Leila, obviously. Mike has a sister, so she'll be involved, and my mom is basically forcing me to ask my cousins, Shirin and Ally, but they're actually cool, so I don't mind. Then I want to ask Kara."

"Oh, yay! I haven't seen her in years." Parisa had met Kara on the set of her first reality show gig, *Strike a Pose*, where Kara had been a contestant who'd walked the runway competing for a modeling contract. Now she was a big-time model who lived in New York and traveled the world.

"I know; she's hardly ever in LA these days."

"So you'll have six bridesmaids."

"Yep."

That was a lot, wasn't it? Maybe not. I didn't know much about weddings or how they worked. I'd have to start doing some research. "Have you set a date yet?"

"Not an exact date," she said, "but we want to do it in June."

"Of next year?" That gave me plenty of time to get up to speed on current wedding trends.

"No. This year."

That did not give me much time at all. "That's soon."

"Yeah, but I really don't want to drag the engagement out longer than necessary. You know me: once I decide to do something, I wanna get it done. If I had my way, we'd be going to the Little White Wedding Chapel tomorrow, but our families would kill us. Six months is just enough time to book a halfway-decent place and buy a dress and send out invitations. And, of course, have an epic bachelorette party."

She nudged me with her elbow and giggled. Forcing out a laugh, I reached for my champagne flute and took a big swallow to camouflage the panic rising in my chest.

The chatbot redesign was scheduled to go live in June. For the next six months, I was planning to devote 110 percent of my time and effort to proving my worth at Virtuality. Now I had to find space on my schedule for a bachelorette party.

And dress fittings.

And a bridal brunch.

And whatever else a dutiful maid of honor was supposed to take part in.

Parisa furrowed her brow. "Is everything okay?"

"Yeah, why?"

"You look a little queasy. Maybe you should take it easy on the champagne."

She was right. I should've taken it easy on the champagne. But drinking was an easy way to stem the tide of anxious thoughts that were rapidly consuming my brain. Thoughts I couldn't share with Parisa. As her maid of honor, I was supposed to ease her burdens, not pile more problems on her plate.

So instead, I lifted my glass, slapped on a smile, and told her, "I'm totally fine."

That was my last clear memory of the night.

CHAPTER THREE

Here's a fun fact: champagne gets you drunk faster than other alcoholic beverages. It's true. The bubbles increase the pressure in your digestive system, which makes your body absorb the alcohol faster. In other words, a little bit of fizzy French booze goes a long way toward getting you lit.

Which explains why I didn't even have to finish that second flute before my memories started getting all fuzzy and fragmented. Fortunately (or perhaps unfortunately), Parisa helped me fill in the gaps. As soon as I woke up the next morning, I called her for details.

"You tried to dance on the bar."

I groaned and turned over, burying my face in the pillow. Vespa was an upscale, trendy dining establishment, not some stanky dive. What on earth was I thinking?

"Please tell me I didn't actually go through with it."

"No, of course not," she said. "I told you I had you covered. Brandon and I had to physically restrain you, though."

My stomach lurched. "Brandon saw all this happening?"

"Oh yeah. You spent a lot of time chatting him up."

"What was I saying?"

"I'm not totally sure. You were talking so fast I couldn't always follow along."

This was a nightmare. "Why did you let me do that?"

"It's not like I could stop you. The yip-yap just kept coming out of your mouth. It was pretty entertaining, though. At one point, you squeezed his bicep and asked him if he ever had to fight with any wild animals on *Off the Grid.*"

Her giggle pierced the softest parts of my brain. "This isn't funny."

"It's kind of funny."

"How did I get home?"

"We split a ride share. I dropped you off first to make sure you were safe." She giggled again. "You made the driver play this awful Post Malone song on repeat the entire ride."

"What is wrong with me?"

"Hey, I warned you to take it easy on the champagne."

"I only had two glasses!" Though, come to think of it, I couldn't remember what had happened after I'd drunk that second one. "Didn't I?"

"You sneaked a third glass when I got up to go to the bathroom. I cut you off after that."

"Thanks. I'm sorry I was such a mess."

"Don't be sorry. It could've been way worse." She paused, then added, "At least you didn't break a tooth."

I rolled onto my back, gripped by a sudden wave of nausea. The tip of my tongue reflexively stroked the back of my top left incisor. Or, rather, the porcelain crown that had replaced my top left incisor. I'd broken the real one back in college, when I'd fallen off that bar I'd been dancing on.

It happened early on during my freshman year. High school had been rough, socially speaking, but at least I'd had Parisa. Once I got to college, though, I was on my own. If I wanted to make friends, I had to put myself out there, and mingling with strangers and making small talk proved to be challenging. It was always so hard for me to start a conversation. It wasn't that I was shy, exactly. More like I was terrified of being judged and, ultimately, rejected.

But I soon found a way to cope with my fear: drinking. I'd purposely avoided alcohol all through high school; my mother was a big drinker, and let's just say I didn't want to end up like her. College was a different story, though. Every event was dripping with alcohol. It felt completely unavoidable. Also? It was the perfect social lubricant. With every sip I took, I became more relaxed and chatty and totally unworried about what people thought about me.

My roommate, Angelica, fast became my drinking buddy. We'd go to bars and clubs and parties, then stumble back to our dorm room in the early morning hours. Too often, we'd take turns holding each other's hair back as we puked.

One night in September, we went to a frat party together. It was in a filthy house with an unfinished basement stacked with kegs and kegs of beer. There were so many people, so many good-looking guys. The thought of talking to them terrified me. So the moment I walked in the door, I filled a red Solo cup to the brim with whatever beer was in those kegs and kept drinking until I blacked out.

I don't remember much about what happened after that. All I know is that I thought it would be a good idea to dance on a makeshift bar in that filthy unfinished basement. At some point, I fell off and smacked my face on the hard wooden edge of a pool table, busting open my bottom lip and obliterating my left front tooth. I have vague memories of writhing around on the concrete floor as my mouth filled with blood. My vision was blurry, since my glasses had flown off my face, but I could tell there were strangers standing over me, whispering. A few even laughed. Their cell phones were out, recording my misery as I launched into a full-scale anxiety attack, screaming and crying and carrying on.

Angelica took me to the hospital in a cab. The nurse gave me some Ativan to calm my nerves, then sent me home with seven stitches and a referral to a local cosmetic dentist. When my dad saw the insurance claims, he was furious. I had to pay him back every last penny of the

Kristin Rockaway

medical bills. Worse still, he told me I was turning out to be just like my mom.

As if bleeding and panicking in the middle of a frat party weren't bad enough, videos of my injury started making the rounds. Soon, there wasn't a single person on campus who hadn't witnessed Nicole Palmieri making an absolute ass of herself in the basement of the Sigma Alpha Epsilon house.

That was the last time Angelica and I had gone out drinking. In fact, I'd stopped drinking altogether and thrown myself into my schoolwork instead. Studying was far more rewarding than socializing. In class, you were never judged for your looks or your personality or your willingness to do a keg stand. You were judged solely on your efforts. Do a good job, get a good grade. It was all so cut and dried. And there was zero chance of breaking a tooth.

"That was a bad joke," Parisa said, cutting through the infinite silence. "Sorry."

"No, it's fine. I just have a headache."

"Get on Instacart and order some Gatorade, coconut water, and a bunch of bananas. You'll feel better in no time."

After ending the call, I did just that, then opened my calendar app to check my schedule for the day:

Saturday, January 9
8:00 a.m.: 10-minute morning meditation
8:10 a.m.: Shower & get ready
8:45 a.m.: Breakfast @ the dining hall
9:00 a.m.: Work (see task list)

My pulse instantly spiked. Considering it was currently 11:42 a.m., my morning plans were already shot to shit.

I hated when this happened. Normally, I was a very "live and die by the schedule" type of person. Some people called me "uptight" (Parisa) or "a stress case" (also Parisa), but organizing my time into manageable, predetermined chunks helped me know what to expect from my days. And that made me feel like I had a handle on things. Like I was in control of my own life.

Thankfully, today's scheduling snafu was an easy problem to solve. I'd planned to work until six, then grab dinner at the dining hall before going home and bingeing Netflix until I passed out. To compensate for my wasted morning, I pushed everything forward four hours so meditation started at noon and work ended at ten. If I stayed up late, there was still a chance I could sneak in a decent Netflix binge.

The simple act of rearranging my schedule calmed my nerves. My heart rate returned to normal; my anxiety subsided. Everything was right with the world.

Plus, I had a few minutes to spare before my first task began. Just enough time to take a quick snooze, which would hopefully relieve the remnants of this hangover.

No sooner had I closed my eyes than my phone dinged with an incoming text:

> You doing okay today?

It was from an LA area code, but I didn't recognize the number. Probably spam or a misdial. I ignored it and set my phone down on the mattress beside me, but thirty seconds later, it dinged again:

> I think I found one of your earrings behind the bar.

My eyes darted to the jewelry dish on my nightstand, where a single chandelier earring rested, its mate nowhere to be seen.

Good Lord.

With trembling thumbs, I texted Parisa: Did you give Brandon my number?!?

No, she responded. You gave it to him. You actually snatched his phone from his back pocket and typed it in yourself. Honestly, I've never been prouder of you.

Three glasses of champagne. That was all it took to transform me from a socially anxious introvert to a man-chasing blabbermouth.

I wanted nothing more than to pretend last night had never happened. That Brandon Phelps didn't know my name or my number or my embarrassingly low tolerance for alcohol. But he did, and there was no undoing that now. So I texted him a sincere, sober apology.

> Thank you so much.

> And I'm really sorry about last night.

> I don't usually drink like that.

> I don't usually drink at all.

There's nothing to apologize for.

I've seen way worse, trust me.

Although no one has ever tried to dance on our bar before.

That was a first. 😆

I wanted to crawl into a hole and never come out.

> BTW I've got your earring,
> so whenever you wanna pick it up, just swing
> by Vespa.
>
> Or I can drop it off.
>
> If that's easier for you.

No.

Text message apologies were one thing, but there was no way I could come face to face with Brandon ever again. The embarrassment would melt me from the inside out.

> That's okay, they were cheap.
>
> You can just throw it away.
>
> Thanks, though.

Three dots bounced on the screen, then disappeared, then reappeared. With all the typing going on, I expected a long reply, but all he sent was a thumbs-up emoji. Then nothing.

There. That wasn't so bad. Now I could put that unpleasant evening behind me forever. Hopefully, no one had been recording my nonsense. If I became fodder for yet another viral video, I might have to consider faking my own death and starting over with a pseudonym.

According to my phone, it was now 11:58, which gave me two minutes of peace before my day began in earnest.

Two minutes of peace that Parisa promptly disrupted with a text.

> Did Brandon call you or something?
>
> He texted.

Told me he found one of my earrings.

😆

He offered to return it to me but I told him to throw it away.

I'm too mortified to face him.

I am never going back to Vespa.

Um, yeah you are.

For my bridal brunch.

OMG.

Please hold it somewhere else.

Sorry . . . I already booked it.

You're kidding.

Right?

No, I had to snag it. That place books up fast, I was lucky they had an opening!

Made a deposit this morning, invites go out next week.

Love you! 💜

The clock flipped to noon.

I swiped over to my meditation app and loaded a ten-minute guided session themed around calming your nerves. As the narrator instructed me to breathe *in-two-three-four* and *out-two-three-four*, I scanned my body for feelings of physical tension, trying my best to commit her words to memory so I could recall them whenever I needed them.

Then I set all thoughts of Parisa and her wedding aside and got ready for a long day of work.

CHAPTER FOUR

The following Tuesday, I was the first person to arrive for the chatbot project kickoff meeting. I took a seat toward the front of the conference table, eager to let the project manager know exactly how motivated I was to do a good job. When she walked in, I introduced myself. "Hi, I'm the design lead, Nicole Palmieri."

"I'm Anna." She nodded curtly, regarding my outstretched hand as if it were contaminated, then began setting up her presentation.

As the room filled up, I stole glances around the conference table. I'd seen most of these people around the office, but I'd never actually talked to any of them before. I wondered if they were gunning for promotions of their own.

Then again, maybe they were already senior members of their respective teams. No one else looked the slightest bit nervous. Certainly not as nervous as I felt.

In-two-three-four, out-two-three-four.

"Welcome, everyone." Anna had a faint Russian accent and a strong, confident voice. It reverberated around the tiny conference room and made people sit up and take notice. I wished I had that kind of voice. "We're here to kick off one of this year's most highly anticipated projects. It's going to be a lot of work in a short period of time, implementing new features that will take Virtuality's chatbot product to the next level. I've been assured by each of your directors that you are the best candidates to get the job done. I assume you're all ready for the challenge that lies ahead."

She made deliberate eye contact with every person in the room. When her blue eyes landed on me, I flinched and shrank down into my chair. But I had to remind myself there was no need to be nervous. After all, Jon must've told her I was the best candidate for the job. I deserved to be here, even if Charles thought otherwise.

"Our sales team just signed the contract last week, and we're ready to hit the ground running. So without further ado, I present to you our newest client." Anna tapped her tablet, and the monitor flashed with the logo for Krueger-Middleton, the company that provided health insurance for all Virtuality's employees.

"Krueger-Middleton is the fastest-growing managed medical-care system in the United States. Last year, their health plan and hospitals reported a combined fifty-six billion dollars in net revenue, and they're predicted to grow at least eight percent in the next two years. To maintain their competitive edge, they want to employ a customized Virtuality chatbot that will empower patients to take charge of their health care."

Interesting. Our intelligent chatbots were already used in a wide variety of industries. They helped people book flights or diagnose car problems or investigate fraudulent credit card activity, all through straightforward text messaging. The conversations were so natural, so personalized, most people who interacted with them had no idea there wasn't an actual human on the other end.

As Anna advanced through her presentation, though, I started to get nervous. Our product was designed for customer-service inquiries— making appointments, paying bills, that sort of thing. But Krueger wanted it to diagnose illnesses and deliver treatment plans. They wanted more than a chatbot; they wanted a doctor bot. And as the design lead, it was my job to make it intuitive and easy to use.

Jon hadn't been kidding when he'd said it was going to be a lot of work.

"Naturally," Anna said, "this means the conversations will need to change. Krueger's chatbot must be familiar with medical terminology, communicate with both authority and empathy, and determine when human intervention is necessary. We'll need to conduct interviews, both with administrators and medical professionals, to get our messaging right. This will require quite a bit of time working on site with the client, particularly for you."

She pointed at me. Conducting interviews with clients was a regular part of my job, but I generally did them over video chats or phone calls. Rarely did I ever have to make an on-site visit. Those were always reserved for the more senior team members. "Will there be any traveling involved?"

"Many of Krueger's offices are located in the LA area, but their headquarters are in Oakland, and they do have a major hub in Phoenix. So yes, there will be some travel involved. We've already developed a tentative schedule, which I'll share with you when the meeting is over."

"Great." How exciting! I never traveled anywhere. Not that Oakland or Phoenix were all that far, but still, it'd be nice to have a change of scenery.

"In and of itself," Anna said, "this is a lucrative business opportunity. But we also have the opportunity to revolutionize health care as we know it. This could lead to very big things, not just for Virtuality but for the entire human race."

In hindsight, this statement seemed a bit grandiose. But in the moment, I was shaking with enthusiasm. Because I truly believed Virtuality could change the world for the better. I envisioned this chatbot being used to help people who didn't have immediate access to medical care, like those living in remote rural regions. A few simple text messages could help them prevent a minor ailment from becoming a major catastrophe. And I would be partly responsible for making it happen!

"As I said before," she continued, "we're working on an extremely tight timeline, with a hard go-live date of June fifth. You can review all the interim deadlines on the project plan I'll be distributing as soon as we disperse."

Anna ended the meeting, and I left the conference room with my body buzzing and my brain overflowing. There was so much to process, so much to plan. I'd dive in as soon as lunch was over.

In the dining hall, Dwayne had my usual Tuesday-afternoon quinoa salad at the ready—"Extra avocado, just the way you like it, Nicole!" I thanked him and headed to our table in the back left corner, where Vimi and Ben were already sitting.

"Hey," I said, dropping into an open chair. "How are you guys?"

Vimi scrubbed a hand over her face. "Tired."

"Same." Ben gave me the once-over with his bloodshot eyes. "You look awfully chipper, though."

"Do I?" Now that he mentioned it, I realized I was smiling.

"Yeah." Vimi narrowed her eyes suspiciously. "What gives?"

"I'm in a good mood, that's all. Jon assigned me to this new project for a big health care company. It's gonna be a lot of work, but it seems really cool. I'm excited."

"Is that the Krueger-Middleton chatbot?"

"You've heard of it?"

Ben nodded. "Charles was complaining about how he wanted to work on it. I'm glad you got the lead design role instead of him."

"Seriously," Vimi said. "That guy's a total tool."

"Do you think this means you'll get a promotion?" Ben asked.

I froze with my fork lifted halfway to my mouth. I wasn't sure whether to admit that I was gunning for a promotion. Ben and Vimi were my friends, but they were also my colleagues, and at Virtuality, that introduced an uncomfortably competitive dynamic. Not that I thought they'd sabotage me, but there were just certain things you didn't speak about around the office. You never bad-mouthed the company's strategy, told anyone the size of your paycheck, or shared your aspirations for climbing the org chart. Besides, what if they wanted the promotion I was gunning for? Then it would make things awkward and tense.

To play it safe, I shrugged. "I don't know."

"Who's the project manager?" Ben asked, stabbing a fork into his bowl of pasta.

"Anna . . . something. I forget her last name. I've never worked with her before."

"Anna Nikolaevsky?"

"Yes, that's it."

Vimi and Ben shuddered simultaneously.

Uh-oh. "She's bad?"

"She's intense," Vimi said.

"Just don't piss her off," Ben added. "I once went around her to ask a client to clarify a requirement, and she threw me off the project."

Yikes.

I could *not* get thrown off this project if I wanted a promotion. I was going to have to make Anna happy, right from the start. So I housed my quinoa salad as quickly as possible, then returned to my desk, ready to get down to business and organize my thoughts.

First, a document titled *Chatbot Kickoff Brain Dump* containing stream of consciousness–style ramblings about everything I'd learned in the meeting and all the ideas I had for making the project a success. Next, a to-do list with action items, like researching Krueger-Middleton and the health care industry in general.

Finally, I opened my calendar and set my schedule for the next five months, culminating in the big go-live date of June 5. It was the first Saturday of the month. One hundred and forty-four days from now. A lot could happen in 144 days.

And a lot would *have* to happen, according to these requirements. As I plugged time estimates for each task into my calendar, I quickly realized that between this and all the travel I'd be doing, I'd need to work a lot of nights and weekends to get this project finished on time. Which was fine, really, since I already worked a lot of nights and weekends. But now there was just no room in the schedule to account for errors. I had to get things right the first time. No mistakes, no excuses.

Maybe I shouldn't have been so quick to dismiss Charles's offer to help.

No! That was quitter talk. I was perfectly capable of doing this on my own. All I had to do was push myself a little harder, a little further, and that promotion was as good as mine.

I was halfway through scheduling the month of March when an email notification popped up on my phone screen. It was a Paperless Post invitation from Roxana Shahin, a.k.a. Roxy, a.k.a. Parisa's little sister.

~

She Said Yes!
Please join us for a party honoring the engagement of

Parisa Shahin

&

Michael Lundgren

Date & Time:
Sunday, January 24, at 12:00 p.m.

Venue:
Vespa
8109 Beverly Boulevard
Los Angeles, California

Attire:

California Brunch Chic
RSVP to Roxana Shahin by Sunday, January 17

∽

There was a lot to unpack here.

First, what on earth was "California Brunch Chic" attire?

Second, why was Roxy sending out the invitations for the bridal brunch? I figured if Parisa needed help, she would've asked me for it, but should I have preemptively stepped in and offered to do this? Not even a week had passed, and I was already proving to be a shitty maid of honor.

Third, and perhaps most concerning, why were there forty-three people on the guest list? Parisa had said she was only inviting ten.

I texted her: Hey, just saw the invite for your bridal brunch and . . . I have questions.

Two seconds later, the phone was buzzing in my hand.

"I'm going to murder my sister."

"Okay, back up a second," I said. "What happened?"

"I told my mother we weren't having an engagement party, and she flipped out on me. Then she called Mike's mother, and the two of them decided to hijack the bridal brunch and turn it into this big ordeal. So of course Roxy stepped in and took over planning it because she can't mind her own business. Did you see that 'California Brunch Chic' bullshit?"

"Can you call it off?"

"It's too late. The invites just went out. I'd look ridiculous if I canceled it now. Plus, Mike's parents are already annoyed because I refuse to get married in a church. I don't want to make things worse with them." She heaved a world-weary sigh.

"Well, is there anything I can do to help you? Should I step in and help plan the party? I feel bad that I let this happen."

"No, don't even get involved in this ridiculous party. Let them handle it. And you have nothing to feel bad about; this wasn't your fault."

"Yeah, but I'm your maid of honor. It's my job to protect you from stuff like this, isn't it? I should be keeping all these rogue family members in line or something."

She laughed. "There isn't a person alive who could keep my family members in line. And now with Mike's mom in the mix? Wait until you meet her. She gives my mom a run for her money."

I laughed, too, because I didn't want to let on how absolutely terrified I was. As if dealing with Roxy and Leila and their mom wasn't going to be challenging enough, now I had Parisa's future mother-in-law to contend with. I wasn't cut out for contention and conflict. Why couldn't everyone just be nice to one another?

"Honestly," she said, "if they want to throw an engagement party, I say let them go nuts. As long as they don't make it my problem. Or *your* problem. Wedding planning does not interest me at all. There's only one thing I really care about."

"What's that?"

"The bachelorette party. I want an epic, amazing throwdown in Vegas. Fine dining, bottle service, poolside cabana, suite with a view. I wanna keep it classy, so no strip clubs or anything. You know what I like, so I want you to plan it for me."

"Absolutely!" I had no idea how to plan a bachelorette party. I'd never even been to Vegas. But for Parisa, I would do my best.

"Yay!" She let out an excited squeal. "It's gonna be so great. My last hurrah." There were voices in the background, and Parisa said, "Oh shit, Nicole, I gotta go. There's a false-eyelash emergency. I'll talk to you later. Love you."

"Love you," I said, to dead air.

My phone screen reverted to the bridal-brunch invitation—or, rather, the engagement-party invitation. I selected *Will Attend* and tapped the link to add the event to my calendar. Instantly, the app warned me of a conflict; one of my chatbot tasks was already scheduled for that day. I'd blocked out six hours for it, from 10:00 a.m. to 4:00 p.m.

No worries. I could simply move it to the evening hours, from 5:00 p.m. to 11:00 p.m. Surely the party would be over by 5:00 p.m., right? All I'd have to sacrifice was a nighttime Netflix binge. And probably some sleep.

But there'd be a lot more wedding-related stuff to cram into my schedule over the next few months. Unfortunately, there wasn't a lot of free space to cram it into.

Still, I convinced myself everything was going to be fine. I'd just have to take it one event at a time. First up: this bridal brunch turned engagement party. Parisa was stressed out about her family seizing the reins, but I was sure she'd have a blast. And so would I. All I had to do was avoid the bar and hide under a table every time Brandon walked into the room.

No problem. Everything was going to be fine.

CHAPTER FIVE

The back room at Vespa looked like something out of an event planner's Instagram account. By the entrance, there was a sign propped on an easel that read **WELCOME TO PARISA AND MICHAEL'S ENGAGEMENT PARTY** in big brush lettering. Beside it was a table covered with place cards. Apparently, this was an assigned-seating sort of situation.

I found mine—*Nicole Palmieri, Table 2*—and stepped inside. There were already a lot of people here, which was surprising, since I was fifteen minutes early. On second glance, though, I saw they were all busy setting things up. Hanging garlands and fluffing up flower arrangements. I probably should've arrived even earlier to help out. Yet another strike against me, the world's shittiest maid of honor.

"Nicole!" Parisa ran toward me. Or rather trotted, since the platform heels she wore weren't conducive to running. She hugged me, then said in a low voice, "Thank God you're here. My family's driving me bonkers."

I peered over her shoulder to see Roxy and Leila squabbling over where to place a bouquet of confetti balloons. "Did your sisters do all this decorating?"

"Yes. It's so over the top, isn't it?"

"I don't think so." I'd been picturing something slightly more understated for this brunch, like a casual gathering where you could choose your own seat, but this was actually pretty nice. I kind of wished Roxy and Leila had included me in the planning, though. Of course, it wasn't like I had any time for that. Besides, from the grimace on Parisa's face, she wasn't exactly thrilled with what was going on around her. "Are the decorations really bothering you that much?"

"Yes. No. I don't know. *That's* definitely bothering me, though." She gestured to the corner, where a few neatly wrapped presents sat on a long table. "My mother set up a registry for me. This was supposed to be a small brunch for the bridal party, not a way to get more gifts. Everyone's already going to give me stuff at the wedding. It's double-dipping."

"Don't worry, I think engagement-party gifts are pretty standard." At least, that was what I'd read on the Knot. A few days earlier, I'd started my maid of honor research at full force. I'd even found a checklist online that included duties like going dress shopping and assembling invitations. It was immensely helpful in organizing my schedule.

The checklist also said my number one priority was to be a good, supportive friend. Weddings were stressful, and brides could get easily overwhelmed. So even though Parisa was feeling less than positive about this whole engagement party, I still needed to make sure she relaxed and had a good time. "Can I get you a drink or something?" I asked.

"Oh, thanks, but I already ordered one. It better come soon. I need it before my mother-in-law gets here."

"Where is she?"

"Mike's grabbing her from the hotel right now. She drove up from Orange County with his dad and sister last night."

Oh, right. I'd forgotten her future sister-in-law would be in the bridal party. "How old is his sister, anyway?"

"Sixteen."

"So I guess she won't be going to Vegas?"

"Sadly, no." Parisa didn't look very sad about it. Frankly, I wasn't very sad about it either. The fewer people I had to coordinate for the bachelorette party, the easier it would be. "It'll just be you, me, my cousins, and Kara. And my sisters, unless I can convince them to stay home, but that's unlikely. Oh, here it is!"

Her whole face lit up, and I turned to see what she was beaming at: a pink cocktail with a salted rim and lime wedge. Then I saw who was holding the cocktail, and my stomach dropped to my knees.

It was Brandon, looking as wickedly handsome as ever. His biceps were practically bursting through his fitted blue button-down. How were the sleeves not ripping at the seams?

"Here's your paloma," he said, handing the drink to Parisa, who immediately took a long, desperate swig. He looked at me, and the corner of his mouth quirked up. "Nicole. It's good to see you again."

What I wanted to say was, *Good to see you, too.* What came out of my mouth was, "Uh . . ."

My awkwardness didn't seem to faze him. "Can I get you something to drink?"

"Uh . . . ," I said again. Parisa elbowed me in the ribs, dislodging whatever had clogged up my ability to form a complete sentence. "I'm not really drinking today. For . . . obvious reasons."

The back of my neck grew hot and sweaty, as I remembered the fool I'd made of myself the other night. Brandon smiled warmly. "How about something nonalcoholic, then? We've got a whole craft-mocktail menu."

"Oh." A mocktail sounded festive. "That'd be great."

"Do you prefer spicy, citrusy, or sweet?"

"Spicy, please. And thanks."

"No problem." With an amused glance at Parisa draining the last of her drink, he asked, "Can I get you another one?"

She nodded and shoved the empty glass into his hand. "Just keep them coming all afternoon."

As Brandon and his bulging biceps walked away, Parisa said, "He likes you."

"He pities me."

"No, he doesn't. He thinks you're cute."

There was a difference between cute and pathetic, but before I could explain that to Parisa, her mother, Farnaz, stalked over to us. "Parisa, *joon*, please settle this argument with your sisters."

"Mom, I don't give a shit about the balloons." That paloma must've gone straight to Parisa's head for her to say the word *shit* in front of her mother.

"Language! They're trying to make this nice for you, since you don't care about making it nice for yourself." She said a few words in Persian that made Parisa go red in the face. Whatever they were, Parisa didn't have a comeback. She just grumbled and trotted off toward her sisters.

Suddenly, I was alone with her mom. I hadn't seen Farnaz in months . . . actually, it was probably more like years. Maybe at Parisa's cosmetology-school graduation ceremony? She looked exactly the same as she had when we were in grade school. Black hair, red lips, firm skin, full bust, thin waist. The woman never aged.

"Nicole, it's so good to see you, darling." She offered a hug, which I returned. "Parisa says you're working hard. Are you still at the big tech firm?"

"Yes. I've been at Virtuality for almost five years now."

"That's wonderful. And are you dating anyone?"

"No." I didn't feel the need to elaborate. Fortunately, she didn't press the issue.

"How are your parents?"

To be honest, I would've preferred to discuss my nonexistent dating life. I hadn't spoken to Mom or Dad since Christmas, which had been a miserable experience for everyone involved, although it wasn't different from any other holiday we spent together. Dad had overcooked the turkey; Mom had gotten drunk and cried in the pantry; I'd cut out early and stress-eaten a tin of gingerbread cookies on the drive home.

"They're fine," I said.

"Is your mother doing okay?"

On the surface, this was a simple question, but it was hard to tell what she meant by *okay*. If she meant, *Is your mom alive?* then the answer was yes. If she meant, *Has your mom gotten her shit together?* then it was a hard no. I didn't feel like asking her to clarify, so I just shrugged.

The look of pity on her face made me want to fall through the floor. This was why I never talked about my family with anyone. There was no hiding it from Farnaz, though. She already knew all about my mom and her problems; the whole Shahin family did. Mostly because I'd spent an absurd amount of time at their house when I was younger, just to get away from the drama that was going on at my own home. Parisa's sisters were always mean, and her mom gave new meaning to the term *helicopter parent*, but being around them had made me feel somewhat stable. At least no one ever got wasted and cried in the pantry at the Shahins'.

Brandon returned with a smile on his face and a highball glass in his hand, which he presented to me with a flourish. "Here you go: a ginger-jalapeño spritz."

Slices of small green pepper floated in the pale fizzy drink, and a lime wedge hung off the rim. It looked like any other fancy cocktail. I took a long sip through the striped straw, and my salivary glands began to tingle. Bubbles popped against the roof of my mouth, and my tongue prickled against the tang of the ginger. The jalapeño burned; the icy liquid soothed. This wasn't just a mocktail; it was an experience.

"This is insanely delicious," I said. Then quickly turned to Farnaz and added, "It's nonalcoholic."

There was that look of pity again.

"I'm glad you like it," Brandon said. He paused a beat, like there was something else he wanted to say to me, but before he could get the words out, someone across the room yelled, "We're here!"

An older white woman with a blonde bob and a designer caftan walked in, her arms spread wide, as if we'd all been awaiting her arrival. Trailing behind her were an older man and a teenage girl with long strawberry-blonde hair and freckles on her nose. Mike brought up the rear, looking like he needed a nap.

Farnaz stepped forward with her hand extended. "You must be Francine. It's so lovely to finally meet you."

The woman in the caftan—who I assumed was Mike's mom—ignored Farnaz's invitation for a handshake and instead pulled her in for a hug. "Farnaz," she said. "I cannot believe we didn't do this sooner." She stepped back and gestured to her family. "I'd like you to meet my husband, Ray, and this is my daughter, Abigail."

Ray waved meekly while Abigail looked up and smiled. "It's nice to meet you, Mrs. Shahin."

"Please," she said, "call me Farnaz."

Brandon clapped his hands and said, "Can I get anyone a drink?"

"Yes, please," Francine said. "I'd love a glass of champagne."

"Seven and seven," Ray said. His voice was gruffer than I expected it to be.

Abigail smiled sweetly. "I'll have a glass of rosé, please."

Brandon nodded. "Okay. Are you twenty-one?"

"No, she is not," Francine said. "She'll have a Shirley Temple."

Abigail scowled and buried her freckled nose in her phone.

"I'll have a server bring those to you now." Brandon flashed me a grin, and I watched him walk away. Those pants he was wearing were expertly fitted. Particularly around the rear.

Once he was gone, I felt sort of lonely. Which was ridiculous, I knew, because he was working and I was a guest, and also because we barely even knew each other. But now Mike had wandered off to talk to some guys who I assumed were groomsmen, and Francine and Farnaz were engaged in what seemed to be an extremely important motherly discussion, and Ray and Abigail were circling the hors d'oeuvres trays. So it was just me, alone, holding my ginger-jalapeño spritz.

Parisa was still arguing with her sisters over those balloons. Part of me wondered if I should go over and try to mediate the situation. I hated the idea of getting between Parisa and her sisters, but I *was* the maid of honor. It was my job to smooth over issues with the bridesmaids. To help take the stress off the bride.

All right, that was it. I'd do it. Just one more sip of my drink and—

POP!

"What is wrong with you?"

"I didn't realize it was gonna pop!"

"It's a balloon, Roxana! Of course it's gonna pop if you poke at it!"

"Do you even know how expensive these were?"

"No one told you to spend money on these stupid balloons!"

Oh no. I should've acted sooner. Still, better late than never. I raced to the scene of the balloon carnage, where confetti and bits of latex littered the floor. "Can I help with something?"

Roxy's big brown eyes narrowed to slits. "*Now* you decide to offer help."

"Don't be so rude," Parisa said.

"I'm just saying, she's the maid of honor, and she hasn't done anything for this party."

"Because I told her not to get involved. This was supposed to be a simple brunch with a few people, not a big blowout. You and Mom wanted this, not me."

Leila rolled her eyes. "So sorry we're excited to celebrate your engagement."

As Parisa continued sparring with her sisters, I silently bent down and swept up the detritus with my hands. That way I was doing something constructive, while also staying out of the line of fire. I tossed the remnants into a small trash bin in the corner of the room, and when I returned, they were still bickering. Time to do my maid of honor duty.

"You know," I cut in, "I think this bouquet would look nice on the gift table. Right in the center, with all the cards and presents gathered around it."

"That's a great idea," Parisa said. "Thank you for *helping*, Nicole." She gave Leila and Roxy a pointed look, then pulled me away. "Come, let me introduce you to the bridesmaids you'll actually *like* spending time with."

Three women were already seated at table two. I slid into an empty chair and set my drink down as Parisa introduced us. "Nicole, these are my cousins, Shirin and Ally, and you already know Kara."

"It's nice to meet you. And great to see you again, Kara."

Parisa's cousins were as gorgeous as she was, with the same olive skin and sleek black hair, though Shirin's hair was long and wavy, while Ally's was trimmed into an adorable pixie cut. Kara was breathtakingly beautiful, too—a Black woman with lustrous dark skin and thick curls dyed blonde at the ends.

Mike called to Parisa from across the room. She turned to us and said, "I'll be back."

When she left, Shirin said, "Nicole, my cousin has told us so much about you."

"All good things," Ally added.

I mocked wiping sweat from my brow. "That's a relief."

"You've known Parisa since you were little kids, right?" Shirin asked.

"Yeah. We went to school together from kindergarten to twelfth grade."

Ally turned to Kara and asked, "How do you know Parisa?"

"She did my makeup on *Strike a Pose*."

"Omigod," Ally said, her eyes practically bugging out of her head. "Now I know why you look so familiar. I watched that whole season! You look different, though. Like your hair was shorter back then, maybe? And you had a septum ring?"

Kara grinned coyly, a deep dimple appearing in her flawless cheek. "Good memory."

"You were totally robbed," Ally said. "Jane did not deserve to win."

"That's all right. I've been walking every single New York Fashion Week for the past three years, so everything worked out for me in the end."

"What do you do, Nicole?" Shirin asked. "Are you in the business, too?"

The unnamed "business" being show business, of course. "No, I'm a user experience designer for Virtuality."

"Oh. My ex-boyfriend works there," Shirin said. "Do you know Charles Ingot?"

Ugh, Charles. "Yeah, actually, we're in the same department."

"Didn't you say he hated it there?" Ally asked.

"No, he loved it there," Shirin said. "*I* was the one who hated it. He worked insane hours. I finally told him he had to scale it back on the weekends or we were through, and . . . well, you see what happened there. He cried like a baby when I dumped him."

Yikes.

"Forgive my ignorance," Kara said, "but what's a user experience designer?"

"You're not ignorant; it's kind of a weird job title. Basically, I'm responsible for making software more user friendly. You know when you go to a website and it's hard to find what you're looking for? The menus don't make any sense, and the colors are awful, and you have to scroll for ten minutes to get to the bottom of the page? It's my job to fix that kind of stuff."

"So you're a web designer?"

"Not exactly. I mean, I can build websites; I've been doing that for years. But in my day-to-day job at Virtuality, I'm just telling the people who *do* build the websites how to build them in a way that won't make people want to tear out their hair. Right now, though, I'm working on a chatbot, which is—"

"Hey, bitches!"

Oh, good. Leila and Roxy were here. They sat down in the two empty seats at the table. "This is it!" Roxy exclaimed. "The whole bridal party!"

"No, we're missing Mike's sister," I said. "She's still over by the hors d'oeuvres table."

"Whatever, she's a kid." Leila brushed her perfectly highlighted hair over her shoulder. "How's everybody doing?"

Shirin and Ally replied in unison with an underwhelmed, "Great." I took another long sip of my drink.

Roxy pointed one lacquered red nail in my direction. "What are you drinking? It looks good."

"It's called a ginger-jalapeño spritz."

"What's in it, tequila? Rum?"

"Um, actually, it's nonalcoholic."

"Oh, are you doing Dry January, too?" Kara asked. "I tried, but I only lasted until the third."

"Anyway," Roxy said, crossing her arms on the table and affecting an air of authority, "now that we're all here together, we need to talk. Since my sister is having the shortest engagement in history, we've gotta get cracking on the planning pronto. Nicole, as the maid of honor, I trust you've got a handle on the situation?"

"Yes, I do." Thank God for that checklist from the Knot.

"Great! So has Parisa put together a mood board yet?"

My checklist said nothing about a mood board. "What is that?"

Roxy and Leila exchanged a look. Instantly, I felt incompetent. "We'll handle the mood board," Leila said. "What about the wedding website; have you set that up?"

That *was* on my checklist, but I hadn't started on it yet. "No."

"Well, what *have* you done?"

"I've been doing a lot of research," I said. From their twin icy glares, it was clear that wasn't enough. It had only been two and a half weeks since Parisa had announced her engagement. How much was I supposed to have done? Desperate to feel like I wasn't completely useless, I said, "I'm also putting together a plan for the bachelorette party in Vegas."

"Oooh, Vegas!" Kara squealed in delight.

Roxy snickered. "There are a lot of other, more important things we need to focus on before we get to the bachelorette party."

"Parisa told me it was very important to her."

"Parisa's not the only person involved in this wedding."

"Well, obviously Mike's involved. But the groomsmen are handling his bachelor party." Unless I was supposed to be involved in that, too?

"We're talking about the actual wedding, Nicole." Leila's tone was getting pissy now. "It's less than six months away, and they haven't even picked a venue yet."

"Have they settled on a date?" I asked.

"No," Roxy said, "and that's a problem, because soon all the venues are going to be booked up."

"If they're not booked up already," Leila added.

"Right," Roxy said. "We need to tour places immediately. Parisa was dragging her feet, so I went ahead and made some appointments for next weekend, if anyone else wants to come with us."

"Parisa didn't mention that to me." Damn. I was supposed to be in Oakland next weekend for work.

Leila pursed her lips. "If you don't want to go, Nicole, just say so."

"No, it's not that I don't want to go; it's just—"

Roxy cut me off. "We're checking out the Belleview Ballroom and the Grand Palace Banquet Hall."

Knowing Parisa as well as I did, I could imagine her getting married on a beach or in a garden or at a cabin in the woods. Not at a place with the words *ballroom* or *banquet* in the name. If she was upset about the "California Brunch Chic" attire at this engagement party, I didn't want to know how angry she'd be if her mother insisted on putting down a nonrefundable deposit for a reception venue she hated.

"Is this a standard kind of thing?" I asked. "For the whole bridal party to tag along on tours of reception venues? It seems like something the bride and groom should do together, alone. So they can decide if it's right for them without feeling any sort of external pressure." *Like from her pushy sisters and overbearing mother.*

"They need help with this," Leila said. "They have no idea what they're doing."

"Exactly," Roxy added. "If we didn't set these appointments up for them, they never would have done it for themselves. And there are very few venues left in LA with availabilities in June that can accommodate up to two hundred guests."

Two hundred guests? "She told me they wanted a small, simple wedding."

"Mom wants something big."

"But it's not your mother's wedding. It's Parisa and Mike's. It should be about what *they* want, not about what anyone else wants for them."

"This is about more than what they want." Leila's voice shot across the table like a flying dagger. "This is about the whole family. She's our oldest sister, my parents' first child. This is a big deal for all of us."

"Family is important," Roxy said. "Parisa understands that. She wants to have this wedding for everyone. But I know you don't understand that, given your whole crazy situation." She punctuated that last word with a flick of her wrist, like I was a piece of dirt she was brushing away.

An awkward silence descended around the table. Or maybe it wasn't awkward for anyone but me. I didn't know how to respond. All I had wanted to do was advocate for my best friend, and I was met with the lowest of blows.

With nothing to say, I sipped my drink, taking long pulls through the straw and swallowing until the entire glass was drained. My eyes stung from the heat of the jalapeño. Tears sprang from nowhere. I shouldn't have worn mascara today.

"Excuse me, I have to go to the bathroom." The words came out so weak I'm not sure anyone heard me.

Mercifully, the restroom was empty. I stared down my reflection in the mirror, dabbing at the corners of my eyes to keep the mascara from running. Roxy was being pointlessly cruel, and I knew I should've let her words roll right off my back. My family's problems were not my fault, but she'd unknowingly poked at a soft, sensitive space deep in my brain that thought maybe I should've been trying to fix them. Families were supposed to stick together. I had abandoned ship immediately after high school, returning only for the occasional uncomfortable holiday dinner and running away as soon as it was done. Did that make me selfish? Cowardly?

This was neither the time nor the place for an existential crisis. I was the maid of honor, dammit. I needed to be out there, smiling and schmoozing with the rest of the bridal party. It was time to get it together.

In-two-three-four, out-two-three-four. One more quick swipe at my lower lashes, and I was good to go.

With a plastered-on smile, I threw open the restroom door and stopped short when I saw Brandon standing in the hallway.

"Hi," he said, then quickly added, "Sorry, is this weird that I'm waiting for you outside the bathroom door? I'm not trying to be weird. You just looked upset when you went in there, and I wanted to make sure you were okay."

That was sweet of him. "Thanks. I'm fine. Weddings are stressful, that's all."

"I get it. Especially all the family stuff. I know Parisa was stressing out about her mom when you guys were here the other night. Worried that she was gonna try to take over the whole thing."

"She was?" Another thing I didn't remember.

He nodded. "Yeah, but you were doing a really good job of calming her down. Telling her it would all be okay. You're a good friend. Makes sense why she picked you to be her maid of honor."

My heart fluttered inside my chest. Finally, an affirmation that I wasn't incompetent. That I *was* the right choice, even if Roxy and Leila resented me for it. "That's nice to hear."

"I wouldn't say it if it weren't true. Oh, also, I wanted to give you this." He reached into his front pocket and pulled out my earring, then dangled it in front of me. "I know you said to throw it away, but I was holding out hope that I'd see you again. So here you go."

He placed it in my palm. It still held the warmth of his body.

"Thank you so much." I clasped my fingers around it, and when he met my gaze, the warmth traveled up my arm and settled in the center of my chest. Suddenly, I wished I had more to say. Though the silence between us was comfortable. I could stand here in this foyer for hours, just staring into his gray eyes.

"You should get back in there," he said. "You've got an important job to do."

He was right. I *did* have an important job. Parisa was counting on me, and I wasn't going to let her down.

"Thanks again." My voice sounded wispy and weak. Reluctantly, I broke his gaze and turned to head back to the party. As I walked away, there was a burning sensation in the center of my back, like someone was aiming a spotlight directly on me. I glanced over my shoulder and saw Brandon's eyes smoldering from across the room.

CHAPTER SIX

Conversations can be tricky. Mostly because our emotions can get in the way of our ability to think rationally and communicate clearly. If you're nervous, you might stumble over your speech or say the wrong thing. If you're angry, you might misinterpret someone's words or lash out with spiteful commentary. Then nobody gets their point across, and one or more participants may end up running away to the bathroom in tears.

Actually, let me clarify that first statement: Conversations *with humans* can be tricky. Conversations with computers, however, are almost always much less complicated. Computers don't have emotions. They operate on logic. Conditional statements and binary choices. A rational justification for every remark.

Of course, computers don't inherently understand how to be good conversation partners. Humans have to teach them. Which is precisely what I was doing for Krueger-Middleton's new chatbot. It was my responsibility to ensure every interaction with their virtual medical professionals was relevant, informative, and, above all, pleasant.

This wasn't as easy as it sounded. Lots of people were going to come to this chatbot with their emotions running high. They'd have questions about their health, but because of anxiety or anger or fear, they might mistype or veer off on a tangent. The chatbot had to calm them down, steer the conversation in the right direction, and provide answers, quickly and efficiently.

Essentially, a chatbot hated conflict. Kind of like me.

But while I preferred to avoid conflict altogether, chatbots needed to face it head-on before de-escalating. Seeing as I had no clue how to do that, I had to perform a bit of research before I could properly tackle this project. As I pored over articles on how to navigate difficult conversations, I thought of a thousand different ways I could've responded to Roxy's comment about family that did not involve running away to the bathroom in tears. If only I'd have learned these conflict-resolution techniques a week earlier. Not that I'd have had the courage to use them.

By Thursday, I'd finished the bulk of my research and started compiling an agenda for my upcoming trip to Krueger's headquarters in Oakland. To make the most of my time on site, I wanted to prep as much as possible beforehand. That meant checklists, questionnaires, and—of course—detailed daily schedules. I was also constantly checking in on our group chat for the project; my Slack notifications were blowing up left and right. When my phone dinged in the late morning, I assumed it was another Krueger-related message. Turned out it wasn't work related at all:

> Roxy Shahin (roxana.shahin@geemail.com) has invited you to join the Slack workspace Parisa's Bridal Party. Join now to start collaborating!

My shoulders reflexively hunched up toward my ears. I took a deep breath and rolled them back. There was no need to be tense right now. Roxy wasn't here, and furthermore, her words couldn't hurt me unless I allowed them to. Besides, this was a positive thing. Having a group chat to keep all our wedding-related correspondence in one place was a smart move. I didn't know why I hadn't thought of it.

I tapped on "Accept Invite," and the Slack interface filled my screen. A menu along the left-hand side listed channels, which allowed us to organize our discussion into different topics. There were at least ten of them, with labels like *#dresses*, *#invitations*, and *#bridal-shower*. Roxy had really thought this through.

Though I did notice one glaring omission from the list. There wasn't a channel set up to discuss the bachelorette party. Happy to finally feel useful, I created one. I intended to do most of the planning—Parisa had said she wanted me to take the reins—but the whole group still needed to coordinate on things like travel dates and budgets.

In the #reception channel, there was a lengthy conversation under-way. From the time stamps, they'd all started chatting yesterday. So why had I only gotten this invitation five minutes ago?

I scrolled back to read through everything they'd said so far. Most of it pertained to the venues they'd selected to tour this weekend. Both appointments were on Sunday afternoon.

> **Leila:** we're doing belleview at 1 and grand palace at 3:30
> **Shirin:** sorry i can't make it
> **Kara:** i can't 😔 i'm in nyc rn
> **Ally:** 😢 We'll miss you.
> **Roxy:** What about you nicole? Will you be gracing us with your presence?

The last message had been posted ten minutes ago. That was when Roxy must've realized that she'd forgotten to send me an invitation.

> **Nicole:** I'm so sorry, I can't make it. I'll be flying to Oakland that afternoon for work.

I felt like I was failing Parisa. Not only had I allowed her sisters to commandeer these tours of the wedding venues, but now I wasn't even going to be there to support her through what would undoubtedly be an extremely stressful afternoon with her family.

Immediately, I sent her a guilt-ridden text:

I'm really sorry I'm not going to be there on Sunday.

Be where on Sunday?

The tours. Of the wedding venues?

Oh, right. I totally forgot about that.

Whatever, don't stress.

I don't even care about the venue, honestly.

Really?

Yeah. I told you, if it were up to us, we'd have eloped a week ago. We're only doing this whole party thing to make our families happy.

Leila's words echoed in my memory. *This is about the whole family. Family is important.* So important, it seemed, that Parisa was willing to throw up her hands and let them take over every aspect of one of the most significant events in her life. Every aspect except for the bachelorette party, that was.

If family was this important, then maybe Roxy and Leila had a right to feel snubbed. I wasn't a family member, yet I'd been given an important, respected role in the wedding. And let's be honest: I wasn't exactly crushing it.

Do you really think I should be your maid of honor?

Almost instantly, the phone started buzzing with an incoming call. Parisa sounded crestfallen when she asked, "Do you not want to do it anymore?"

"No, no, of course I do." I tried to keep my voice down so no one around me in the office could overhear. "I just feel bad."

"What do you feel bad about?"

"I get the feeling Roxy and Leila resent me."

"Of course they do. They resent everything about this wedding. Trust me, it has nothing to do with you and everything to do with them."

"Then why are you so cool with letting them take over all the plans?"

"Because it's easier. I talked to my therapist about this at length, and I don't care enough about the details of this party to fight with my sisters every step of the way. I got all upset about them hijacking the engagement party, but it was a waste of worry because it turned out to be fine. I'm sure the wedding will be fine, too."

She was probably right. Even if the festivities weren't going to reek of Parisa's unique style and personal taste, they'd almost certainly be well organized. The Slack workspace was an indicator of how much thought her sisters had been putting into the whole thing. "The group chat will be really useful."

"Oh, the Slack thing?" Parisa snickered. "I ignored the invite. I can't deal with them talking about this twenty-four seven. I suggest you ignore it, too."

How was I supposed to ignore it? There would presumably be important information in those chat threads that I'd have to pay attention to. Details about dress fittings and shower invitations. And I'd just added that channel about the bachelorette party to help us coordinate our travel plans.

Plus, even if her sisters were being insufferable, I didn't want to completely tap out of the planning process. Maybe I'd be able to inject some Parisa-specific touches into this wedding without pissing off her sisters.

"I just want your big day to be special," I said.

"You know," she said, expertly changing the subject, "you're gonna need a date to my wedding."

"I think I'll be fine flying solo."

"Why don't you ask Brandon?"

"Brandon has no interest in me."

"He saved your earring."

My palm tingled, right in the spot where he'd placed the earring, still warm from his body. "We haven't spoken since your engagement party."

"So text him. He's probably waiting for you to make the next move."

Was he? I'd simply assumed he was being polite by returning my earring, but perhaps there was more to it than that. After all, he'd waited outside the bathroom to make sure I was okay. And we had definitely shared a moment with all that mutual staring into each other's eyes. Hadn't we?

"What should I say to him?" I asked.

"Why don't you just—" A commotion broke out on the other end of the phone line, and Parisa suddenly said, "Oh shit, the talent's getting shiny; I've gotta run. Love you."

"Love you, too."

My phone screen flashed with the words *CALL ENDED* before fading to black. Damn. I really wished Parisa would've finished that sentence. Now I had no idea what to say to Brandon. I swiped over to my texts and typed the words: Hi there!

Too eager.

I deleted the exclamation point and put a period in its place: Hi there.

Too distant.

I deleted the word *there* so it just said: Hi

Too creepy.

Could I have been any worse at this?

I trashed the text to Brandon and sent one to Vimi and Ben instead: Anyone up for an early lunch? Vimi said, Can't. Swamped. Ben said, Sure. Five minutes later, the two of us were seated at our usual table in the back left corner with piping-hot bowls of the Thursday special, chicken-tortilla soup. Dwayne had thrown in a few extra chips for me, and I crunched on them while listening to Ben talk about his new workout routine.

"Have you tried those new treadmill desks in the gym?" he asked.

"You know I don't go to the gym."

"Well, you should. We're not getting any younger." I shot him a death glare. "Don't give me that look; it's important to stay active. That's why the treadmill desk is so great. You can walk while you work. Kill two birds with one stone."

"When did you start this?"

"About two weeks ago. Cass and I do it together. It's become our daily 'us time.'" Cass was Ben's girlfriend. She also worked for Virtuality, and as a software engineer, her workload was even more bananas than ours. We were always trying to get her to join us for lunch, but she barely ever took a break. Which made me feel sort of guilty for taking these breaks myself. Maybe I should've been working through all my lunch hours, too.

Suddenly, Ben muttered, "Don't look behind you," then hunched over and stared down into his soup. Unable to control myself, I looked behind me, then regretted it the moment I made eye contact with Charles.

Ugh, Charles.

He smiled toothlessly and said, "Hey, guys."

"Hi." Weird. Charles never came up to us in the dining hall. He usually walked by our table without acknowledging our existence.

Lately, though, it seemed like he was stalking me around the office. "What's up?"

"Nicole, I heard you're headed to Oakland this weekend."

Oh. That was what this was about. It must've been eating him up inside that I'd gotten assigned to the Krueger project instead of him. "Yeah, I'm flying out Sunday afternoon."

"How long are you there for?"

"All week."

"Sounds like you'll be busy." He hesitated, stuffing his hands in his pockets, then resting them on his hips. Finally, he asked, "Do you think you'll be able to get it all done in one week?"

"I'm gonna have to. The following week, they're sending me to Phoenix."

"Really? Wow." His smile faltered momentarily. "Well, if you need a hand, I can talk to Jon about joining you."

Ben snorted, then quickly covered it with an overly dramatic cough. "Thanks," I said, "but I think I've got it under control."

Charles looked from me to Ben and back again. His smile transformed to a self-important smirk. "It's strange that they're entrusting such a significant project to a junior designer."

What an asshole. We both knew I was more than qualified to handle it.

I couldn't deal with him harassing me about this until June. Maybe there was a way to get him to leave me alone. Like, say, if he knew I was hanging around with the girl who'd broken his heart.

"I met Shirin this weekend."

His eyes went wide with surprise. "Shirin Abassi?"

I nodded, trying not to feel too smug. "She's my best friend's cousin. When she heard I worked for Virtuality, she asked if I knew you. Funny coincidence, right?"

"Yeah. Funny." His voice sounded distant.

"Anyway, my best friend is getting married this summer. I'm the maid of honor and Shirin is a bridesmaid, so we'll be spending a *lot* of time together. Getting to know each other really well."

"That's great." He slowly backed away, looking so defeated I almost felt bad for him. Almost. "I've got a meeting now, but good luck in Oakland."

"Thanks," I called after him as he disappeared across the dining hall. Then I turned to Ben and rolled my eyes. "What a douche."

"What was that all about? Who's Shirin?"

"His ex-girlfriend. Apparently, she dumped him because he spent too much time at work, and he was completely broken up about it."

I expected Ben to snort again, but instead he frowned. "I can't stand the guy, but I'm sympathetic. I've dated women in the past who just don't get what the Virtuality culture is all about. That's why Cass and I work so well. She understands it because she's a part of it."

"Right." There were more than a few couples around here who'd met at Virtuality. I'd dipped my toes in the office dating pool a couple of times, too, but the relationships always fizzled out as quickly as they started. The only thing I ever had in common with those guys was work. There was never any spark. No warm feeling in the center of my chest that burst into flames when we touched. That was what I wanted. A bright, burning blaze.

Kind of like how I felt when Brandon looked at me.

As Ben extolled the virtues of dating coworkers, I slurped my soup and wondered if he and Cass had that burst-into-flames kind of feeling when they were together. Considering their special "us time" consisted of working side by side on treadmill desks, their relationship didn't sound particularly fiery.

When lunch was over, I returned to my desk determined to concentrate. But my mind kept slipping back to Brandon. Let's say Parisa was right, and he *was* waiting for me to make the next move. If I texted him now, what exactly was I supposed to say? We'd only hung out twice. I barely remembered anything about the first time, and the second time he'd witnessed me crying outside a bathroom. Those weren't things I ever wanted to discuss again.

Maybe I could start with a question. One of those articles I'd read about chatbot design said that asking good questions could lead to deeper, more effective conversations. And there was actually something I wanted to know.

Before I could overthink it, I tapped his contact information and sent him a text: How do you make that ginger jalapeño spritz?

There. That was easy enough.

But as the seconds passed by with no reply, my stomach started feeling all tight and achy. What if Brandon saw my message and instantly swiped it away without reading? I certainly wouldn't have blamed him. As far as he knew, I was kind of a mess. He probably had me saved in his contacts as *Drunky McCries-a-Lot.*

A moment later, my phone dinged with a text. Brandon had written me back!

Let me show you.

Come to Vespa tonight and I'll give you a private mixology lesson.

8ish okay?

Ooh, a private mixology lesson! It sounded kind of dirty. Of course, it wouldn't be. We were meeting in his place of business on a busy Thursday evening. It wasn't like we'd be making out behind the bar.

Not that I'd mind that.

I swiped over to my calendar app and checked out my schedule for tonight. I'd blocked out a whole four hours for work, from six to ten. Since I was prepping for this trip to Oakland, all my evenings this week were jam packed.

But this was a private mixology lesson. How could I possibly say no?

With a few taps, I reduced this evening's work block from four hours to two and added a new entry at eight o'clock labeled *Private Mixology Lesson with Brandon.*

Then I texted him: 8 is perfect. Wouldn't miss it for the world!

CHAPTER SEVEN

At seven thirty, I ran home to change. After throwing on yet another kind-of-schmancy outfit—a satin camisole, cigarette pants, strappy sandals, and my favorite rose-gold glasses—I headed over to Vespa. When I arrived, the hostess asked me if I had a reservation.

"I'm here to meet Brandon?" It came out like a question.

"Right this way." She escorted me to the bar with a smile and said, "I'll let him know you're here."

"Thanks." I sat down on a corner stool and instantly recognized the bartender as the same woman who'd served us champagne during my first visit here. As she poured ingredients into a cocktail shaker, I caught her eye and waved. One of her perfectly manicured eyebrows arched skyward; then she turned away and acted as if I weren't there.

Yikes. Apparently, she had no intention of serving me again. I must've been a real jerk to her that night.

"Hey there." Brandon's voice came from behind me. I swiveled around and found myself face to face with his broad, solid chest. He was wearing another one of those fitted shirts that tested the limits of cotton fabric. Especially in the shoulder area.

"Hey," I said, tilting my head back to see his face. He had three days' worth of stubble and an easy smile that made his gray eyes twinkle. That warm spot formed in the center of my chest again. "How's it going?"

"Not bad. Just finished my shift, so I'm all yours. Ready to learn how to make some mocktails?"

I cast an anxious glance down the bar, where the bartender wielded a soda gun like a weapon. "Do you think we'd be getting in her way? She looks busy, and I don't wanna bother her."

"Nah, Kelsey won't mind. Besides, we won't take up much space. Stay right here." He walked a few feet away, then lifted the counter hatch and ducked behind the bar. On his way back, he grabbed a coaster and placed it in front of me. "Should we start with the ginger-jalapeño spritz? Or are you feeling something different tonight?"

"I'm not sure. What are my other options?"

He spread a menu before me, pointing to a section on the right-hand side labeled *Mocktails*. There were at least half a dozen to choose from, with names like Strawberry Fields and Rosemary Smash. One sang to me above all the others. "How about the Coconut-Cucumber Cooler?"

"You got it." He plucked a glass from the shelf and set it down on the coaster. "Let me show you how it's done."

Brandon launched into a detailed demonstration of how to make the perfect mocktail. He showed me how to muddle cucumber with mint leaves and how to determine the right ratio of coconut water to lime juice. The whole time, I felt like I was watching a cooking show. He had such a magnetic presence; it was clear why those producers had selected him for *Off the Grid*. I bet he was amazing on camera.

Finally, he slipped a fringed slice of cucumber onto the rim of the glass and set it down with a flourish. "Voilà."

"Let's see how it is." I brought the glass to my lips and took a long, thirsty sip. My taste buds tingled at the combination of flavors. The perfect balance of sharp and sweet.

"What do you think?" he asked.

"It's delicious. I love that you have so many interesting mocktails on your menu. Most places just have, like, a lavender lemonade and that's it."

"Yeah, I suggested the change last year. I read a stat in some industry journal that more and more people are cutting back on their alcohol consumption, sometimes going completely dry for long stretches of time. But just because you're not drinking doesn't mean you can't go out and have a great time, right?" He leaned in and lowered his voice. "Plus, there's money in mocktails. We can charge more for this than a club soda, you know what I mean?"

"How forward thinking of you. You're an excellent businessman. *And* an excellent bartender." I tapped the edge of my glass with my fingernail. "Did you design these drinks yourself?"

"I had some help from Kelsey." He nodded toward the other end of the bar, where she was throttling a cocktail shaker and giving me the stink eye. I quickly looked away. "She's a certified mixologist, so she knows a lot more than I do. I only tended bar for a little while before I made the jump to management."

"How long have you been a manager?"

"About two and a half years. Before I started at Vespa, I worked at a bunch of other bars and restaurants around LA."

"So when did you do that survivor-man reality show?" I took another sip. Mmm, tasty.

His cheeks turned pink, and he let out a stilted laugh. "*Off the Grid* was five years back. Feels like a lot longer, though."

"Did you actually audition for that, or did a talent scout find you in the forest, foraging for berries?"

Another laugh, this one heartier. "My brother saw the casting call and dared me to apply. I didn't think I had a chance, but I got in."

"And you wound up winning."

"Which I'm still surprised about, honestly. Every other contestant spent months preparing in expensive wilderness camps. I just showed up and hoped for the best."

"You're a natural, then. You could be the next Bear Grylls."

He shook his head. "Nah. I live for the outdoors, but I'm done being in front of a camera." As I drained the last of my Coconut-Cucumber Cooler, he asked, "What's next?"

I perused the menu. "Um . . . how about the Sunshine Swizzle?"

"Coming right up." He flipped a cocktail shaker like they did in the movies, his bicep flexing beneath his shirt sleeve as he expertly caught it in one hand. My cheeks burned as I thought about other ways to put his dexterity to good use.

As he filled the shaker with ice from the bin, Kelsey approached, still looking surly. "Can you make me two sidecars for table twelve?"

"Not really, I'm in the middle of something." His eyes darted toward me and back again. "I clocked out at eight."

With a scowl, she said, "Look, it's getting busy in here, so if you're not gonna help, then get out of the way." She brushed past him to grab a bottle from the well before huffing back toward where she'd come from.

I couldn't imagine talking to my boss like that. I actually envied her. Maybe if I had half her shameless gall, I'd have asked Jon for a promotion two years ago.

Brandon dumped the ice out of the shaker and said, "You know, I've got all the stuff I need to make these drinks at my place. Wanna go there?" He held up three fingers in a Scout's salute and said, "I promise, no funny business."

Frankly, I wouldn't have minded some funny business. Watching him carefully craft this drink had been a real turn-on. All the stirring and shaking, the muddling and mixing. His muscles were practically begging to be freed from the confines of that button-down.

Perhaps once we got to his place, he'd change his mind.

The evening was unseasonably warm, so we walked the three blocks to his apartment. I expected a typical bachelor pad, one with mismatched furniture and a ginormous flat-screen TV, but when he opened the door, my mouth fell open in shock. As we crossed the threshold, we suddenly teleported out of LA and into a log cabin somewhere deep in the woods. A really well-appointed log cabin.

The entryway opened up to a spacious living room with wide-plank wood floors and a stone fireplace. The couch was cozy, with overstuffed pillows and what looked like a hand-crocheted afghan hanging over the back. A cedar trunk functioned as a coffee table, and a chandelier crafted from antlers hung overhead.

"Welcome to my little cabin in the city," he said.

My eyes were wide with wonder. "This is . . . something else."

"You think it's weird, don't you?"

"No, I think it's really cool. I've never seen an apartment like this in LA." I walked the length of the room, taking it all in. A sliding barn door led to an updated bathroom—was that a claw-foot tub inside?—and an oil painting of a mountainous landscape hung above the fireplace. I pointed to it. "Is that the feeling you're trying to evoke? Because if you are, it's working."

"Yep. That's Idyllwild. My favorite place in the whole world."

I'd heard of Idyllwild, but I'd never been there. It wasn't far, maybe a two-hour drive, kind of near Palm Springs but in the mountains. Not long ago, I'd seen a viral video about their odd choice of government official. "Isn't that the town that has a dog for a mayor?"

He nodded, beaming. "That's right, Mayor Max. Technically, he's Max the Second. Max the First died a while back. He reminds me of the dog I had when I was a kid, Charlie. He was a golden retriever." His eyes went wistful at the memory of his childhood friend. "I miss having a dog."

"I love dogs. I've always wanted one, but my parents wouldn't let me have one growing up. I've thought about getting one now that I'm an adult who can make my own decisions, but with my work schedule being so crazy, I feel like I wouldn't be able to give it the time it deserves."

"You work for a tech company, right?"

"Virtuality."

He shook his head. "I've never heard of it."

Weird. I thought Virtuality was a household name. Then again, I lived and breathed this company. My perspective was probably the teensiest bit skewed.

"Why is your work schedule so crazy?" he asked. "It's not like a nine-to-five kind of thing?"

Oh, that was funny. I couldn't help but laugh, though it came out sounding sort of bitter. Less lighthearted giggle, more resentful bark. "No, it's most definitely *not* nine to five. Even when I'm not physically in the office, I'm still on email from the moment I wake up in the morning until the moment I go to sleep at night. Plus, I'm up for a promotion right now, so things are extra intense." The very mention of work made me itchy to check my phone for unread messages. I'd bet anything Anna was still at her desk right now, grinding away on the Krueger project.

"That's a lot," he says. "Don't you ever get burned out?"

"No." I didn't really buy into the concept of burnout. No matter how full my plate was, I always felt better when I had too much to do rather than too little. Being productive gave me a sense of control and accomplishment. Sure, I'd get overwhelmed from time to time, but that was why I had my schedule. To help me keep track of the things that were important to me and fit them all neatly into my meticulously organized days.

Which reminded me, I had to rearrange my plan for tomorrow morning to account for tonight's impromptu outing with Brandon.

"Well, right now it's time to take your mind off of work and kick back with a mocktail. Still up for that Sunshine Swizzle?"

"You know it."

The kitchen evoked the same woodland vibes as the rest of the apartment. Pine cabinets, a farmhouse sink, a rustic bar cart filled with bottles and bartending utensils. I sat at the long dining table and ran my hands over the knotty wood surface.

As Brandon assembled the ingredients to make my drink—a shaker, some sugar, two kinds of juice—I thumbed through a magazine left open on the tabletop. The centerfold was a map with the words *Explore Idyllwild* printed across the top.

"Have you been to Idyllwild recently?" I asked.

"Yep. Just last week."

"How often do you go?"

"Usually about once a month, but lately I've been going a lot more." He filled the shaker with crushed ice from the refrigerator door, then flashed a wide smile. "I'm starting a business out there."

"What kind of business?"

"A brewpub. My brother, Eric, lives in Idyllwild. He's been brewing beer for ages, and now he wants to open his own place. And since I have a lot of management experience, he asked me to handle the business end of things. Couldn't think of a better partner than my bro, honestly. Family's everything, you know what I mean?"

"Yeah." I didn't, but I wasn't about to go down that road on a first date.

"Anyway," he continued, pouring juice into the shaker, "we've been scoping out locations and finally found the right spot. Signed the deed last week, and now we've gotta hire some workers to renovate. In the meantime, I'll be putting together menus and recruiting employees and figuring out a marketing plan. There's a lot of work to do in a short amount of time."

I swallowed hard against the rising discomfort in my stomach. "So this is happening soon?"

"We're aiming to open in June. I'm putting my two weeks' notice into Vespa on Monday so I can focus on the launch. This business is a real dream come true for me. I'm gonna give it everything I've got."

He capped the shaker and jiggled it wildly. A raucous rattling filled the room, making it hard for me to parse out my very jumbled thoughts. Finally, he stopped, and as he strained the liquid into two tumblers, the pieces slowly fell into place. If he was quitting his job in LA and opening a business in Idyllwild . . .

"Are you moving away?" I asked.

"To my favorite place in the whole world." The smile on his face was infectious, so much so that I couldn't help but smile myself, even though I wasn't feeling particularly happy about this revelation. "I've got my eye on a few cabins, but I wanna see if anything else comes on the market in the next couple of months. My real estate agent said March is a good time to buy. Lots of inventory after the winter thaw. Until then, I'll be back and forth between here and there."

He lifted both drinks and handed one to me. "Bottoms up," he said, and then we clinked our glasses and sipped.

I'm sure the Sunshine Swizzle was every bit as delicious as the other mocktails I'd sampled, but I didn't really taste it. My brain was too busy processing this new and unsettling information.

If Brandon was about to upend his life and move to the mountains, it wasn't the best idea to get romantically involved with him. Long-distance relationships took a lot of work. Long phone calls. Long drives. Long stretches of time without seeing one another. So many limitations and so much that was out of my control.

This was our first date, and the odds were already stacking up against us. Best to cut out now, before I got emotionally invested and, ultimately, hurt.

Because I knew I would get hurt. In fact, I already felt a sharp pang deep in the pit of my stomach. Something tense and tight, like a clenched fist. It was the weight of disappointment, mourning the loss of a love that I'd yet to experience, that I'd hoped I might finally find in Brandon. And if I felt this way now, how much more painful would it have been to *actually* fall in love, deeply and without reserve, only to have it end when we discovered we couldn't make it work?

It'd be excruciating. Mind bending. Debilitating.

I needed to get out of here.

In one swift movement, I tilted my head back and chugged my swizzle like I was slamming a beer bong. When I wiped my lips on the back of my hand, Brandon's gray eyes went wide. "Uh . . ."

"I'm really sorry," I said, already on my feet. "But I've gotta get home and do some work." Not exactly a lie, considering my jam-packed schedule. Still, it was an abrupt and ridiculous way to end things. Couldn't I have thought of something a little less awkward?

Too late now. I walked toward the front door, with Brandon following closely behind. He placed his hand on the doorknob but didn't turn it. I stared down at his fingers so I wouldn't have to look him in the eyes.

"Did I say something wrong?" he asked.

"No, why?"

"Well, I thought we were having a good time, and then you suddenly downed your drink and said you had to take off. What happened?"

There was no reason not to tell him the truth. I took a deep breath and finally met his gaze. "Look, Brandon, I really like you. I think you're a great guy, and I would absolutely love to get to know you better. But if you're moving away in a couple of months, then I don't really see the point."

His eyebrows knotted together. "The point?"

"Yes. The point of you and me getting to know each other."

"Isn't that the point in itself? Just getting to know each other."

"Right. But if we spend lots of time together and get close and catch feelings and then you move away? I know it's putting the cart before the horse, but I just don't think it's a good idea to get involved. Romantically speaking."

He released his grip on the doorknob and took a step closer to me. I caught a whiff of his cologne. It smelled earthy, like a freshly trimmed tree. The signature scent of a mountain man. It made the tiny hairs on the back of my neck stand at attention.

"Do we have to jump ahead like that?" he said. "This is our first date. We're having fun. Maybe it'd be okay to just take it one day at a time."

His eyes burned into mine, and the heat traveled through me, settling in the center of my chest. For a moment, I thought it might be worth it to risk getting hurt for the chance to experience that burst-into-flames feeling.

Then the fist in the pit of my stomach clenched tighter, igniting a war between my heart and my gut. Emotion versus reason. What I wanted versus what I could control.

Some people found joy in taking things one day at a time, not worrying about the what-ifs and the maybes. I wasn't one of those people. I needed stability, certainty, the ability to plan ahead. This not knowing? It wasn't going to work for me.

"I can't. I'm sorry."

His entire stance suddenly changed. He deflated, like a tire that had been slashed. "Okay."

"Thanks for having me over tonight. And thanks for the drinks. They were really amazing."

"You're welcome." He looked so sad standing there. Eyes drooping, mouth turned down at the corners, muscles flexing beneath the thin fabric of his shirt.

Maybe I was making the wrong decision. Maybe I'd never find anyone else who looked at me the way Brandon did, all blazing heat and fire. I wanted that burst-into-flames feeling, but if I ended things now, at least I knew I wouldn't get burned.

So I spun around, and I walked out the door.

CHAPTER EIGHT

Remember when I said I didn't buy into the concept of burnout? I take that back, at least when it comes to wedding planning.

To be fair, though, planning Parisa's wedding probably would've been a far less draining experience without the constant barrage of Slack notifications. It seemed as if my phone dinged every five minutes with some inane or imperious comment from Parisa's sisters. Leila complained that Parisa wasn't assembling her guest list fast enough. Roxy said she hated the color scheme I'd used on the wedding website and demanded I change it twelve times. They both posted a trillion different photos of bridesmaid dresses and asked for our opinions on every single one.

At first, I tried to keep up with it all in real time, but eventually I had to tap out. For two weeks, I was on site in Oakland, then Phoenix, in back-to-back meetings with executives from Krueger. I couldn't interrupt my workdays to give feedback on whether I preferred a strapless or off-the-shoulder neckline.

But there *was* important stuff in there, stuff I couldn't just ignore. So every night, when I returned to my hotel room, I'd spend a half hour or so reviewing all the messages that had accumulated during the day to extract the information that was relevant to me.

Like the date of the wedding. Mike and Parisa had settled on Saturday, June 26, which was a huge relief, because it was well *after* the Krueger project went live. I'd have the whole week to rest and rejuvenate before the big day, without having to worry about working late nights or being on call. Maybe I'd even ask Jon for a day or two off to help me mentally prepare.

Her mother and sisters had also settled on a venue: the Grand Palace Banquet Hall. From the photos on the website, the space looked very un-Parisa-like. Tufted chairs and crystal chandeliers and drapes hanging in random places. When I texted Parisa to see if she was cool with their decision, her response was, I told you, I don't care. Okay, then.

To keep me on track, I set up a recurring event in my calendar called *Review Slack Messages* every evening, from ten to ten thirty. Most of the time, I was done with my work by then; if not, I just took a short break. With this system in place, the whole situation—ignoring notifications all day, checking in at night—seemed to be working out fine.

Roxy, however, didn't agree.

The Monday after I returned from Phoenix, I was sitting at my desk when a DM from Roxy popped up on my phone:

> Nicole, I noticed you haven't been active on our Slack chats during the day. It would be nice if you didn't wait 12 hours to respond when we asked you a question. As maid of honor, you're supposed to be the leader of the bridal party, but it feels like you don't even care about this wedding at all.

I clenched my fists to keep from responding with a string of curse words I'd later regret. Because I had to remember the most important part of this job: being a good friend to Parisa. It was my responsibility to keep her stress levels low, to protect her from bullshit like this. If I blew up on her sisters, they'd complain to Farnaz, who would make Parisa's life miserable. I couldn't do that to her.

What I wanted to do was pretend I'd never seen this message. What I needed to do was de-escalate and redirect. Just like a chatbot.

I sat there for a few minutes, pondering exactly how a chatbot would respond. What would be the most effective way to remove the pesky emotions from this conversation and defuse any imminent conflict?

Then I realized I didn't have to ponder this at all. Because I could use an *actual* chatbot.

It was the perfect solution, really. A chatbot could stand in for me during the day, giving canned answers and words of encouragement from my Slack account. The bridal party—and Roxy and Leila, in particular—would feel like I was an active participant in the chat. And each night, I could check in for real and get up to speed on any critical information I needed to know about.

Fortunately, setting up a simple chatbot didn't take that much effort. First, I ran a scan of the existing log to help the bot establish some context and familiarize itself with the topics at hand. I also instructed it to pay special attention to my contributions so it would learn how to mimic my unique voice.

Then I had to give it some triggers, which were essentially keywords that would kick the chatbot into action. For example, if someone typed *Nicole* or *website* or *bachelorette party*, the chatbot would generate a response that looked like it was coming from me. It would also echo general sentiments of disappointment or enthusiasm, to align with what other people were saying. It wouldn't be perfect, but it'd be enough to appease Roxy. Hopefully.

When I was done, I tested it in an emulator, throwing random phrases at it to see how it would respond.

Me: Nicole, can you change the background from that awful taupe color to a bright lime green?
Chatbot: Of course. I'll take care of it as soon as I get off of work.
Me: Should we do roses or peonies for the bridesmaid bouquets?

> **Chatbot:** I trust your judgment. Let's do what you think is best.
>
> **Me:** I can't believe Parisa hasn't sent out save the dates yet.
>
> **Chatbot:** *sigh* I know. I'll talk to her about it ASAP.

There. Immediate answers with zero conflict. That would totally shut Roxy up.

I replied to her DM:

> Roxy, you're right, and I'm sorry. I've been so busy with work that I've neglected to keep up with the chat. From now on, I'll make sure to check in much more regularly, and respond in a timely manner. Thank you!

It was a far nicer response than Roxy deserved, in my opinion, but I'd be getting the last laugh. Because I had no intention of spending my entire day glued to the Slack chat, reading her snotty remarks. This chatbot was going to do it for me.

The moment before I turned it on, though, I felt a prickle of apprehension. It wasn't that I was worried anyone would find out. These Virtuality chatbots were top of the line; they'd been used for years on scores of corporate clients and were virtually bulletproof in terms of accuracy.

More than anything, it just *felt* wrong. All day long, everyone else would be chatting away, thinking they were talking to me, when in reality this AI software would be evaluating their conversations and spitting back appropriate computer-generated messages. Basically, I'd be lying to the bridal party.

But I didn't have any other choice. Roxy was being completely unreasonable, and this was a simple way to make everybody happy. Besides, I didn't have time to get bogged down in some moral quandary. I was operating on a tight schedule here.

I clicked the button to activate the chatbot and kept the window open to monitor the first few interactions. Soon enough, Roxy came on with some news about wedding dress shopping.

> **Roxy:** Tried to get Parisa in at Bergman's to pick out a gown but they're booked up until July. 😠
> **Leila:** Of course they are. They're Bergman's.
> **Shirin:** Isn't that the shop featured on that reality show about weddings?
> **Ally:** Oh, The Bridal Boutique! I love that show!
> **Roxy:** Yes. Was hoping to get us featured but no such luck.
> **Leila:** That sucks.
> **Shirin:** Yeah, I'm sorry. 😥

I watched with glee as my chatbot chimed in.

> **Nicole:** That's too bad.

A perfect echo of empathy!
The conversation continued:

> **Leila:** Where else are you looking?
> **Roxy:** I called around a few other places and booked us a session at Gloria's Bridal in Glendale. Sunday the 28th at 2PM. Can you all make it?
> **Shirin:** Yep.
> **Kara:** Sorry I'll be in New York all week. 😕
> **Ally:** I'll be there.
> **Leila:** Me too.
> **Nicole:** I'll put it on my schedule!

Bam. Virtual Nicole was killing it.

I shut down Slack and opened my calendar to create an entry for this appointment at Gloria's. Then I shifted my focus toward work, which was what I should've been doing this past half hour instead of messing around with this Slack chatbot.

Right now, the only chatbot that mattered was the one I was designing for Krueger-Middleton. During my business trips, I'd spoken to dozens of people about what their chatbot was supposed to say. Now, I had to translate that feedback into a flowchart that tracked the possibilities for their most commonly encountered conversations.

I'd just entered "the zone"—totally immersed in the task at hand—when a text appeared on my phone from Vimi: Lunch?

Can't, I replied. Swamped.

> Ben's skipping out, too.

> I think I'm just gonna grab a to-go box.

> Want one?

> The muffulettas always go fast on Mondays.

Sure, thanks!

Can you ask Dwayne to hold the mortadella?

Five minutes later, my phone dinged with another text. Probably Vimi letting me know that the dining hall was already out of muffulettas.

When I checked, though, it was actually Parisa: Are you back in town or are you still traveling for work?

I'm home. Got in yesterday.

> How was Phoenix?

Didn't really see anything aside from the client's office and my hotel room.

What's going on with you?

Just relaxing.

Had a long day on set yesterday.

What show are you working on now?

A baking competition called Donut Warriors.

Ooh delicious!

Yeah I ate my weight in bear claws last week.

Speaking of reality show competitions . . . any word from your survivor man lately?

Okay, here's the thing: I hadn't exactly told Parisa about what had happened the last time Brandon and I had hung out.

I mean, I'd told her most of it. That he'd made me delicious drinks, and that his apartment was styled like a log cabin, and that we hadn't engaged in any funny business even though I'd kind of wanted to. I also told her he was moving to Idyllwild, but I conveniently left out the part where I'd slammed my swizzle and run for the exit, shutting the door on any potential romantic future between us. Because I knew she'd tell me I was being ridiculous, and I didn't feel like arguing with her. The next day, I flew off to Oakland, hoping she'd forget all about Brandon by the time I came back.

Obviously, she had not.

Nope. Haven't heard from him.

Really? That's weird.

How did you guys end things?

Like did he say he'd call you?

I did not want to talk about this right now.

I don't think it's going to work out between us.

Wait . . .

You blew him off, didn't you?

I didn't blow him off.

I just said it wasn't a good idea for us to see each other if he was moving out of town.

He's only moving two hours away!

Mike and I did long distance for a whole year when he was living in Chicago, and that was a four-hour flight.

It's too hard.

I don't have time for it with my job.

Nicole!

You need a life outside the office!

Stop using your job as an excuse to avoid a relationship!

I didn't respond. We'd had this conversation a million times already, and there was no need to rehash it. Besides, I wasn't using this as an excuse. Parisa had her way of doing things, and I had mine. End of story.

Tossing my phone aside, I tried to turn my attention back to this flowchart. But now that Parisa had mentioned Brandon, I couldn't stop thinking about the last time we'd hung out together. Images of him floated through my brain: The way he'd smiled when he'd talked about Idyllwild. The way his bicep had flexed when he'd flipped that cocktail shaker. The way his gray eyes had burned into mine.

I'm not sure how long I was sitting there, staring into space, fantasizing about what Brandon might look like without a shirt, before Vimi came back with my lunch.

"Muffuletta here, minus the mortadella." She held the sandwich aloft, then furrowed her brow. "What's wrong?"

"Nothing, why?"

"You're all flushed."

Instinctively, I pressed my fingertips to my cheek. It was warm to the touch. "Oh."

"Are you having hot flashes? I always get them when I'm stressed out."

"Maybe."

"Try going for a run or something. It'll help relieve the stress. Did you see those new treadmill desks in the gym?"

Was I the only person in this office who wasn't exercising while I worked? Regardless, I took the sandwich from her hand and said, "Thanks."

It wasn't stress that was causing my cheeks to flush. That heat was coming from a wholly different source. Just *thinking* about Brandon was enough to raise my body temperature.

I wondered what he was doing right now. Was he finished with Vespa already? Had renovations started on his new brewpub? Complicated feelings aside, I was genuinely interested in his new business venture and his life in general. Maybe we could still maintain a platonic friendship. Would it be weird to send him a friendly text, just to see what he was up to?

Maybe. But that didn't stop me from doing it.

> Hey!

> Just checking in to see how things are going with the new brewpub.

> Hope you're doing well!

The moment I hit send, I cringed. There was no statement more meaningless and cliché than *Hope you're doing well.* It was the opening sentence of every work email I ever sent. Was I *that* incapable of casual communication?

Thankfully, Brandon didn't seem to mind, because he wrote me back almost immediately.

> Hey, good to hear from you!

> The contractors start demolition next Monday so renovations are almost underway.

> Working on a menu and marketing plan now.

> Also, there's this: mountainairbrewpub.com

Wow, he'd already put together a website. Good for him! I tapped the link, eager to see how his business was claiming its little corner of the internet.

Oh. Oh no.

This website was atrocious.

It wasn't even a full website. It was merely a placeholder for what was to come. But what should've been a clean, simple landing page managed to be an overly complicated eyesore.

The logo was nicely designed—a minimalistic mountain and pine tree with the words *Mountain Air Brewpub* underneath—yet it was placed off center, beneath a bright-red banner that screamed *Coming Soon!* against a forest-green background. The side banner contained a bunch of dead links. And was I hearing things, or were there *birds* chirping in the background?

In this day and age, there was no excuse for such a crudely designed website, and it would reflect poorly on Brandon's brand. I didn't know if he'd created this himself or if—heaven forbid—he was paying someone for it. All I knew was I couldn't allow him to let this janky mess show up in a Google search for his new brewpub.

Dating Brandon was out of the question; there were too many what-ifs and maybes. But there was no reason he and I couldn't keep things platonic and work together in a professional capacity.

I texted him back: I have a business proposition for you.

CHAPTER NINE

"I don't understand."

Brandon and I were sitting at his kitchen table, reviewing wireframes for the new Mountain Air Brewpub website. I'd thrown them together the night before—just some simple black-and-white layouts of each page to give him an idea of what it would look like. I'd thought they were clear, but from the wrinkle in his forehead, I could see I'd thought wrong.

"What don't you understand?" I asked, scanning the wireframes for anything that might look confusing. "Is it the navigation menu? Because we can always change it."

"No, the menu is great. Everything's great, honestly. I'm blown away by what you did here. This is so much more than I expected."

"It's not that big of a deal." The back of my neck suddenly felt hot and sweaty. Had I gone overboard? "Really, this is a super basic business website."

"It seems way more than basic to me. I mean, you've included a whole online-ordering section." He waved his hands over the papers that were spread out between us. "I just don't get it."

"What don't you get?"

"You said you had a business proposition for me. But how is this a business proposition if you don't want me to pay you for your work?"

"You can't pay me. I'm pretty sure that would violate this moonlighting clause I have in my employment contract with Virtuality. I'm not supposed to take on any side jobs. An unpaid favor for a friend, though? That's totally allowed."

He shook his head. "This is a really big favor."

"Well, to be honest, I have an ulterior motive. You know how I'm up for a promotion at work? To get it, I have to build a portfolio that includes stuff like letters of recommendation and written personal statements and side projects that are relevant to my job."

"For a promotion?" He let out a low whistle. "That sounds more like a college application."

"I know; it's pretty intense. Anyway, I haven't worked on any side projects recently, so this is the perfect opportunity to develop something fresh for my portfolio."

"So this would be a mutually beneficial relationship."

"A *business* relationship." The words came out quickly. Perhaps a little too quickly, because Brandon gave me this weird side-eye and a little smile.

"Okay," he said. "This is great, then. How long do you think it'll take you to get the site up and running?"

"I can probably get the bones of it up by the end of the week. Work is slow right now, so I can get it all done before things pick up again. As you and your brother finalize your menus and take photos of the finished space and stuff, we can update the templates."

That look of skepticism returned. "Are you sure this isn't too much? I know you're busy at work; I don't want to pile more stuff on your plate."

"You're not piling anything on my plate. I offered to do this, remember? Plus, it really isn't all that much work. I know it might seem like a lot, but I've been doing this kind of thing for a while now. I can bang out a website much quicker than you think."

He picked up a wireframe and studied the empty boxes and placeholder text. "Exactly how long have you been doing this?"

"Web design? Probably around eight years. I started in college, as a side gig to earn extra cash."

"You're really good at it. This is a million times better than the website we have now."

That was the understatement of the year. "Who designed that, anyway?"

"My brother. He thought we could save money by using one of those free website builders. I didn't have the heart to tell him it looked terrible."

"You and your brother are pretty close, huh? I mean, you must be to go into business together."

"We are. He's the one who introduced me to Idyllwild. He's been living there for about a year now, but before that, he was all over the place: Oregon, Utah, Northern California. It's been years since we lived in the same zip code. I'm looking forward to being near him again."

His gaze went soft around the edges, and I felt a stab of envy. Here was another person for whom family was sacred and essential. The bond between siblings was something I could never understand.

"I'm an only child," I said. "I kind of hate it. I always wanted a sibling."

"I can't imagine what my life would've been like without my brother." His voice grew quiet as he said, "We went through some shit growing up."

"What kind of shit?"

The muscles in his jaw clenched, and his gaze suddenly hardened. "My parents are alcoholics. Our childhood was . . . not ideal."

A lightness overcame me. I gripped the table to keep myself from floating away. "My mom's an alcoholic, too."

"So you get it." His lips curved into a smile. Not a happy, radiant, glowing smile but a sad smile. The smile of someone who understood the struggles you'd gone through, the complex, frustrating pain you'd endured and probably always would. Someone who didn't require an explanation of what it was like to grow up in a highly dysfunctional home and who knew pity was a waste of emotion.

Someone who got it.

"Yeah, I get it," I said. "My dad doesn't really drink, but he's always been cold and distant. He was constantly cheating on my mom, which made me feel bad for her, but also resentful. Like I felt it was her fault for not having her shit together. Obviously, now that I'm older, I know the truth is way more complicated than that. But it would've been easier if I'd had a brother or sister to go through it with. Then I wouldn't have felt so alone all the time."

Brandon reached across the table. Gently, tentatively, he caressed the back of my hand. The touch was so soft, but the result was like flint striking steel.

"That must've been hard for you," he said.

"It was." My voice sounded smoky. "You understand what it's like, though."

"Yeah, but at least I had Eric. And Charlie." When I narrowed my eyes in confusion, he laughed. "My dog, remember?"

"Oh yeah." With Brandon touching me, I was having a hard time remembering anything. Specifically, I couldn't remember why I'd decided dating him would be such a bad idea.

I knew he was still interested. I could feel it in the way his fingertips fluttered against my skin. This was more than just a friendly, comforting pat on the back of my hand. This was an invitation.

He angled his body toward mine. "What's your relationship with your parents like now?"

"Not great. I only really see them on holidays, and it's always a terrible time."

"I completely understand. That's why I stopped speaking to my parents."

"It's definitely crossed my mind to cut them off, but then I feel like I'd be abandoning them. As it is, I probably don't spend as much time with them as I should. They need help, you know? To fix their problems."

"No way." He gave my hand a tender squeeze. "You *cannot* fix their problems. That's the first thing I learned in therapy."

So Brandon was in therapy, too. Sometimes it felt like I was the only person in this city who didn't have a therapist.

I knew I could benefit from it. I wasn't too naive to understand that there were some deep-seated issues I needed to address. But the idea of sitting in a room with a complete stranger, pouring my guts out about private matters I didn't even want to *think* about, much less talk about, made me so uncomfortable that I'd simply resigned myself to a lifetime of low-level pervasive anxiety and miserable Thanksgivings.

"Anyway," he said, "I think family isn't made up of the people who raised you or who share your genetics or your last name or anything like that. It's the people who share your beliefs and your values, who build you up instead of trying to hold you down. The people who love you for who you are and who always want what's best for you."

"Chosen family," I said.

He nodded. "Exactly."

"I feel that way about Parisa. Like she's my chosen family. She's been there for me my whole life. When things were bad with my mom, she gave me a safe space to escape to. She's always looking out for me, always making time to listen. Sometimes I think she cares more about my own happiness than I do."

"You don't care about your own happiness?"

He leaned in, his voice low and husky, his face mere inches from mine. My gaze dropped to the tabletop, and I watched his thumb stroke the back of my hand, stoking a fire beneath my skin.

This was dangerous territory. I was the one who'd said it was pointless to get to know each other, yet I'd just spent the last fifteen minutes confessing my innermost feelings. What was I doing? I had my reasons for not letting myself get involved with Brandon. And they were good reasons! Not excuses, like Parisa said.

Besides, it wasn't that I didn't want to be happy. It was that I didn't want to be sad. I needed to feel safe and stable, not exposed and vulnerable. But when I lifted my gaze and met Brandon's burning eyes, I felt like I might spontaneously combust.

In a flash, I was on my feet, standing with such force that my chair toppled backward. "Oops, sorry," I said, scrambling to pick it back up.

"Are you okay?" Brandon stood to help me, his palm finding the small of my back. "What happened?"

"Nothing, I'm fine." I straightened my glasses and smoothed my hair. *Don't look at him, don't look at him.* "It's just . . . I should go."

As I gathered the wireframes into a messy, uneven pile, Brandon asked, "Do you have everything you need?"

"Yes. I'll get to work on the website right away." This was turning out to be a replay of the last time I'd bolted from his apartment in a nervous frenzy. But I couldn't help it. I had to run away from these uncomfortable emotions and pretend they didn't exist. Stuff them into some neglected crevice in the back of my brain and let it scar over. That was the only way I could feel safe again.

With my stack of papers tucked neatly under my arm, I walked to the front door. Brandon trailed behind and asked, "So you'll be in touch when the website is ready for my review?"

"Absolutely." I spun on the ball of my foot, purposely avoiding eye contact. Instead, I looked at Brandon's chest. He wasn't wearing a button-down today. Instead, he wore a tight-fitting graphic tee printed with the words HIKE MORE, WORRY LESS. It felt accusatory. "I'll text you later this week, okay?"

When he didn't answer, I looked up to find him staring at me intently, his eyes on fire, his top teeth grazing his bottom lip. Instantly, I turned away, taking deep breaths to calm the rising ache in the center of my chest. *In-two-three-four, out-two-three-four.*

Finally, he said, "Okay."

"See ya," I said, then fled his apartment and walked down the hall.

Only after the elevator doors closed behind me could I finally take a deep breath. As I exhaled the tension and the fear, I came to the conclusion that Brandon and I could never have a platonic friendship, or even a strictly professional partnership.

Because every time we were together, I wanted to burst into flames.

CHAPTER TEN

Every night that week, I stayed up late working on the Mountain Air website. Despite it being a personal project, I treated it like any other work-related task: a technical challenge with little to no emotional attachment. Granted, I did have a moment of weakness when putting together the *Our Team* page, which included a high-res headshot of Brandon and his brother. As I centered the image on the screen, I stopped to stare into Brandon's gray eyes, letting myself get lost in the fantasy of what it would be like to run my fingertips along his stubbly cheeks.

Most of the time, though, I was very self-disciplined.

When the site was ready, I texted Brandon the link to review. Moments later, he replied:

> This is incredible!
>
> Gonna send to Eric now.
>
> I'm sure he'll love it, too.
>
> Thanks again for being awesome.
>
>

I tried not to read too much into that heart-covered smiley face. And I *definitely* did not acknowledge that odd little pitter-patter tapping around in my chest.

Once the website was squared away, I threw myself headfirst into the Krueger project, which was ramping up quite rapidly. Our task list was growing by the day, and Anna started leading the team in daily stand-up meetings to review our progress, which meant I always had to be on point. With my promotion at stake, falling behind wasn't an option.

For the first time in my Virtuality career, I started pulling all-nighters. Sometimes, when I was desperate for a rest, I'd catch a quick nap in one of the sleep pods on the fifth floor. And I finally checked out the employee gym. Not to work out, of course, but to freshen up in the locker room from time to time. I kept a travel toiletry kit in my desk now, with a toothbrush and deodorant and the four skin-care products I used on my face each night.

One evening at around ten o'clock, I was applying glycolic acid serum to my forehead when Cass walked into the locker room. She had a toiletry kit of her own, which she plopped on the counter beside me.

"Hey," she said. "How's it going?"

"Good, how about you? I haven't seen you around lately. Have you been busy?"

"Yep." She pulled a roll of floss from her bag and tore off a long strand. "You know how it is."

Indeed, I did. The hectic schedule and extreme workload we endured was unfathomable to people who didn't work here. It's why Parisa was always hounding me to get a life and Brandon warned me about burnout. But Virtuality employees inherently understood each other. There was no need to explain or defend or feel guilty. We just got it.

That was why Ben said he and Cass worked so well. And I admit, their relationship sounded pretty nice. I bet everything between them was so easy, so drama-free. Maybe it was time for me to dip my toe back into the old office dating pool. Surely there must be *someone* here I'd spark with. The new guy on the infrastructure team was pretty cute.

"How long have you and Ben been together now?" I asked.

Between flosses, she said, "It was a year yesterday."

"Oh my gosh, I didn't know. Happy anniversary." Funny, Ben hadn't mentioned it. "What did you guys do to celebrate?"

She flashed me a befuddled look in the mirror. "Nothing. I mean, we had our daily 'us time' at the gym, but other than that, it was just another day. I had to monitor a go-live last night, anyway."

"Oh." She'd worked right through their anniversary? That was depressing. Though she didn't look particularly depressed about it. Maybe she and Ben were just one of those couples that didn't make a big deal out of their anniversary. I'd never heard of those couples, but they must exist.

The next day, I ate dinner with Ben and Vimi in the dining hall—it was one of those not-so-rare occasions when we were all working late. As we sat there feasting on Dwayne's famous lasagna, I congratulated Ben on his anniversary.

"Has it really been a year?" Vimi said. "That went by so fast."

"Yeah. It did." Ben pushed his pasta around his plate, looking sullen.

"Is everything okay?" I asked.

He shrugged one shoulder. "Things are fine. It's just . . . I thought she might want to go to dinner to celebrate, somewhere besides the dining hall. So I made surprise reservations at this schmancy place on Beverly. Have you guys ever been to Vespa?"

"Yes." That odd little pitter-patter in my chest started up again. "They have really good desserts."

"I read that on Eater," he said. "Anyway, when I told her about it, I thought she'd be excited, but she said she couldn't go. I guess there was some big go-live she had to babysit. So then I suggested we do something special in the dining hall—you know how Dwayne makes those awesome cakes on request? But she told me not to bother. That she didn't want to make a big deal out of it. Isn't that weird?"

"Maybe a little," Vimi said. "Did you talk to her about it?"

He shook his head. "Nah, we haven't really had a chance."

"What about during your daily treadmill dates?" I said.

"The gym is always packed. This isn't exactly the kind of conversation I want to have in front of a hundred of our coworkers."

Vimi frowned. "That sucks. I'm sorry."

"Me, too."

"It's fine," Ben said, but from the despondent expression on his face, he was certainly not feeling fine.

Turned out dating a Virtuality colleague didn't mean your life was drama-free. Romantic relationships were always full of emotional land mines.

As I shoveled a forkful of lasagna into my mouth, my phone dinged with a text from Parisa:

> Where are you???

I double-checked my schedule, worried that I'd forgotten some important wedding-related event that was supposed to take place tonight. All I saw was a big block of time labeled *Work*.

Maybe she'd meant to send this text to Mike. Or maybe something was really wrong.

> What is it? Are you okay?

> I'm about to murder my mother and sisters and possibly also my future mother-in-law.

> Have they trapped you in some annoying

text chain about the wedding?

No, they've trapped me in the dressing room.

With THIS monstrosity of a gown.

She sent a photo of herself wearing a wedding dress, a selfie she'd taken in a full-length, three-way mirror. From every angle, this gown was hideous. Big floofy bows on each shoulder. Tiny silk roses all over the bodice. A full pleated skirt with a ruffled flounce. Why had she even agreed to put this on?

When did you take this photo?

Two seconds ago.

We're all at Bergman's.

Why aren't you here?

No, that couldn't be. The dress fitting was at Gloria's on Sunday, not at Bergman's and not today. That was what my schedule said. My schedule was never wrong.

Despite how busy I'd been, I was still keeping up with the Slack chat every single night, and there was never any mention of an appointment at Bergman's. Had I missed it somehow? Frantically, I pulled up the app. Under the #dresses channel, there was a slew of unread messages from earlier this morning.

> **Roxy:** Good news, bitches! Bergman's just called me with a last minute opening for tonight at 6:30.
> **Ally:** No way. Are they filming for the show???
> **Roxy:** Of course not, that's a completely separate application.

Ally: 😒 Do you think Roland will be there, at least?

Roxy: I certainly hope so! It's his store, after all.

Ally: OMG this is so exciting.

Leila: Nice work, Roxy! Can't wait to do this thing!

Roxy: I already told Parisa and she's good with the time. I understand this is very last minute, but I trust you all can make it?

Ally: Wouldn't miss it!

Leila: Obvs.

Shirin: I can make it!

Nicole: Sure! It's in my calendar.

Dammit. The chatbot had confirmed I'd be there.

Instantly, I texted Parisa:

> I am so sorry.

> I completely lost track of time.

> Running out the door now.

> Be there as soon as I can!

Hurry, please!

I'm afraid to leave the dressing room.

What a disaster.

"I've gotta go." I leaped out of my chair without an explanation, leaving my half-eaten lasagna behind. I ran back to my desk, threw my purse over my shoulder, and made a beeline for the stairs. As I turned the corner at the end of the hall, I collided with a beady-eyed bearded man.

Ugh, Charles.

"In a hurry?" He chuckled at his own bad joke.

"Kind of." I adjusted the strap of my bag, waiting for him to step aside. When he didn't, I said, "Is there something you need from me, or . . ."

He cast a leisurely glance at his smart watch. "Are you leaving already?"

I wasn't sure why Charles felt the need to keep tabs on my schedule; he wasn't my boss. Maybe he was looking for a way to get me kicked off the Krueger project so he could snag it for himself. I couldn't let him know what I was really up to. "I'm working from home. There are too many distractions here; I need some quiet."

He pulled a face like he'd sucked on a lemon, clearly disappointed that he hadn't caught me cutting out early. Though, really, was six forty-five such an objectively unreasonable time to leave the office? Yes, cutting out of work early meant I'd fall behind on my task list, but there was no way I could miss out on wedding dress shopping. Parisa needed me there to save her from whatever nonsense her family was putting her through. I'd just have to clock back in after I left Bergman's and hope to somehow double my productivity tonight.

No point in giving it any more thought. I'd already wasted too much time with this bozo, so I pushed past him and ran toward my car in the underground parking lot.

LA traffic being what it was, it took me forty-five minutes to get to Bergman's. I threw my car in the overpriced valet and was in a full nervous sweat by the time I reached the front door. This place was so fancy I had to be buzzed in, and the receptionist grimaced a little when she saw the sweat stains blooming from my armpits. "I'm with Parisa Shahin," I said.

"She's at Platform Twelve," she said, and then her eyes fell to the computer screen before her. "But according to the schedule, she only has ten more minutes before the next bride arrives. You'd better hurry."

Platform 12 was in the far back corner of the showroom, which was massive and arranged like a labyrinth. I wove my way through the mannequins and freestanding mirrors, sidestepping employees who pushed racks of dresses hastily across the floor. Scattered throughout were brides-to-be perched on miniature stages, posing in front of their friends and family, who sat on velvet couches, offering feedback and sipping champagne. Between the bright white lights and the echo of voices and the pervasive smell of flowery air freshener, I was feeling a bit overwhelmed. This store was an assault on the senses.

Finally, I caught sight of Platform 12. Roxy and Leila sat on either arm of the royal-blue couch, flanking the other guests like guardian statues. Shirin and Ally were there, alongside Farnaz, Francine, and Mike's sister, whose name I'd unfortunately forgotten. Off to the side, an hors d'oeuvres tray sat empty, the complimentary bottle of champagne drained dry.

"Hi, everyone," I said, breathlessly. "I'm so sorry I'm late."

Roxy sneered in my direction. "It's about time. Parisa's trying on her last dress right now."

I squeezed into a tiny open space on the couch next to Mike's sister, whispering, "I'm so sorry; I've forgotten your name."

She smiled back, perfectly pleasant. "Don't worry about it. I'm Abigail."

"Where's Kara?" I asked, this time with my voice at full volume.

"She's in New York all week, remember?" Ally said.

"Honestly," Roxy said, "I don't know why she's even a bridesmaid. She barely contributes to our conversations."

"Well, she *is* a famous model," Ally said. "She's got a lot of work to do."

Leila and Roxy both rolled their eyes.

"Enough of this," Farnaz cut in, tapping a clipboard she held in her hand with handwritten notes. "What do we think of the dresses Parisa has tried on so far? The one with the mermaid silhouette is my favorite, by far."

Francine grimaced. "Oh, really? I thought that one was *very* unflattering."

Farnaz scowled. "Unflattering how?"

"It bunched up under her bosom and made her look like she had a gut."

Now I was scowling, too. Apparently, Mike's mother wasn't a member of the body-positivity movement. Parisa had struggled for years with her body image and had only recently found peace. I sincerely hoped this woman wasn't going to make her feel bad about herself and undo all the progress she had made.

"I liked the third one," Leila said. "The lace details were so beautiful."

"Me, too," added Roxy. "But the one with the silk roses on the bodice was *so* gorgeous."

That must've been the dress Parisa was wearing in the photo she'd sent me. The one she'd deemed a "monstrosity."

"You know," Abigail said, "I thought that dress had a little too much—"

"What is taking her so long in there?" Roxy interrupted as if Abigail hadn't spoken at all. Abigail slouched back into the couch, and Roxy stood up, craning her neck to look around the showroom. "Where's Roland already? Our time's almost up here."

"Who's Roland?" I asked, which elicited another eye roll from Roxy and Leila.

Ally's eyes went wide, though. "Haven't you ever seen *The Bridal Boutique*?" When I shook my head, they went even wider. "Roland's the lead fashion consultant on the show. He tends to the brides and helps them find their perfect wedding gown."

Shirin leaned over and touched my knee. "Truthfully, he's not so great. The stuff he's been pulling for Parisa is way off base for her."

"Shh!" Ally swatted at Shirin's arm. "Here he comes!"

Roland was a petite man in a three-piece purple suit. He moved with fluid grace, gliding across the showroom as if on roller skates. "Have we made a decision yet?" He was smiling, all bright-white teeth and frozen forehead, but he gave off a tense vibe, like he'd seen one too many indecisive brides today and was going to lose his shit any minute.

"She's been in there forever," Roxy said. "I don't know what's going on."

He rapped on the dressing room door. "Parisa? Sweetheart? Everything all right in there?"

"I'm done," she called out from the other side. Her voice sounded muffled and sort of wobbly. "I'm not getting this dress."

"Well, sweetheart," he said, "let's at least see it before you make a decision. Come out here and look in the three-way mirror, under the lights. You'll get a better view that way."

"No, I'm good," she said. "You can all go home now."

Leila and Roxy simultaneously groaned while Farnaz shot out of her seat. "This is ridiculous," she said, then shoved Roland aside and tried to open the door. "Get out here now. We need to see it."

As they argued back and forth in Persian, I whipped out my phone and sent Parisa a text: Hey, I'm here. Do you need me to come in there with you?

A moment later, she called out, "Nicole, come here! *Just* Nicole."

Farnaz stepped aside as I approached the dressing room and tapped softly on the door with my fingernails. In a flash, Parisa stuck her arm out and yanked me inside, then slammed the door closed again.

There was barely enough room in here for the both of us. The train of the dress took up most of the empty floor space. I had to stack one foot on top of the other so I didn't trample the delicate chiffon under my sneakers.

Parisa looked absolutely beautiful, though, like a goddess who'd descended from the clouds. The gown was off white with a deep sweetheart neckline and an open back. The lace detail on the bodice swirled like waves, and the full tulle skirt shimmered like starlight.

Suddenly, this whole wedding thing felt a lot more real. Tears sprang to my eyes as I took in this vision of my radiant best friend, the bride-to-be, who was mere months away from marrying the man who would hopefully make her happy for the rest of her life.

"You are so stunning," I said. My voice wavered a bit, and I felt sort of silly, until I realized Parisa was on the verge of crying, too. Except I wasn't so sure those were happy tears she was about to shed. "What's wrong?"

She flung her arms wide. "I hate this dress. I hate all these dresses."

"The one with the roses and bows was truly terrible, but this one is gorgeous. It suits you perfectly, all ethereal and elegant." She turned around to look in the mirror, and I glanced at her reflection. "What don't you like about it?"

She pressed a nervous hand to her stomach, then pinched at the flesh under her arms. "You don't think I look bad?"

Rage rose within me. "Is Francine body shaming you? Because if she is, I will march up to her and shout her right out of the store."

"No, that's not it," she said, cracking the smallest of smiles. "But I appreciate your willingness to throw down for me. I think I'm just feeling overwhelmed. The wedding didn't feel real until now, do you know what I mean?"

I nodded and placed a comforting hand on her shoulder. "I was thinking the same thing myself."

"Yeah." She took a deep, shaky breath, her eyes still glued to her reflection. "Standing here in a wedding dress. It's all really happening. And it's happening so fast."

Okay, I knew what was going on now: prewedding jitters. I'd read about this in my extensive maid of honor research. The stress of planning a wedding, including the pressure to please family and future in-laws, could lead to intense feelings of anxiety. Fortunately, I'd found a helpful guide to talking the bride through an episode like this.

"It's perfectly normal to feel this way," I said, my voice calm and even, trying my best to soothe her nerves. "You're taking a huge step forward in life. That's understandably overwhelming."

"They're not making things any easier for me." She gestured angrily to the door. "I'm doing this whole thing just to make them happy, but it's like nothing I do is ever enough."

"Do you want me to ask them to leave?"

Parisa spun around, her big brown eyes full of hope. "That would be amazing. Would you be comfortable doing that?"

"Of course." The idea of telling her mother and sisters and future mother-in-law to buzz off made me feel anything but comfortable, but for Parisa, I'd step out of my comfort zone. "Give me one second."

I slipped out of the dressing room and into the lion's den. Farnaz, Francine, Roxy, and Leila were already on their feet, hovering around me. Roxy snarled, "What's going on in there?"

"Um . . ." I froze, unable to speak with these four pairs of hostile eyes trained on me. They were waiting for an answer, though. I had to give them one.

In-two-three-four, out-two-three-four.

"Parisa has asked me to ask you all to leave."

There. That wasn't so bad.

"What?" Farnaz yelled so loudly I jumped.

Francine looked around at the others before squinting at me. "I don't understand."

"She's just feeling a bit overwhelmed," I said. "I think she needs some space to process . . . everything."

Roxy snatched her purse from the back of the couch. "Whatever. This is so typical of her."

"*So* typical." Leila sucked her teeth and shook her head, and the two of them stormed toward the exit. Shirin smiled apologetically as she left, with Ally trailing behind taking covert photos of Roland, who was now tending to another bride across the showroom.

It took another moment for Farnaz and Francine to collect their belongings, all the while muttering about how "absurd" and "dramatic" Parisa was being. But Parisa was one of the least dramatic people I knew. If anything, everyone else was being dramatic.

Finally, Farnaz gave me a kiss on the cheek and said, "I hope she doesn't give you too much trouble."

Francine waved goodbye. Abigail followed her out the door, turning back with a regretful look on her face. "Bye, Nicole."

"Bye," I said.

After everyone had finally left, I returned to the dressing room, hiding my shaking hands behind my back. "They're gone," I said.

"Thank you so much." Parisa was still wearing the gown, smiling, looking radiant. "That was really awesome of you."

"That's what I'm here for."

She faced the mirror and turned slowly from side to side, admiring the sparkly skirt as it flowed back and forth. "I've decided you're right about this dress. It's actually really stunning. And I think it might be the one. What do you think?"

"I think you're right."

Parisa spun around. "Thank you for being here for me."

Tears welled in my eyes again. "I'll always be here for you. I'm sorry I was so late today."

"Don't even worry about it. You didn't miss anything except for some fugly dresses. And you came just when I needed you. Like you always do." She smoothed her hands down the lace front of her gown. "I guess I should ring up Roland. Tell him I made a decision."

"I'll go get him."

Roland was standing beside the abandoned Platform 12, his face contorted with rage. When he saw me, he forced that same frozen smile and said in a strained voice, "We need this space for our next guest. Has your sister made a decision?"

"Oh, actually . . ." I was about to correct him. But then I thought back to what Brandon had said about chosen family. How it wasn't made up of the people who shared your genetics but the people who loved you, who nurtured you, and who always had your back. That was me and Parisa. We weren't sisters in blood or in name, but we were the next best thing. We were almost-sisters.

"Yes," I said. "She's found the perfect dress."

CHAPTER ELEVEN

Life chugged along, according to schedule. This, of course, translated to work, work, and more work. Fortunately, Krueger seemed happy with everything we'd delivered so far. Whenever Anna responded to one of my emails with *Good job,* I suddenly felt taller, stronger, more powerful. It made me want to work even harder, stay even later at the office. I lived for the dopamine hit of praise for a job well done.

One Friday morning, Anna called our daily stand-up meeting in the hallway outside her office. These usually lasted no more than ten minutes, with each of us running through what we'd accomplished thus far and what we were planning to work on next. The engineers went first, then the data people, then the guy from operations. Finally, Anna turned to me and said, "Nicole, let's talk about design for a minute."

"Sure," I said, ready to rattle off my list of completed and pending tasks. "Yesterday, I made a lot of headway on the welcome messaging, and—"

"Hold on a second." She frowned slightly. "Last night, our sales team got an email from Vince in the Oakland office. He's the VP of customer relations for Krueger. Did you meet with him when you were out there?"

"I believe so." Honestly, it was a struggle to remember the name of every single person I'd encountered on that whirlwind trip. "What did he say?"

Her frown deepened. "Unfortunately, he's not too happy with what we've provided so far."

I shook my head. Surely I must've misheard her. "I don't understand."

"He listed a number of concerns." She peered down at her tablet and scrolled down the screen. "The placement of the buttons, the style of the conversation bubbles, the tone of the messages in many of the conversation flows."

So basically everything. "But all the feedback I've been getting so far has been positive. They approved the conversation flows, and I designed everything else according to spec. What happened?"

"I guess there's been some internal miscommunication on their end." She ran a hand roughly along her forehead. "We have to sort it out. Vince is pretty angry, so the sales team is flying up to Oakland on Monday morning to see if they can smooth this over and get clarity on their real requirements."

"Do they need me to go, too? Because I can be there, no problem."

"No." The word came out sharp as a knife. "Best to let sales handle this. They're experienced in dealing with dissatisfied clients."

Yikes. The client was dissatisfied with the design I'd delivered, and they didn't want me to be part of the conversation to fix it? This did not bode well for me. Not at all.

My fingertips tingled and started to go numb. I wiggled them discreetly. "What should I do in the meantime? Should I keep going as planned with our project schedule or—"

"No." Another knife slash. "Right now, your tasks are in a holding pattern. I'll let you know the plan by Monday evening. If all goes well, we'll get the client to commit to a new set of specs. Then we can reassess your task list."

Reassess? Did that mean I'd have to start from scratch? If I had to put things back on my to-do list that I'd already marked as done, I wouldn't possibly be able to finish on time.

"Does this mean we're extending the project timeline?"

She sneered at me, as if I'd insulted her. "Our go-live date of June fifth is firm. That's what we promised, and that's what we need to deliver. No matter what."

The meeting ended abruptly, and I wandered down the hallway feeling completely untethered. All this time, I'd thought I was doing such a great job on this project, but in reality, the client hated everything I'd turned in. It wasn't necessarily my fault—Anna had said there was probably an internal miscommunication on their end—but the optics were bad. If the client was ultimately dissatisfied with the design, that fell squarely on my shoulders. What would the promotion committee think?

Maybe Jon could set things straight. I marched to his office and found him sitting behind his desk with the door open. "Do you have a minute?"

He looked up from his computer. "Nicole. Sure. What's going on?"

I closed the door behind me and took a seat in his guest chair. "I need to talk to you about the Krueger project."

"Is something wrong?" He winced, undoubtedly seized with regret for assigning me to this project.

"Well, I'm not sure. Things were going along great; then Anna told me the client sent an angry email to sales saying they're dissatisfied with the design. I did everything according to spec, though. They're just changing their requirements on the fly."

He nodded, unfazed. "It happens."

"But I'm supposed to be using this project as a way to justify my promotion. If the client isn't happy, even if I did everything right, will the committee still hold that against me?"

I'd been hoping for a little consolation. Maybe a few pearls of wisdom from this director who'd been around the Virtuality block a couple of times. At the very least, it would've been nice to have an assurance that Jon would put in a good word for me. All he did, though, was throw up his hands. "There are a lot of forces at play," he said. "The promotion committee will review your whole application before making a decision."

That wasn't an answer. It was a punt.

I left his office fuming about how ridiculous this whole promotion process was. I could work my hardest, devote every waking moment to the pursuit of this goal, and still be passed over simply because I'd been assigned to a project for an unreasonable client. All those hours would be wasted. All this stress would be for nothing.

In situations like this, I'd usually stuff my frustrations into a neglected crevice of my brain, then dive into work in an effort to forget all about them. But there was no work to do right now. My tasks were on hold. My daily schedule was irrelevant.

I pulled out my phone to text Vimi and Ben and see if either of them were up for a cup of coffee. Then I thought better of it. No doubt they'd pick up on my weird, anxious state, and I couldn't talk to them about what was bugging me. They didn't know I was up for this promotion, so they wouldn't understand what was really at stake. And around here, there was so much secrecy surrounding the promotion process that I wasn't even sure we were *allowed* to talk about it. As colleagues, I knew there were limitations on our friendship, but I'd never sensed it so acutely before. For the first time in this office, I felt really and truly alone.

I was overcome with a sudden urge to go home. There was no work for me to do, so what was the point in sticking around? Then again, there was nothing for me to do at home either. I supposed I could binge Netflix or read a book or something, but in my empty apartment, I'd be even *more* alone than I was here.

Rather than leave, I went to the dining hall to eat my feelings. It wasn't even ten o'clock yet, which meant Dwayne was still manning the omelet bar. When I approached the counter, he flashed me a wide, welcoming smile.

"Hey, Nicole, how's it going?"

"Not bad, how about you?"

"Can't complain. What'll it be this morning? The usual?"

"The usual" meant spinach and jack cheese with a splash of Tapatío. But I needed something different, something richer and greasier, to help soothe the pain of this morning's events.

"I'll have an omelet stuffed with brie and bacon, please," I said. "And smother it in hollandaise sauce."

I grabbed a coffee and an apple fritter, too, then went to sit down. Unfortunately, my usual table in the back corner was occupied by two people I didn't recognize. Annoying. When I spun around in search of a different seat, I accidentally made eye contact with Charles, who was sitting at a two-top right in front of me.

"Hi, Nicole."

Ugh, Charles.

"Hi."

He gestured to the chair across from him. "Care to join me?"

My first instinct was to tell him no, but the longer I stood there, the more enticing that empty chair looked. Everyone else in the dining hall was sitting with at least one other person. And in that moment, I was so terrified of being alone that sharing a meal with Charles didn't sound *too* terrible.

"Sure." I smiled tightly and set my tray down on the table. "Thanks."

"How are things going with the chatbot project?"

"Great." He did *not* need to know what was really going on. "How are things with you?"

"Busy, as usual. You know how it is. Hard to find the time just to eat breakfast." He pointed to his half-eaten pitaya bowl.

"Yeah, totally." This omelet was my second breakfast of the day, seeing as I had nothing but time on my hands right now.

"So . . ." He cleared his throat, scratched the back of his neck. I fully expected him to make some obnoxious comment about my lack of qualifications or junior-designer status, but instead he came out with, "How's Shirin doing?"

"Fine." Truthfully, I wasn't sure how Shirin was doing. I didn't know her all that well. We'd spoken only briefly at the engagement party and at Bergman's. She seemed like she was doing okay without Charles, but suddenly I wondered if Charles was doing okay without her. From the looks of it, not really. He had this hangdog expression on his face. Like he was the saddest, loneliest man in the universe.

"Do you two talk at all?" I dug the side of my fork into the omelet and watched brie ooze out all over my plate. Delicious.

"Unfortunately, no. We had a rough breakup. I'm sure she told you all about how it went down."

"Not really. She mentioned something about you working long hours, but that's it." Also the part where he'd cried like a baby, but I figured I'd spare him that detail.

"I suppose that's the crux of it." He cleared his throat again. "It *was* my fault. The breakup, I mean. She wanted us to spend more time together, and who could blame her, right? If you want to build a relationship, you have to prioritize it. You have to be there for the other person. I wasn't there for her."

I nodded and slowly chewed my food. This conversation was becoming uncomfortably emotional, exposing a side of Charles I'd never seen and wasn't sure I wanted to see. But he appeared to be going through some sort of catharsis, or possibly crisis, and I felt like it would be rude to interrupt.

"She didn't understand what it's like to work for Virtuality," he continued. "How cutthroat it is. One misstep, and they're already hiring your replacement. Eventually, she gave me an ultimatum: my job or our relationship. It didn't seem fair. It still doesn't seem fair. But I have to admit, sometimes I wonder if I made the right choice."

As I took another bacony bite, I began to see Charles in a whole new light. I'd only ever thought of him as my professional nemesis, but maybe he wasn't such a bad guy, after all. Yes, he'd been hired into a position that should've been mine, but it wasn't his fault I'd never gotten a promotion. That was just how things worked around here. If you wanted to get promoted, you had to advocate for yourself. And I'd never self-advocated until now.

"Anyway," Charles said, "the next time you see Shirin, tell her I said hi. If you don't mind."

"Of course I don't mind. I'll definitely let her know you're thinking of her."

He smiled sheepishly, then picked up his tray and headed for the exit.

I sat by myself for a while, polishing off the rest of my omelet and my apple fritter. The whole time, I couldn't stop picturing how sad Charles had looked when he'd talked about ending things with Shirin. He must have really loved her.

Was it possible he loved his job more? Or was it simply that he needed someone who understood the unique challenges we faced here at Virtuality? If so, he'd be better off dating someone like Cass. Then they could both work right through their anniversary, and no one would be upset about it.

The rest of the day dragged on aimlessly. With no work to do, I was restless and lost, keeping busy with random podcasts and scrolling through social media. The good news was it was Friday, which meant I had something on my schedule to look forward to: our regular Friday-night game tournament.

Vimi, Ben, and I, along with a few other members of the design team, gathered in the game room at seven o'clock. It was a massive space on the third floor, filled with Ping-Pong tables, pinball machines, foosball, air hockey, and about a dozen different arcade video games. The video games were swapped out every few weeks or so to keep things interesting. Tonight, we were playing the newest addition, *Mortal Kombat*.

By now, the initial shock of the Krueger news had worn off, so I was better able to camouflage my anxiety. Plus, everyone was so engrossed in the competition there wasn't time for idle conversation. We were too focused on beating the crap out of each other.

I wasn't one for gratuitous violence, but it was intensely cathartic to take my frustrations out on these pixelated characters. Every virtual round-house kick or elbow strike brought a new wave of emotional release. When I finished one guy with a fatal spinal rip, I squealed with unbridled glee.

"You're on fire tonight," Vimi said, throwing me a high five.

"What can I say? I'm in the zone."

As I celebrated the gruesome victory, my phone buzzed with a text message from Brandon: Hey! How's it going?

Our last text exchange had been over a week ago. He'd told me his brother loved the new website, I'd sent him a thumbs-up emoji, and we'd left it at that. I hadn't expected to hear from him so soon, but maybe he'd settled on a menu or something and needed me to update the site. I texted him back.

> Good!
>
> How are you?

Great!

I wanted to thank you again for all the hard work you put into the Mountain Air website.

> You're welcome!
>
> Like I said, it wasn't entirely altruistic.

Well, I also wanted to tell you we have a new business partner, and we've asked him to give us his feedback on the site.

Oh no. I couldn't deal with another fickle client today. Someone else changing their requirements at the last minute or telling me they hated what I'd done. I sagged against the wall, trying not to let this bit of news send me spiraling into self-doubt.

Seconds later, Brandon sent a picture of a dog. A cute little dog with light-brown fur and button ears and a tongue that hung out on the side.

Say hello to Hops, the newest co-owner of Mountain Air Brewpub.

He told me to tell you he thinks your work is "paw-some." ☺

You got a dog???

Adopted him yesterday at a rescue in Encino.

He's adorable! 🐾

I'll be in town all weekend.

Wanna meet him?

Of course I wanted to meet him. He was quite possibly one of the cutest dogs I'd ever seen in my life.

But being around Brandon was risky business. I'd already established that I couldn't be friends with him. Whether I liked it or not, my feelings for him were more than platonic.

Then again, I didn't have anything better to do this weekend. With this Krueger project on hold, my schedule was wide open. And I didn't want to spend my Saturday alone.

Definitely!

What are you up to tomorrow?

Hanging out with you.

"Okay, spill it."

Vimi's voice was low in my ear. When I looked up, she was practically standing on top of me, her eyes twinkling with mischief.

I shoved my phone in my back pocket, hiding the evidence. "Spill what?"

"You're texting a guy, aren't you?"

"What makes you say that?"

She gestured to my face. "You're completely flushed again."

"Am I?" This was becoming a real problem.

"Yes, and I'm dying to know: Is it the new guy in infrastructure? Because he is totally hot."

I shook my head. "No. It's someone else. He's just a friend, though."

"Right. Just a friend." She winked, then twiddled her fingers nervously. "So does that mean I can make a play for infrastructure guy? I don't want to step on any toes."

"Go for it." At this point, I couldn't even remember what the guy in infrastructure looked like. The only guy I could picture was the only guy I'd ever sparked with—Brandon Phelps.

CHAPTER TWELVE

I'd never been what you'd call an "outdoorsy" person. My life mostly took place indoors, in various states of inertia—sitting at my desk or lying in my bed or eating at my usual table in the dining hall. So when Brandon suggested we go for a hike late Saturday morning, I was nervous but also excited. Hiking meant exploring new terrain, and right about now, I desperately needed a change of scenery.

We made plans to meet at a trailhead in the Hollywood Hills. Seeing as I never ventured over to this area, I didn't know where I was going, and my GPS kept trying to get me to turn down roads that were closed to the general public. By the time I finally oriented myself and found a parking space, I was ten minutes late.

Brandon didn't seem to mind, though. Standing in front of the entrance gate, he was all sparkly gray eyes and smiles. He looked ruggedly handsome in his hiking shorts, which showed off his thick, toned calves. I'd never thought calves were a particularly sexy body part before, yet here I was, struggling not to gawk.

But something else snatched my attention right away. Something small and brown and furry. Hops excitedly circled Brandon's feet, and as I approached, he let out an enthusiastic little yelp. I couldn't help but giggle.

"Oh my gosh, you are so cute!" When I bent down to greet him, he hurried over to sniff, then lick, my face. His coat was short and soft, much softer than I'd expected, and his big brown eyes glinted in the bright morning sun.

"Isn't he great?" Brandon crouched down beside me. One whiff of his woodsy cologne, and my body temperature started to rise. "I was planning to adopt a bigger dog, but this little guy called to me as soon as I walked in the shelter. I couldn't say no."

"How could you? He's absolutely perfect." I scratched behind his ear, and his long pink tongue flopped out to the side. His tail was wagging so hard I was afraid he might sprain it. "How much does he weigh?"

"About fourteen pounds. I've gotta get him a car seat for the front of my truck so he can travel safe. We'll be doing a lot of road trips together, won't we, boy?"

"Right." Lots of long drives between LA and Idyllwild. Because in a matter of months—or maybe weeks?—Brandon was moving away. I needed to keep reminding myself of that. It seemed so easy to forget.

"Hopefully, Hops likes to hike. This one should be pretty easy. Wide path, gentle grade."

"Good. I need an easy hike. I don't get out on the trails much. Or at all. Am I even dressed appropriately for this?" I stood up and gestured to my leggings and sneakers.

"Let's see." As he stood, his gaze traveled the length of my body. Slowly, as if carefully evaluating every inch. His eyes burned through my clothes, scorching my skin, lingering on my mouth, before he licked his lips and said, "You look great."

A shiver shook through me. *Don't feel what you're feeling. He's moving away.*

We pushed through the gate and made our way up the smooth dirt pathway. There was grass on one side, low brush on the other. As we continued on, I could tell we were climbing a hill, but it was a slow, gradual ascent, perfect for someone like me whose idea of an intense workout was walking up three flights of stairs.

"Do you come here a lot?" I asked.

"Not really. I do most of my hiking outside of the city. But I figured this was a good one to start out with for Hops. And for you."

Brandon's lips curved into a mischievous grin as his fingers grazed my forearm, sending my body temperature soaring. Sweat beaded under my arms and pooled in the backs of my knees. I wiped my brow with the back of my hand and asked, "How are things going with Mountain Air?"

"Good! The renovations are moving along nicely, and we're starting to put together ideas for the menu. I'm actually out here this week to go over the drink selection with Kelsey."

"Kelsey from Vespa?"

"Yeah," he said. "She's designing some beer cocktails for us. If things go well, she might move out to Idyllwild and work for us full time."

That was a long way to move for a bartending job. I thought back to the casual way she'd spoken to him, how annoyed she'd been when he'd been making me those mocktails. At the time, I'd assumed she didn't want me there because of my previous drunken shenanigans, but could there have been more to it than that?

Maybe she and Brandon had a history together. Maybe she was moving to the mountains just to be close to him. My stomach clenched at the thought of them snuggling up together on some cozy cabin couch.

Don't be jealous. You'll only get hurt.

We walked along in silence for a while, Hops sniffing feverishly at every shrub, marking his territory as we went. My legs ached the higher we climbed, my breath coming in huffs and puffs.

Then we turned a corner, and the whole city came into view. A blanket of apartment buildings and houses and storefronts spread out beneath us, interspersed with the occasional tree. In the distance, the skyscrapers of downtown LA jutted toward the sky. It all seemed fuzzy through the layers of haze that were ubiquitous in this city.

As we approached an overlook, a sudden cramp seized my side, right below my rib cage. I groaned and came to a stop.

"Are you okay?" Brandon rushed back to me and touched his palm between my shoulder blades, which did little to help the whole breathless situation. The heat from his hand radiated clear through to my heart, its beats coming fast and fluttery.

"I'm fine," I said, pressing my knuckles against my ribs. "It's just a side stitch, I think."

"Let's rest for a second." He pulled a bottle of water from his backpack and handed it to me. "Here, have a drink. You're probably dehydrated."

I downed half the bottle in one gulp. The cold water felt good as it slid down my throat, easing the pain. Brandon watched me with concern in his eyes. "Are you sure you're okay?"

"Yeah." How embarrassing. Brandon had barely broken a sweat; meanwhile I was cramping up and panting harder than Hops. "I'm sorry. I told you I don't get out much. Hiking isn't really my thing."

He pinched his lips together. "I'm sorry. I didn't mean to drag you out to do something you didn't want to do."

"No, no. That's not what I mean." I touched his arm in what was supposed to be a reassuring gesture but nearly melted at the feel of solid muscle beneath my fingertips. His bicep was even firmer than I'd dreamed it would be. Ignoring the quivering sensation in my thighs, I retracted my hand and continued. "I'm really happy to be out here, doing this. It's nice to have a change of scenery and be outdoors for once. Usually, I'm more indoorsy than outdoorsy."

With a laugh, he said, "What do you usually do for fun indoors, then?"

Good question. What *did* I do for fun? I didn't really have any hobbies, unless you counted bingeing Netflix. When I wasn't working, I was sleeping or eating in the dining hall. There was the occasional night out with Parisa. I did have my regular Friday-night game tournament, though.

"I guess you could say I'm a bit of a gamer," I said.

"Really?" He raised one eyebrow. "That's kinda cool. Are you more, like, a first-person shooter fan or an *Animal Crossing* aficionado?"

"Neither, really. I'm into vintage arcade games. *Donkey Kong*, *Pac-Man*, *Asteroids*, that kind of thing. I also like pinball, and I'm pretty kick ass at air hockey, too."

"That's awesome. Where do you play?"

"Virtuality has an incredible game room."

"So you only play at work?"

"Yeah, but my friends and I have a tournament every Friday night." He blinked at me, like he couldn't quite understand what I was saying. Yes, I spent every Friday night at the office, but I was having fun!

Suddenly, I heard Parisa's voice in my head, calling me strange for having no boundaries between my work life and my social life. I didn't want Brandon to think I was strange. Quickly, I said, "I mean, I'd love to have my own game room, but right now, I'm living in a studio apartment. There's barely enough space for my bed, never mind a pinball machine."

He nodded. "I completely understand. That's another reason I'm looking forward to having a home outside of the city. The housing market is off the rails here; I could never afford anything bigger than my tiny one-bedroom. It'll be nice to have the extra space. I've actually got an appointment with my real estate agent in Idyllwild on Wednesday to look at a few places."

Right. Of course. Brandon was leaving LA. Soon. Selling his condo and departing forever, in a matter of weeks. We'd been talking about it all morning, so why did I still keep forgetting about it? I was acting like if I put it out of my mind, his plans to move to the mountains would magically change, and he'd stay. Which was absolutely ludicrous.

I took a long sip of water, wondering if I'd ever see his cabin-themed apartment again.

"Well," I said, swallowing hard, "an upside to the off-the-rails housing market is that your condo will probably sell lightning fast. It's super unique and in a great location."

"Oh, I'm not selling my condo."

"You're not?"

"Nah. I put a lot of work into it; I'm kind of attached. Don't get me wrong, I'm looking forward to putting down roots in Idyllwild, but I might find a good reason to come back here eventually. I'm gonna rent it out for six months and then see what happens after that." The corner of his mouth quirked up as his gray eyes searched my face. "Who knows what the future holds?"

The correct answer: Nobody. Not Brandon, not me. And I hated the not knowing. It made me feel helpless and frightened and completely out of control.

But if I ever wanted to fall in love—and I *did* want to fall in love, deeply and without reserve—I needed to learn to be okay with that. Because whether I met someone in my office or on the internet, whether they lived down the street or on the other side of the country, being in a relationship would always involve risk. The risk of getting my heart broken. Of sharing my feelings. Of being judged and, ultimately, rejected.

I didn't know what the future would hold. All I knew was when Brandon looked at me, every nerve ending in my body jolted to life. Every skin cell tingled; every muscle quaked. And I didn't want to let that go.

As if reading my thoughts, he reached toward me, gently lacing his fingers through mine. At his touch, white-hot sparks ignited a fast-burning flame that traveled up my arm, shot across my collarbone, and settled in the center of my chest. My gaze fell to his mouth, soft and inviting. He bit his lower lip and leaned toward me, slowly, surrounding me in his earthy scent.

I wanted Brandon Phelps so badly.

But a voice in the back of my head whispered: *Don't do this. You'll get hurt.*

I wriggled free of his grasp, stepping back, panting hard.

The hurt in his eyes was unmistakable. He scrubbed his hand through his hair and sighed. "Nicole, the last thing I want to do is push myself on you or make you feel pressured or uncomfortable in any way. But I'm having a hard time figuring out exactly how you feel about me."

There were so many things I could've said to him. I could've told him how touched I was that he'd saved my earring or how much it meant to me that he'd made sure I was okay when I was crying at Parisa's engagement party. I could've told him how impressed I was by his work ethic and entrepreneurial spirit, especially in light of how difficult I knew his childhood must've been. I could've told him how every flex of his biceps made my knees weak, how his eyes had the power to set me on fire.

I could've said all this and more. But, as usual, emotions got in the way of my ability to communicate clearly. And all I could say was, "I'm afraid."

He inhaled deeply, exhaled slowly. "So am I."

"You are?"

"Of course. Putting my heart out there isn't easy. What if it gets stomped on?"

My mouth fell open, but shock had stolen my voice. Why had it never occurred to me that Brandon was just as scared as I was? That the risk of getting hurt was as great for him as it was for me?

"Then again," he said, "what if it doesn't?"

His eyes burned like supernovas, outshining the galaxy. I wanted to tell him I'd never stomp on his heart. That I'd cradle it closely and treat it with care, that I'd entrust him with mine if he'd promise the same.

But the words got jammed somewhere deep beneath my vocal cords, held down by the weight of emotion.

So I spoke without words.

Stepping forward to close the space between us, I reached up and ran my fingertips along his cheek. The stubble prickled my skin, but there was an unexpected softness there, too. Brandon's hands found my waist, pulling me closer so our hips pressed together. My breath was heavy, laden with anticipation, the desire to know the unknown. I sipped in his scent and opened my mouth.

When our lips touched, it was flint striking steel.

CHAPTER THIRTEEN

I'd never thought I'd want a hike to last forever, but the morning raced by all too quickly. We held hands as we walked the rest of the trail, then stopped at the peak to take in the scenery and steal a few lingering kisses. Before we turned around, Brandon snapped a selfie of the two of us, our faces pressed together with the cityscape as our backdrop.

When we reached the entrance gate, Brandon walked me to my car, Hops trotting along beside him. I was hoping he'd ask if I wanted to grab brunch or even just sit in the back seat and make out for a few more hours. Instead, he said, "I've gotta get going. I promised my bro I'd drive to Idyllwild tonight so we can do a walk-through of the property first thing tomorrow."

"Oh. Sure." My heart sank to my stomach like a cinder block. "I had a lot of fun today. Thanks so much for planning this."

"Next time, I'll bring you to one of my favorite spots. This little hidden gem in the valley. The trail is a little more strenuous, but I think you can probably handle it."

Next time. Those two words made my heart sprout wings, frantically fluttering as it flew back up to the center of my chest. "I can definitely handle it."

He brushed a tendril of hair behind my ear and fixed me with his brilliant gray eyes. Our mouths met, open and hungry. With our tongues twining and hands searching, I forgot we were out in public, until a sharp bark popped our bubble of lust.

Hops pulled at his leash, snapping and snarling at a golden retriever approaching from across the parking lot. Brandon tried to quiet him with firm, fatherly commands, but Hops didn't stop barking until the other dog had disappeared down the trail. "We've got some work to do, I see."

I knelt down and scratched under Hops's chin, careful to avoid his dangling, drool-covered tongue. "He's a good boy. He's just getting used to his new situation. Right, Hops?"

"Yeah. Change is hard."

Brandon looked at Hops adoringly, then slid his gaze over to me. Heat rose in my belly, and I licked my lips, preparing to pick up where we'd left off. Then a Subaru pulled into the lot and parked two spots over. The back door immediately opened, children spilling out, howling and whining. The moment was over. Time to go home.

"I'll text you later," Brandon said, before giving me a soft, tender kiss. It was quick and chaste, but it left my lips tingling.

In fact, they were still tingling the next morning when I got an urgent text from Parisa:

> Hey, I know this is totally last minute, but any chance you have some time today to help me assemble wedding invitations? I can't put it off any longer.

You're in luck, I responded. My schedule's completely clear.

An hour later, I was knocking on her front door. Mike answered with a smile and a "Hey, Nicole!"

"Hey!" Instantly, the scent of warm sugar filled my nostrils. "Are you guys baking something?"

"No," Mike said, closing the door behind me. "They shot the season finale of *Donut Warriors* last night and sent Parisa home with a few parting gifts."

I rounded the corner into their open-concept apartment and found the source of the mouthwatering smell. Donuts, everywhere. Arranged neatly in boxes and trays, they covered every counter and surface.

"I'd say this is more than a few." These weren't your run-of-the-mill old-fashioneds either. These were designer donuts, each one a distinctive and undoubtedly delicious work of art, covered in toppings that spanned the colors of the rainbow. Yellow glaze, pink icing, red and blue and green sprinkles. Chocolate chips and blueberries and bits of crumbled bacon. Some looked like they were stuffed with buttercream or compote. My stomach roared, demanding samples.

"Hey!" Parisa emerged from the bedroom, her hair damp and smelling of coconut shampoo. She hugged me and said, "Help yourself to some donuts, please. There's no way we're going to eat all this."

"Speak for yourself," Mike said.

Parisa playfully swatted him on the arm. "You should bring some to work with you." Mike was a film producer, so he'd be spending his Sunday on set somewhere. Like Parisa, his schedule was dictated by whatever production he was working on.

"Maybe." He plucked a fat chocolate one from a platter and swallowed half of it in one enormous bite. White frosting oozed from the center, and a big glop of it landed on his chin. Parisa giggled and swiped the mess off with one finger, then kissed away the remnants. Before she could walk away, he dipped his head slightly and caught her lips for one more kiss.

Mike and Parisa's chemistry was off the charts. It always had been, from the moment they'd met. As far as I was concerned, they had the archetypal relationship. One built on love, mutual respect, and blazing animal magnetism.

"Help me clean off the table before you go?" Parisa asked him. "We need space to assemble the invitations."

"Sure thing." He crammed the rest of the donut into his mouth and started moving boxes off the dining table. When I stepped forward to help, he waved me off. "Don't worry, Nicole. I got it."

"Do you want a cup of coffee?" Parisa was standing in the kitchen with a K-Cup pod in one hand and a mug in the other, waiting for me to give her the green light.

"Yeah, but I can make it."

"No, don't worry. Just relax."

"Okay." I hated standing around doing nothing while everyone else made themselves useful. Then again, it was nice to hang back and watch Parisa and Mike do their thing. They were so in sync, effortlessly bobbing and weaving around each other in this tiny kitchen space, almost like they were performing a tightly choreographed dance.

I found myself daydreaming about Brandon, wondering if we would ever move together that gracefully. But that was putting the cart before the horse again. Mike and Parisa had been building their relationship for years, while Brandon and I had only shared a few passionate kisses. Still, it felt good to ponder an unknown future. For once, the not knowing was welcome.

After the dining table was cleared, Mike grabbed two boxes of donuts and planted a lingering kiss on Parisa's lips. "I'll see you later, baby," he said, then smiled over at me. "Bye, Nicole."

"Bye." When he was gone, I turned my attention to a platter of donuts on the kitchen counter. My mouth watered as I surveyed the options. "Should I go for the one smothered in crushed Oreos or the one with the peanut butter frosting?"

"The peanut butter one," Parisa said. "There's jelly inside. It won first place."

"Say no more." I picked up a PB&J donut and sank my teeth into the soft, sweet dough. A burst of strawberry jelly hit my tongue. Instantly, I felt the inaugural twitch of an oncoming sugar rush. "Omigod, this is so good."

"That's what everyone was saying."

"Didn't you have one?" The question came out muffled with all that donut in my mouth.

"No. After four weeks of filming, I'm kind of bored of donuts."

"What?" Parisa had the world's strongest sweet tooth. One time, in eighth grade, she'd eaten two movie-theater-size boxes of Gobstoppers in one sitting. Then she'd thrown up. "I didn't think that was possible."

She shrugged. "Now that I dropped all this money on a wedding gown, I've gotta make sure I can fit into it."

Uh-oh. This sounded worrisome. It wasn't unheard of for brides to diet before their big day, but Parisa had a history of taking her diets to the extreme. Calorie restriction, compulsive exercising, even shady hormone injections. With this wedding on the horizon, she was under a lot of stress, which made her vulnerable to slipping back into old habits.

She set her coffee mug down on the dining room table, and one glance inside confirmed my suspicions. That wasn't coffee. It was hot water with a thin slice of lemon floating on top. Her beverage of choice when she was trying to lose weight.

"Are you dieting again?" I tried to keep my voice calm and even. If she felt I was badgering her, I knew she'd shut down. "Is this about what your mother-in-law said?"

"No." Her knuckles went white as she gripped her mug. "It's just that gown was so expensive. I need to look good in it."

"Of course you're going to look good in it. You'd look stunning in a potato sack."

She gazed down into her lemon water without saying a word.

"Have you talked to your therapist about this?"

"Naomi's on vacation." Chewing the inside of her cheek, she raised her big brown eyes to meet mine. "I promise I'll talk to her about it when she gets back next week, okay?"

"Okay." I took another bite of my donut and unwittingly moaned. "Are you sure you don't want to try this? It's seriously incredible."

"You enjoy it," she said. "I've got, like, four more where that came from."

I polished it off greedily, then washed my hands and joined Parisa at the dining room table, where she'd already set down my mug of coffee. "Where are the invites?"

"Let me grab them." Parisa went to the hall closet and returned with an enormous box that looked like it could've held a sheet cake. She lifted the cover to reveal stacks upon stacks of fancy paper products. "There's instructions on how to assemble them here."

I'd never realized how elaborate a wedding invitation could be. This one had eight components: an outer envelope, an inner envelope, a ceremony card, a reception card, the RSVP and its corresponding envelope, a note with directions and information about accommodations, and, inexplicably, a blank sheet of tissue paper.

"The good news is," she said, "the outer envelopes are already printed with the addresses. All we need to do is put everything together."

"Easy peasy." This might seem strange, but of all the wedding-related responsibilities I'd been tasked with, this was the one I'd been most looking forward to. There were no people to deal with, no awkward or uncomfortable social situations to navigate. It was just me and my best friend, sitting side by side, stuffing and stamping envelopes.

We lined up the eight components in order of assembly, alongside two envelope moisteners and a thick packet of stamps. Then we rolled up our sleeves and got down to business.

"This stack is huge," I said. "How many people are invited?"

"Honestly, I have no idea. A hundred and fifty, maybe?"

"Wow. I don't think I even *know* a hundred and fifty people."

"I don't know most of these people." She slipped an envelope off the top of the pile and read the name on the label. "Gregory Meyers. No clue who that is."

"So why is he invited to your wedding?"

"You know why."

"Right." There was no point in having this conversation again. Parisa was having this party for her family. They chose the guest list, the venue, and, from the looks of it, these gaudy invitations.

It seemed completely wrong to me that such a significant day in Parisa's life would reflect so little of who she really was. But if this was what she wanted, then this was how it would be. Instead of arguing with her, I tucked a tiny RSVP card under its tiny corresponding envelope and placed it on top of the tissue paper, just like the assembly instructions told me to.

"You've been so busy lately," Parisa said. "I'm surprised you could get the day off of work to do this."

My fingers tightened around an envelope, crumpling the clean, creamy paper in my grip. I'd been so distracted by Brandon over these past twenty-four hours that I hadn't given a single thought to work. I hadn't stressed about the Krueger project or obsessed over my promotion. Now it all came rushing back, an anxious tidal wave seizing my body and submerging my brain.

"Are you okay?" Parisa looked concerned, eyes darting from my scowling face to the squashed envelope in my hand. I was never very good at hiding my emotions, especially from Parisa. Even when I couldn't verbalize it, she knew when I was feeling angry or scared or nervous, and she always made it her mission to help me feel better. To solve whatever problem was causing me grief.

But this wasn't a problem Parisa could solve. And if I told her what was going on, I knew what she'd say: *You work too much. Your company doesn't treat you well. You should leave them and get a job somewhere else.* That wasn't what I needed to hear right now. She didn't understand why Virtuality was so important to me, and she never would.

So I shook my head and smoothed the envelope against the tabletop with the palm of my hand. "Yeah, I'm totally fine. I've just got the weekend off, that's all."

"Really?" Her eyebrows shot up in surprise.

"Yeah." The envelope was pretty flat by now. Only one little crease in the corner. Good enough. "I haven't been in the office since Friday."

"That's great. I'm glad the company's finally doing right by you. What'd you do yesterday, just relax?"

A slow smirk spread across my face. "Actually, I went hiking."

"You took a Saturday off to go *hiking*? Who are you, and what have you done with my best friend?"

"Well, I didn't go alone." As I told Parisa all about my morning with Brandon—the views of the city from the Hollywood Hills, the kisses we'd shared that had left my lips tingling—her brown eyes went wide, and she let out a squeal of delight.

"Omigod, Nicole! This is so exciting." She smiled tenderly, affecting a glow that was almost maternal. "I'm really glad you changed your mind about him. I can already tell he's gonna be good for you. Your face brightens just talking about him. Like he lights a fire inside you."

I pressed my fingertips to my cheeks. Predictably, they felt warm to the touch.

Morning wore on into afternoon as we talked and stacked and folded and stuffed and stamped. We'd sealed dozens of envelopes, yet we'd barely made a dent in the towering piles.

"I still can't believe how many people are invited," I said.

Parisa shook her head. "You know my mom. She's gotta invite her colleagues and her old college friends from Iran and every second cousin twice removed. For her, it's all about showing off. It's ridiculous, I know, but it's easier this way."

"Right." She kept saying it was easier this way, but nothing about this seemed easy. I shuddered to think how hard things would've been if she'd actually stood up to her mother and said no.

I slid what seemed like my four thousandth outer envelope off the top of the stack. The name on the label was vaguely familiar. "Arash and Elizabeth Karami. Who are these people? I swear I know them."

"Karami?" Parisa snatched the envelope out of my hand, and her tan skin went pale as she looked at it. "I cannot believe she invited them. She hasn't even spoken to them in years."

All at once, I realized why I knew the name: Sam Karami was Parisa's first boyfriend. They'd met when she was sixteen and dated for five years. To say it was an unhealthy relationship would be an understatement. Sam's constant putdowns and subtle snubs bordered on emotional abuse. As far as I was concerned, he was responsible for how badly she struggled with her body image. He called her fat, pinching the skin on her stomach and beneath her arms while telling her to cut back on carbs. It was always in private, never where anyone could see. She didn't even tell me about it until they were already two years in. I told her to leave him, that she deserved better, but like too many of us in our teenage years, she wasn't convinced of her own worth.

Their parents were close, though, so when Parisa finally gained the confidence to kick him to the curb, Farnaz was distraught. She tried to convince Parisa to change her mind, and when that didn't work, she hounded her for months, telling her she'd made a huge mistake that she'd live to regret.

Soon, Parisa met Mike, who was infinitely more loving and inarguably a better fit for her than Sam had ever been. My best friend blossomed in this relationship, learning to love herself and embrace new experiences, new adventures. At first, Farnaz had been resistant to this strange guy who wasn't Sam, but eventually she'd come around to love and accept him.

Or I'd thought she had.

"Why would she invite them?" I asked, knowing exactly why she would. To irritate Parisa. To show her that she still thought her daughter had made the wrong choice.

I could accept that Parisa was fine with letting her family call the shots on planning the wedding. I could stay quiet while they ordered gaudy invitations and fought over balloon centerpieces and asked me to change the color scheme of the website fifty times. But I could not allow them to cast an ugly shadow over her special day by inviting the parents of her terrible ex-boyfriend.

"We're not sending this out," I said. A satisfying rip echoed around the room as I tore the envelope in half.

Parisa didn't argue. "My mom's gonna be pissed."

"She won't even know." I gestured toward the enormous stack of envelopes. "This guest list is out of control. There's no way she'll be able to keep track of it all. You're the one handling the RSVPs. If she asks, just tell her they responded no. Besides, you just said they haven't spoken in years. She can't reasonably expect them to come to your wedding."

"My mom's not reasonable." She glanced down at the torn-up envelope, which I'd shredded into tiny pieces. "Thank you for this."

"You're welcome." I slipped another envelope off the top of the stack. "Now let's hurry up and finish. I want another donut, but I can't eat it until I'm done. Otherwise, I'll get sticky fingerprints all over this fancy paper."

She smiled at me as she brought the lemon water to her lips. "I think when we're done, I'll have a donut, too."

CHAPTER FOURTEEN

Taking the weekend off work was a last-minute change to my schedule. Normally, last-minute schedule changes made me feel tense, but this was different. Stepping away from the office, getting out in nature, spending time with my best friend—it all did wonders for my stress levels. A calmness settled over me, one I hadn't experienced in who knew how long. My shoulders relaxed; my jaw unclenched. I felt like I could breathe more deeply.

But my newfound peace of mind came to a screeching halt the moment my alarm went off on Monday morning. Because today was the day I would find out my fate. Would I get the chance to prove myself for a promotion, or would I be chucked off the Krueger project immediately? Just the thought of being relegated indefinitely to the role of junior designer made me queasy.

This was the first time I could ever remember dreading going in to work. It was a weight in the center of my chest, keeping me glued to my sheets, pinned beneath my blankets. I wanted to stay here in bed for the rest of the day.

That wasn't an option, though. I had responsibilities and obligations. Blowing them off would make my bad situation infinitely worse. So I threw back the covers and reluctantly went out to face reality.

When I got to the office, there wasn't much for me to do besides sit around and refresh my email, waiting for a message from Anna that never showed. At noon, Vimi texted Ben and me: Lunch? Ben responded with a 👍, and I responded, Sure. I couldn't stay at my desk staring at my empty inbox for one more second.

As always, Mondays meant the muffuletta special in the Virtuality dining hall. Sliding my tray along the cafeteria counter, though, I found I didn't have much of an appetite. That queasiness from this morning still hadn't subsided.

Dwayne frowned when I turned down the sandwich.

"Everything okay?" he asked. "You look a little pale."

"I'm feeling a little under the weather," I said. "Nothing serious. Just an upset stomach."

"Stress'll do that to you."

I almost asked Dwayne how he knew I was stressed. Then I realized: everyone here was stressed at all times. It was common to see people rushing in and out of the dining hall, tugging at their hair in frustration, barely looking up from their phones as they ate their food. Dwayne must've seen a lot from his spot behind the counter.

"Wait here a second," he said, before disappearing into the kitchen. A moment later, he returned with a plate of toast and a mug of tea. "It's lemon ginger. Drink it slowly."

He smiled, and it felt like a hug. Suddenly, I felt extraordinarily lucky. Working here was stressful, but it helped to know there were people here looking out for me. People like Dwayne and Vimi and Ben. It reminded me how Virtuality was kind of like a family.

I set the items on my tray and said, "Thank you so much."

"Not a problem. And take it easy. Try to schedule a day off soon, if you can."

"Definitely." As in, *I will definitely not be able to schedule a day off anytime soon.*

We sat down at our usual table in the back left corner, and as I crunched into a slice of toast, Vimi said, "I spoke to the new guy in infrastructure."

"Oh! How'd it go?"

She pulled a sour face. "He's got a girlfriend."

"Does she work for Virtuality, too?" Ben asked, taking a big bite of his sandwich.

"I don't think so."

"Then it's not gonna last," he said, with an unsettling degree of confidence. Especially considering how upset he'd been over his own anniversary debacle.

"How are things going with Cass?" I asked. "Did you guys ever talk about what happened last week?"

"Yes. And we both agreed that we need to take some time away from the office. Just the two of us. No work."

"That's nice," Vimi said, in a dreamy lilt. "What're you guys gonna do?"

"We're taking a long weekend out of town. I got an Airbnb in Big Bear, a cabin right on the lake. Super secluded. I'm not even sure the place has Wi-Fi."

Wow. The idea of being disconnected from the internet for an entire weekend sounded like a nightmare. Not to mention it was unheard of around here. Ben had been working for Virtuality almost as long as I had, and I couldn't remember a time when he'd been completely unplugged from the office. Even if he'd technically been "on vacation."

"Cabins are so romantic," Vimi said.

"Yeah, they are." Visions of Brandon's apartment floated through my mind. His stone fireplace and his comfy couch and his claw-foot tub. I wondered if his bedroom was cabin themed, too. "When are you going?"

"Not for a month. The first day we could both get off was Friday, April sixteenth."

That reminded me, I needed to request April 16 off, too—it was the first day of Parisa's three-day bachelorette weekend, which I still needed to plan. Right now, the only detail we'd solidified was the date. I made a mental note to get a conversation going in the #bachelorette-party channel of our Slack chat. After the disaster at Bergman's, I'd disabled the chatbot and had been making more of an effort to check in periodically throughout the day. But aside from a couple of snarky remarks from Roxy and Leila regarding Parisa's decision to let the bridesmaids choose their own dresses (*Tacky! Lazy!*), it had been uncharacteristically quiet.

With the Krueger project falling to pieces, though, would Jon even approve a day off for me? Not to mention that flitting off to Vegas when my promotion was at stake didn't seem like the sharpest career move.

Still, I couldn't let Parisa down. I'd have to make this trip happen for her. Even if it meant working around the clock until then.

"You okay?" Vimi looked at me with her eyebrows scrunched together. "You seem upset."

I gestured to my tea and toast. "My stomach's bugging me. Plus, I just remembered I have to ask for a day off, and now I'm worried that it won't get approved."

Ben wiped a droplet of olive salad from his chin. "Don't worry. I'm sure it'll be fine. Jon approved my request right away, no questions asked."

"Good to know." I sipped my tea, glancing at Ben over the edge of my mug. He looked so unbothered by the idea of taking a day off. Then again, he probably wasn't up for a promotion.

Or was he? That was the thing about working at Virtuality. The secrecy surrounding the promotion process made it impossible for us to speak honestly. We couldn't ask each other for advice or talk things through or even just vent.

And I needed to vent. I needed to talk things through and ask for advice, specifically from people who understood where I was coming from. Ben and Vimi were my colleagues, but they were also my friends. Surely we could discuss this in confidence.

I glanced around to make sure there was no one else in earshot. Then I leaned over, and in a low voice, I asked, "Can I talk to you guys about something confidential?"

"Of course." Vimi's eyes glittered. "Who is he?"

"No, it's not about that. It's about work." I cleared my throat and lowered my voice further. "Have you guys ever been up for a promotion?"

At the exact same time, their eyes bulged from their skulls, and their lips pressed into thin lines. It would've been a hilarious sight if I weren't currently so petrified.

"Look," I said, "I know we're not supposed to talk about this kind of thing. But I'm working toward a promotion right now, and I'm freaking out. The process is absolutely bonkers, and—"

"I know," Ben said. "The written statements, the personal projects, the letters of rec—"

"The committee!" Vimi's voice was a little too loud. She winced, looking over her shoulders to ensure nobody had overheard. Then she whispered, "It's worse than applying to college."

"So you've both been through this before?"

"Twice," Ben said.

"Only once for me," Vimi said. "The first time was so traumatic I didn't bother to try again."

Suddenly, I wished I hadn't said anything. "It was really that bad?"

She nodded sharply. "I was assigned to a big project that completely collapsed halfway through. It wasn't my fault—you know how it is around here: management is constantly shifting priorities, clients change their minds on a whim—but when it came time to present my accomplishments to the committee, they said my contributions to the company weren't quantifiable and thus weren't significant enough to justify a promotion."

"What did Jon say?"

"He was worse than useless."

"Did he give you that 'there's a lot of forces at play' line?'" Ben asked.

"Yup."

"He gave me that line, too!" I drummed my fingernails against the tabletop, overwhelmingly frustrated with how futile this seemed. Was it even worth the effort to try? "Does anyone *ever* get promoted around here?"

"Cass did," Ben said. "But she's in engineering, so it's different."

"Do they not have to deal with a promotion committee?"

"Oh, they do, but the engineers are the golden children of Virtuality. You know that. Besides, she's got the strongest work ethic of anyone I've ever met. I mean, she worked through our anniversary, for crying out loud."

Ben took an angry bite of his muffuletta. Clearly, he and Cass still had some issues to resolve. Hopefully that long weekend in the woods would be good for them.

After a moment of somewhat awkward silence, Ben asked, "Do you ever fantasize about quitting? Just marching into Jon's office and telling him you're done?"

"No." I didn't hesitate. I couldn't imagine my life without this company, these people, this dining hall. My work badge was as essential as my passport or my social security card. It identified who I was and where I belonged.

Vimi thought for a second, then said, "Sometimes. But I don't know where else I would go. Working for Virtuality is the ultimate achievement, you know what I mean? Jumping ship to another company would be like taking a step backward in my career. I could stay a junior designer here for ten more years, and it'd still look better on my résumé than having a senior job at a less prestigious company."

Ben slouched over his plate. "Yeah. I guess you're right."

Our lunch conversation was indeed a downer, but I still felt better when I left the dining hall, because at least now I knew I wasn't alone. Even if I never got promoted, I'd rather be at Virtuality than anywhere else. This was my home. My coworkers were my family.

As the afternoon wore on with no update from Anna, I resigned myself to being a junior designer for the foreseeable future. It was disappointing, but it certainly wasn't the end of the world. In fact, now that I didn't have to worry about putting together this promotion portfolio, I felt freer and less anxious. It was one less item on my to-do list, one less project on my schedule. I'd have more time to plan Las Vegas and hang out with Brandon. This was a good thing.

If I kept telling myself this was a good thing, eventually I'd have to believe it, right?

At five forty-five, I was already winding down, preparing to leave the office, when an email from Anna popped up on my screen. I couldn't double-click it fast enough.

> Nicole,
>
> Sales did a good job smoothing things over. Krueger has agreed to make several modifications to their chatbot requirements. We'll need to adjust the conversation to meet the new specifications document, which is attached to this email. Please review and give me your estimates at your earliest convenience.
>
> FYI The client acknowledged this was not our fault, but an internal miscommunication on their end. This may buy us more time for implementation.
>
> Stay tuned.
> -A

I nearly leaped from my chair and kissed the computer screen.

My chances at scoring this promotion were still alive and well, and now I was more determined than ever to make it happen. If Cass could do it, so could I. Because I had a strong work ethic, too, and I was essential to this company—as essential as it was to me. I'd do whatever it took to prove that.

With a smile on my face, I stood up and headed toward the dining hall. It was time to grab a quick dinner to go; I'd be eating at my desk while reviewing these specifications. From the size of the document, I could already tell it was going to be a late night. But I also knew it was going to be worth it.

CHAPTER FIFTEEN

I started pulling all-nighters again.

Over the next couple of weeks, that toiletry kit in my desk got put to good use. Some mornings, when I was brushing my teeth, I ran into Cass in the locker room. We'd share generic pleasantries and toothpasty smiles, but we never really talked. For one thing, she always looked distracted, like her mind was working through some programming problem even as she rinsed out her toothbrush. For another, I didn't want to mention Ben, afraid it could lead to some awkward conversation about the state of their relationship, which I suspected might be shaky, since Cass would stay in the office through all hours of the night, while Ben usually cut out after dinner.

Don't get me wrong, though. I didn't think they had to spend every waking moment together. In fact, time apart could be healthy for a relationship. I was learning that firsthand.

Brandon and I hadn't seen each other since those kisses in the Hollywood Hills. While I was stuck in the office redesigning this chatbot, he'd been stuck in Idyllwild overseeing construction on the brewpub. Despite the miles between us, though, we still managed to stay connected. During the day, we exchanged flirty text messages and Snaps, and every night we had a standing video-chat date at nine o'clock sharp. Finally, I had a legitimate reason to use those soundproof privacy booths Virtuality had installed on each floor.

It all had me thinking that maybe our long-distance relationship wouldn't be so hard after all. That we could totally make it work.

One Friday morning, Brandon sent me a text: Headed back to L.A. tonight! Are you free to hang out?

I twirled my desk chair around and around, erupting into a fit of giddy giggles. Even though we were indeed rocking the long-distance thing, there was truly no replacement for Brandon in the flesh. Instantly, I dreamed about burying my face in the crook of his neck and breathing in his earthy scent.

> For you? Of course I'm free!

> What time do you think you'll be back?

8ish?

I'll have a better idea once I'm on the road and I can see what traffic's like.

> I can't wait to see you.

> Come straight to my place!

I'll have Hops with me.

Is that okay?

> Yes! I miss him, too. ☺

I swiped over to my calendar app, prepared to create an entry for this evening labeled *Brandon!* 🐾. But then I realized there was already something on my schedule for tonight. It was Friday, which meant game night with the design team. As the reigning *Mortal Kombat* champion, I was expected to be there to defend my crown. And probably get back to work right after I finished kicking ass.

Clearly, though, being with Brandon took precedence. We hadn't seen each other in almost two weeks. I needed to touch him, to smell him, to kiss his lips. All the things I couldn't do over the phone. Ben and Vimi would completely understand.

I texted them: Guys, I'm sorry but I've gotta skip out on the tournament tonight.

Vimi:

Again? 😔

Ben:

I'm beginning to think you don't like us anymore, Palmieri.

I love you guys, I swear.

But Brandon is back in town tonight.

I haven't seen him in two weeks.

Vimi:

Oh! That's different.

Of course you've gotta spend time with your man!

Ben:

😈

Vimi:

Don't be bitter, Ben.

We'll find someone else to fill in.

Ben:

Who?

Vimi:

I can see if Abram is free.

Who's Abram?

Vimi:

The hot guy in infrastructure. 😉

???

I thought he had a girlfriend.

Ben:

I told you, that's not gonna last.

Vimi:

He does work awfully long hours.

😈

I knew Vimi was trying to be funny, but her scheming devil face left a sinking feeling in the pit of my stomach. Was she *trying* to get Abram to ditch his girlfriend? A few weeks ago, I probably would've egged her on, but now it felt like a personal attack. Like maybe someone was trying to get Brandon to ditch me. Someone he worked closely with. Like Kelsey.

Now I was just being paranoid. And wasting time, to boot. I put down my phone and turned my attention back to work so I could get out of the office at a reasonable hour tonight.

At seven forty-five, Brandon texted: I'm a half-hour away. There were still a ton of unchecked tasks on my to-do list, but they'd have to wait until morning. My man was on his way to my place, and I needed to make it look presentable.

I raced home as fast as I could and did a lightning-fast cleanup of my apartment. Fortunately, it wasn't very messy, though frankly there wasn't much to make a mess of. My studio was sparsely furnished—a bed, a couch, a coffee table—and since I wasn't around all that often, there wasn't much clutter. Just some empty boxes from various deliveries I'd had over the past couple of weeks. I stacked those neatly beside the door and jumped in the shower.

When Brandon arrived, my hair was still wet. I hadn't had a chance to put on makeup, either, but I didn't care. I ran to the door as fast as I could and flung it wide. The sight of him on my threshold left me light headed. Biceps bulging from the bottoms of his T-shirt sleeves. Gray eyes burning straight through to my heart.

My vocal cords jammed again, like there was a cork in there preventing any words from coming out. But I didn't need words, anyway. Not when Brandon was standing here in front of me, begging to be held. I threw my arms around his neck and pressed my mouth to his, conveying a message that was clear and unambiguous: *It's good to see you. I've missed you. I'm so glad you're back in town.*

Minutes passed, or maybe it was hours. An entire day could've come and gone while I tasted Brandon's lips, running my hands up and down the length of his solid chest. I probably would've kept on kissing him, too, if Hops hadn't interrupted us with a high-pitched bark. I stepped back to see him sitting impatiently at my feet, tail wagging, eyes pleading for attention.

"It's good to see you, too!" I said, kneeling down to scratch under his furry chin.

I welcomed them inside and put a bowl of water down for Hops, who drank it with gusto. Brandon set his duffel bag beside it, then slowly surveyed my apartment. "So this is your place."

"Yeah. It's small, I know."

"I like it. It's efficient." He smiled at me, and my insides melted to goo. "Did you just move in?"

"No, I've lived here for almost five years."

"Oh." There was a slight furrow to his brow as he looked around again, almost like he was searching for something he'd missed the first time. "It doesn't seem very lived in."

I followed his gaze, trying to see my apartment through his eyes, and I realized there were no personal touches. No knickknacks collecting dust on a shelf, no pictures hanging on the wall, not even a decorative throw pillow on the couch.

My cheeks burned with shame. Here was a man who clearly cared about his home, who put an extraordinary amount of thought and effort into the decor. What must he think about me, a woman who couldn't even be bothered to paint her walls anything other than the same stark, soulless white they had been when she'd moved in?

I made a mental note to schedule a trip to IKEA as soon as I had a free afternoon. And maybe hire a painter, too.

"I'm not here much," I said, by way of explanation. "Long workdays and everything."

Brandon nodded without a trace of judgment in his face. Hops, however, sniffed around with disdain, looking for a bed or a soft place to lie down. With no throw rugs or floor pillows in sight, he climbed into one of the empty delivery boxes next to my door and curled into a sleepy ball.

"He's tuckered out from the long ride," Brandon said.

"Are you tired, too?"

"Not tired but hungry."

"Oh." It just occurred to me that I was a terrible hostess who hadn't bought any snacks or drinks for her guest. In my fridge, there was only a half-empty bottle of Gatorade and a few frozen dinners. That left only one choice. "Should we order in?"

Thanks to Grubhub, the sushi place down the street would be delivering our dinner in thirty-five to forty-five minutes. While we waited, we cuddled on the couch, and Brandon caught me up on the latest developments at the Mountain Air Brewpub's construction site.

"They finished the patio today." He fished his phone out of his pocket and scrolled through the camera roll. "Here, take a look."

I leaned in close to peer over his shoulder, purposely squeezing his bicep as I studied the photos of the completed patio. It was a long covered deck that wrapped around the second story of the building. The railing was lined with a bar-top table, offering an expansive view of the forest, almost as if you were hovering in the treetops. "Wow. This is beautiful."

"Pictures don't really do it justice. Being there is a whole experience, with the birds chirping and the pine trees rustling."

"Well, I can't wait to see it in person."

A light flashed behind his eyes. "Wanna come visit next weekend?"

"Oh." I really *did* want to see it in person, but next weekend was way too soon. "I can't."

"Why not?"

"I've gotta work. I'm super behind on this project, and my promotion basically hinges on whether it's a success, so I can't take any time off until it's done. I still haven't asked for the day off to go to Parisa's bachelorette party because I'm afraid my boss will tell me no."

"You don't have to take any time off. Just drive out after you get off of work on Friday and go home on Sunday night."

I barked out a laugh. "I'm working next weekend. And this weekend. Aside from Parisa's bachelorette party, I'm working every weekend until this project goes live."

The light in his eyes flickered and faded, and I felt an overwhelming sense of guilt. Getting this promotion was my top priority, but it couldn't be my *only* priority. This brewpub was Brandon's dream, and I wanted to support that. To support him. After all, he was entrusting me with his heart. I needed to treat it with care.

"Listen." I took his hand in both of mine, tracing the peaks and valleys of his knuckles with the tips of my fingers. "The project goes live on June fifth. After that, I'm all yours."

One side of his mouth turned upward in a subtle half smile. "Do you think you'll be able to make it to the grand opening? It's June nineteenth."

"Absolutely." To show him how serious I was, I picked up my phone from where it sat on the coffee table and opened my calendar app. My schedule for Saturday, June 19, was completely clear. So I tapped out an entry labeled *Mountain Air Brewpub Grand Opening!*—and I sealed my promise with a kiss.

One kiss led to another, which led to a full-fledged make-out session on my couch. As we pressed our bodies together, I cherished every sensation. The scent of his warm, woodsy skin. The taste of his sweet lips. The gentle, yearning pressure of his tongue. I'd thought I was satisfied with the status of our long-distance relationship, the video chats where I could hear his voice and see his face, but now I wasn't so sure. No connection could compare to being in the same room with Brandon, breathing the same air and feeling his fragile heart beating steadily through the thin fabric of his shirt. This was everything.

I could've kept on kissing him forever if the Grubhub delivery person hadn't knocked on my door. We stopped abruptly yet reluctantly, and after smoothing my shirt and straightening my glasses, I grabbed the food and set our feast on the counter for consumption: edamame, shishito peppers, shrimp tempura, and a chef's special assortment of sushi. My stomach grumbled as we filled our plates and returned to the couch.

"So," Brandon said, stripping an edamame pod of its beans, "where are you going for Parisa's bachelorette party?"

"Vegas." My pulse instantly spiked. Planning this trip was my most important responsibility. Out of all the wedding-related events, Parisa said this was the one thing she cared about. It needed to be perfect. And I didn't know what I was doing.

At least I'd managed to book the flight; Parisa and I were leaving out of LAX at eight forty-five that morning. Roxy had complained that it was too early—"I won't even be out of bed before nine o'clock!"—so she'd decided to book a later flight with her sister and cousins. But I still hadn't reserved a hotel or made dinner plans. Every time I started researching places to stay or things to do, I became overwhelmed by the sheer amount of information the internet had to offer and shut my browser down in a tizzy.

"What's wrong?" Brandon asked. Apparently, my worry was written all over my face. "Do you not like Vegas?"

"I don't know if I like it or not; I've never been there. But I'm supposed to be planning the whole trip, Parisa has very particular tastes, and I have no idea where to begin."

"Let me help you, then. I've got so many contacts out there through the business. We can put together a weekend that's perfect for her."

I groaned with relief. "That would be amazing. Thank you."

"It's no problem at all." He flashed an easy smile, and my limbs felt all tingly. "What does Parisa want to do? Does she want the typical bachelorette thing at a strip club or—"

"No! She definitely doesn't want a strip club. She was very clear about that."

With a chuckle, he said, "Okay. Something more upscale, then?"

"Her specific requests were fine dining, bottle service, poolside cabana, and a suite with a view."

"We can make that all happen. I know a travel agent who can hook you up with a discount on a suite and dinner reservations. Plus, a buddy of mine does VIP bookings at all the big clubs. Does she like EDM?"

"She loves EDM. Her dream in life is to see Tiësto spin live. He's got a residency at Omnia, but bottle service is astronomically expensive."

"Don't worry; I'll get you a hookup," he said, popping a shishito pepper in his mouth.

"Wow. Thank you. Are these connections all people you met through the bar business?"

He swallowed hard. "No, I meant I knew them through show business."

"Oh. I didn't realize you were more involved than just that one season of *Off the Grid*."

"Well, I wasn't intending to be, but then these opportunities started falling in my lap. Promotional stuff, paid appearances, hosting gigs, that sort of thing. I wasn't crazy about being on camera, but it felt good to be in demand. Plus, the money was great. The environment, though . . . that was pretty toxic."

"Toxic how?"

Brandon's ears turned a deep shade of pink, and I wished I could take the question back. In fact, I almost told him to forget all about it before he said, "I was hanging out with the wrong people. Slipping into unhealthy habits. Lots of drinking. Some drugs. That wasn't what I wanted for my life. It reminded me too much of how my parents were. And I always swore to myself I'd never end up like them. So I decided it was best to remove myself from the situation completely."

The tip of my tongue touched the back of my fake front tooth. "I know exactly what you mean. I had this accident in college, drank way too much and busted my face open. When my dad found out, he told me I was turning out to be just like my mom."

He set his plate down on the coffee table and slid closer to me, fixing me with his gray eyes. "You know that's not true, right?"

"Of course." The words came out wobbly and weak. Even to my own ear, they didn't sound convincing. Because they weren't completely true. "There's still a big part of me that's afraid, though. Alcoholism runs in families, you know? It's a huge reason why I don't drink."

"I get it, Nicole, believe me. But we're not our parents. We're carving out completely different lives for ourselves. We're choosing our own families. We're deciding our own futures."

He reached over to squeeze my hand. I squeezed it back, my heart brimming with so much gratitude I didn't think my chest could contain it all. This man understood me, possibly more than anyone else in this whole world. Without needing an explanation or a justification, he cut right to the core of my deepest fears and disarmed them with his gentle touch and his earnest, powerful words.

Brandon saw me—the true me, the hidden me—and he knew my past wouldn't determine my future. And as we sat there, hand in hand, I could swear I saw my future in the depths of his gray eyes.

CHAPTER SIXTEEN

With Brandon's help, I was able to make all the reservations for Parisa's bachelorette weekend that night—complete with fine dining, bottle service, and poolside cabanas, just like she'd requested. Having those plans in place made me feel about a thousand pounds lighter. Everything was set. This trip was going to be epic.

Yet it took me another two weeks to work up the nerve to request the time off work. And I had reason to be nervous: promotion concerns aside, vacations were generally frowned upon here. People hardly took time off; in fact, a lot of my colleagues routinely stopped accruing vacation days because they hit their caps. Rather than complain, they wore it like a badge of honor. Admittedly, I did, too. I hadn't taken a day off in over two years, and that had only been because I'd had a severe case of food poisoning.

Still, Parisa was counting on me, so I needed to stop procrastinating and just suck it up. As soon as I arrived in the office that morning, I submitted my request through Virtuality's time-tracking software and crossed my fingers that it would all miraculously work out.

Five minutes later, an email arrived in my inbox:

> Your time-off request for FRIDAY, APRIL 16TH, has been APPROVED.

All that worry, for nothing.

I strolled into the daily stand-up meeting with my chin held high, feeling good about life, thinking everything was going so well. Then Anna announced some changes to the project schedule, and everything went to shit.

"Due to internal miscommunication on the client side," she said, "Krueger has decided to push our delivery date forward by two weeks. The project will now be going live on Saturday, June nineteenth."

A ringing resounded somewhere deep inside my brain. I didn't have to consult my calendar to know June 19 was already booked. That was the grand opening of Brandon's brewpub, and I'd promised him I'd be there.

No problem, though. I'd most definitely have to be on call to handle emergencies, but I could do that remotely. All I had to do was bring my laptop with me to Idyllwild and—

"Due to the urgency and high-profile nature of this project," Anna continued, "we're going to need every member of the team assembled in the office that day to oversee the deployment together."

"I'm sorry, what?" Uh-oh. I didn't mean to say that aloud.

Anna jerked her head in my direction, her pointy nose crinkled as if a foul odor filled the air. "Is there a problem with this?"

Everyone else turned to stare at me, their eager eyes awaiting my response. There was only one acceptable answer. "No, of course not."

She resumed her speech, but I couldn't understand a word she said. All I heard was the frantic whoosh of blood rushing through my veins.

This wasn't happening. This *couldn't* be happening. I'd made a promise. I'd sealed it with a kiss.

In that moment, my mind conjured some far-fetched ideas. Cloning. Holograms. Quantum entanglement. Anything that might allow me to be in two places at one time. I was so lost in my science fiction fantasies I didn't even know Anna was addressing me until she yelled, "Nicole? Hello? I'm talking to you!"

Yikes. "Sorry, I was thinking about . . . something."

"As I was saying, we've scheduled the usability tests with the client. You'll need to administer those and deliver an analysis to the rest of the team."

"Great." Usability tests allowed us to see whether our design was effective by watching how users interacted with our software. "When will those be?"

"The morning of Friday, April sixteenth."

"No." I didn't mean to say that either. But I certainly meant it.

Anna looked at me like I'd lost my mind. "Excuse me?"

"I'm sorry. What I meant to say is, we'll need to reschedule the tests. I'm on vacation that day."

"Vacation." The way she said the word, I wasn't sure she actually knew the definition. "And who approved that?"

"Jon. He's my direct supervisor. All my vacation approvals go through him."

"Well, he should have cleared it with me first."

"Oh, I thought he did." That wasn't exactly true. I'd actually never thought twice about whether he'd run it by Anna. Regardless, it was too late now. "Can we move the tests forward to Monday the nineteenth?"

"No, we cannot. We've already negotiated the new delivery dates; we cannot push out their tests, too." She spoke to me like I was an obstinate child, even though I was pretty sure she wasn't that much older than me. "You'll have to reschedule your vacation."

"I can't. I have flights and hotel reservations. It's a whole thing with a big group of people."

She pursed her lips, her cheeks blazing bright red, and that was when I realized there was no way to win this. Either I disappointed Parisa or I thoroughly pissed off Anna. If I chose the former, I'd jeopardize the most meaningful relationship I'd ever had. If I chose the latter, I'd jeopardize my promotion and possibly even my job. Like Charles had said, one misstep and they were already hiring your replacement.

And there were plenty of other user experience designers who were qualified to fill my position.

Oh. That gave me an idea.

"What if I could get someone else to cover for me?"

"That won't work. You're the only designer who knows the ins and outs of this project."

"There's someone in my department who's completely qualified to stand in for me. I can get them up to speed with no problem. Besides, all they'll need to do is take detailed notes and ask the right questions. They'll record it for me, and I can handle the analysis when I return."

Anna scowled, but she didn't argue, so as soon as the meeting was over, I dashed off to Vimi's desk. She was wearing a headset and a look of disgust. When she spotted me, she mashed the mute button on her phone and said, "This new project I'm on is the worst. Five hours of pointless conference calls every damn day."

"I need a huge favor. Can you oversee some usability tests for me when I go to Vegas?"

"Sure." She clicked around on her laptop and brought up her schedule. "What's the date?"

"Friday, April sixteenth. It'll probably take all morning, but I can't imagine it going past noon."

She sucked in a breath through clenched teeth. "Fuck, I'm sorry. I have a conference call scheduled from nine to eleven that day. This same stupid client."

A wave of nausea washed over me. "What am I gonna do?"

"Ask Ben; I'm sure he'll cover for you."

"He's going away that weekend, too. The cabin with Cass, remember?"

"Oh, right. Isn't there anyone else on the team you can ask?"

"Not really. No one else has the same knowledge of chatbots or conversation design. Except . . ." I couldn't even bring myself to say his name.

Vimi knew exactly who I meant, though. "Charles."

"There's no way he'll do me any favors. He's already salty that I was assigned the project instead of him."

"Are you kidding? He'd totally do it, just to claim he had a hand in making Krueger a success."

That was part of the problem. I didn't want Charles stealing my thunder. Though maybe I was overreacting. It was one measly set of usability tests. Even if he tried, he couldn't reasonably take credit for all the hundreds of hours of work I'd already put into this project. And I was pretty sure he'd try.

But at this point, I didn't have much of a choice. I needed the day off. Parisa was counting on me. So I swallowed my pride and went off in search of Charles.

I found him sitting by himself in the dining hall, staring at his phone with his AirPods in his ears, cramming forkfuls of salad into his face.

"Hey, Charles," I said. He didn't hear me, so I knocked sharply on the edge of his table. The rat-a-tat-tat startled him into awareness, and he looked up at me in shock.

"Nicole." He pulled his AirPods out of his ears and set them on the table beside his phone. "What's going on?"

"Is it okay if I join you?"

"Of course." He eyed me as I sat down. "How are things with the Krueger project?"

"That's what I wanted to talk to you about, actually. I need your help."

His eyes went wide, almost hungry, and for an instant, I second-guessed my decision. Then I took a deep breath and reminded myself why I was doing this. For Parisa.

"They're conducting usability tests with the client on April sixteenth, but I've got plans to be out of the office that day. I was wondering if you'd be able to fill in for me."

"Why won't you be in the office?"

"I'm going to Las Vegas, just for a long weekend. I'll be back by Monday. All you'd need to do is give instructions to the users, monitor their behavior as they engage in a few interactions with the chatbot, and ask them relevant questions. I'll even write out a script for you, so it should be super straightforward. And I'll be available by phone the whole time, so you can call me whenever you have a question."

"I've run my fair share of usability tests," he said, snorting. "I think I know how it's done."

"So you'll do it?"

He didn't answer yes or no. Instead, he asked, "What are you going to Vegas for?"

"A bachelorette party. You know, for my best friend, who's getting married."

"Will Shirin be there?"

"She's a bridesmaid, so yeah."

He looked down into his salad and stabbed a cherry tomato with his fork. Then he put it in his mouth and chewed slowly and thoughtfully as he considered his response.

"I know you must have a lot of your own work," I said. "But I promise this shouldn't take you more than two hours. Three hours, max. You don't have to do any analysis afterward. Just record your screencasts with audio and upload it to the shared drive. I'll review it all when I get back."

Another forkful of salad went into his mouth. Chew, chew, chew. Still no response.

"When you take your next vacation, I'll totally cover for you." This was an easy promise for me to make, knowing Charles would likely never take a vacation. I realized I meant it, though. "We should be able to take vacations around here without people freaking out. You know, I haven't taken a day off in over two years. Isn't that absurd?"

He swallowed his food and frowned. "Shirin was always trying to get me to take time off, and I never did. I probably should have. If I had, maybe we'd still be together."

There was a crumb caught in the side of his beard, a piece of crouton or something. I felt like I should tell him about it, but I didn't want to make him feel uncomfortable. Things were awkward enough as it was.

Finally, he sighed and said, "I'll do it."

"Oh, thank you." It took a great deal of effort to keep from lunging across the table and hugging him.

"On one condition," he said.

My desire to hug him immediately vanished. Of course there'd be strings attached. Why had I assumed otherwise?

"What do you need?" I asked, my voice heavy with dread.

He set his fork down and steepled his fingers. "I want you to convince Shirin to take me back."

CHAPTER SEVENTEEN

My romantic history was, in a word, sparse. I could count the number of guys I'd dated on one hand, the number of guys I'd slept with on one finger. Brandon and I hadn't even had sex yet. That being the case, I was hardly qualified to go messing around in other people's love lives.

But Charles wasn't leaving me any other choice. I needed that day off. So I told him I'd try my very best to convince Shirin to take him back, even though I didn't think he had a chance in hell.

It wasn't that I didn't empathize. I knew what it was like to work for Virtuality, how the company seeped through your skin and flowed through your veins. It was more than just a job; it was a lifestyle.

And I also knew what it was like to fall head over heels for someone. To catch yourself daydreaming about their smile or their scent when you should've been focusing on your work. To burst into flames every time you touched.

I understood Charles's predicament on a deeply personal level. That was why I knew he didn't stand a chance. Because I'd recently come to the realization that Brandon and I didn't stand a chance either.

Only two weeks earlier, I'd been convinced I saw my future in his eyes. But that was the last time we'd been in the same room together. The next day, he'd shown his apartment to some prospective tenants, then immediately driven back to Idyllwild to deal with some unexpected permitting issues related to the brewpub. He'd been there ever since, and I'd been here in LA, working nonstop, remembering exactly why I was hesitant to pursue a long-distance relationship in the first place. It was hard being apart. Calls weren't a substitute for kisses; texts couldn't take the place of a touch.

I missed him, viscerally.

Though, in a way, I was grateful for the space between us. It made it easier for me to conceal the truth. As far as Brandon knew, I was still going to Idyllwild for the grand opening of Mountain Air, and for now, I wanted to keep it that way. So I smiled my way through our video chats and hid my trembling hands off camera. Eventually, I'd have to confess I was breaking the promise I'd made to him, but I wanted to do it in person.

Of course, I had no idea when that would be. He was supposed to come back to LA the day before I left for Vegas, but earlier that morning, he texted to cancel: I'm so sorry. My bro scheduled some last minute meeting with a bunch of local vendors tomorrow. I can't miss it. ☹️

I replied, It's OK 🖤, I totally understand! even as a wave of disappointment crashed over my shoulders. When it receded, though, I experienced the sweet release of relief. Suddenly, I didn't feel quite so guilty about missing his grand opening. He understood what it was like to be under pressure, to *need* to be at work for reasons beyond his control. He'd recognize that sometimes promises had to be broken.

That night, I cut out of the office at a reasonable hour (seven thirty was considered reasonable these days) and headed home to pack my suitcase. True to form, I'd made a detailed list of everything I needed to bring to ensure the whole weekend went according to plan. Aside from my own belongings, I packed some swag for the whole group. Nothing cheesy or penis covered; just a few small items to help make the experience more fun. Temporary tattoos that identified each member of the bridal party; heart-shaped sunglasses for our day at the pool; hangover kits, complete with ibuprofen, antacid, and hydrating sheet masks.

I even printed itineraries, detailing the entire schedule of events:

~

Parisa's Bachelorette Weekend

April 16—18

Friday
8:30 PM: Dinner at Costa di Mare
11:00 PM: VIP table at XS, Encore

Saturday
12:00 PM: Pool cabana at Cosmopolitan
8:00 PM: Dinner at Beauty & Essex
11:00 PM: VIP booth at Omnia, Caesars Palace

Sunday
11:00 AM: Massages and facials at Spa Bellagio
2:30 PM: Farewell lunch at Yardbird
5:00 PM: Depart for airport

~

Though I hadn't yet shared it with the rest of the bridal party. Parisa wanted the details of this weekend to be a surprise, and I couldn't risk one of her loudmouthed sisters spilling the beans before we even got to the airport.

That reminded me, I should probably make sure everyone knew when and where to meet the next day. I pulled up Slack, ready to tap out a quick little message with the hotel info, but stopped when I saw an exchange that nearly made my head explode:

> **Roxy:** I booked us tickets for Hunk-O-Rama!
> **Leila:** Whoooooooo!
> **Roxy:** Got the VIP package, which means we get unlimited drinks, Parisa gets to sit in the "stripper hot seat," and we all get to go backstage after the show. 😜
> **Shirin:** Yay! So fun!
> **Ally:** This sounds like a nightmare.
> **Leila:** Oh, come on. You can suck it up for one night.
> **Roxy:** Yeah, if you're gonna be a killjoy, then just stay home.

No. No, no, no. Under no circumstances were we taking Parisa to a strip show or a strip club or a strip anything. Certainly nothing with a "stripper hot seat." This weekend, there would be no men in shiny thongs waving sweaty balls in her face. We were keeping this classy. Just the way Parisa wanted it.

> **Nicole:** I'm sorry to say this, but we're not going to Hunk-O-Rama.
> **Ally:** Thank you! Finally, a voice of reason.
> **Roxy:** Yeah, we are. I already bought the tickets.
> **Nicole:** No, we're not. Parisa was very clear about the way she wanted this weekend to go down, and she specifically said she didn't want to go to a strip club.
> **Leila:** This isn't a strip club, it's a strip *show*. 😒
> **Nicole:** I've already got our whole weekend planned out. Dinner reservations, a pool cabana, a table at Omnia, a spa day . . .
> **Shirin:** Ooh, a spa day!
> **Ally:** Is Kara going? I haven't seen her in this chat at all.

Leila: Me neither. I don't even know if she's still a bridesmaid.

Nicole: Kara will be there. She's flying in from New York, so she'll arrive a little later in the day on Friday.

Leila: When did you make all these arrangements?

Roxy: Yeah, you did this in secret. It would've been nice if you'd consulted us first.

I purposely hadn't consulted them because I didn't want them sabotaging my perfect plans. I had every hour of the trip mapped out, from the moment we arrived to the moment we left. Roxy and Leila might have commandeered every other aspect of this wedding, but this was the one thing that Parisa said she cared about, and I wasn't going to let them mess it up.

Nicole: I've printed itineraries. I'll hand them out as soon as we meet at the suite. Don't forget, it's at the Cosmopolitan, and check-in is at 2PM.

Roxy: Well, make sure you add Hunk-O-Rama to the itinerary! It's Saturday night at 10PM.

Nicole: Again, I'm sorry, but Hunk-O-Rama is not happening.

Roxy: 😠 These tickets are non-refundable!!!

Nicole: I'm sure you can resell them on StubHub or something.

Honestly, I didn't know if there was a resale market for male strip shows in Las Vegas, but I also didn't care. Instead of continuing to argue, I shut down the Slack app and returned to packing my bag.

Five minutes later, somebody knocked on my door. I assumed it was a delivery person who had the wrong apartment number, so I casually poked my head out into the hallway to redirect them. When I saw who was standing there, though, I shrieked.

It was Brandon.

"Hi." He smiled, glowing, and I flung myself into his arms. It had been so long since I'd seen him—too long. I pressed my mouth against his, inhaling his scent and tasting his lips, devouring him with all my senses. There was no thought involved, only instinct. The fulfillment of an animalistic craving.

After a minute, I came up for air and led him inside, relishing the sight of him standing in my apartment. "What are you doing here?"

He squeezed my waist gently with his strong hands. "I needed to see you."

"But what about your big meeting?"

"I rescheduled it for Monday. The vendors can wait. This"—he pressed a tender kiss to my lips—"can't. I wanted to catch you before you left for Vegas so you wouldn't be tempted to run off with a stripper."

"Not a chance." I leaned in to kiss him again, but then I realized something was missing. Or rather *someone* was missing. "Where's Hops?"

"I left him in Idyllwild with Eric. It's a long ride, and I think it's pretty hard on him."

"Oh." Maybe the ride was hard on Brandon, too. "I can't believe you came all this way. And canceled your meeting! You shouldn't have done that just for me."

"Of course I should've. This"—another kiss, this one lingering and succulent—"makes it worth every second on the road."

I pulled him closer, resting my ear against his broad, solid chest so I could listen to the soothing thunk-thunk of his heart. "I'm so happy you're here."

"So am I. And I have a surprise."

"You being here isn't a big enough surprise?"

"Just wait." He stepped back and pulled his phone from his pocket, swiping through until he found a photo. "Look at this."

It was a gorgeous log cabin. Like something out of a fairy tale, with an A-frame roof and floor-to-ceiling windows, surrounded by majestic pine trees.

"What is this?"

"Your new weekend-getaway home."

I blinked blankly, taking a moment to connect the dots. "Did you buy this cabin?"

"Yep. In thirty days, it'll be all mine."

"Wow." The word came out sounding detached, squeezed flat by the pressure in my throat. I'd known this moment was coming, but now it was real. The photographic evidence was right here. Brandon was actually moving away, putting permanent roots down in a city that wasn't Los Angeles.

But Idyllwild was his favorite place in the whole world, and from the smile on his face, he was clearly overjoyed. I didn't want him to see my disappointment or my fear. So I smiled, too, and forced out an enthusiastic, "Congratulations!"

"Thanks. I'm really pumped; it's exactly what I wanted. Take a look at the inside." He swiped through his camera roll, showing me photos of exposed beams and wood floors and ceilings that seemed impossibly high. The backyard was a wide expanse of grass, surrounded by acres of forest.

"This is stunning."

"Wait until you see it in person. By the time Mountain Air opens for business, I'll be all moved in."

"That's awesome." I spun away, futzing around with my open suit-case to distract from the panic rising in my chest. Now was the time to tell him I wasn't going to be at the grand opening. I'd been waiting to break the news until we were face to face. There was no excuse to hide the truth anymore.

But I couldn't bring myself to do it. Not when he'd gone out of his way to surprise me like this. He'd rescheduled his meeting and driven two hours just to see me before I flitted off to Vegas. Only a jerk would choose this moment to break a promise to him.

"Are you all set with your plans for the weekend?" he asked.

"Yes, thanks to you." I grabbed an itinerary from the stack beside my suitcase and handed it to him. "Parisa's going to be so excited when she sees this."

"This is amazing." He studied the paper before placing it back on the stack. "You really went above and beyond for her."

"Well, none of this would be happening without your help. I was totally lost. You pulled all the strings for me."

"It was nothing, really. Hey, what time are you checking in? There's something special I want to arrange in the room for when you arrive."

"Another surprise?" I'd never been subjected to this level of kindness. To be honest, it was overwhelming. The pressure that had started in my throat was creeping higher, into my cheeks. I couldn't get my thoughts straight. They were a muddled mess, tangled up in emotion, and instead of smiling or saying thanks, I wound up blurting out a shaky, "I don't deserve you."

It was an offhand comment. At least, that was what I told myself. But Brandon saw right through that lie. He wrinkled his brow and narrowed his eyes, searching my face for an explanation. I tried to turn away again, but he stopped me with a gentle squeeze on my shoulder. "What are you talking about?"

There was nowhere to hide now. My trembling hands were on full display. I was exposed and vulnerable, and Brandon's eyes were about to light me on fire. The answer spilled off my lips. "You are so thoughtful and beyond generous, and you have done so many nice things for me. And I've done nothing to deserve to be treated so well."

"What?" He took a step forward, closing the space between us, grasping my hands as if he were saving me from falling off a ledge. His eyes were no longer gray; they were incandescent. "Are you serious? You're the most thoughtful woman I've ever known. Look at everything you're doing for Parisa, planning this outstanding weekend for her and helping her through the stress with her family. Not to mention you saved me and my brother from embarrassing ourselves on the internet. That website you designed would've cost us thousands of dollars, but you did it for free. And look at the life you've built for yourself. Despite everything you've endured in your past, you're thriving. You're an incredible person, Nicole. You're amazing. You deserve the world. I wish you could see that."

He cupped my face in his hands, his big thumbs stroking the sensitive spots beneath my earlobes. His touch released the pressure that had been building inside me. I opened my mouth and sighed it all out.

As I exhaled, Brandon's lips brushed over mine, breathing me in. Suddenly, I became aware of every inch of my skin, all of it tingling in anticipation. My heart pounded an urgent rhythm beneath my ribs, and somewhere deep in my brain, a quiet voice whispered, *You deserve this.*

So I gave in.

We kissed fervently, feverishly, tongues searching and hands grasping. Breaths came hard and fast as we drank each other in. There was a gravity to our kisses, like this wasn't just a want but a *need.* Before I knew it, I was on my bed, on my back, with Brandon hovering above me, his fingers slipping beneath the bottom of my shirt.

I knew where we were headed. Lying here with my legs wrapped around his hips and his lips trailing fire down my neck, there was only one direction this could go. Every muscle ached for him, and every nerve ending flared. I wanted Brandon; I *needed* Brandon.

But that quiet voice in my brain was gone now, and all I could think was how I didn't deserve this at all. Because I wasn't thoughtful; I was selfish. I'd promised him I'd be at the grand opening of Mountain Air, but now I knew there was no way I could be there. Even though he'd foregone a work commitment for me, I couldn't do the same for him. I couldn't choose him over work, not right now, not when so much was at stake.

And the worst part of all was that I didn't even have the guts to tell him.

Panting, I pulled back, hastily breaking the kiss. Instantly, Brandon's eyes filled with worry. "Are you okay? Did I do something?"

"No, no." I crawled backward on the bed, inching out from beneath him. "I'm fine. You're fine."

He knelt on the floor, head tilted in confusion. "What happened?"

"I . . ." Words escaped me. Now was the time to tell him everything, to explain why I couldn't keep my promise to him, to defend my commitment to Virtuality. But it was pointless, wasn't it? He would never understand. Just like Shirin had never understood Charles.

We didn't stand a chance.

"I'm just not ready," I said, copping out in the most pathetic way possible.

"Oh. Okay." He sighed and scrubbed his hand through his hair.

"I'm sorry."

"Please, don't be sorry. If you're not ready, you're not ready." Brandon leaned forward, resting his hand softly on my knee. "And when you are ready, I'll be here."

His gaze was a caress. So gentle and so understanding. I wanted to bathe in his gray eyes forever. But I knew forever wasn't an option. Because I didn't deserve him.

CHAPTER EIGHTEEN

You know those people who casually roll into the airport five minutes before their flights are about to depart? That wasn't me. I was the exact opposite, the one who needed to be at the gate a full hour before take-off. It wasn't rational, I knew, but nothing about flying seemed rational to me. The invasiveness of body scanners, the possibility of being randomly bumped from an oversold flight, the very idea of hurtling through space in a steel tube suffused with recycled air. It was all so nerve racking. Arriving early left time for unforeseen complications and, most importantly, gave me a moment to catch my breath.

I'd already been sitting at the gate for forty-five minutes, practicing my deep-breathing exercises, when Parisa finally showed up. She looked radiant as she crossed the concourse, wheeling her designer suitcase behind her. We simultaneously squealed as we hugged each other. "It's happening!"

"I know!" I clapped my hands like an excited toddler. "This is going to be the best weekend ever. I've got so much good stuff planned. Do you want to see the itinerary now or later?"

"You printed an itinerary?"

"Of course I did. Have we met?"

I slipped one from the folder inside my tote bag and placed it in her outstretched hand. Her face lit up as she read through it. "VIP at Omnia! Omigod, please tell me the resident DJ is—"

"—Tiësto."

She squealed again. "This is so amazing, Nicole. I knew I could count on you to make this exactly the way I wanted it to be."

My chest swelled with pride. I'd knocked my biggest maid of honor responsibility out of the park. And there was still one surprise left in store. "There's something else that's not on the itinerary. Since we're getting in a bit earlier than everyone else today, I set up a special brunch at Bouchon, just for us."

Bouchon was a French restaurant in the Venetian headed by Thomas Keller, a famous and much-revered chef. It was high class and haute cuisine, and reservations were hard to come by. Fortunately, Brandon knew the GM, who'd promised to hook us up with a two-top on their terrace. There'd be oysters and caviar and *soupe à l'oignon*. Parisa always loved a French feast.

"Omigod, you are the best!" She flung her arms around me, swaying us from side to side, and I couldn't help but laugh. I was so happy to have this alone time with her before the rest of the bridal party arrived. We hadn't spent much time together lately, not since that morning we'd assembled the invitations, and I felt like I was failing on the "good, supportive friend" front. This would be a chance for us to reconnect.

Then, from across the concourse, an obnoxious voice bellowed, "Hey, bitches!"

No. It couldn't be.

But it was. Roxy trotted toward us, dragging an enormous suitcase that was most definitely not going to fit in the overhead compartment. Beside her was Leila, with an equally huge suitcase. Shirin and Ally trailed behind, with far more reasonably sized carry-ons.

"I didn't realize they were on our flight," Parisa mumbled.

"They're not," I mumbled back, just as Roxy pulled up next to us.

"Are we ready to get this party started or *what*?" she hollered, then reached into the front pouch of her overstuffed suitcase, procuring a plastic tiara with a polyester veil. With a flourish, she plopped it atop Parisa's head. "Here's your crown, Your Majesty!"

Parisa fondled the edge of the veil, inspecting the frayed trim, and did a double take when she saw the pink plastic penises pinned to the fabric. There were dozens of them, lined up in obscene little rows.

"They light up," Roxy said. "You just have to flip the switch on the headpiece like this."

She tried to turn it on, but Parisa smacked her hand away, then tore the tiara off and shoved it at her. "Put this back. We are in an airport, for God's sake."

Roxy scowled. "You're such a prude."

Time to do my maid of honor duty and defuse this situation. In the most saccharine of tones, I said, "What a surprise to see you, Roxy. I thought you were all taking a much-later flight."

"We were going to," Leila said. "But we didn't want to miss out on whatever you guys were doing."

"Also," Shirin added, "this flight was so much cheaper."

"Yeah, because no one in their right mind is flying at nine o'clock in the morning." Roxy pouted, slamming her retractable suitcase handle into its base. "It's too early for this. I need coffee," she said, then trotted off toward Starbucks, still holding the penis veil in her hand.

No problem. Everything was going to be fine.

And it was, for a while. On the flight, Parisa and I sat together, with everyone else scattered around the plane. As we buckled ourselves in for the ride, Parisa muttered, "I hope my sisters don't mess up this trip."

"They won't," I said. "They can't. I planned everything out. There's a whole schedule of events that we're going to stick to. Don't worry."

"I wish I didn't have to have them in my bridal party."

"You don't mean that. They're your sisters. They're pains in the ass, but you know you love them."

"I love them, but I don't want to travel to Vegas with them." She huffed out a sigh and fiddled mindlessly with the latch on the tray table. "Everything has gotten so out of control. The reception, the dress, the flowers, the family. Sometimes, I fantasize about calling the whole thing off."

"That's normal," I said, recalling what I'd read about prewedding jitters. "Most brides feel this way at some point in the wedding-planning process. Just keep thinking about how wonderful it's going to be when you and Mike finally say *I do*."

She slouched back in her chair and stared out the window, watching the baggage handlers carelessly toss suitcases under the plane. Then she turned back to me, her face brightening. "Hey, is there a beverage service on this flight?"

"I think there's enough time for one drink."

"That's all I need," she said. "Just one, to take the edge off."

Once airborne, though, Parisa scored two servings of vodka for her one Bloody Mary. And when the flight attendant found out it was her bachelorette party, she slipped her the extra bottle of Tito's with, "This one's on me, girl." By the time the plane landed, there was a wobble to Parisa's walk.

As we waited for our bags at the carousel, Roxy asked, "Should we split some Lyfts or something?"

"There's actually a limo coming to pick us up," I said.

"Oh!" Finally, something I said made her smile. "Let's drop our bags at the hotel, and then maybe we can do a little bar crawl on the Strip. I could go for a yard-long margarita."

"Mmm," Leila said. "That sounds good."

Parisa's mouth fell open in horror. There was no way I could let this happen.

"Actually," I said, "Parisa and I have brunch reservations. I didn't think you guys were going to be here this early, so I got the two of us a table at Bouchon."

Ally's eyes went wide. "Oh, I've always wanted to eat at a Thomas Keller restaurant."

"That sounds fine, I guess," Roxy said.

"Well, I'm not sure they can accommodate all of us. The reservations are for two, and they're always pretty booked up."

Leila shrugged. "So? Let's do something else."

I froze, unsure of how to handle this situation. Parisa looked disappointed, Roxy looked annoyed, Leila looked indifferent, and Shirin and Ally looked like they just wanted someone to make a decision already. My perfectly printed itinerary did not account for a snafu such as this.

"Let me see if there's anything I can do," I said. Maybe Brandon could get his contact over at Bouchon to throw together a bigger table. I felt bad bothering him about this when he'd already done more than enough, but for Parisa, I had to try. I pulled out my phone to send him a text and found a message from Charles waiting for me: Any progress with Shirin?

Jeez. I'd barely touched down in Nevada, and he was already asking me for updates? I shot back, Nothing yet. I'll keep you posted.

"Nicole, is that your bag?" Parisa pointed toward my suitcase rumbling down the conveyor belt. I shoved my phone in my purse and yanked at the handle with both hands.

"That's everything, right?" Shirin said.

"Looks like it," Ally said.

"Let's get this limo, bitches!" Roxy marched toward the exit, where a man held a sign that read **PARISA'S BACHELORETTE PARTY**. My mood instantly lifted. How could you feel anything but giddy as you crawled into the back of a luxury stretch limo?

Inside, there were leather seats and a bottle of champagne chilling in the cooler. Shirin popped the cork and poured plastic cups all around. I took one, just to partake in the toast. We held our flutes high as the driver whisked us out of the airport and into the city.

"To Parisa's last hurrah!" I said.

"Cheers!"

I set my cup in the holder, and as everyone else took their first fizzy sips, my phone buzzed with a text from Vimi. Uh . . . everything okay with Krueger?

My pulse instantly spiked. I think so . . . why?

Charles just marched past my desk bitching about it, she replied. Not sure if there's an actual problem or if he's simply being his usual charming self.

Shit.

Thanks for the heads up, I replied, then immediately texted Charles.

> Is everything going okay with Krueger?

> Vimi said you might be having a problem.

We've hit a wall in testing.

> What kind of wall?

I don't know how the chatbot's supposed to respond to these utterances.

> Check the conversation flow diagram.

> It has all the answers.

I don't know where that is.

> It's on the shared drive.

> I showed you this yesterday.

No, you didn't.

Yes, I had. But there was no point in getting in a pissing match with him when he obviously hadn't been paying attention to what I'd said. I spent the next fifteen minutes explaining where to find the diagram and how to interpret it, things he should have already known how to do as a senior designer. I found myself getting infuriated all over again that he had been hired into this role, while I'd been repeatedly passed over for a promotion.

"Who are you texting?" Ally asked. "You seem really angry."

Her voice shocked me back to the present. Lost in this argument with Charles, I'd almost forgotten I was in a limousine in Las Vegas. "Something blew up at work."

"I thought you took the day off," Parisa said.

"I did, and this guy was supposed to cover for me, but he's doing a really shitty job of it." I glanced over at Shirin, who was halfway done with her glass of champagne. "It's Charles, actually."

She snickered. "Not surprising. He was never good at keeping his promises."

Yikes. Shirin definitely wasn't going to give Charles another chance. Not that I was particularly interested in advocating for him. Our deal was that he'd take over these tests so I could have the day off. But I *wasn't* getting the day off. I was holding his hand through this whole process when I should've been enjoying my break.

My phone buzzed again, and I returned to my angry texting. It went on for so long I didn't even realize we'd pulled into the drop-off area in front of the hotel. Parisa had to poke me in the ribs to get my attention. "We're here."

"Where?" I didn't even look up from my phone.

She grunted. "I think it's finally time to stage that intervention."

That made me look up. "I'm sorry. This guy is such a douche; I'm so mad that he can't handle this on his own. He's gonna mess up the whole project."

"Listen, your company will function just fine without you for one damn weekend." Her eyebrows scrunched together. "It's my bachelorette party, Nicole. This is a once-in-a-lifetime event. Please, be present for it."

She was right. Virtuality would continue to thrive without me there, even if these usability tests weren't a roaring success. Whether they'd continue to employ me was another story. But I'd made a promise to Parisa, and I'd already broken enough promises this week.

I texted Charles: I have to go now. Please figure this out on your own. Then I dropped my phone back in my purse and led the bridal party to the registration desk.

"Welcome to the Cosmopolitan," the clerk said. "How can I help you this morning?"

"We're here to check in to one of the Chelsea Suites," I said, slapping my Amex down on the cool marble countertop. "My name is Nicole Palmieri."

She smiled and said, "Fabulous."

This suite was most definitely fabulous. There were three big bedrooms, an expansive common area, a wraparound balcony overlooking the Strip. In the kitchenette, a bottle of champagne awaited us beside a tray of chocolate-covered strawberries and a note that read, CONGRATULATIONS, PARISA!

This must've been the surprise Brandon was talking about. I really didn't deserve him.

Taking a big, luscious bite of a strawberry, I slipped the printed itineraries from my bag and spread them out on the coffee table. Shirin picked one up and said, "Wow. You've got a whole schedule and everything. Nice touch, Nicole."

"Yeah," added Ally. "You've done such a great job planning this trip."

"Thanks. Only the best for the bride, right?" I glanced over at Parisa, who was gazing wistfully out the window with a faraway smile on her face. It made me happy to see her so satisfied. At least I'd done something right.

"I'm starving!" Roxy whined, flipping open the room service menu and flopping down on the couch. "What should we eat for lunch?"

"What about a buffet?" Leila offered.

Roxy made a gagging sound. "No, thanks."

"Were you able to get a bigger table at Bouchon?" Parisa asked.

Oh no. I'd gotten so distracted by Charles and his ineptitude that I'd completely forgotten to text Brandon about the reservation. It was probably too late now, and I didn't want to admit to Parisa that I'd dropped the ball because of a work emergency. She was already annoyed that I'd been working today.

"No, I'm sorry. I couldn't." Not exactly a lie.

"You're not gonna go without us, are you?" Leila wasn't asking me; she was asking Parisa. Her eyes were wide and watery, and I could tell Parisa was torn.

This was the point where I should've put on my big maid of honor pants and intervened, to save the bride from having to make such a difficult decision. But, of course, I didn't. Because I always cowered at the first sign of conflict.

Instead, Parisa said, "No, let's stay together."

"Yard-long time!" Roxy whooped and threw her hands in the air.

"I thought you were hungry," Shirin said.

"A yard-long margarita is a meal in itself."

As everyone dispersed to get ready for their afternoon on the Strip, I pulled Parisa aside to apologize. "I'm so sorry our plans got messed up."

"Don't worry about it." She gave me a small smile, then gestured to the printed itinerary on the table. "According to this, the first official event doesn't start until eight thirty, so technically everything's still going according to plan."

She was right. It was. And I'd do everything in my power to keep it that way. Just as soon as we returned from this unscheduled bar crawl along the Las Vegas Strip.

CHAPTER NINETEEN

The thing about having an unscheduled bar crawl is that it's really hard to get back on schedule after it's over. Because by then, everybody's rip-roaring drunk.

On the plus side, Parisa seemed to be having a good time. First, she knocked back a giant margarita at—where else?—Margaritaville, where we dined on fried pickles and loaded nachos before heading out onto Las Vegas Boulevard. From there, we bounced from casino to casino, drinking shots of whiskey at O'Shea's and frozen daiquiris from swirly machines at Fat Tuesday. At one point, Roxy dared Parisa to shotgun a beer, which she did with surprising agility, considering how much alcohol was already in her system.

By six o'clock, it was time to start heading back to the suite to clean up for dinner. As the only sober member of the crew, I had to wrangle everybody in the direction of our hotel and, once there, motivate them to get in the shower instead of passing out in their dirty bar-crawl clothes. This was not an easy task.

Thankfully, Kara arrived shortly before seven, injecting new life into the party. She sparkled, as if she'd just stepped off a movie set instead of a cross-country flight. As she walked flawlessly in five-inch heels, her curls bounced off her shoulders, and her skin glowed. With this drop-dead-gorgeous model joining our group, everyone else suddenly had an incentive to get off their asses and glam themselves up, too.

We were only five minutes late to our reservations at Costa di Mare, which was actually right on time according to their seating schedule.

Our table for seven was outside, beneath a canopy of lights, right next to an artificial lagoon. In a matter of hours, we'd gone from day drinking in Vegas to dining seaside in Italy. Sort of.

The server approached our table, welcoming us to the "four-star award-winning restaurant" and reciting the daily specials. The branzino with baby broccoli sounded particularly scrumptious. "Can I start you ladies off with anything to drink?" he asked. "Perhaps a bottle of wine?"

"With this group?" Leila said. "I'd say more like five bottles."

Everyone laughed, and a discussion ensued over what kind of wine they should start with. Three people said red; three people said white. I said nothing because I didn't have a horse in this race, but Kara turned to me and said, "You're the tiebreaker, Nicole. Which one do you want?"

Before I could open my mouth to answer, Roxy yelled across the table, "Nicole doesn't drink." Her tone was contemptuous, like I was ruining the evening with my teetotaling prissiness.

A small voice in the back of my head whispered, *Just have one.* But I knew better than to trust it. One always turned to two, and two always turned to trouble. I was not my mother. I was choosing a different path.

Ultimately, they settled on rosé. When the server went around the table, pouring it into long-stemmed glasses, I covered mine with my hand and said, "No, thank you."

Kara leaned over, her brown eyes regarding me with concern. She whispered, "Are you in AA?"

"Um . . ." I wasn't sure why Kara thought that was an appropriate question to ask. After all, the second *A* in AA stood for *anonymous.*

"It's totally okay," she said, this time a bit louder. "So are half the people I work with."

Ignoring my desire to crawl under the table, I said, "I'm not. Alcohol just doesn't agree with me, that's all."

"Yeah, just ask her dentist." That was Roxy, who broke out into a fit of cackles while Leila snickered beside her. Everyone else looked confused. Parisa scowled and said, "Will you stop?"

"It's fine." It wasn't fine, but this was far more awkward than it needed to be. So I turned to Kara, Shirin, and Ally and explained. "When I was in college, I got really drunk, fell off a bar, and busted my front tooth. The whole thing was caught on camera and passed around the school. It was mortifying, and after that, I swore off drinking."

I tried not to notice Roxy whispering in Leila's ear as Kara patted my arm and said, "I totally get it. Two years ago, I was at one of Leonardo DiCaprio's yacht parties in Saint-Tropez when I got wasted and had a nip slip that ended up in *Tatler*."

Mercifully, Shirin tapped her fork against the edge of her wineglass, bringing an abrupt end to this uncomfortable conversation. "Should we have a toast?"

"Excellent idea!" Roxy stood up, glass in hand, the self-appointed leader. She tossed her long hair over one shoulder and cleared her throat. "So. First of all, welcome. Thank you all for coming here to celebrate my sister, Parisa, as she begins this new phase of her life."

Parisa smiled weakly and stared down into her glass.

"She is the first of the Shahin sisters to get married," Roxy continued, "which is obviously a really big deal for us. We're all so proud of her, and we're so happy to welcome Mike into the family."

Shirin and Ally exchanged a stealthy glance as Roxy prattled on about the first time she'd met Mike and how she'd known he was "the one" for Parisa right away. The sentiment was nice, but it seemed out of place here in this restaurant, after a day of downing yard-long frozen drinks. It was the kind of toast usually reserved for a wedding. The toast that was usually given by the maid of honor.

"Anyway," she said, turning to Parisa with tears in her eyes. "I wanted to tell you I love you and I'm so proud of you, and I'm so excited to see my big sister getting married."

"Cheers!" we practically screamed, so overjoyed were we that this sermon had come to an end. Everyone clinked their glasses of wine, while I toasted with my sparkling water.

"Nicole, no!" Roxy shrieked, her voice so jarring that my hand shook. Water sloshed over the sides of the glass and dripped down my fingers.

"What is it?" I looked around frantically for any sign of danger. Had I leaned too close to the candle on the table and caught my hair on fire? Was there a murder hornet hovering above my head?

"You can't toast with water," she said. "It's bad luck."

Oh. I'd heard this superstition before. Toasting with water—or any nonalcoholic drink, for that matter—could doom you to seven years of bad sex or lead you to a watery grave or condemn you to some other horrible fate. It was ridiculous, to say the least, but this wasn't the time to argue. I just nodded and put my glass down, fighting the urge to run off to the bathroom and hide.

Parisa was pissed, though. "What is wrong with you, Roxana?"

Roxy looked hurt. "I'm trying to protect you. Do you want bad luck hanging over your bachelorette party? Or worse, your marriage?"

"Okay," Ally said, spreading her hands out in a gesture of calm. "Let's not get carried away. This is not a big deal. Just forget it."

From the snarl on Parisa's face, I didn't think she was prepared to forget it. Thankfully, the server swooped in to save us with a cheerful, "Have we decided on our entrées yet, ladies?"

We went around the table, ordering short ribs and spaghetti and sea bass. I ordered the branzino special. Roxy ordered two more bottles of wine. I asked for a refill on my water.

After the server collected our menus, the mood at the table began to shift, and the conversation flowed. I listened but didn't contribute. I was never much of a conversationalist; in fact, I was always amazed by how easily people made small talk about the most inconsequential topics.

I suppose there were things I could've said. I could've commented on the menu or wondered out loud about what the VIP booth was going to be like when we got to XS. But it was hard to find an entry point into the conversation. Someone else always had something funnier or more interesting to add than I did. Plus, I wasn't exactly brimming with self-confidence after that whole "toasting with water" debacle.

At one point, I pulled out my phone. It wasn't something I consciously thought about doing; it was an instinctual move. My phone provided an easy means of escape, a way to remove myself from this situation without getting out of my chair.

When I looked at my screen, though, I immediately regretted it. Because there was a text waiting for me from Charles: **Any updates on Shirin?**

I'd been so distracted by this afternoon's unplanned bar crawl that I'd completely put anything and everything work related out of my mind, including Charles. Now, it all came rushing back, along with a fresh wave of panic. He hadn't mentioned anything about the usability tests, the results, or the client's reaction. At once, I was furious with myself for blowing it off and trusting him to handle it correctly.

Ignoring his question, I asked, **How did the tests go?**

Fine.

How did the client respond to the interface?

I told you, fine.

Do you foresee significant changes to the design?

I don't know.

All I did was run the tests.

You said you were doing the analysis.

Now what's going on with Shirin?

It was still clear to me that Charles didn't stand a chance with Shirin. She didn't have anything nice to say about him; that was for sure. Still, aside from that irritating text exchange we'd had in the limo, Charles had held up his end of the bargain. Apparently, the tests had gone fine. At the very least, I could have a chat with her about him.

Nothing yet, I replied. Will let you know in a few.

"Please tell me you're not working, Nicole." Parisa's exasperated voice carried across the table. I looked up to see her frowning at me.

"I'm not, I promise." I made a big show of shoving my phone back in my purse. "I was just texting someone, that's all."

Her frown morphed into a mischievous smile. "Brandon?"

"Who's Brandon?" Shirin asked. "Is that your boyfriend?"

"Remember that hot guy from the engagement party?" Parisa said. "The manager at Vespa?"

Roxy whipped her head around and glared at me. "You're dating the guy from *Off the Grid*?"

"Kind of," I said.

"There's nothing 'kind of' about it," Parisa said, her brown eyes glittering. "Brandon is most definitely your boyfriend."

He most definitely was not. We'd never used the terms *boyfriend* or *girlfriend*, never talked about any sort of concrete future together. The only long-term plan we'd made was for me to visit him in Idyllwild for Mountain Air's grand opening, and that wasn't actually going to happen. Not that I'd informed him of that yet.

And now that I thought about it, I hadn't texted him once since I'd landed in Vegas, not even to thank him for the champagne and strawberries he'd so generously ordered to the suite. Sure, I'd been distracted, but that was no excuse. What kind of thoughtless person was I?

As Roxy easily steered the conversation away from me and back to herself, I pulled my phone out of my purse and shot off a text to Brandon.

> Hey!
>
> I'm sorry I haven't texted sooner.
>
> Things have been crazy here.
>
> Thank you so much for the champagne and strawberries. And for everything, really.
>
> I'm thinking about you.
>
> Hope you're having a great night.

He responded instantly:

> No worries, I figured you were busy. ☺
>
> Glad the champagne arrived.
>
> Hope you're having a great time.

Then, two seconds later: I miss you.

Heat radiated to the tips of my fingers and toes, and I felt a flush creep up my neck and into my cheeks. Brandon wasn't my boyfriend; I knew that. But I couldn't deny that burst-into-flames feeling.

With a smile on my face, I wrote back, Miss you too.

As I pressed send, the food arrived, so I tucked my phone away for the duration of the meal. After I'd connected with Brandon, my mood improved, and I started to relax and enjoy myself. Whenever Roxy made a snide comment, I ignored her, choosing instead to focus on my delicious branzino, which was grilled and seasoned to perfection. The wine flowed around me, the conversation getting louder and slightly more slurred. I smiled all the way through to dessert, which was a delectable lemon panna cotta with raspberry coulis.

After dinner, we wandered through the Wynn casino, rubbernecking behind the players at the craps table and spinning a few nickel slots. Emboldened by the wine, Parisa sat down at the roulette wheel and dropped twenty-five bucks on the number twenty-six—as in the twenty-sixth of June, the day of her wedding. She lost, and Roxy clucked her tongue. "Told you not to toast with water."

The entrance to XS nightclub beckoned from across the casino floor. There was a long line to get in, crowded with women in tight dresses and men in tight shirts. One flash of our VIP passes, and the bouncer let us skip to the front, leading us straight to our private couch in the main ballroom.

Parisa beamed, her bright-white teeth shining through the darkness of the club. "How did you score such a good table? These are, like, thousands of dollars."

"Brandon hooked me up," I said, sliding into the seat next to her.

"Okay, bitches," Roxy announced. "It's time!"

And thus began the parade of penis paraphernalia. First, the penis veil from the airport, then a light-up penis necklace, a hot-pink penis whistle on a chain, and a novelty sash that screamed *SAME PENIS FOREVER* in big bubbly letters. I wasn't sure how Roxy had managed to cram quite so much phallic crap into her tiny little clubbing purse.

Under more sober circumstances, Parisa probably would've scoffed. Now, she only giggled as her sisters draped her in plastic penises. Everyone laughed and snapped photos, and I felt a twinge of disappointment because I'd forgotten to give out the temporary tattoos I'd brought with me. Those would've been cute. Tomorrow I'd remember them, for sure.

The server poured us drinks—vodka all around. Except for me, of course, who stuck with sparkling water. Roxy popped a penis straw in each glass. It had tiny little testicles and protruding veins.

Shirin took a long penis-y sip from her screwdriver, then grimaced as she swallowed and tossed the straw to the side. "Blech. This thing has gotta be made from toxic chemicals."

I tossed mine aside, too, though nobody else seemed to mind the taste. They were drinking through their straws and bouncing to the music.

"It's so cool that your boyfriend hooked us up with this table," Shirin said, leaning close to my ear so I could hear her over the noise. "He must be really well connected."

"Yeah." He always played it so humble, just a guy who loved the mountains and his dog, but he obviously knew a lot of people. People who could get us reservations at restaurants that were booked up for months or thousand-dollar tables at the hottest nightclubs. The fact that he didn't make a big deal about what a big deal he was made me like him even more.

"How long have you been dating?"

"About six weeks or so. It's still pretty new."

"That's the best part of a relationship," she said, with this dreamy look in her eyes. "When you're still getting to know each other and having so much amazing sex."

"Totally." My eyes fell to the penis straws abandoned on the table, thinking about what had happened last night, how I'd pushed him away. If we'd kept going, I bet the sex really would've been amazing.

"I'm in that phase right now, actually," she said.

"Oh. You're seeing someone new?"

"His name's Mateo. Hands down, the best sex I've ever had in my life."

So much for convincing her to give Charles another chance. "That's awesome. Congratulations."

"It's more than good sex, though. He's kind; he's patient; he really listens when I talk. That's so rare, you know? After the way things ended with Charles, it's so nice to be with someone who really *wants* to be with me."

"I'm sure Charles wanted to be with you," I said. "His work is just so demanding."

She snorted. "Bullshit. He's not performing surgery or saving lives. He's designing software for a tech company that makes rich people richer." Instantly, she covered her mouth with one hand. "I'm sorry. I don't mean to say your work isn't important."

I'll admit her words stung a bit, but I tried not to let it show. "It's okay. I get it. But Virtuality isn't some evil tech company. We do a lot of really good things. I'm actually working on a project right now that has the potential to save lives."

"That's great." From her thin-lipped smile, I could tell she wasn't convinced. It took all my self-restraint not to launch into a detailed description of everything Krueger's chatbot was capable of doing: diagnosing illnesses, recommending treatments, offering empathy and assistance to people who couldn't get to a doctor for whatever reason. But that wasn't what Shirin wanted to talk about right now.

"The thing is," she continued, "if he'd wanted to spend time with me, he would have found a way. He could've pushed back more at work. He just didn't want to. His job was more important to him than I was."

"In theory, I agree, but Virtuality is such a competitive place to work. One misstep—"

"—and they're already hiring your replacement. Yeah, he told me that, too. And if that's the kind of job he wants to have, then great. That's his choice. But I need someone who's gonna be there for me. He was always canceling our dates, and when he was around, he might as well have been at the office, since he was constantly checking his email. No matter what was going on in our relationship, his work always took precedence. You know he even missed my birthday party?"

"Really?"

"Mm-hmm. He said there was some 'go-live' he couldn't miss. That's when I was like, 'I'm done. Choose your job or choose me.' He chose his job." She shrugged one shoulder. "Now that I'm with Mateo, though, I can't say I'm mad about it. He helped me get over Charles real fast."

"Right." A ripple of nausea passed over me. I'd be missing Brandon's grand opening because of Krueger's go-live. Did that mean an ultimatum was coming my way, too?

The music surged, a blast of drums and synth, a bass line that rattled my bones. Parisa popped out of her seat and shimmied her way to the dance floor, the penises on her veil bouncing behind her. She motioned for the rest of us to join in, so I gulped down my water and followed her lead, leaving all thoughts of Virtuality and Brandon behind. I couldn't solve that problem tonight, but I could do my very best to stay present for Parisa.

CHAPTER TWENTY

The next morning, I woke up at ten o'clock, feeling surprisingly energetic. Everyone else was still asleep, so I went quietly to the kitchenette to put on a pot of coffee, then set out my homemade hangover kits and bottles of water on the counter. The way the rest of the bridal party had stumbled back to the room last night, they'd probably need them.

When the coffee finished brewing, I poured myself a cup, grabbed my phone, and sat outside on the wraparound terrace, taking in the sights of the Strip. We were right next door to the Bellagio, which meant an unobstructed view of the fountains. Across the street, there was the Paris Las Vegas hotel, with its hot-air balloon sculpture and half-size replica of the Eiffel Tower. Beyond, there were rows upon rows of towering buildings, casinos with neon lights that glittered brightly even on a sunny day. Mountain ranges loomed in the distance, a striking natural contrast to the glitzy artifice of this city.

The mountains reminded me of Brandon. I texted him a photo of the view and captioned it: Good morning from Las Vegas.

A few minutes later, my phone buzzed with what I expected to be a reply from Brandon, but instead it was a text from Charles: Any updates on Shirin?

Ugh, Charles. This guy was relentless. There was no point in hiding the truth, and beyond that, I wanted him to leave me alone. So I wrote back: I'm really sorry to tell you this but she's seeing someone else and I think it's pretty serious.

He didn't respond. Hopefully, that put an end to it.

A banging came from inside the suite. I entered to find Parisa standing in the kitchenette, chugging a bottle of water. She swallowed, moaned, then chugged some more.

"There's some Advil in the hangover kit," I said.

She moaned again, then tore open the packet and swallowed two pills. "I don't even remember coming back to the hotel last night."

"You were in rare form."

"Did I do anything embarrassing?"

"Not at all." I refilled my coffee and poured her a cup, too. "How are you feeling?"

"Not great, but I've been worse. Just a bad headache, honestly. Give me an hour and two more cups of this"—she gestured to her mug—"and I'll be ready to go. What's in store for today? I forgot what was on the itinerary."

"Cabanas by the pool at noon, then dinner at Beauty and Essex, followed by VIP at Omnia."

"That's right! Tiësto!" She squealed a little, then groaned and held her head. "I've gotta get my shit together."

A knock came at the door, short and sharp. Parisa's eyes went wide with anticipation. "Ooh, did you order room service?"

"No, but that's a good idea. It must be housekeeping. I probably forgot to put the *Do Not Disturb* sign on the door last night. Let me ask them if they can come back later."

"Would you see if they'll give us extra washcloths? Roxy and Leila ruined all of ours taking off their makeup last night."

"Sure thing." I opened the door, but it wasn't housekeeping standing in the hallway. It was a teenage girl with a duffel bag slung over one shoulder. She had long strawberry-blonde hair and bright hazel eyes and a sprinkling of freckles across her nose.

"Hi!" she said, as if I should have recognized her.

A split second later, I did. "Abigail?"

"Thank goodness this is the right room. I accidentally went to the twenty-fifth floor instead of the twenty-fourth floor at first, and let me tell you, those people upstairs are *not* friendly."

I should've invited her in, but I couldn't speak. I just stood there with my mouth hanging open, trying to process what I was seeing: Parisa's sixteen-year-old future sister-in-law, here in Las Vegas, apparently all by herself. Part of me wondered if this was some stress-induced hallucination. But when Parisa gasped behind me, I knew it was all too real.

"Abigail?" She rushed up and pushed me aside. "What are you doing here?"

Her face fell slightly as she adjusted the strap of her bag. "I wanted to celebrate with you guys."

"How did you even get here?"

"MaxBus. It's only fifteen bucks from downtown Irvine to the Strip."

"You were wandering around on the Strip by yourself?" She grabbed Abigail by the forearm and yanked her into the room. "Get in here."

I closed the door behind us, still in a state of disbelief. "Do your parents know you're here?"

Abigail rolled her eyes. "Please. They think I'm at Laurel's house for the weekend. It's not like they're gonna check in on me either. Dad's working, and Mom's doing some yogathon in Laguna."

"Well, I have to call her," Parisa said.

"No, don't!"

"She will kill me if she finds out you came to Vegas and I didn't tell her."

"She doesn't have to know. She'll never find out!"

Parisa held her head in both hands and squeezed her eyes shut tight. "I don't understand, Abigail. Why are you here?"

"I told you. I wanted to celebrate with you." She dropped her duffel bag on the floor with a loud thud. "I'm a bridesmaid. I should've been invited to the bachelorette party."

"You're sixteen. You can't gamble or drink. You shouldn't be here." Parisa opened her eyes, fixing Abigail with an exasperated look. "I've gotta take you home."

"No!" Abigail and I both yelled at the same time, and she flashed me a grateful smile, like I was on her side. But this wasn't about Abigail. This was about Parisa. This bachelorette weekend was important to her, and it was my responsibility to make sure she had a good time. No one was going to ruin it. Not Roxy or Leila, not Charles, and certainly not this little twerp.

I turned to Parisa and gave her shoulders a reassuring squeeze. "You are not going to cut your party short. Abigail can come with us to the pool today, and I'll see about adding another person to our dinner reservation."

"What about the club tonight? She obviously can't come with us."

"Oh, I totally can," Abigail said. "I've got a fake ID."

"No!" This time it was Parisa and I shouting simultaneously.

"Give us a second," I said, then pulled Parisa out onto the balcony, where Abigail couldn't hear us. "She can stay here by herself."

"She just lied to her parents and crossed state lines. Do you think we can trust her to stay here alone?"

"So I'll stay here, too, and make sure she doesn't leave."

Parisa frowned. "But then you don't get to have any fun."

"I'll be fine. The most important thing is that you have a good time tonight. It's your last hurrah, remember?"

To be perfectly honest, I wasn't *that* disappointed about missing out on the club. The night before had been kind of a nightmare, herding drunk people through the casino and into cabs. Of course, looking after a defiant teenager didn't sound like a rollicking good time, either, but it was the only way Parisa was going to enjoy herself tonight without worrying about Mike's little sister going wild in Vegas.

"I don't know," Parisa said, her frown deepening.

We looked through the sliding glass door at Abigail, who was picking through the penis-themed novelties on the coffee table. She wrapped her lips around the bright-pink penis whistle, and the shrill sound echoed out onto the balcony.

Parisa grabbed her head again. "Omigod."

"Don't worry. I've got this under control." I marched back into the suite and confiscated the whistle. "Be quiet—people are still sleeping."

The damage had already been done. Roxy staggered out of her bedroom, sleep mask pushed up onto her forehead. "Nicole, why the hell are you blowing that thing so early?"

"It wasn't me." I tossed the whistle back onto the coffee table as Roxy registered the new and unexpected guest.

"Aren't you Mike's little sister?"

Abigail waved. "Hi."

"Aren't you, like, twelve?"

"She's sixteen," Parisa said, stomping over to us. "And her name is Abigail."

Seemingly uninterested in where Abigail had come from or why she was here, Roxy stretched her arms over her head, revealing her taut, tanned stomach. "Can we order some room service or something? I'm hungry."

"That's a fantastic idea."

As the rest of the bridal party stirred from their slumber, I flipped through the room service menu and ordered some continental break-fast–style fare: fruit platters, pastry baskets, and orange juice and champagne for mimosas. After a while, the shock of Abigail's arrival wore off, and we all relaxed into the comfy living room couches. We ate and drank and enjoyed the view, and I had to admit, there was something nice about having the entire bridal party together without the added stress of a dress to buy or a speech to give. It was easy. It was comfortable.

That easy, comfortable feeling extended into the afternoon. We made our way to the Boulevard Pool, where a reserved cabana awaited us. Inside, there was a TV, a fridge stocked with water and soda, lots of fresh towels, and a comfortable couch. We also had a couple of lounge chairs reserved poolside and dedicated waitstaff who would bring us whatever else we wanted.

Mostly, that was frozen drinks. Margaritas and mudslides and daiquiris. Abigail tried to order a frosé but was roundly rejected, so she settled for a virgin piña colada, just like mine.

According to every travel blog I'd read, April was the perfect time to visit Vegas, and the weather today proved them right. It was sunny but not oppressively hot. A warm desert breeze rustled the curtains framing the entrance to the cabana. After spraying down with sunscreen, everyone took their drinks and heart-shaped sunglasses and meandered to the edge of the pool.

Everyone except for Abigail, that was. She lingered behind on the couch, staring at the TV screen and sipping her piña colada. The confidence she'd displayed this morning was gone, replaced with a wide-eyed anxiety that I recognized all too well.

I sat down beside her. "Everything okay?"

She nodded, the straw still in her mouth.

"You don't wanna go in the pool?"

Her eyes drifted over my shoulder and out through the curtains, taking in the crowd. Music pumped out of speakers all around us, the low, thumping bass that was omnipresent in this city. People laughed and splashed and danced. Roxy and Leila had their drinks raised above their heads in a toast to no one in particular.

"I can't wait until I'm twenty-one," Abigail said.

"Why? So you can drink?"

She gave me this *Well, duh!* face that made me feel old and uncool. Which I was, in a way. Whatever. "Drinking's not all that great."

"I don't need the patronizing *say no to alcohol* speech, okay? I'm not a child."

"I didn't say you were a child, and I'm not trying to be patronizing." I held up my half-melted virgin piña colada. "There's no alcohol in this. I don't drink."

She leaned in and whispered, "Are you in AA?"

This again. "No. Alcohol doesn't agree with me. That's all."

Except that wasn't all, and Abigail knew it. She fixed me with her hazel eyes, squinting like the truth was written in teeny-tiny letters on my face that she couldn't quite read. So I decided to tell her the real reason I didn't drink. "I got super wasted in college and busted my face open, and the video of it went viral. After that, I swore off drinking."

She was still squinting, still trying to discern the truth. She thought there was more to the story. And she was right.

"Plus, I don't want to end up like my mom." It was weird to come out and admit that so casually, to someone I barely knew. I could hardly even admit it to myself.

"Is your mom in AA?" she asked.

"I wish. I could never convince her to go. The closest I came was in high school. I drove her to a meeting in the next town over, but when we got there, she refused to get out of the car."

"Wow." She took a long pull from her frosty drink. "That must've been hard."

"It was, but I'm fine now."

"Isn't it weird not drinking? Like, don't you ever feel left out?"

"All the time. It's better than busting my face open, though."

She laughed, then abruptly stopped herself. "Sorry."

"Don't be. It's funny in hindsight. I just don't ever want to get to that place again. I really only drink because it makes it easier for me to talk to people. I have a hard time with that."

"Really? Because we've been talking for a while, and you're not drinking, and you seem totally comfortable."

"It depends on who I'm talking to or what kind of situation I'm in. When I'm in big groups of people or there are a lot of strangers around or there's a lot at stake, I get nervous." I nudged her with my elbow. "But you're easy to talk to. You're what I'd call an exceptional conversation partner."

She smiled, and suddenly, I was happy Abigail had crashed our bachelorette weekend. She was, after all, part of our bridal party, and while she had behaved recklessly, she only wanted to be included in the festivities. I felt a strange camaraderie with her. Possibly because we were the only two sober people at this pool.

Parisa in particular was drinking heavily today. At one point, I saw her doing shots with some random dudes at the swim-up bar. Which was her prerogative—this was her last hurrah!—but I kept an eye on her at all times to make sure nothing bad happened. She could slip in a puddle and split her head open, or one of those random dudes could sneak something in her drink. There were so many things that could go wrong. I had to take care of her and keep her safe.

The afternoon wore on, eventually turning to early evening, when we packed up our belongings and headed to the room to get ready for dinner. We added an extra person to our reservation with no problem, so at eight o'clock, all eight of us rolled into the faux-pawnshop storefront that served as the hidden entrance to Beauty & Essex.

The food was phenomenal. Grilled cheese dumplings served in porcelain spoons filled with tomato soup. Rice balls stuffed with wild mushrooms and goat cheese. Empanadas and sliders and deep-fried shrimp. And, of course, a lot of drinks.

When Parisa got the hiccups, that was when I really started to worry. She was usually so composed, even while drunk, and always knew to pace herself so she didn't get too out of control. Today had been so different. The mimosas in the room, the shots at the pool, the constant stream of cocktails at dinner. She'd been drinking for hours, nonstop. Maybe it was time to pump the brakes.

I leaned over to Shirin and asked, "Do you think we should cut Parisa off?"

Roxy instantly cut in. "Stop trying to control her."

"I'm not trying to control her, but look." I waved my hand in Parisa's direction. Her eyes were starting to close. "She was so excited about seeing Tiësto tonight; I don't want her to miss it because she's blacked out."

Roxy huffed and reluctantly conceded. "I'll get her some water. But you should probably take this one"—she jerked her head toward Abigail—"back to the room now. It's past her bedtime."

Abigail frowned. I felt bad for her. She'd been perfectly pleasant all day and had nothing but wonderful things to say about dinner. There was no need for Roxy to be so nasty.

But Roxy was Roxy. She'd always be nasty. And unfortunately, she *did* have a point. We needed to wrap things up here so they could claim the table at Omnia. "The reservation is under Parisa's name," I said. "She's got a booth on the balcony. Just text me if there are any problems, okay? And please make sure she doesn't drink any more."

Roxy rolled her eyes. I took that as a yes and escorted Abigail back to our suite. The restaurant was in the Cosmopolitan, so it was a short but winding walk through the casino to get to the elevator. Inside, I swiped my card and pressed the number twenty-four, then stared at the digital screen displaying advertisements for upcoming concerts and dive-in movies.

"What's wrong?" Abigail asked.

"Nothing, why?"

"You're tapping your foot like crazy."

Was I? Sure enough, there was a tap-tap-tapping in the air, and it was indeed coming from the tip of my toe beating a steady rhythm against the floor. I pressed the sole of my foot down hard to make it stop.

"I'm nervous about Parisa, that's all."

"She did look pretty drunk."

"I know. She never gets that drunk. I don't know what she was thinking."

I clenched my fist, my fingernails digging into my palm, as bitterness bubbled up from the pit of my stomach. This was no longer a bachelorette party. This was a babysitting job. And I wasn't just talking about Abigail. I was talking about Parisa, too.

In my life, I'd had plenty of experience babysitting drunk people. Or, rather, one drunk person: my mom. All those times my dad had been "working late," I'd stayed glued to her side, just to make sure nothing bad happened. So many nights sitting next to her on the couch as she cried about how unhappy she was in her marriage. Rolling her over onto her side after she passed out so she didn't aspirate vomit in her sleep. Hiding the wine bottles while she snored, in the vain hope that it would somehow curb her drinking.

It was always my job to take care of my mom, to keep her safe. That was a lot for me to take on. But Parisa had always been my haven, providing an escape from the oppressive weight of worry my mother had heaped upon my shoulders.

Now Parisa was the source of that worry. And I couldn't help but feel the tiniest bit resentful.

I closed my eyes and took a deep breath—*in-two-three-four, out-two-three-four*—then slowly unclenched my fist, wiggling my fingers, as I reminded myself that this wasn't the same kind of situation at all. With my mother, it was a persistent, pervasive worry that had permeated every aspect of my life. But this was only one weekend in Vegas, and Parisa had merely suffered a momentary lapse in judgment.

Parisa wasn't my mother. And I wasn't my mother either. My tongue stroked the back of my fake front tooth, a permanent reminder of my own lapse in judgment. A mistake that did not define me, an event in my past that did not decide my future.

The elevator dinged, and I opened my eyes. As the doors rumbled open, Abigail said, "Why don't you go back to them? Go to the club."

"I can't. I promised Parisa I'd stay with you." I stepped into the hallway, but Abigail stayed put, one hand holding the doors. "Come on. She'll be upset if I leave you alone."

"She's too drunk to even remember I'm here right now," she said. "Look, I promise I won't go anywhere. I don't want to get you in trouble, but I don't want Parisa to get in trouble either. You should go to her."

Abigail was right. And it was funny: I trusted her to keep her word more than I trusted Roxy and Leila to take care of Parisa. As maid of honor, my number one priority was to be a good, supportive friend at all times. Tonight, that meant keeping her from dancing on any tables and potentially breaking a tooth.

"Thanks, Abigail." I handed her the key to the room and hopped back in the elevator as she hopped off. We waved goodbye between the closing doors.

As the elevator whooshed me back down to the ground floor, I pulled out my phone to text Roxy: Headed to Omnia now. Abigail's staying alone. Everything okay with the reservations?

She didn't respond right away. I was already outside, in line for a ride share, when my phone finally buzzed with her reply: Actually, there's been a change of plans . . .

Then she sent a photo of Parisa wearing her penis veil, standing next to an oiled-up, half-naked man. Her eyes looked unfocused, like she wasn't exactly sure where she was or what she was doing there.

But I knew exactly where she was: Hunk-O-Rama.

CHAPTER
TWENTY-ONE

I don't know what I expected. It wasn't like the name Hunk-O-Rama evoked a sense of class and sophistication. But when the driver pulled into the parking lot of some seedy strip mall behind the Circus Circus casino, I was convinced she had the wrong address.

"Are you sure this is it?" There wasn't much here. A few blacked-out storefronts and something that looked like a warehouse.

"You wanted the Hunk-O-Rama male revue, right?" Her voice was hoarse and phlegmy.

"Yes, but I don't see it."

She drove around the back of the warehouse, where there was a big black door, above which hung a blue neon sign that read **HUNKS**. "Here you go," she said, tapping the button on her app to stop the ride. "Have a good time. I heard these guys are the wildest hunks in town."

When I stepped into the club, the first thing I noticed was the pervasive smell of Axe body spray. It shot up my nose and clung to my clothes. They must've been pumping it in through the ventilation system.

The second thing I noticed was the giant golden penis. It was six feet long with a pink saddle strapped on top, and it bucked like a mechanical bull. There was a woman riding it, her body jerking back and forth with each haphazard movement. Suddenly, the giant penis lurched, and she flew to the padded floor like a rag doll.

I ventured farther inside to find a sea of women standing around, clutching drinks and chattering exuberantly. Half of them wore polyester penis veils. It was going to be impossible to find Parisa in here.

Fortunately, Shirin found me first. I heard her screaming my name over the din of bass and babble, then turned to see the whole group gathered in a corner behind a velvet rope, beside a sign that said **VIP**. I pushed through the crowd, and a burly, shirtless bouncer waved me inside.

"Isn't this *wild*?" Shirin said.

"I heard these are the wildest hunks in town," I said.

"Did you see that giant penis?" Leila asked.

"I'm gonna ride it!" Roxy screamed.

Ally and Kara were standing off to the side, engrossed in conversation and sucking on their drinks through cocktail straws. But I didn't see the guest of honor. "Where's Parisa?"

Roxy gestured over her shoulder. "Little Miss Party Pooper is over there."

Sure enough, she was leaning against the back wall, yawning. So much for this being her special night.

I hurried over and squeezed her hand. "Hey, are you okay?"

Her eyes were cloudy, as if I'd woken her from a nap. "Yeah, I'm fine, but what the hell are we doing here? We're supposed to be at Omnia tonight."

"They kidnapped you," I said. "Should we get outta here?"

She yawned again. "Honestly, Nicole, I'm so tired; I just wanna go back to the room." Her eyes went wide as she remembered the eighth member of our party was missing. "Wait. Where's Abigail?"

"At the suite. Don't worry about her. She promised me she'd stay put, and I believe her." I peered around, wondering if maybe I could sneak Parisa to the exit. Roxy and Leila were currently distracted by a man in a bow tie and thong who was making his way around the room.

If we left now, they wouldn't realize we were gone until we were halfway back to the Cosmopolitan.

Before I could finalize our escape plans, though, the lights dimmed. Howls rose all around us, and a cheesy synth melody blared through the speakers. An unseen announcer asked, "Who's ready for some hunks?"

The howling intensified, but that wasn't enough for Mr. Announcer Man. He repeated the question, roaring, as if punctuating each word with an exclamation point: "I said: Who's! Ready! For! Some! Hunks!?"

A horrible screeching tore through the club, like two hundred women were possessed by a demon. Leila's eyes bugged out of her head, Roxy's face was purple, and Shirin jumped up and down. Kara and Ally were nowhere to be seen. Parisa yawned yet again.

Theatrical smoke billowed from the center of the dance floor. Like magic, five men appeared in the clearing fog. They were a bizarro version of the Village People, decked out in cliché costumes: a cowboy, a sailor, a construction worker, a firefighter, and some sort of S&M dungeon master. But instead of breaking out into song, they simply started humping the floor.

As the show progressed, each man gave a solo performance in which he undulated and pumped his hips and eventually stripped down to a G-string. Mercifully, there was little audience interaction; the guys would wink and throw their clothes into the crowd, occasionally allowing grabby women to caress their sweaty chests, but for the most part, the show was hands off.

Roxy, Leila, and Shirin remained enthralled throughout, while I hung back against the wall with Parisa, making sure she didn't pass out or puke all over herself. This was the worst possible way this evening could've gone. Most likely, the host at Omnia had already given our table away. Who knew how many strings Brandon had had to pull to get it for us? And we didn't bother to show.

As if sensing my dismay from across state lines, Brandon chose that moment to send me a text: How's your night going?

I snapped a photo of the cowboy stripper performing lasso tricks in his assless chaps and sent it as a reply.

Dammit, you ran off with a stripper?

Just what I was afraid of . . .

Not exactly.

Parisa's sister hijacked my plans.

Now we're at the Hunk-O-Rama male revue instead of our table at Omnia.

Yikes.

Yup.

Parisa's super drunk, too.

She needs to go to bed.

I'm sorry.

What for?

You set me up with this amazing VIP package and now we're not even going to show up.

Don't worry about it.

You can't really schedule Vegas, anyway.

You kind of have to just let it happen.

So I've learned.

Hope your night's going better than mine.

It's going very well, actually.

Closing some business deals as we speak.

On a Saturday night?

And you said I work too much . . .

Well, I wouldn't exactly call it work . . .

He sent a selfie, and at the sight of his beautiful face, my knees turned to gelatin. He had that three-day stubble I loved so much, and his gray eyes burned right through the camera lens. There was a fancy cocktail in his hand, a slice of lime hanging off the rim of a copper mug. A woman was laughing in the background. She seemed vaguely familiar. Then I realized it was Kelsey, the bartender from Vespa who'd served me the night I'd behaved like a total fool.

Are you at Vespa tonight?

Yep. And I have great news.

I've convinced Kelsey to quit her job and follow us to Idyllwild.

She's Mountain Air's new master mixologist!

Oh.

The edges of my vision got all splotchy, and my stomach turned to stone. There was no reason to be jealous, though. Brandon and Kelsey were only working together. This was simply a business relationship.

A business relationship in which both people were completely upending their lives and moving to a new town to build a brewpub together and probably live in very close proximity to one another, too.

"All right, ladies!" The announcer was back on the mike, enthusiastic as ever. "It's about time to . . . pull! It! Out!"

Good Lord. Were they actually going to do full-frontal nudity at this thing? If so, I was about to take my bottle of water and scram.

However, it soon became clear that "It!" referred to a makeshift throne the performers were dragging across the dance floor. The announcer yelled, "One lucky lady gets to sit in the Hot Seat tonight!"

Screams erupted around the club as Parisa grimaced and held her head. "Ugh, that sounds like a nightmare."

It sure did. And from what I remembered of the bridal party's Slack chat, Parisa was scheduled to be tonight's lucky lady. "There's something you should know," I said. "Roxy and Leila planned this whole thing, and they were talking about—"

"Can we get Parisa Shahin to the dance floor?"

When the announcer said her name, the color drained from her face. "Are you kidding me?"

"I told them not to do this. I said we were going to Omnia, but they wouldn't—"

"Parisa?" The announcer sounded concerned. "Your sisters want to wish you a happy bachelorette party and are sending you off from singlehood in style. Please, come on down to the Hot Seat now and let our hunks go wild on you!"

"Omigod, no." She shielded her face with her hands. I searched frantically for an emergency exit, maybe even a window we could jump through to freedom, but it was too late. Leila was already tugging on her arm while Roxy yelled, "What is wrong with you? Go up there!"

There was no time to protest. The bouncer pulled back the velvet rope at the same time Roxy shoved Parisa toward the dance floor with both hands. Before I could process what was happening, Parisa was sitting in the Hot Seat, which upon further inspection appeared to be a repurposed barstool covered in tinsel.

The audience cheered and whooped as Parisa sat there, mortified, with a mostly naked stripper grinding against her. He finished his lap dance with an impressive wide-legged handstand, which allowed him to wiggle his taint directly under her nose. When she stood up and staggered away, her skin was a sickly shade of green.

"Give it up for Parisa, everybody!" The crowd shrieked, more riled up than ever. Parisa made a beeline for her sisters.

"What the hell did you do that for?"

"Because it was hilarious!" Roxy said.

Leila pointed and laughed. "You should've seen your face. You looked like you were gonna throw up."

Parisa scowled. "You know I hate this kind of shit."

"Lighten up!" Leila said. "It's your bachelorette party."

"Exactly. It's *my* bachelorette party, not yours."

"Obviously." Roxy rolled her eyes.

Parisa tore off her penis veil and flung it to the floor. "You know what? This is why I made Nicole my maid of honor."

Uh-oh. I did *not* want to get dragged into this sisterly spat. Not to mention people around us were starting to stare. I put my hands out between them and said, "Okay, that's enough, you guys." But they ignored me.

"Some maid of honor!" Roxy yelled. "She hasn't been around for anything. She didn't come look at the venues; she was late to the dress fitting; she barely participates in the Slack chats."

"So? That's not important to me."

Leila looked hurt. "It isn't?"

"Of course it isn't," Roxy said. "Because she's selfish."

Parisa flinched, like she'd been slapped. Then she spun around, knocking the velvet rope to the floor as she sprinted away.

"I thought she was having a good time," Leila said, genuinely disappointed.

"She never wanted this," I said. "I told you that."

"You're such a fucking know-it-all." Roxy sneered at me. "I never understood why my sister thinks you're so great."

To be honest, I didn't know either. If I'd been doing my job as maid of honor correctly, we wouldn't have ended up in this situation. But this wasn't about Roxy, and it wasn't about me. This was about Parisa. And right now, she needed my help.

I ran off to find her, checking the bar first, then the bathroom. An awful retching sound coming from the second stall alerted me to her whereabouts. When it subsided, I tapped on the door. "You okay in there?"

The toilet flushed, and she came out, face sweaty and hair tangled. Dark circles sagged beneath her tear-filled eyes.

"This whole thing is so stupid," she cried.

"I know, it's ridiculous. I'm sorry I allowed this to happen. Let's leave. It's not too late to catch Tiësto, and—"

"No, I'm not talking about the strip show. Well, the strip show is stupid, too. But I'm talking about the wedding. Everything snowballed out of control so fast. I don't even want to have it anymore."

I thought back to that article on prewedding jitters, searching my memory for some piece of advice that would serve me well. There was never any mention of a drunken confessional in the Hunk-O-Rama bathroom, so I improvised. "You don't really mean that. You're just upset right now, that's all."

"No, I mean it." Her voice was stronger now, like she was sober all of a sudden. "I want to call the wedding off. I've talked about this with Mike already, how sick I am of the whole thing. He said he'd support whatever decision I made. Maybe I can convince him to fly out here tonight. We can go to the Little White Wedding Chapel tomorrow.

That's all I really want, anyway. Just me and him. No frills. You can serve as our witness. In Vegas, you only need one. I checked."

Apparently, she'd given this some forethought. "You said you wanted to do the big wedding for your family."

"Screw my family." Her tears had turned to full-fledged, red-cheeked rage. "If they don't care about what I want, then I don't care about what they want."

There was fire in Parisa's eyes. Like she was really about to call her mother and cancel the whole thing.

"Please don't make any decisions right now," I said. "You've been drinking all day, and you're tired and emotional. Sleep on it and see how you feel in the morning."

She swallowed hard, considering my words, then wordlessly bent over the sink to splash her face with water from the tap. Droplets dripped down her chin and soaked her shirt. As she blotted her skin with a one-ply paper towel from the automatic dispenser, we made eye contact in the mirror.

"Fine," she said, tossing the balled-up paper towel in the trash. "But as soon as I wake up tomorrow, I'm calling Mike. Mark my words: we're canceling this wedding."

CHAPTER
TWENTY-TWO

I'd been friends with Parisa for a long time, so I knew a lot about her, things that not many other people knew. I knew about the nose job she'd gotten the summer after high school and the one-night stand she'd had with a washed-up boy bander. I knew she was wildly intelligent but also wildly impulsive.

And I also knew that once she made up her mind about something, there was no convincing her otherwise. In fact, trying to talk her out of an impulsive decision often backfired, and she'd go running full force toward whatever it was I was cautioning her to avoid. That was how she'd wound up with that cockeyed Tinker Bell tattoo on her ass.

So even though calling off the wedding would've created a cascading disaster of epic proportions, I knew I couldn't come right out and tell her that. I needed to give her the time and the space to arrive at the conclusion herself.

And it most *definitely* would have been a disaster to call off the wedding. There were the nonrefundable venue deposits. The dress that couldn't be returned. The invitations that had already been sent out and the RSVPs that had already come in. I understood her anxiety, her desire to throw in the towel. I'd fantasized about calling it quits on this wedding, too. But it was only that: a fantasy. Not something I'd ever actually do. Because I knew Parisa was counting on me.

All night, I tossed and turned, worrying about what would happen in the morning. When the first glints of sunlight peeked over the desert mountains, I gave up my vain attempt to sleep. I got out of bed, put on a pot of coffee, and sat nervously on the balcony, waiting for Parisa to wake up.

Halfway through my second cup of joe, the sliding door opened, and Abigail poked her head outside. "Mind if I join you?"

"Of course not. There's coffee in the kitchen, if you want."

She held up a mug. "Way ahead of you."

"How'd you sleep?"

"Good." She sat down in the chair beside me, resting her bare feet on the bars of the balcony railing. "When did you get back last night? I didn't hear you guys come in."

"Parisa and I came back pretty early. I'm not sure about everyone else."

"How was Tiësto?"

"We missed him. Roxy and Leila wound up taking us to some strip show, and things kind of deteriorated after that."

Abigail laughed. "Strippers? That's so un-Parisa."

"See? Even you know that's not something Parisa would like. I don't understand why her sisters thought it was a good idea."

She glanced over her shoulder, then whispered, "Her sisters are mean. Especially Roxy."

"No kidding. Last night, Parisa was so upset with them that she threatened to call off the wedding."

Her jaw dropped. "Omigod, is she really calling off the wedding?"

"No." I sipped my coffee. "Maybe. I hope not, though."

"But why would she call off the wedding because her sisters are mean? She should just throw them out of the bridal party. That's what I'd do, anyway."

"It's complicated. The Shahins have a strong sense of family, and I think her mother would be devastated if Parisa didn't include them as bridesmaids. She told me if it weren't for the family, she and your brother would probably just elope."

"Really?"

"Yup." I nodded. "Parisa isn't enjoying any part of this wedding planning."

"Then why is she doing it?"

"I told you, because of family. She's doing it to please her mom. And your mom. Everyone except herself and Mike."

"Wow. Then they *should* call it off."

"At this point, there's too much money on the line. They've already paid for so many things they can't get refunded."

"So? Our families aren't getting married; they are. They should do what makes them happy. I mean, you only get one life. Live it the way you wanna live it."

Abigail had a point. The deposits, the gown, the hotel block: these were already sunk costs. Parisa always said time was our most precious commodity. Was it worth spending two more months of her life being absolutely miserable because of money that had already been spent?

In fact, the more I thought about it, the more I realized that calling off the wedding might not be such a bad idea. Parisa could plan the tiny, intimate elopement of her dreams, and everyone else could just deal. And no matter what, I'd continue to be the good, supportive friend that she needed me to be.

So a few minutes later, when she came out on the balcony, I was completely prepared to back her up. "Hey, Abigail," she said, "would you mind giving me and Nicole a minute alone? We need to talk in private."

"Of course." Abigail walked inside, throwing me a meaningful look before closing the sliding door behind her.

Parisa sat down and stared out onto the Strip. She was quiet for a minute, before she said, "I'm really sorry about last night."

"You've got nothing to be sorry for. Yesterday was beyond crazy."

"Yeah, but I shouldn't have had so much to drink. I should've paced myself better. It was irresponsible and unfair to you, because you wound up having to babysit me all day."

"Hey, you've done it for me. Remember that first night at Vespa?"

"That is so not the same. You had, like, three glasses of champagne. I was drinking for ten hours straight. Plus, I know it's hard for you. Because of everything you've dealt with."

By that, of course, she meant all the times I'd had to babysit my mother. When I was younger, I never told anyone else what was happening at home—except for Parisa. She was the only person I trusted. And she honored that trust with her love and support, holding me when I needed to cry, telling me jokes when I needed to laugh, giving me a safe space to land when I needed to escape. She never asked me to explain how I felt. She just understood.

So I knew she was feeling guilty about last night. I could see it in the droop of her big brown eyes. But I wasn't mad at her. It had only been a momentary lapse in judgment. We all had them. Including me.

"It's fine," I said.

"No, it's not. And I'm sorry." She took a deep breath and puffed up her cheeks as she blew it out. "I'm stressed out and confused. This goddamn wedding is taking so much more emotional energy than I thought it would."

"Well, if you do decide to call it off, I'm here for you."

She furrowed her brow. "Oh, are you talking about my tantrum last night? I didn't mean that. There's no way I can call off the wedding."

"You could, if you really wanted to. It would be awkward and inconvenient, but not impossible."

"Don't be ridiculous."

"Maybe it sounds ridiculous, but you seemed so incredibly unhappy last night. I'd hate to see you spend the next two months feeling the same way."

"Look, I was drunk. I was being dramatic and said stuff I didn't mean."

She bored into me with her big brown eyes, flaring her nostrils and pursing her lips. It was the same look she'd given me in the tattoo parlor six years ago, right after I'd told her that putting Tinker Bell on her ass was a bad choice. I could tell it was time to back off.

"Okay," I said. "But if there's anything you want to talk about, I'm here. No judgment."

She nodded and stared out into the desert again. "I can't believe Abigail took a bus out here all by herself. I need to book her a ticket on our flight home. I hope there are still seats available."

"I'm sure there are. There were plenty of open ones on our flight out here."

"Mike can drive her home from the airport." She scrubbed her palm over her face. "God, I hope Francine doesn't find out."

"She won't. Abigail's a handful, but I think she knows how to be discreet."

"I guess. What time do we land, again?"

"Eightish."

"So not too late. Are you gonna see Brandon tonight?"

"Hadn't planned on it."

She raised her eyebrows. "Seriously? You haven't seen each other all weekend. This is the perfect opportunity for some hot reunion sex."

"Uh . . ." I wasn't sure I wanted to admit this to her, but, "We haven't had sex yet."

I thought her eyebrows were going to rocket right off her forehead. "Are you kidding? It's been weeks. What are you waiting for?"

"I don't know." No, that wasn't true. "I guess, deep down, I'm afraid we won't work out. And if we sleep together, I'll be that much more hurt when we inevitably break up."

"From everything you've told me, he seems like the perfect guy. Why are you so afraid?"

"He's moving."

She threw up her hands in exasperation. "Only two hours away!"

"Still, it's been really hard. We talk and text all the time, but it's not the same as being together in the same room, you know what I mean? I miss him. Like, physically."

"Well, it doesn't sound like you two are getting very physical."

"We do other stuff. We hug, we cuddle, we kiss. His kisses are . . ." I trailed off, struggling to find the words to describe how it felt when Brandon's mouth was on mine. "They're like fire. I've never experienced that with anyone before."

Her lips curved into a sympathetic smile. "Long distance isn't easy, I know. If you find someone like that, though, it's worth the effort. When Mike was living in Chicago, it was so hard to be physically apart from him for those long stretches of time. But we always made sure to be together for the big important stuff."

"Like what?"

"Birthdays, anniversaries. Special occasions like that."

I gnawed my lower lip, thinking of the very special occasion I was going to be missing out on. "That's not always possible."

"You have to make it possible."

"I can't!" My voice sounded frantic. I reined it in and continued in a far more even tone. "He asked me to go to the opening of his brewpub in Idyllwild, but I can't make it because there's a big go-live happening at work that day." She opened her mouth, and I held up my hand to stop her. "Before you start lecturing me about how terrible my company is and how I spend too much time in the office, let me explain that if this project fails, I won't get promoted. The project manager told everyone to be in the office that day, and I can't just tell her no."

"Can't you get someone to cover for you, though? That's how you got the day off to come to Vegas."

"Maybe." There's no way I'd ask Charles to cover for me again, but I supposed I could ask Vimi or Ben. Then again, a deployment was far more complicated than running a couple of usability tests. This was the culmination of months of hard work, with a million moving pieces. I couldn't expect anyone else to oversee it. "I'm not really sure that's an option."

She let out an exasperated sigh. "Look, I know your job is important to you, Nicole, but it can't be your whole life. Otherwise, you'll wake up a few years from now and realize you wasted your entire twenties."

"Are you calling my career a waste of time?"

"No, but let me ask you a question: Why do you want this promotion so badly?"

"Because. It's a promotion."

"Right, but what does that mean, exactly? What does the promotion get you that you don't already have?"

"More money. More responsibility. More clout."

"And will those things make you happy?"

"Yes, of course." Although now that I stopped to think about it, I wasn't so sure. Money was important, but it wasn't everything. And would I actually have more clout? Look at Charles. He was a senior designer—the job title I was gunning for—and he wasn't exactly a power player at Virtuality.

So why did I *really* want this promotion?

The sliding door opened, and Shirin stuck her head out. "Hey there. How are you two doing?"

What a relief. Now we could end this uncomfortable conversation. "Not bad. Did you guys end up at Omnia last night?"

"Nope." She stepped out and closed the door behind her. "Roxy and Leila got into some monumental fight, so I abandoned them to go play three-card poker at Caesars Palace. I won two hundred and fifty bucks!"

"Congrats!" Parisa said. "What happened to Kara and Ally?"

She bit back a smile, like she was holding on to the world's most exciting secret. Then she whispered, "When I came back to the room, they were making out on the couch. I think they're really into each other."

Huh. I hadn't seen that one coming. At least something good had come out of this disaster of a weekend.

"Anyway," she said, "we should probably get everyone up and going soon, no? Our spa appointments are in an hour."

Parisa sighed. "A massage sounds so perfect right now."

"I'll give you the reservation information," I said. "I'm giving my appointment to Abigail."

"What? No! You worked so hard to plan this weekend; you deserve to pamper yourself a little."

"No, she's been feeling really left out, and I want her to feel included. Plus, it'll give me time to pack up."

Parisa squeezed my hand. "You're the best, Nicole."

I didn't feel like the best. I felt like a mess. "You should go wake everyone up. Get them moving so you're not late."

After they retreated into the suite, I stayed on the balcony, empty coffee mug in hand, staring out over the Strip. It almost looked peaceful down there. So different than the unbridled debauchery of last night.

This trip had gone so differently than I'd planned. Brandon had said you couldn't really schedule Vegas, that you just had to let it happen, and it turned out he was right. If I hadn't come into this trip with a perfectly printed itinerary, would things have gone better for us? Maybe trying to control every last detail had made it all spin more wildly out of control.

I had control issues; I knew that. It was why I scheduled every hour of every day. And it was also why I was afraid to take things to the next level with Brandon. I couldn't control the way I felt about him, and that terrified me.

But what was the alternative? I certainly didn't want to end up like Charles, alone and pining, only realizing what I could've had after it was no longer a possibility. I'd set up this choice between my career and my relationship, but it was a false choice. Parisa was right. I was using it as an excuse.

In that moment, I vowed to stop making excuses. I wouldn't shut down this relationship before it even started. It was time to say yes instead of no.

It was time for some hot reunion sex.

If he was game for it, of course. I whipped out my phone and texted him: My flight lands at 8. Can I swing by your place after I land?

I'd probably swing by my own place first, to brush my teeth and wash the airplane grime off me. If we were going to get naked, I wanted to look and smell my best. I started mentally planning everything I'd do this evening, from the moment the wheels touched down at LAX to the moment I showed up at Brandon's front door. But my plans were dashed as soon as I got his reply: Won't be home. 😔 I'm leaving for Idyllwild in a couple hours. Gonna be there until Friday afternoon. Next weekend?

The weight of disappointment settled in the pit of my stomach. No hot reunion sex to be had. Worse yet, another week without Brandon.

But I had to be okay with that. This was part of being in a relationship. I couldn't predict his every move. I couldn't schedule everything all the time. I had to learn to relinquish control.

I wrote back: Next weekend, for sure. And, of course, I put it in my calendar. A four-hour block of time on Saturday night labeled *Brandon* ♥.

CHAPTER
TWENTY-THREE

My weekend in Vegas had been so filled with drama that I couldn't wait to get back to the relative calm and monotony of a day in the office. On Monday morning, I showed up extra early, eager to review the results of the usability tests. Anna would undoubtedly expect a detailed analysis in today's stand-up meeting, so I only had a couple of hours to put together a coherent, comprehensive report.

It was a lot of work to do in a short period of time, and I was most definitely cutting it close. Truthfully, I should've started it the night before, as soon as I got home from the airport, but I was so tired from the long day of travel that all I'd wanted to do was go to sleep. So I had.

And now I was regretting it.

Because I couldn't find the project documents. Charles had been asked to record screencasts of the tests and save them to a shared drive. But they weren't there. No notes or feedback either. Nothing but the scripts and conversation flows I'd provided him with.

I leaped out of my chair and ran to Charles's desk, but he was nowhere to be seen. So I texted him: Where are the screencasts???? No response. I texted him again: Hello? and then called him twice. Each time, it rang for thirty seconds before going to voice mail.

I was about ready to dig up his home address and pound on his front door when he finally decided to reply: They're in the shared drive.

No they're not.

Yes they are.

I looked again, searching through every single folder, thinking maybe he'd saved them to the wrong directory. After five minutes of frantic, fruitless clicking, I called him, and he answered with an exasperated sigh. "I put them in the shared drive," he said. "Just like you asked me to."

"I'm telling you, they're not there. Did you accidentally save them to your own hard drive instead?"

He snickered. "I think I know the difference between my own computer and a network drive."

"Then where the hell are they?" I wasn't one to raise my voice at my coworkers. I wasn't one to raise my voice at all. But I was so freaked out by the thought of these tests being lost forever that I couldn't control myself.

He was completely indifferent to my rising panic, though. "I don't know what to tell you, Nicole."

"You told me you would cover for me."

"And I did. I administered the usability tests, and I saved the screencasts to the shared drive."

I kept closing and reopening the folder, as if they'd magically appear out of nowhere. "Well, did you take any notes or anything?"

"No, I didn't take any notes." He sounded offended by the very suggestion. "I wasted enough of my time on those tests as it was. I had my own work to do; I couldn't spend my whole day covering for you."

"I didn't ask you to spend the whole day covering for me. I only asked you to spare a couple of hours. And you agreed."

"Well, *you* agreed to be on call to answer my questions, but then you told me to figure it out on my own."

"But you said the tests went fine." My mouth went dry as a sudden realization hit me. "Charles, did you intentionally not save the screencasts to the shared drive? Are you screwing me over on purpose?"

"That's a bold accusation, Nicole. Besides, I'm not the one who took the weekend off during an important project to go party in Vegas. I would never do anything like that."

No, he probably wouldn't. And he wouldn't admit to sabotaging me, either, but I knew the truth.

Maybe it was because I had failed to convince Shirin to take him back. Maybe it was because the culture at Virtuality framed colleagues as competitors rather than collaborators. Whatever the reason, it was my own fault. I shouldn't have trusted him. How could I have been so naive?

I didn't even get the satisfaction of ending the call first, because when I looked down at my phone screen, it was already blinking with the *Call Ended* message. Now I was alone with my mistakes and an empty folder where a dozen usability tests should've been.

What was I supposed to do now? My daily stand-up meeting for this project was at ten o'clock. In less than three hours, I'd have to admit my massive failure in front of the entire project team. We'd have to reschedule the tests with the client, all because the lead designer had spent her weekend surrounded by strippers and booze instead of tending to the needs of their critically important project.

I'd never screwed up this badly before, never been this flagrantly negligent. What would the consequences be? Would I lose out on this promotion? Or would it be much worse than that? Just considering the possibilities stole my breath away.

Suddenly, it was like someone pressed a pause button in my brain. I couldn't think or move or speak. The only thing I could do was stare straight ahead, at the empty folder on my screen, the blank white space where the recordings should've been.

I stared until the edges of my vision went blurry, disconnecting from my thoughts, my surroundings, my emotions. At a quarter to ten, I finally snapped out of it when my computer chimed and a reminder message burst into the center of my screen: *Daily stand-up meeting with Anna re: Krueger.*

Dammit. In a flash, I pocketed my phone and ran upstairs to Anna's desk, where she was scrolling through some documentation on her screen. "Hey, Anna, can I talk to you for a second?"

She spun around in her swivel chair and fixed me with her cold blue eyes. "I'm finishing something up right now. The meeting will begin shortly."

"This can't really wait for the meeting. It's about the usability tests."

"We're discussing that in the meeting. I want the whole team to be there to hear your analysis."

"Well, I wasn't able to analyze anything."

Pink splotches spread across her pale cheeks. "You said you'd handle the analysis when you returned."

"And I was completely prepared to do that. But Charles didn't save the screencasts properly, so I can't see what happened during the tests. He didn't take any notes either." I rolled my eyes at this last statement, indicating how thoughtless and ridiculous it was to administer usability tests without jotting down key observations. Not that it would absolve me of any blame.

The color in Anna's cheeks spread up into her temples and down along her jaw, until her whole face resembled the flesh of a Ruby Red grapefruit. "This is unacceptable."

Immediately, I went into fix-it mode. "What if we rescheduled the tests for this afternoon? I could do the analysis this evening, and then we'd only be behind by one day." Though, technically, it'd be two days, since I'd have to postpone the tasks on today's to-do list until tomorrow. And then pull an all-nighter to catch up on those.

It didn't matter, though, because Anna wasn't interested in my proposal. "Do you understand how incompetent that will make us look? Not to mention now we're behind on the project schedule." She slapped an open palm on her desk, and I jolted at the sound.

I wrung my hands, desperate to clean up the terrible mess I'd made. "Maybe we can brainstorm a solution with the rest of the team at our meeting."

"Don't come to the meeting this morning." Her voice was as sharp as the blade of a guillotine. "I don't want the rest of the team knowing about this colossal fuckup. They need to keep their eyes moving forward, not worrying about how behind we are. I'll talk to sales and figure this out. In the meantime, I'm going to have a little chat with Jon."

"A chat?" This was not good. Not good at all. Was she going to yell at him for letting me take the day off? Or complain to him about how badly I'd screwed up? I could lose the project, the promotion. Possibly even my job.

"Leave," she said. "Now. I have to finish what I was doing before you interrupted me with this bullshit. I still have a meeting to run in five minutes."

As I walked away, my heart started to pound like a double bass drum. Fast, furious, and unbelievably loud—so loud that it drowned out every other sound. I couldn't hear my footsteps on the stairs or the creaking of my chair as I sat back down at my desk. All I heard was the deep, fuzzy thunk-thunk-thunk-thunk of my heartbeat going wild with worry over what was going to happen to my future at Virtuality.

All at once, I felt short of breath, as if there weren't enough air in the room to fill my lungs. I fell back on my tried-and-true breathing exercises—*in-two-three-four, out-two-three-four*—but they only made me feel light headed and dizzy. My throat tightened, and beads of sweat dripped down my neck and into my cleavage. Everything in my line of sight started to sway and swivel. Was the building about to collapse on me?

With clammy palms, I gripped the edge of my desk to steady myself. When the room eventually stopped moving, I closed my eyes and rested my forehead against the cool laminate of the desktop. The sensation calmed me so I could finally breathe deeply. My heartbeat slowed, no longer the racing rhythm of a heavy metal song but the slow, painful pounding of a death march.

"Nicole, are you okay?"

I cracked one eye open and saw Vimi hovering above me, her eyebrows drawn together. "I think so," I said. "I don't know."

"Do you have a headache or something?"

"Not really." I forced myself up into a sitting position, holding my heavy head in my hands. "I had this weird thing where I couldn't breathe and the room started to spin. It felt like I was having a heart attack or something."

"Maybe you should go to the doctor."

She was probably right, but I couldn't leave the office now. Once Anna spoke to Jon about the usability-test debacle, he'd undoubtedly want to meet with me, and being MIA would not be a good look. I needed to get it together, stat.

"No," I said. "I'll be fine. I'm already feeling better."

"Well, I'm gonna grab some breakfast. Wanna come with? Or I can bring something back for you from the dining hall?"

Just thinking of food made my stomach turn. "No, thanks."

"Okay. Let me know if you need anything, though."

"I will."

As soon as Vimi left, I set my head down on my desk again, consumed by a fresh wave of panic. My heart started that double time drumbeat again, and my breath got all shaky. Maybe I really *did* need to see a doctor. If only Virtuality had a doctor on site.

Although, now that I thought about it, they sort of did. Not a human doctor, but a chatbot doctor.

Krueger's custom chatbot wasn't ready for public consumption yet. We still had to fix some security issues and, of course, review those missing usability tests, but the AI engine was mostly complete. That meant it could more or less provide accurate diagnoses and suggest potential treatment plans. The data we used was reliable—far more reliable than whatever random website Google might pull up—so I knew I could trust it. Probably. It was worth a shot, anyway. Better than dying alone at my desk.

I fired it up, and it greeted me with our standard messaging:

> Thank you for reaching out to our virtual physician service.

> How may I help you today?

>> I'm not feeling well.

> I'm sorry you are not feeling well.

> If this is a life-threatening emergency, you should call 911.

> Do you feel your life is in danger?

>> Maybe.

> Please tell me your symptoms and I will do my best to help you feel better.

>> Sweating, racing heart, shortness of breath, tightness in throat, feelings of impending doom.

> Hmm.

> I have a few more questions that will help me narrow it down.

> Have you taken any recreational drugs in the past 24 hours?

No.

Could you be pregnant?

No.

Do you smoke or have you previously smoked?

No.

Are you currently under extreme stress?

Yes.

Hmm, that sounds challenging for you.

Please explain your stressful situation.

I hesitated, not knowing if I should delve into too many details. I wasn't afraid of anyone finding out; due to privacy concerns, the chat logs weren't saved anywhere on our systems. But writing it all out would be an admission of a truth I wasn't sure I was ready to face. Namely, that my life was spiraling out of control, and my perfectly organized schedule couldn't fix it.

Then again, this could be the therapy session I knew I needed. Sitting in a room talking to a stranger was a terrifying prospect. Sitting at my desk typing to a chatbot was more my speed. So I decided to go for it and take a deep dive into the finer aspects of my personal life. As I described my angst over work and this wedding and Brandon, the words flowed from my fingertips, and the chatbot kept me going by asking relevant questions at all the right times.

It might have seemed strange to pour my heart out to a computer, but that was part of what made it so appealing. There wasn't an actual person on the other end, only an AI engine parsing my words with zero emotion and zero judgment.

After quite a bit of back-and-forth, the chatbot paused, displaying a bouncing ellipsis I'd designed to mimic the effect of a chat partner typing. Of course, there was no chat partner; the app merely needed time behind the scenes to perform an elaborate database query and create a diagnosis and treatment plan. Which made me a little nervous, to be honest. Was it going to refer me to a live, human therapist? If it was, I wasn't ready for that yet.

Finally, it spat out the answer:

> It sounds like you may be suffering from ANXIETY. ANXIETY is your body's reaction to stressful situations and can manifest in the symptoms you have described.

> It sounds like your ANXIETY may stem from COMPETING PRIORITIES and you may be at high risk of BURNOUT.

> I have a few suggestions on how to manage your ANXIETY and reduce your STRESS. Please follow the link below to get your customized proposal of care.

With a trembling finger, I clicked the link to review the information compiled by the chatbot. There was an overview of anxiety, including symptoms and likely causes, tips on how to handle a panic attack—which was apparently what I'd experienced—and a laundry list of ways to cope with anxious feelings and prevent them from happening in the first place.

Most of the strategies were things I'd already known. Deep-breathing exercises and meditating and managing your time. I already did those things, and they obviously weren't working. There was a visualization exercise—*Picture your happy place!*—that seemed like it would've been helpful in the moment, but now that the panic attack had passed, it didn't do me much good.

I was beginning to feel like this advice was totally useless. Then I saw something that gave me a glimmer of hope: the prioritization matrix.

The prioritization matrix was an exercise that required me to assign a number to each of my commitments—whether work related or personal—based on some combination of how important and urgent it was. To calculate the value, I had to ask myself a question: What was the specific, measurable impact of this commitment on helping me achieve my goals in life? If the number was high, it meant I should focus my effort and attention there. If the number was low, I should clear it off my schedule forever.

I loved this. It was objective, logical, and straightforward, stripping away all the complicated and frustrating emotions, boiling everything down to indisputable numerical data. My heart rate instantly calmed, and I started taking stock of everything I had on my plate.

First, there was the Krueger project. Obviously, it was extremely important, and because of our hard-and-fast deadline, it was extremely urgent, too. The specific, measurable impact would be getting a promotion (or, at the very least, keeping my job), which would most certainly help me achieve my career goals. And working for Virtuality was the epitome of career goals. High score.

Next, Parisa's wedding. This was important because my friendship with Parisa was so important. Urgent, too, because the date was fast approaching—only two months away now. The specific, measurable impact was, of course, Parisa and Mike getting married. Even though it wouldn't necessarily be the wedding of their dreams, I was still responsible for supporting Parisa through it all. High score, coming in slightly below the Krueger project.

Finally, there was Brandon.

Broad, burly, wickedly handsome Brandon. My cheeks burned when I imagined his steely gray eyes, the taste of his lips, the cedary smell of his skin. It was a visceral response, a primal yearning. Every cell in my body wanted him, *needed* him.

But I was straying off course with that line of thinking. Wanting, needing, yearning: those emotional responses were irrelevant here. All that mattered was my answer to this simple, straightforward question.

Except, in this case, it wasn't very simple or straightforward. Because I didn't know the specific, measurable impact of our burgeoning relationship. There was no goal other than to be together. How could I possibly quantify that burst-into-flames feeling?

Being with Brandon *felt* important and urgent. But this exercise wasn't about feelings; it was about facts. And when I subtracted all the muddled, messy emotion from the situation and looked at the straight-up, clear-cut data—specific, measurable data—Brandon's score was pitifully low.

According to this matrix, there was no room for Brandon on my schedule.

CHAPTER
TWENTY-FOUR

Normally, I wasn't one to dispute the facts. You could never win an argument against logical, rational data. But something about this prioritization matrix didn't sit right with me.

True, if I broke up with Brandon, my life would be less stressful. I'd have fewer schedule conflicts. Specifically, I wouldn't have to worry about where I was going to be on Saturday, June 19. I would be in the office, by default.

But my life would also be less joyful. Because being around Brandon made me radiate joy. It flowed through my blood vessels; it seeped out my pores. Just thinking about him made my cheeks burn with the desire to see him again.

Feelings didn't factor into this exercise, but shouldn't my happiness have counted for something?

It was a question I pondered for the next several hours, while trying in vain to get some work done. Which was a lost cause. Between this stupid matrix and the missing screencasts, my concentration was shot. At least I didn't have another panic attack, though. Vimi came by to check on me a few times, and I assured her I was fine. Because I was. Physically, anyway.

Then, late in the evening, the screencast recordings magically appeared in the shared drive, right where they were supposed to be. Apparently, Vimi had overheard Jon having a tense talk with Charles, after which he'd miraculously "found" them. All that panic for nothing. Crisis averted.

Although that meant I had to get cracking on the analysis, stat—as well as catch up on all the stuff I'd been slacking on all day. I worked through the night and into the morning, then finally caught an hour-long nap in the sleep pod before starting work all over again on Tuesday. I worked through all my meals, barely getting up from my desk until Wednesday, when Vimi and Ben finally convinced me to join them for lunch.

As I sat down with my beef bulgogi bowl (sans green onions, thanks to Dwayne), Vimi asked, "How are you doing, Nicole?"

"Yeah, we haven't seen you all week," Ben said. "Krueger being a pain in the ass?"

"Not really. I just fell behind after taking the weekend off."

"Me, too. Finally got caught up last night."

"Oh, right. I forgot you were going away with Cass. How was Big Bear?"

"Really great. I was nervous about the whole no-Wi-Fi thing at first, but it wound up being exactly what we both needed. Just the two of us, no distractions." He stared off wistfully into the distance. "We made a vow to do it more often. I've got my eye on a beach house in San Clemente for the first weekend in June."

"That's nice," I said, though truthfully it was hard not to sulk. Ben was already planning his next romantic three-day weekend. Meanwhile, after the mess of these usability tests, I probably wouldn't be approved for another vacation day as long as I worked for Virtuality.

"I missed both of you while you were gone," Vimi said, one side of her mouth curling up in a devilish grin. "But I did get to spend some quality one-on-one time with Abram, so it wasn't all bad."

"What do you mean, quality one-on-one time?" I asked.

"We hung out on Friday night in the game room. He's surprisingly good at *Pac-Man*, but I kicked his ass at *Donkey Kong*."

"Oh. I thought you meant something else."

"Unfortunately no, we haven't hooked up. But I'm hoping that's not far off." She waggled her eyebrows. "He broke up with his girlfriend."

"Told you it wasn't gonna last," Ben said.

"You called it," she said. "He said they were constantly fighting over his work hours ever since he started here. Apparently, she was already asking him to quit and find a new job."

Yikes. Another relationship destroyed by Virtuality's culture of working till you dropped. I couldn't help but wonder if Brandon and I were doomed to the same fate.

"Anyway," she continued, "he was really broken up about it, so I was just a shoulder for him to cry on."

"Give it another week or two, and he'll be ready to move on," Ben said.

Vimi crossed her fingers. "Here's hoping."

Instantly, I pictured Kelsey tending bar at Brandon's brewpub on the night of his grand opening, being his shoulder to cry on since I wouldn't be there. Maybe she'd be crossing her fingers, hoping he'd ditch me to move on with her. And who could blame him if he did?

What little I'd eaten of my lunch began to churn inside my stomach. I pushed aside the tray and got to my feet. "I've gotta go. I just remembered I have a meeting in five minutes."

Ignoring their questioning looks, I hustled back to my desk and stared blankly at my computer screen. When it came to my relationship with Brandon, all signs pointed to ruin. But I still wanted him. Still *needed* him. In fact, I couldn't get him out of my mind. I pulled out my phone and sent him a text: Thinking of you.

As I waited for a reply, a thought occurred to me, unbidden and unwelcome: What if Brandon gave me an ultimatum, too? What if he forced me to choose between my job and him? A nightmarish scenario, to be sure. Especially because I already knew how I'd respond.

I wouldn't choose Brandon.

This wasn't just a job. Virtuality was my whole world. The linchpin of my career, the epicenter of my social life, the place where I ate all my meals and sometimes even slept. Without this company, I didn't even know who I was.

When Parisa had asked me why I wanted this promotion, I couldn't give her a straight answer. But now I knew. It was because I wanted to prove myself here. To feel validated. To know Virtuality valued me as much as I valued them.

I wanted to be with Brandon, but not if it meant sacrificing my chance at this promotion. And certainly not if it meant sacrificing Virtuality.

My phone buzzed with his reply: Me too. Can't wait for Saturday.

Neither can I, I replied, but that wasn't entirely true. Even though I yearned to be in his presence, I was also sort of dreading it. Because I'd finally have to tell him where I was going to be on Saturday, June 19. And it wasn't Idyllwild.

◆ ◆ ◆

Saturday night, I showed up on Brandon's doorstep with a whole speech memorized. An eloquent explanation of why I couldn't be at the grand opening of his brewpub, why I was breaking this promise I'd made to him. If I didn't prepare what to say beforehand, I was afraid I might stammer or stumble over my words. I needed to remain calm, focused, unemotional.

Problem was, the moment he opened the door, remaining unemotional was an impossibility. Because being around him made me radiate joy. When I saw him standing there in his tight-fitting T-shirt, gray eyes sparkling like fireworks, my whole body lit up. I forgot everything I'd planned to say, and I kissed him.

It was a kiss that swept me off my feet. Quite literally, because Brandon scooped me up in his big, burly arms. Instinctively, I wrapped my legs around him and melted into his warm embrace. The smell of his skin was electrifying; the taste of his tongue sent shock waves all the way down to my toes.

He walked backward into his apartment, holding me tight, our lips never parting as he kicked the door closed with his heel. My fingers sank into the thick hair at the crown of his head, tugging gently. My teeth grazed his lips. My thighs squeezed his hips. This wasn't just a want; it was a *need*.

But when he set me down on his couch, I opened my eyes and saw something I was wholly unprepared for.

Cardboard boxes. Tons of them, everywhere. Some were folded flat, some were assembled, and some were even taped closed and labeled with bright-red marker. *KITCHEN. FRAGILE.*

"You're already packing?"

Brandon looked a little dazed from the abrupt ending to our heated kiss. He shook his head as he sat next to me and said, "Yeah. I mean, I'm doing it little by little, since I'm not here all the time."

"When's your move-in date?"

"May fifteenth."

Three weeks away. "That's so soon."

"Yeah. I was gonna wait a little longer, but the new tenants want to be in before the end of next month, so I need to clear out."

The temperature in the room promptly plummeted, leaving me cold. This was actually happening. Brandon was saying goodbye to LA, for good. I'd known it was coming, but thus far it had been in some abstract future. Seeing these boxes made it real. Immediate.

He caressed the sensitive inner flesh of my forearm, drawing small circles along my skin with his fingertips. "Listen, Idyllwild's not that far away, you know? And I think you're gonna love it at the cabin. There's this really cool loft space that I'm thinking about making into a game room. I'll try to have it set up by the time you come for the grand opening and—"

"I can't go."

The words were like a bolt of lightning, shocking us both into silence. I should've expanded on my hasty declaration, but I couldn't recall a single segment of my perfectly prepared speech.

Brandon opened his mouth, but nothing came out. Then he cleared his throat and tried again. "What do you mean?"

I swallowed hard. "I can't go to the grand opening of Mountain Air. I'm really sorry. I have to work that day. The go-live for that really important project, the one my promotion hinges on? It was moved to June nineteenth. The project manager is demanding that everyone on the team be in the office to oversee it."

"Well, can't you get someone to cover for you?"

"Not after what happened when I was in Vegas. The guy who covered for me screwed up royally. I could've gotten fired."

"For someone else's screwup?"

I spread my hands wide and shrugged. There was no good explanation. Actually, now that I said it out loud, it seemed completely absurd. But that was the way things were. It was out of my control.

Lately, it seemed like *everything* was out of my control. Even things that were usually so simple, like my work performance or my friendship with Parisa, had become messy and complicated. And I couldn't bear the way Brandon was looking at me right now, like he couldn't believe he'd put his heart out there just for me to stomp all over it. I truly didn't deserve him.

"I'm so sorry." My apology was strangled by the pressure in my throat, the lump that was expanding by the millisecond. Hot tears pooled in my eyes, clouding my vision.

Brandon's face became a blur, but his voice was clear when he said, "It's okay, it's okay."

He pulled me to him, and I cried softly into his chest, tears dampening the soft cotton of his T-shirt.

"No, it's not okay," I said. "I promised you I'd be there."

"But I understand why you can't be."

I sat back and pushed my glasses up on my face, wiping my eyes with my fingertips. "You do?"

"Of course. I'd be lying if I said I wasn't disappointed. But this promotion is a big deal. I know your career is important to you."

Fresh tears formed, spilling down my cheeks. Brandon wiped one away with the pad of his thumb. "I don't want to lose you," I said.

"You're not going to lose me."

"I was so afraid to tell you. I thought you'd make me choose."

He cringed, like I'd insulted him. "Choose between me and your job? Are you serious?"

"It's happened to people I know. A lot of them, actually."

"Then those relationships were doomed from the start." He took my head in both his hands and fixed me with his stare, the fire in his eyes burning wild. "Nicole, I would never ask you to give up something that important to you. I want to be with you, and that means all of you. Not just the part that's convenient for me, but all the inconvenient stuff, too. We're carving out lives for ourselves, building our own futures. I want to be part of your future. Don't you want to be part of mine?"

He searched my eyes, then my lips, waiting for an answer. My heart started pounding like a double bass drum. This wasn't a panic attack, and it wasn't anxiety either. It was the swift, sudden realization that there was nothing more important or urgent than telling Brandon how I felt. That I could see my future in the depths of his gray eyes.

But as usual, I couldn't speak. Emotion stole my voice.

So I spoke without words.

I pressed my palms to his broad chest, gripped his shirt in my fists, and pulled him toward me, urgently. Our mouths collided, a combustion of longing and lust. He pressed me against the couch cushions, and as I lay on my back, wrapping my legs around his waist, I released an unwitting moan. This pent-up desire was ready to be unleashed. And I deserved it.

Minutes later, our clothes were scattered around his wide-plank wood floors.

CHAPTER
TWENTY-FIVE

Three weeks went by in a flash. A blur of late nights working in the office and early mornings tangled up in Brandon's bedsheets. He was in town more often than usual, preparing for his move. And while it brought me no joy to see those empty boxes around his apartment slowly get packed and taped, I was happy for every opportunity to see him, touch him, taste him. I drank him in until my senses overflowed.

On Friday, May 14, I cut out of work at seven o'clock and headed straight to Brandon's. It was the last night we'd ever spend there, at least for the foreseeable future. Moving day was tomorrow.

We gave the apartment a proper send-off. Sex everywhere: on the floor in front of the fireplace, bent over the kitchen countertop, soaped up under the shower as we stood in his claw-foot tub. It was so much, yet not enough, and I resented my past self for letting fear stand in the way of doing this sooner.

The next morning, I woke up with my head on Brandon's chest, the soft thunk-thunk of his heartbeat resounding in my ear. He was already awake, his fingers playing with the tendrils of my hair. When I stirred, he smiled down at me.

"Hey," he said. "How'd you sleep?"

"Good. You?"

"Not so great." His gray eyes slid toward the ceiling. "I'm gonna miss it here."

"Well, if you miss it that much, you can come back when your tenants move out. It's only a six-month lease."

"A year, actually."

I sat up, alarmed at this new information. "When did you decide that?"

"My brother talked me into it. He said he'll need my help on site for a while to get the business up and running, especially through the winter months, when things might slow down. I figured I might as well lock in a tenant so I wouldn't have to worry about it later on."

"Oh." I'd somehow fooled myself into thinking he'd only be gone for six months. That once this lease was up, he'd move back to LA, and we'd pick up right where we'd left off. But now the earliest he'd even consider returning would be a year from now, and who knew if he'd actually come back, anyway?

"Hey." He took my chin in his thick fingers and tilted my face down to look at him. He was insanely handsome first thing in the morning, with his hair all tousled and his eyes reflecting the remnants of his dreams. "We're going to make this work. Let's just take it one day at a time, okay?"

One day at a time. That was *so* not how I liked to do things. But staring at Brandon right now, I realized all that mattered was this one day, this one moment, this one man in this room. So I straddled his hips, and I seized the day.

Two hours later, the movers arrived. I kissed Brandon goodbye on his doorstep, then went straight to the office, where I stayed until the sun went down, distracting myself with work so I wouldn't think about the fact that he was gone. Later that night, as I ate dinner alone in the dining hall, he sent me a text. A photo of his brand-new living room, with its exposed beams and impossibly high ceilings. There were moving boxes everywhere, Hops sniffing them suspiciously. **Made it!** he said.

Miss you already, I replied, then immediately went back to work so I couldn't dwell on how lonely I felt.

The next day, I drove over to Parisa's apartment for the hair-and-makeup trial. Every article I'd read about wedding planning said only the bride was supposed to participate in the hair-and-makeup trial. But, of course, Roxy and Leila had demanded we *all* get a day of primping and preening, and since Parisa hadn't felt like getting in yet another argument with her sisters, she'd simply hired a bunch of her industry friends to come in and make us pretty.

When I arrived, her apartment was bustling. The air was thick with the scent of flat irons and hair spray. Pop music blared through the sound system, barely audible over the blow-dryers and incessant chatter. Everyone was here: Leila and Roxy, Shirin and Ally, Abigail, Francine, Farnaz, even Kara, which was surprising, since she was always out of town on some modeling assignment.

"You're here!" Parisa yelled from across the living room, her mouth barely moving as a makeup artist spackled on about a pound of foundation. "Grab some coffee. You're up next."

I poured myself a cup from a silver carafe on the kitchen counter, then walked over to where she was perched on a stool. Her long dark hair was in big fat rollers, and her false eyelashes fluffed out like black down feathers. "How's it going?" I asked.

"My mother's driving me batshit, but other than that I'm fine."

Farnaz stood sour faced in the corner, critiquing a hair stylist who was curling Leila's locks. "What's she doing now?" I asked.

"Nothing. Everything." Her nostrils flared slightly as she took a deep breath. "Whatever. How's Brandon?"

"Good. He left for Idyllwild yesterday. For good."

"When are you going to visit?"

"I'm not sure."

"Well, when's the grand opening of his brewpub?"

I sipped my coffee so I didn't have to respond right away. This was not what I wanted to talk about. Besides, Brandon and I had agreed to take this one day at a time. I was focused on today, not five weeks from now.

Parisa narrowed her eyes. "You *are* going to his grand opening, aren't you?"

Swallowing hard, I said, "I can't."

"What? Why not?"

"I told you, my big project is going live that day and—"

"So why can't you get someone to cover for you?"

"Because I did that in Vegas, and it was a total shit show. Look, I already talked to Brandon about this, and I apologized and he was fine with it. Don't start making me feel bad all over again."

She looked uncharacteristically sheepish as she said, "Sorry."

"It's fine. It's just . . . it's not like I'm happy about it, you know? I *want* to be there."

"Can't you go before then?"

"Not really. I'll be working every weekend until this project is over. Then your wedding's the following weekend. That puts us in July."

Parisa opened her mouth, most likely to launch into some lecture about how I worked too much—the same lecture she'd given me a dozen times before. Fortunately, the makeup artist came to my rescue, brandishing a large brush in her face. "Be perfectly still. No more talking."

A moment later, an Asian woman with oversize tortoiseshell glasses and a wide friendly smile tapped me on the shoulder. "Are you the maid of honor?"

"Yes, hi. I'm Nicole."

"I'm Leilani. I'll be doing your hair. Do you have any photos?"

"Photos?"

"Inspiration photos. Styles you wanna try or aesthetics you like. Also, a photo of your dress would be great, too. That way we can decide what works not just for your hair type but for your whole look."

"Uh, no. I didn't realize I was supposed to bring any photos." Also, I hadn't bought my dress yet. Better get on that soon.

Her friendly smile went tight around the edges. "That's okay. We'll figure something out." She tousled my hair, inspecting it from all angles. "Are you looking for an updo, or do you want to wear it down?"

"I don't know." I hadn't given much thought to it, which I now realized was a mistake. "Whatever's easier, I guess?"

She grunted, clearly dissatisfied with my lack of direction. "Let's just curl it and take it from there."

After wrapping my hair in jumbo hot rollers, Leilani said, "Let that sit for twenty minutes," then moved on to Abigail, who had a phone full of inspiration photos at the ready.

I wandered over to the kitchen counter to refill my now-empty coffee cup and found Shirin nibbling on a blueberry muffin. Her curly hair was swept into a soft, romantic twist with a few sprigs of baby's breath peeking out. "You look gorgeous," I said.

"Thanks! Leilani did such a good job. I haven't seen you since Vegas; how're you doing?"

"Not bad. Work's still crazy, but you know. Hanging in there." I was tempted to tell her what an ass her ex-boyfriend was, but then I realized there was no point, since she already knew. "How about you?"

"Good. Nothing new with me. Ally and Kara, on the other hand . . ." Her gaze drifted over to the couch, where the two of them were shamelessly canoodling, like they existed in their own little world. Suddenly, it made sense why Kara was here. "You know they moved in together?"

"Already? They've only been dating for, like, a month."

Shirin shrugged one shoulder. "Yeah, but when you know, you know. They're so good together. I don't think I've ever seen my sister that happy."

"But doesn't Kara live in New York?"

"She was bicoastal, and she still sort of is, but I think she gave up her place in Manhattan. She travels a lot for work, anyway, but she's here pretty much every weekend now."

"Wow." Following your new girlfriend to another city was a bold move.

"And how are things with your boyfriend?" she asked.

"Good." No need to tell her he was moving to another city this weekend and I was *not* following him.

"Nicole!" Francine called to me from across the room. "Come here, darling—I have a question for you."

Oh, Lord. I was in no mood to make chitchat with Parisa's future mother-in-law. I took a big swig of coffee for courage and strode over with a plastered-on smile.

"Hi, Francine, good to see you," I said, then waved at Abigail, who was sitting beside her, getting her hair braided.

"Lovely to see you, too. Listen, I'm curious: Which dress did Parisa go with? I can't seem to get a straight answer out of her."

If Parisa wasn't telling her, then maybe she didn't want her to know. Maybe after the way Francine had body shamed her at Bergman's, she didn't want to hear her opinion.

Farnaz sidled over to eavesdrop on our conversation. Apparently, Parisa wasn't telling *anybody* which dress she'd decided on. And I certainly wasn't going to break her confidence. So I squinted, like I was trying really hard to remember. "I can't recall."

"Was it the one with the silk roses?" Francine asked.

"I hope it was the one with the mermaid silhouette," Farnaz said.

Francine grimaced. "No, that was the unflattering one."

"None of them were unflattering." My voice was surprisingly firm. I wasn't looking to argue, but I also wasn't going to let this woman tear down all the hard work Parisa had done to improve her body image. "She looked beautiful in all of them."

"Of course she looked beautiful," Francine said. "She's a beautiful woman. I just meant her gut was—"

"Can you please not talk about her body that way?" I said, still firm but somewhat hushed. I didn't want Parisa to overhear this nonsense.

Francine couldn't take a hint. "I'm only speaking in her best interests. Every woman wants to look their best on their wedding day. You understand what I mean, don't you, Farnaz?"

I expected Farnaz to jump to her daughter's defense. Instead, she cocked her head to the side and said, "That's what shapewear is for."

"Omigod!" Abigail burst forth with an irritated sigh. "Will you two stop?"

"Excuse me, young lady." Francine scowled at her daughter. "Don't speak to me like that. And absolutely do *not* speak to Farnaz like that. Apologize this instant."

"I will not. You're both being ridiculous and mean."

Francine gasped. Leilani kept braiding Abigail's hair like nothing was happening, but I could see her eyes flicker between us, eager to listen in on this juicy squabble.

"No wonder she's not enjoying the wedding planning," Abigail said.

"Who's not enjoying the wedding planning?" Francine asked.

"Parisa."

Oh no. I'd told that to Abigail in confidence. I never thought she'd repeat it in front of her mother. And definitely not in front of Farnaz. They both stood there with confused looks on their faces, like they couldn't quite grasp what she was saying. So Abigail decided to make it clearer.

"She doesn't even want to have a big wedding," she said. "She's only doing it to make the family happy, but you're not even grateful. You're just making her life difficult."

Farnaz and Francine exchanged a look. Then Francine said, "When did she tell you all this?"

"Nicole told me at the bachelorette party."

Oh no.

"The bachelorette party." Francine spoke slowly, her brain process-ing each word as it formed on her tongue. "But that was in Las Vegas."

Abigail gave her mother the *Well, duh!* face. Francine looked to me for an explanation, but I couldn't come up with a lie fast enough. In an instant, she beckoned. "Parisa! Come here for a moment, darling!"

"Not now, Mom," Abigail said, but it was too late. Parisa had already mouthed "Sorry" to the makeup artist and was walking our way. Her skin was completely beige, caked in foundation, one eye ringed with liner like that guy from *A Clockwork Orange*.

I wanted to tell her to turn around and run away, to avert the disas-ter that was about to unfold, but before I could make a sound, Francine exclaimed, "Why didn't you tell me my daughter was in Las Vegas for your bachelorette party?"

Her mouth fell open. She looked to Abigail, then to me, then back to Francine. "I—"

Abigail quickly intervened. "Mom, she didn't even invite me, okay? I took a MaxBus from Irvine and showed up unannounced."

She gasped. "Are you kidding?"

"No. Parisa wanted to take me home right away, and I wouldn't let her."

Francine scowled. "Well, she still should've told me."

"More importantly," Farnaz cut in, "why is Nicole telling Abigail you don't want to have this wedding? You're my firstborn and the first to get married. This is a momentous occasion for the entire family."

"Yes," Francine said, "that, too. Aren't you excited about this, darling?"

"Of course I am." Parisa's asymmetrical glare sliced through me like a razor blade. "I don't know why Nicole said that to her."

Leilani spritzed Abigail's braid with some finishing spray. Too much of it, really, because those fumes were making me woozy. I turned to

Parisa and muttered, "Can I speak to you privately?" Then we marched to her bedroom and shut the door.

"Nicole, what the fuck?"

"I can explain."

"Why did you tell Francine that Abigail came to Vegas?"

"I didn't! Abigail told her herself."

"Then why did you tell Abigail I didn't want to have the wedding?"

"Because it's true. It was the morning after the Hunk-O-Rama mess, and you were a train wreck and I was upset, and she was there and so I vented. I'm sorry."

"God dammit." She plopped down on the bed so hard one of the curlers fell out of her hair. "This is a fucking nightmare."

I sat down next to her—carefully, so my curlers stayed in place. "Maybe it's time to stop torturing yourself. Maybe it wouldn't be the worst thing to call the wedding off."

She glowered at me. "You're out of your mind, Nicole. All the RSVPs have been received. I got my dress already; the favors are ordered; the venue is booked. I cannot back out now."

"Yes, you can. You can do whatever you want to do. This wedding belongs to you and Mike, not your families. Don't let them dictate how you celebrate. You only get one life, you know? You should live it the way you want to live it."

When Abigail had said those words to me on the balcony of our suite at the Cosmopolitan, I'd found them inspiring and wise. Enlightening, even.

Sadly, Parisa did not agree. She scoffed and said, "You should take your own advice."

"What's that supposed to mean?"

"You're not exactly calling the shots in your own life. Virtuality dictates everything you do."

"That's different. It's my job. I have to show up."

"Twenty-four seven?"

"Sometimes. Unless I wanna get fired."

"So let them fire you. You're a genius with a ton of experience. You can get a job anywhere you want."

She was right. With my expertise and experience, there were plenty of tech companies I could work for. But I didn't want to work anywhere else. I wanted to work for Virtuality. Like I said, without them, I didn't even know who I was.

"I don't want another job."

"Then admit that it's a choice. Because there are plenty of ways for you to make a good living that don't require you to sleep in your office. But you *like* sleeping in your office because if you work all the time, then you never have to make room in your life for anything else."

Her words stung like a slap in the face. "That is so not true, and you know that. I've made time to participate in all the wedding stuff—all the bullshit that you don't even want!—because you're so important to me. But my career is important to me, too, and—"

"Is it? Because in Vegas, when I asked you why you wanted this promotion so badly, you couldn't even give me an honest answer. You know you're not happy, so stop hiding behind your career."

"I'm not hiding."

"Yeah, you are. You're using it to avoid getting close to Brandon. He's an amazing guy who really cares about you, and you can't even take one day off of work to visit his new house. You're missing the grand opening of his brewpub! On a Saturday night!"

"I have to work."

She sucked her teeth and stood up. Another curler fell to the floor, but she didn't reach down to retrieve it.

"Get your priorities in order," she said, before huffing out of the bedroom.

I sat there by myself, staring down at that lone curler, thinking about my priorities. What was urgent, what was important, and what couldn't fit into my schedule. Brandon had told me he wanted all of me, even the stuff that was inconvenient. I'd told him I wanted the same thing, but had I really meant it?

Maybe Parisa was right. Maybe I *was* hiding behind my work. If I was always busy, there was never any time to get caught up in my feelings. And if I didn't feel, I could never get hurt.

Well, it was time to stop hiding. Time to show Brandon that I *did* want all of him.

I burst from the bedroom and barreled toward the front door. Someone called after me, but I just kept on going. Because I was a woman on a mission. A mission to get my man.

When I got to my car, I pulled out my phone and shot Brandon a text: What's your address? I want to send you a housewarming gift.

A minute later, he sent me his address.

I entered it into my GPS.

And I started to drive.

CHAPTER
TWENTY-SIX

The first hour and a half of the drive to Idyllwild went by pretty quickly. I listened to some of my podcast backlog, which kept my mind occupied through the miles and miles of Southern California freeway. Mountains loomed in the distance, growing closer and closer with each passing minute. As I drove farther into the desert, the strip malls turned to brown hills, the Walmarts to sagebrush. Then I turned onto a narrow road with a sign that read, **STEEP GRADES AHEAD**. That was when things got interesting.

My car's engine struggled as I pressed down on the accelerator. This little sedan wasn't used to climbing mountains. Frankly, neither was I, so I took my time, driving carefully around the twisting curves and terrifying turns. At one point, I stole a glance out my side window to take in the view of the desert below. Nothing but breathtaking blue sky and rolling hills. And a sheer drop-off with no guardrail.

I had no idea what the speed limit was—if there were signs, I'd missed them—but I was almost certainly going under it. Several times, I had to pull over onto a turnout so impatient guys in pickup trucks could zoom past me. It was a harrowing, white-knuckled drive, but the higher I climbed, the easier it became. There were trees up here, thousands of them—tall pines with thick branches. Being surrounded by all this lush vegetation calmed me and made me feel safer. Like if I rolled off the road, at least they'd cushion my fall.

Soon, I started seeing homes—or, at least, traces of homes. Fences and driveways and mailboxes. There were trailheads and campgrounds, too, and eventually a sign:

IDYLLWILD
POPULATION: 3,500
ELEVATION: 5,303

I was a long way from Los Angeles.

The GPS led me through a small village that looked like something out of a Hallmark movie. Quaint storefronts and cozy restaurants, a pedestrian park lined with pine trees. People walked their dogs around town. There were so many dogs. No wonder the mayor was a golden retriever.

I drove through the village and onto a rural street, then made a few more turns before my GPS finally announced, "You have arrived at your destination." Which was confusing, because there was nothing but forest here. I inched the car forward until I spotted a small clearing with a dirt road leading into the woods. At the end of that road was the cabin from the photos.

Somewhere inside those four walls, Brandon's heart was beating. I trembled at the thought of being so close to him.

Gravel crackled under my tires as I pulled into the driveway. I threw the car into park, cut the gas, and did a quick check in the rearview mirror.

Omigod. Those rollers were still in my hair.

I unfurled them, one by one, fluffing my curls out into bouncy waves. Not my usual look, but not altogether bad either. Sometimes, different could be good.

Like being here. This mountain town was most definitely different from the congestion of LA. I could sense the change in the air the moment I stepped out of the car. It was fresher, cooler, tinged with the invigorating scent of cedar pines. Colors were brighter here, too, the blue sky more vibrant and the greenery more alive. It was one of the most beautiful places I'd ever seen. In person, at least.

The porch light was on, brightening the path to the front door in the fading late-afternoon sun. Inside, the curtains were drawn, no lights shining through. I rang the bell and bounced on the balls of my feet, impatient for him to appear.

Somewhere off in the forest, a brook babbled continuously. Birds chattered in the trees overhead, and a light breeze rustled the leaves. Other than that, it was quiet. Not a sound coming from inside the house. No footsteps, no barking dog. And now that I stopped to think about it, Brandon's car wasn't parked here either.

My cell phone had no service. Damn. I walked around the property, searching for bars, and finally caught a signal standing all the way out by the main road. When I called him, he answered on the second ring.

"Hey! What's going on?"

"Um . . ." This was suddenly very awkward. In my head, I'd been planning some big romantic gesture. I'd knock on his door and shock him senseless, and then we'd both succumb to unbridled lust. Now that I had to explain it over the phone, it seemed less romantic and more stalkerish. Still, I had to roll with it. "This is gonna sound bananas, but I'm here."

"Here . . . where?"

"In Idyllwild."

He paused. "Seriously?"

"Yeah. I came to your cabin. That was the housewarming gift I was talking about."

"I can't believe this. You actually came?" He whooped with laughter. "This is amazing. I'll be right there."

Five minutes later, Brandon's Jeep turned down the dirt road. He parked next to my car and practically flew down the path to my side.

"You're here!" He picked me up and whirled me around, the crisp mountain air making my bouncy curls billow. When we kissed, electric currents flowed from my lips to the tips of my toes, and I knew at once it was worth every hairpin turn on that mountain to be here in his arms. This was the big romantic gesture I'd been planning, playing out in real time.

He set me down and said, "Your hair's different."

I twirled a ringlet. "Does it look okay?"

"It looks beautiful. *You* look beautiful. It's so good to see you. I can't believe it." He ran the back of his hand down my cheek, like he was testing to make sure I wasn't just a figment of his imagination. "How long have you been planning this surprise?"

"Not long. It was actually sort of spontaneous." So spontaneous, in fact, that I'd only just remembered I hadn't brought a change of clothes or a toothbrush or any of the four skin-care products I used on my face each night. "This is a big weekend for you. I really wanted to see your new place."

Beaming, he held up his key ring. "Come in. Let me show you around."

The cabin was new, yet familiar. There were wide-plank wood floors and a stone fireplace. In the living room, there was the same cedar trunk and cozy couch, the same hand-crocheted afghan hanging over the back. Boxes were stacked all around. But the vertical space—those impossibly high ceilings—created a sensation of boundlessness, like there were no confines and no restrictions to what could happen here.

"I was hoping to get the place set up before you saw it." He led me through the immaculate kitchen and up a spiral staircase to the second floor. "It'll look a lot better without all the boxes."

"It's already amazing." The room at the top of the stairs was a loft overlooking the living room, with french doors that opened up onto a balcony in the treetops. "This space is gorgeous."

"I'm thinking it could be the perfect game room."

"Ooh." My mind went wild envisioning the possibilities. "That alcove would be perfect for a pinball machine."

"I was thinking that, too. And there's plenty of space for a pool table or a foosball table. Or even both."

"That would be so cool."

He wrapped his arms around my shoulders, pulling me close so my back pressed against his broad chest. Together, we surveyed the room, losing ourselves in the fantasy of what the future could bring.

"Yeah," he said. "Then you wouldn't have to play at the office anymore."

My fantasy bubble popped like a balloon. I whirled around and said, "But I like playing at the office."

"Oh. I thought you said you wanted to have your own game room." He stuck out his lower lip, wounded, and I felt like an ungrateful jerk.

"Of course I do; this is so incredible and thoughtful of you. It's just . . . I like playing at work with my friends, too. Our Friday-night game tournaments and everything."

"Right." His brow furrowed for a moment. Then he brightened and said, "Let me show you something else."

He led me down a long hall, pointing out bedrooms and bathrooms and a linen closet. At the end, he opened a door to an L-shaped room lined with windows that showcased the forest. There was a built-in desk and shelving unit. "An office," I said.

"Yep. We could set it up for you the way you like it so you can work remotely."

"What?"

"I don't really need an office, so I figured we could make it yours. I checked with the neighbors, and they said their Wi-Fi connection is always spot on, never any problems. Except sometimes in the winter, with the snowstorms and everything, but it usually only lasts for a day or two. Rarely longer than that."

"Oh." At Virtuality, working remotely was generally frowned upon, but if I did, I needed to have a reliable internet connection that didn't go down for an unspecified period of time. The snowstorm excuse would never fly. Not to mention . . . "Cell coverage is pretty spotty here, huh?"

"It depends on where you're standing." Biting his lower lip, he pulled out his phone and examined the screen. "I've got one bar in here. Oh shit. My brother just texted. I told him I'd be right back." As he tapped out a reply, he said, "Let's go to his place. He and Kelsey are making dinner."

"Kelsey's here?"

"Yeah, she's been living with us for the past couple weeks."

"Us?" The tiny hairs on the nape of my neck stood at attention.

"Well, technically with Eric, but until yesterday I'd been crashing with him, too. Come on." He grabbed my hand, leading me down the spiral staircase and out to his Jeep.

As he backed out of the driveway and turned onto the main road, I couldn't stop thinking about him and his brother and Kelsey, all cozied up under one rustic roof. And now I was joining them for dinner at the last minute. Did I even belong here?

"So," I asked, trying not to sound like a jealous harpy, "are you and Kelsey good friends?"

He glanced over at me. "We're friends. I don't know if I'd say *good* friends, though. She's more like a sister than anything. She and Eric have been dating on and off for, like, five years."

"Oh!" The relief I felt was palpable, so much so that I flopped my head back in the passenger seat and let out a shaky laugh.

"Wait, you didn't think me and Kelsey were ever a thing . . . did you?"

"I wasn't sure. I can tell she doesn't like me. I figured it was because of that drunken night at Vespa, but I didn't know if there was more to it than that."

"Nah, she's just protective of me, you know? Like a big sister. She doesn't want to see me get hurt. But I told her all about how wonderful you are, and she's happy for me. For us." He reached across the center console and linked his fingers through mine, squeezing tightly. "Kelsey and Eric have something really special. They're my model of what a great relationship should be."

"How so?"

"They prioritize their relationship above everything else, but they also encourage each other to follow their dreams. They know how to compromise without sacrificing, if that makes sense."

Seemed to me like Kelsey was sacrificing a lot, though. "Isn't she giving up her life in LA to move to the woods and become your brother's employee?"

"No." His voice was sharp. "I mean, yes, she's leaving LA, and yes, she's working for me and my brother. But she's also getting paid more to do less work in a town that's much cheaper to live in. And the real reason she's going is because she'll have plenty of time and space and money to pursue her true passion, which is painting. Idyllwild has a huge community of artists. She already joined the local alliance."

The Jeep jerked to a stop in the driveway of what I assumed was Eric's house. Another cozy cabin in the woods, just like Brandon's. He took my hand as we walked up the path to the front door, but he didn't say a word. He didn't look at me either.

Something was wrong, but there was no time to ask about it because he was already opening the door.

"Hello?" he called into the living room. Hops ran up to greet us with an excited bark, followed by Kelsey, who wore a warm, welcoming smile.

"Hi! It's so good to see you, Nicole. Your hair looks great."

"Thanks." This was definitely a different Kelsey than the one who'd snubbed me at Vespa. "And thanks for having me for dinner on such short notice."

"Oh, it's no problem. Besides, Eric's doing all the cooking. I'm just setting the table and mixing the drinks." We followed her into the kitchen, where Eric stood over the stove, overseeing three separate burners covered with pots and saucepans. "Can I get you something? A mocktail, perhaps?"

"Water's fine, thanks."

At the sound of my voice, Eric looked over his shoulder. "Oh, hi, Nicole. It's nice to finally meet you."

"Nice to meet you, too. Thanks for having me."

"My pleasure. Brandon said this is your first trip to Idyllwild?"

I nodded as Kelsey set a tall glass of ice water on the counter in front of me. "It is."

"Definitely won't be the last," Kelsey added, with a wink.

"What do you think?" Eric asked.

"About Idyllwild? I think it's beautiful."

"The most beautiful place in the whole world," Brandon said, his voice sounding distant.

"Couldn't you just live here?" Kelsey raised one manicured eyebrow.

"Uh . . . maybe?" This felt like a high-pressure sale. *Move to Idyllwild quick, before you lose Brandon forever!* Sweat beaded along my upper lip and pooled under my arms. I swallowed half the glass of water in one swig.

Brandon meandered over to an easel positioned in front of a floor-to-ceiling window. It held a canvas painted with a half-finished landscape. Trees and sky with a peek of mountain, a reflection of the real-life view. "This one's looking good so far, Kels."

"Really? I'm not crazy about it." She joined him beside the easel, examining the canvas. "I might just scrap the whole thing."

"You say that every time."

"It's part of my creative process."

Brandon chuckled and turned to me. "Kelsey painted the landscape I have in my apartment. Or *had* in my apartment. I've gotta find a good spot for it in the cabin now."

"Dinner's served!" Eric called, and we gathered around the dining table to feast. He served up great big bowls of linguine in a rich cream sauce, dotted with shreds of basil. The heady scent of garlic wafted through the air.

"This smells delicious," I said, my mouth watering in anticipation. "Thanks again for having me."

"I'm the one who should be thanking you," Eric said. "The website you designed for Mountain Air is something else. It really makes us stand out. Some other small business owners in town were asking for your info. I said I didn't know if you were taking on new clients, but I'd ask."

"Actually, I'm not for hire. There's a moonlighting clause in my work contract. This was sort of a one-off. Just a favor for a friend." I glanced sideways at Brandon, but he was staring into his bowl of pasta.

"That's too bad," Eric said. "I bet you could make a killing."

He was probably right. As an undergrad, I'd pulled in a decent amount of money for each website I'd designed. Now, I could turn them around faster and charge even more because of my experience. But as long as I was working for Virtuality, it wasn't an option.

"That reminds me," Brandon said. "We've gotta finalize the menus so we can put them on the website."

Eric blew out a long, frustrated breath. "I know, I know. I haven't gotten around to reviewing them yet. I'm so overwhelmed."

"Dude, I'm living here full-time now; I can take something off your plate. What do you need me to help with?"

"Everything. Between the licenses and the menus and the staffing and the advertising, it seems like it all needs to get done yesterday. I'm pulled in ten different directions, and I don't even know where to start."

"You should use a prioritization matrix," I said.

"What's that?"

"It's a decision-making tool that can help you organize your time and priorities. Basically, you take everything that's demanding your attention and assign it a number based on how urgent and important it

256

is. For example, I was really struggling to balance a bunch of important stuff in my life. I'm up for a promotion at work, I'm the maid of honor in my best friend's wedding, I've got"—I stopped short of saying Brandon's name, instead opting for—"a lot going on. But when I boiled it all down to these objective, uncomplicated numbers, it made it much easier for me to decide what to focus on and what to set on the back burner."

Eric chewed thoughtfully. "That sounds interesting."

"It works. I mean, I had to make some tough decisions, but it really helped me to cut through all the emotion clouding my judgment and just focus on the facts."

"What kinds of tough decisions did you have to make?" Brandon asked. On the surface, the question was innocent. But there was a deeper meaning, something less innocuous. I could tell from the tone of his voice—the way he spit out the word *tough*.

I stumbled over my answer. "Just, you know . . . it was hard. The whole work-life balance thing."

"Of course," Kelsey said. "I totally get it. My hours at Vespa were running me ragged. That's why I'm so happy to be here, working with these guys. I feel like my life belongs to me again, you know what I mean?"

No, I had no idea what she meant. I didn't feel like my life belonged to me, and I hadn't for quite some time. It felt particularly out of my control now, with Brandon avoiding my gaze. He was sitting right next to me, but we might as well have been in separate cities.

As we ate our dinner, the conversation turned to less controversial topics. The unseasonably warm weather. The mural Kelsey was planning to paint on the wall inside Mountain Air. The latest episode of *Donut Warriors*. I didn't say much, just politely ate my pasta, smiling and nodding at all the appropriate times. But the silence between me and Brandon was so uncomfortable that I wished I could teleport out of these woods and back to LA, to the safety and solitude of my one-room apartment. The apartment that didn't feel lived in because I never actually lived in it.

When the meal was finished, we cleared the table, and before anyone could mention dessert, Brandon said, "We're gonna head back to my place. Do you mind keeping Hops again for the night?"

"Not at all." Eric gave him a bear hug with lots of back slaps. "See you at the pub tomorrow."

"Sure. Nine o'clock?"

"Sounds good." He turned to me and smiled warmly. "It was great to have you here, Nicole."

"*So* great." Kelsey opened her arms to me, an invitation for a hug. "I hope we see you up here a lot more often now."

"Totally." I hugged her half-heartedly, then hurried to catch up with Brandon, who was already racing out the door.

We drove back to his cabin in painful silence, the air thick with a tension I didn't fully understand. Twice, I opened my mouth to ask him what was wrong. Twice, my voice faltered. Instead, I stared out the window into the unlit forest. Earlier, this scenery had all been so majestic and vibrant. Now it seemed ominous. Like there was danger lurking somewhere out there.

Gravel crunched beneath the tires as the Jeep inched down his driveway. Brandon cut the engine and killed the headlights, plunging us into darkness.

At first, he said nothing. All I could hear was his breath flowing in and out, steady and insistent. I swallowed, my dry throat stinging against the pressure. Then I finally worked up the nerve to ask, "What did I do?"

He tapped his fingertip on the steering wheel, staring out the window. "I'm not sure."

"Then why are you suddenly so mad at me?"

"I'm not mad, Nicole."

"What is it, then?"

He turned toward me, and the light from the porch glinting off his gray eyes told me everything I needed to know. He wasn't mad. He was hurt.

"Did you give me a number?" he asked.

"What do you mean?"

"On your prioritization matrix," he said. "What objective, uncomplicated number was I?"

I shook my head. "It was stupid; it didn't really help me."

"Do you really want to be with me?"

"Of course! I—"

"Because I feel like I'm just some annoying obligation that's demanding your attention, like you have to struggle to find ways to shoehorn me into the cracks in your schedule. All this time, I've been purposely making space for you in my home—in my life!—and it doesn't seem like you want to be a part of it."

"That's not true."

"It's not? Because you weren't too excited when I showed you around my cabin. You seemed more concerned about missing your Friday-night game tournament than spending a weekend with me. Heaven forbid anything takes you away from your office."

Maybe he hadn't been mad before, but he was definitely getting there now. And honestly, so was I. "You know, you told me you understood how important my job was to me, that you'd never ask me to choose. But now it feels like you suddenly want me to drop everything and move out here to live with you."

"That's not at all what I'm asking for, and it's not what I want. All I want is to feel like I matter to you. I want to be with you, and I thought that's what you wanted, too. But if you're not feeling the same sense of urgency that I am in this relationship, then maybe it's best to end things now."

"What are you talking about? Of course I feel a sense of urgency. That's why I'm here. I dropped everything to drive to the mountains to be with you. I didn't even bring a toothbrush!"

"Because you don't really want to stay."

"How can you say that?"

"You have a toothbrush in your desk at your office. You're more prepared to spend the night with your computer and your coworkers than you are with me. Because your job is more important to you than I am."

"No, it isn't."

"Then where was I on your prioritization matrix? What number did you give me?"

"That's not the point."

"That's the *whole* point. Nicole, I don't want a relationship that's stripped of feeling and boiled down to numbers. This isn't your chatbot; it's real life. It's complicated and emotional and sometimes inconvenient." He gripped the steering wheel with both hands, squeezing until his knuckles turned white. "I should've known this was a mistake from the very beginning."

My stomach twisted into a thick, tender knot. "What are you saying?"

His voice was soft as he said, "You told me you were afraid to get involved. I should've listened. I shouldn't have pushed you."

"But you said you were afraid, too."

"I was. And obviously I had reason to be."

His gray eyes turned to stones, hardened and impenetrable. He'd erected a shield, and frankly, it was justified. I'd stomped all over his heart. Just like he'd feared I would.

In that moment, I should've said something. An apology, a plea for forgiveness, a vow to change for the better. Something to prove I deserved him, to show I'd never meant to cause him pain. But, as usual, emotion got in the way, and I couldn't say anything at all.

Instead, I got out of his Jeep, and I got in my car, and I drove all the way back to LA.

CHAPTER
TWENTY-SEVEN

If driving up the mountain to Idyllwild in broad daylight was scary, then driving down the mountain in the dark of night was something straight out of a horror movie. There were no other cars, no overhead lights. A fine mist obscured the road in front of me; even my fog lights couldn't cut through it. To be safe, I drove a steady ten miles per hour, braking abruptly before every one of those hairpin turns.

The only thing scarier than driving down that mountain was being alone with my thoughts. I blasted the radio, blaring EDM and reggaeton, loud music with fast beats to scramble my brain and prevent me from thinking about what had just happened. Two hours later, I was back in LA.

But I didn't go home. Instead, I went straight to the office, where even in the small hours of the morning, there was always someone hanging around one of the break rooms or snoozing in a sleep pod. Whenever I was here, I was never really alone.

And, of course, Parisa was right: working was a great way to hide from my feelings. Anytime I caught myself recalling the stony look in Brandon's eyes or the desperate way he'd gripped the steering wheel, I simply redirected my attention to my to-do list. All those uncomfortable emotions got stuffed deep down into that neglected crevice of my brain, waiting for the scar tissue to form and bury them forever.

I stayed up all night, too wired to sleep, though eventually the words on my screen started blurring together. Just before nine o'clock in the morning, I was considering a visit to the sleep pods when Vimi texted me and Ben: Anyone up for coffee? Ten minutes later, I was sitting at our usual table in the back left corner, chugging a latte just to keep my eyes open.

"You look beat," Ben said.

"I pulled an all-nighter."

"Krueger's still being a pain in the ass, huh?"

"At least your hair looks nice," Vimi said. "Did you curl it or something?"

"Yeah, I did. Thanks." I'd forgotten all about that. The last time I'd glanced in the mirror, I'd been sitting in my car outside Brandon's cabin, excited to surprise him with my big romantic gesture. Since then, I hadn't combed my hair or changed my clothes. I hadn't even brushed my teeth, despite the toiletry kit in my desk drawer.

"Uh, guys." Ben tapped at his phone, frowning. "What's up with this email from Jon?"

"What email?" I unlocked my own phone to see what he was talking about. Moments ago, Jon had sent a message to the entire design team:

Please meet me in the fourth-floor conference room
in 15 minutes for an impromptu team meeting.

"Weird," I said. "Jon never calls impromptu meetings."

Vimi's eyes nearly bugged out of her head. "Do you think they're doing layoffs?"

"Unlikely," Ben said. "Our latest quarterly earnings report showed our stock price is through the roof."

"Maybe someone hacked our databases or something." Coffee gurgled in my stomach. Whatever this meeting was about, it was not going to be good.

After fifteen minutes of panic and pointless speculation, the three of us made our way to the conference room, where the rest of the design team was already assembled, looking just as nervous as we felt. Jon stood at the front of the room, one hand in his pocket, the other hand closing the door. Then he cleared his throat and started to speak.

"I have an announcement to make. This morning, I submitted my letter of resignation. My last day with Virtuality will be May twenty-eighth. A week from this Friday."

Gasps echoed around the room. Of all the horrors I'd been contemplating, Jon's resignation had never once entered my mind. He'd been working at Virtuality for so long—much longer than me. He was a fixture around this office. Or at least I'd thought he was.

This was a nightmare. I had my issues with the promotion process around here, but Jon had advocated for me. He assigned me to challenging projects and trusted me to get the work done. Reporting to him was comfortable, familiar. Who could ever replace him?

"Over the course of the next two weeks," he continued, "I'll be performing knowledge transfers to ensure complete coverage after I'm gone. Virtuality will begin recruiting my replacement immediately, but until they find a permanent employee, Charles will be operating as the interim director of product design."

No. No, no, no.

Charles was going to be my manager? The man who couldn't figure out how to run some simple usability tests while I was on vacation? My stomach turned as I watched him react to the announcement, with his fingers clasped and a smarmy smile on his face.

This was an absolute nightmare.

"I expect you'll have some questions," Jon said. "If so, please reach out to me via email, and I'll do my best to answer them. But rest assured, you'll be in good hands with Charles."

Ben shot his hand in the air. "Will they be recruiting for the position internally?"

"I suppose so," Jon said. "You'll have to ask HR for more information."

"Where are you going?" Vimi's face was a study in terror.

"I'm relocating to the Bay Area and working at a start-up."

Someone else began to ask, "What about—" but Jon cut them off right away. "Please, if you have any questions, just email me."

Well, this was ridiculous. How could Jon dump this earth-shattering news on us out of nowhere and then refuse to answer any of our questions? The rest of the team stood up, slowly, and began to file out the door. Ben shot me a look of consternation as he and Vimi left the conference room. But I couldn't stand up. I was glued to the chair, in a total daze.

"Are you okay, Nicole?" Jon asked. It was just the two of us now.

"I think I'm in shock."

He nodded. "I know; this is a big adjustment."

"It's a *huge* adjustment."

"Charles will help to bridge the gap until a permanent replacement is found."

Ugh, Charles. "May I ask . . . why did you choose Charles to be the interim director?"

"It wasn't entirely up to me. But he was the person I suggested because he practically lives in the office. He sleeps in the nap pods every night; I'm not even sure he has his own home. He hasn't taken a vacation day the entire time he's worked here either. Being a director means you don't have a life. And that man has no life. He's perfect for the job."

I wondered what that said about Jon. Did he have a life? Was he leaving because he wanted one? There was a significantly more pressing question at hand, though. "What does this mean for my promotion?"

He shrugged and said the same irritating thing he'd said two months earlier. "There are a lot of forces at play."

"You keep saying that, but what does it actually mean?"

With a furtive glance toward the hallway, Jon quietly shut the conference room door. "I'm gonna level with you, Nicole. I don't see you getting promoted anytime soon."

My heart free-fell to my stomach, landing with a thud that made me whimper.

"I'm sorry," he said.

"But why? Because you're leaving?"

"No. Honestly, I have no sway over whether you get a promotion. Managers aren't even allowed to sit on promotion committees for their direct reports."

"That doesn't make any sense."

"There are a lot of things at this company that don't make any sense." He kept his voice low and shot another quick look toward the door. "Did you know I've been trying to get a promotion to senior director for three years now?"

Oh. So Jon was in the same boat as me. "I had no idea."

"And the higher your job title, the harder it is to get a promotion. Exponentially harder. I've been sleeping in the office for weeks, showering in the locker rooms at the employee gym. I haven't had a date night with my husband in God knows how long. I thought it would be a short-term effort, that it would pay off big in the end. But in the last promotion cycle, they turned me down, for the fifth time. Said I didn't bring satisfactory value to the company and that my quantifiable accomplishments did not have a significant impact. I've been giving them all my effort and all my time, and it's never enough."

I felt bad for Jon, but this couldn't have been true for everyone. After all, Cass had gotten promoted. Maybe I would, too. "The Krueger project is going really well now, and it's only a few more weeks until go-live. That's going to make a significant impact, right? Enough to justify a promotion?"

He shrugged again. "It might be. But it also might not be. Even if it is, you'll just be chasing another promotion after that, won't you? And that one will be even harder to get. It's this never-ending cycle. And for what? What's the greater goal?"

I shook my head, trying to make sense of this. All along, I'd been trying to get this promotion because I felt the need to prove myself. I needed validation. But I never stopped to think that there'd always be another promotion to strive for. Truthfully, there was no greater goal I was reaching toward. No vision of an ideal life. I could be running in circles here forever, never attaining that sense of validation, always feeling judged and, ultimately, rejected.

I might have had a schedule, but I didn't have a long-term plan.

"Anyway," he said, "that's what I've been struggling with. That's why I'm quitting. I just wanted to tell you what my experience has been because I thought you deserved to know."

My thoughts were fuzzy, and my tongue felt thick in my mouth, but I managed to force out, "Thanks for being honest with me."

"You're welcome. If you ever decide to move on from Virtuality and need a professional reference, don't hesitate to ask me. I've always enjoyed working with you. If it were up to me, you'd have been promoted three years ago."

Funny, Jon could help me get a job at a different company, but as my direct supervisor here, he held no influence over the trajectory of my career. What kind of messed-up system was that?

I dragged myself back to my desk on leaden feet, my brain aching from a lack of sleep and an overabundance of bad news. My phone buzzed incessantly with texts from Ben and Vimi:

Vimi:

Nicole, where are you?

Ben:

Meet us in the dining hall.

We need to discuss ASAP.

Vimi:

I can't believe that tool Charles is our new boss.

Ben:

It's only temporary.

I have a theory about that.

Vimi:

Nicole, what's going on?

And what were you talking to Jon about???

I ignored them. There was no way I could bring myself to discuss this right now, not with this intense pounding in my head. My heart started pounding, too, a familiar double bass drum that shook me to my core. The edges of my vision went all fuzzy, and I tried to take a deep breath, but there wasn't enough air in the room to fill my lungs.

Oh shit. I was having another panic attack.

I squeezed my eyes shut, thinking back to the last time this had happened, trying desperately to remember what the chatbot had told me to do. Deep breathing, meditation, time management. That useless prioritization matrix.

Then there was the visualization exercise. *Picture your happy place.* You were supposed to envision yourself in the most relaxing surroundings you could possibly think of. Somewhere calm, quiet, and peaceful.

Instantly, my mind went to Idyllwild. The fresh, pine-scented air. A light breeze rustling the trees. A babbling brook in the distance, and a bird singing softly overhead. The vibrant blues and greens of nature. Brandon's gray eyes turning to stone.

This wasn't helping.

I set my head down on my desk, gripping the edges to keep myself from falling out of my chair. Time seemed to slow down and speed up simultaneously. I forced myself to breathe deeply, over and over again. In and out, in and out. Eventually, it passed, leaving nothing but a slick trail of sweat on the back of my neck and a lingering sense of dread.

Desperate for an emergency therapy session, I pulled up the chatbot again. With trembling fingers, I answered the same introductory questions as last time—No, I'm not pregnant. Yes, I am under extreme stress.—until I finally got to the part where I could pour out my feelings.

There was no reluctance this time. I typed as fast as I could, my thoughts flowing in a continuous stream from my brain to my hands and onto the computer screen. My stress over work, my angst about Brandon, my fear of not having a vision for my life. It was cathartic, being able to vent all my innermost worries without anyone listening or judging. This must be why people kept journals.

Except an AI chatbot was so much better than a journal, because it responded to you. When I complained about the lack of control I felt in my life, it asked for specific examples. When I said I wasn't sure if I'd made the right choice with Brandon, it reassured me that we all experienced doubt from time to time. I felt heard and understood. I felt validated.

Eventually, the chatbot did its little bouncing-ellipsis thing while it formulated a diagnosis and treatment plan. I held my breath, waiting for the final reveal.

But I wasn't happy with the results:

> It sounds like you may be suffering from ANXIETY. ANXIETY is your body's reaction to stressful situations and can manifest in the symptoms you have described.

> It sounds like your ANXIETY may stem from COMPETING PRIORITIES and you may be at high risk of BURNOUT.

> I have a few suggestions on how to manage your ANXIETY and reduce your STRESS. Please follow the link below to get your customized proposal of care.

This was the same damn thing it had told me last time. Word for word. Even the contents of the "customized proposal of care" were identical, down to the stupid prioritization matrix.

I decided to try a different tack:

> Do you have additional information?

> What additional information are you looking for?

> Something beyond the customized proposal of care.

> Your customized proposal of care was prepared specifically for you. It contains all the information you need to help control your ANXIETY.

> What if that isn't enough?

> I'm sorry. I don't understand.

Damn. This was an error message that meant the conversation flow had reached a dead end. I knew, because I'd designed it myself. So there was no more information to be gleaned from this chatbot. I'd exhausted the limits of virtual therapy.

What I needed to do was schedule an appointment with a real, live, human therapist. But I was already so overwhelmed; I winced at the thought of adding one more task to my to-do list. Especially one as emotionally taxing as therapy.

So I promised myself I'd deal with it later. After the Krueger go-live and Parisa's wedding. In July, I'd have fewer obligations, more room on my schedule, more time to devote to this.

I just hoped I could get through the next month without another panic attack.

CHAPTER
TWENTY-EIGHT

I binged a lot of Netflix that week.

After Jon's brutally honest take on my chances at this promotion—and the state of my career, in general—I didn't feel like putting a whole lot of effort in at the office. I arrived at nine. I left at six. I slept a whole eight hours every night.

Every so often, my mind drifted to a picture of what my life might look like if I didn't work for Virtuality. True, there'd be no more late nights in the office, no dirty looks from Anna or insults from Charles. But there'd also be no daily chats with Vimi and Ben, no personalized lunches prepared by Dwayne, no Friday-night tournaments in the game room. Nothing familiar. Nowhere I truly belonged.

I could get a paycheck anywhere, but starting over somewhere new, where I didn't know anyone, was a daunting prospect. I'd have to rebuild my reputation from scratch, demonstrate I was a dynamic and dependable employee, make new work friends, open myself up to judgment and potentially rejection. If I stayed at Virtuality, at least I'd feel safe, even if I never did get that promotion.

Although, was it really safe to stay here if Charles was calling the shots? He'd already tried to sabotage me once. With him as my manager, even temporarily, my reputation could suffer for good. The office would no longer be a hiding place. It would be a war zone. And I needed somewhere to take shelter.

So, for the first time in a long time, I turned my attention to things that weren't work related. Like my woefully neglected apartment. I was determined to make it feel lived in and, beyond that, to actually live here. I went wild on Etsy, ordering framed prints for the walls and throw pillows for the couch. I went grocery shopping to fill my fridge with healthy food and my pantry with staples. On Saturday night, I actually made myself dinner. One that wasn't microwaved out of a plastic tray. I couldn't remember the last time that had happened.

My attempt at skillet Alfredo wasn't great, but it wasn't terrible either. Especially not for a first try. I wanted to take a picture of my plate and send it to Parisa—she'd be so proud of me—but we hadn't spoken in nearly a week, and an unsolicited pasta pic didn't seem like the right way to reconnect.

The last time we'd seen each other, I'd stormed out of her apartment with curlers in my hair. We hadn't gone this long without talking since her extreme digital detox in the South Pacific. She was the closest thing I had to family. I needed to know we were okay.

Not to mention her wedding shower was the next day, and with her mother and sister planning the whole thing, it was bound to be bananas. It was time for me to be a good, supportive friend and squash this drama once and for all.

I texted her:

> Hey.

> I'm sorry about everything.

> I shouldn't have told Abigail what you told me in confidence.

> It's okay.

You were stressed out.

And I shouldn't have left the hair trial the way I did.

Well, I shouldn't have snapped at you.

I was stressed out, too. I'm sorry.

BTW Leilani wants her hot rollers back.

Oh, right. They were still sitting in the console of my car.

I'll bring them tomorrow.

Are you excited?

 I guess.

Parisa was bringing the same lack of enthusiasm to her bridal shower as she'd brought to every other aspect of the wedding planning, but there was no point in mentioning it. We'd had this conversation more than once, and it never ended well. Besides, she had her opinions about how I lived my life that I disagreed with, too.

Which was why I didn't mention my disastrous trip to Idyllwild. I didn't want to hear how wrong I was about the prioritization matrix or how I was sabotaging my own happiness for a company that didn't care about me. I already knew all these things. Instead, I sent her a heart emoji and went back to watching TV.

The next morning, I drove to Parisa's parents' house in Brentwood, where her mother was hosting the bridal shower. Since I hadn't been involved in any of the planning, I had no idea what to expect. With the Shahin women running the show, I knew it would be extra, but I wasn't quite prepared for *how* extra.

They'd hired a butler to answer the door. An honest-to-God butler.

He escorted me to their spacious and verdant backyard overlooking the Hollywood Hills. Servers passed trays of hors d'oeuvres while a jazz guitarist played soft instrumentals beside their mediterranean pool. There was a fully staffed bar and more of those confetti balloon centerpieces that had caused such a fuss at the engagement party.

Shirin, Ally, and Kara huddled together around a cocktail table. They waved me over and gave me hugs. "It's so good to see you," Kara said.

"How are you doing?" Ally asked, a look of concern on her face.

"Good. Why?"

"Well, you left Parisa's in such a rush last weekend. Did something happen?"

They stared at me with their mouths open and their brows scrunched together, waiting for an explanation. I didn't know how to respond. I couldn't just blurt out that Parisa didn't want to have this wedding. I'd already betrayed her confidence once, and look where that had gotten us.

"I was going through some personal stuff, that's all." Not exactly a lie.

Shirin frowned. "Everything okay with your boyfriend?"

There was nothing I wanted to discuss less than the mess that was my love life. Except maybe the mess that was my career. Rather than answer, I scanned the backyard and asked, "Where's Parisa?"

"Last I saw, she was fighting with her mother," Kara said, slipping her arm through Ally's.

Shirin leaned in, lowering her voice. "I guess Leila and Roxy don't like the stylists we used last weekend. They want to replace them with someone they found on Instagram. Her mom agrees, but Parisa doesn't want to."

"I don't blame Parisa for being pissed," Kara said. "What do Leila and Roxy even know about hair and makeup? This is one area where they should just butt out."

I wholeheartedly agreed, but I couldn't believe Parisa was pushing back. Up until now, she'd gone along with most everything her mother and sisters had suggested, no matter how misguided it was.

Then again, it made sense that she'd stand her ground on this. She worked in the beauty industry. The people she'd hired were colleagues and friends, and she shouldn't have been expected to shove them aside just because her family wanted her to.

A moment later, Parisa stalked out of the house, her gauzy floral dress flowing behind her like a trail of fire. She made a beeline for our table, then immediately downed the rest of whatever Shirin had been drinking.

"You okay, cousin?" Shirin asked.

"A few more of these, and I will be. That was good—what was it?"

"Kentucky lemonade. There was a lot of bourbon in that; you should go easy."

"Please, I can barely . . ." She trailed off and stared across the yard, her skin going pale. I followed her gaze and saw the butler escorting an older woman into the party.

"Don't let her see me." Parisa crouched behind my back, shielding her face with her hands. "Oh God, what the hell is she doing here?"

"Who is that?" I asked.

"It's Elizabeth. Sam's mom."

"Sam Karami?" As in, her *ex-boyfriend*, Sam Karami?

"Yes. I need to get out of here."

She hightailed it for the house, and I followed closely behind, racing through the living room and kitchen to the back hall outside the bedrooms. Her legs wobbled as she stopped abruptly. Then she whirled around, and her brown eyes were wide with a terror I'd never seen before. In a thin, desperate voice, she said, "I can't do this anymore."

"It's okay," I said. "You're okay."

"No, I'm not, Nicole. Why is she here? I worked so hard to get over all the bad shit Sam put me through. Years of therapy to get my head

Kristin Rockaway

straight, and it still comes creeping back if I'm not careful. And now his mother is here on the day I'm supposed to be celebrating my upcoming marriage to someone else? It's like I can't escape him!"

Her voice was frantic now, almost shrieking, as her breaths came fast and shaky. I gripped her trembling hands, her palms cold and clammy. The tendons on her neck were prominent, her pulse visible, a double time drumbeat quaking beneath her skin.

"Close your eyes," I said.

"What?"

"Close your eyes. I want you to take a few deep breaths with me. It'll calm you down."

She shook her head, like I was being ridiculous, but she did it anyway.

"Now breathe in." I counted slowly to four, watching closely as she inhaled through her nose and then let it all go through her open mouth. We did this together a couple of times, until her pulse slowed and her skin wasn't quite so ashen. Then I said, "Picture your happy place."

"What does that mean?" she asked, eyes still closed.

"Think of a place that's calm and quiet and peaceful. The most relaxing place you can think of."

As I squeezed her hands, her eyelids began to flutter, and I wondered where she'd transported herself. Was it the beach in Fiji, where Mike had asked her to marry him? Or maybe just the comfort and privacy of their bedroom, safe beneath the covers with the man who made her radiate joy.

Instantly, I thought of my happy place. The pine trees, the fresh air, the mountains. Brandon holding me in his big, strong arms.

"What is going on over here?"

Parisa's eyes shot open at the sound of her mother's voice. The visions of our happy places evanesced, replaced with a scowling, scolding Farnaz.

276

"Why aren't you out there entertaining your guests?" she said. "Don't tell me you're still upset about the hair and makeup people. Please, Parisa. Your sisters are right. They made you look like a clown."

"Why is Elizabeth Karami here, Mom?"

"Because I invited her." Her tone was so matter of fact. Like there was no reason to be shocked or bothered, and Parisa was simply being a drama queen.

"The bridal shower is supposed to be for close friends and family. Not my ex-boyfriend's mother. Do you know how that made me feel, to see her walk into the party?"

"Do you know how it made *me* feel when she told me she never received the wedding invitation? I was so embarrassed I immediately invited her to the shower."

Parisa's mouth fell open in disbelief. "Mom, why are you still even talking to her?"

"Just because you decided to break her son's heart doesn't mean that she and I can't maintain our friendship."

"Look, whatever you two do is your business, but there is no reason for her to be here. And there was no reason for her to be invited to my wedding either."

Farnaz balled her fist on her hip. "So you admit you didn't send her an invitation?"

Parisa swallowed hard. I could see the tendons in her neck protrude, her hands clenched into tight, shaky fists. And that was when I knew I was facing my toughest, most important maid of honor duty yet: standing up to the bride's overbearing mother.

With my chin up and my shoulders back, I said, "No, Farnaz. *I* didn't send it."

Farnaz turned to me in slow motion, her red lips snarling. "Excuse me?"

"That's right. It was me. I tore up the envelope. And I'd do it again."

"You had no right to do that," she said, nostrils flaring.

"She had every right to do that," Parisa said, finally finding her voice. "Nicole was looking out for me because she knew how upset I was. In fact, she seems to be the only one who's been looking out for me. That's why I asked her to be my maid of honor. Because I knew she'd be supportive, unlike anybody in this family."

"Your sisters should have been your maids of honor. It's an embarrassment that you didn't choose a family member to stand by your side."

"An embarrassment? To who?" Parisa threw up her hands. "You know what? I don't even want to know the answer to that question. I'm done."

"Good, I'm glad you're done with this ridiculous tantrum. Now you can go out there and entertain your guests."

"No. I mean I'm done with all of this. The wedding is over. I'm calling it off."

Farnaz barked out a sarcastic laugh. "Enough with your nonsense."

Parisa's eyes were wild, burning with untamed fire. "I mean it. It's not happening. It's not worth all the stress. I should've called it off months ago."

For the first time, her mother's confidence faltered. "You cannot call it off now, Parisa. Nothing is refundable."

"I'm fine taking the losses."

"Well, you're not taking all the losses. May I remind you that your father and I paid for the venue? As well as for many other things, including this shower."

"Then Mike and I will pay you back for everything. Every last cent. It's only money. But life is too short for me to be this unhappy."

With that, she flounced down the hallway, her dress flaring around her like flames. Then she left, slamming the front door behind her.

Farnaz and I stood slack jawed for a few seconds, staring at the empty space Parisa had left behind. She massaged her temples, narrowing her eyes like she was trying to understand what had just happened. "My daughter is not serious. Is she?"

"Knowing her," I said, "I'm certain she meant every word."

Finally, Parisa was calling the shots. No more giving in to her family's absurd demands. No more wasting her time on things that didn't matter. Now she and Mike could plan the tiny, intimate elopement of their dreams. And no one could stop them.

Her act of courage was an inspiration. And in that moment, I vowed to call the shots in my own life, too. It was time to stop hiding and to start living out loud.

CHAPTER
TWENTY-NINE

Dear honored guest,

We are writing this email to let you know that our wedding, scheduled to take place on Saturday, June 26, in Los Angeles, California, has been canceled. We are still very much in love and will still be getting married, but we have chosen to do so in a small, private ceremony. Ultimately, the stress of planning a large wedding was too much for us to handle.

Many of you have already spent money on travel arrangements that may be nonrefundable. If this is the case, please let us know, as we are ready and willing to reimburse you for these costs. We will also be returning all gifts that have been sent to us thus far. While your generosity is more than appreciated, we do not feel comfortable accepting gifts.

We understand you may have questions at this time, but we respectfully ask you to reserve them

until a later date, when we are more emotionally
prepared to answer them.

Thank you for your support,
Parisa & Mike

The email went out at midnight. Despite having asked everyone to
hold their questions until a later date, Parisa immediately received no fewer
than twenty responses demanding an explanation. She ignored them all.

The next day, I walked into work with a renewed sense of optimism.
The Krueger project was approaching its final weeks, and I was determined to see it through to its successful completion. Even if I didn't get
promoted, at least I could say I'd tried my very best.

But I also had a whole new perspective on the promotion process.
Up until now, I'd shaped my career goals around climbing the org chart,
higher and higher, until I reached the very top. After talking to Jon,
though, I started to wonder: What if the goal wasn't to rise through the
ranks but to find meaning in the day-to-day work?

Because there was plenty of meaning to be found. I was employed
by one of the most prestigious companies in the tech sector. With my
current project, I was helping to revolutionize health care, making positive contributions to this world, just by showing up to the office every
day. Beyond that, there was Vimi and Ben, Dwayne in the dining hall,
and a whole host of other people and perks to be grateful for. Sure,
Charles would be my manager for the time being, but like Ben had
said, it was only temporary.

And he wasn't in charge just yet. Jon was still my manager, at least
for the next five days. Though I hadn't seen him around the office
much. He and Charles had been holed up in conference rooms, performing knowledge transfers and training. For the rest of the design
team, though, it was business as usual.

During lunch, Ben dropped a bomb on us: "I'm thinking of applying for the director position."

Vimi and I exchanged a quick glance, which was not as discreet as I thought it was.

"What?" Ben said. "You don't think I'm qualified?"

"Of course you're qualified," Vimi said. "It's just . . . you know the way things work around here. The promotion committees and everything."

"Yeah," I said. "They rarely do internal hires. I feel like they'll probably go with an outsider. Like they did with Charles."

Vimi grimaced. "Maybe Charles will stay on as director permanently."

The notion sent a chill up my spine. "God, I hope not."

Ben scowled. "If that asshole can do it, then so can I. I'm throwing my hat in the ring."

"Well, we're rooting for you," I said, in my most encouraging voice, knowing full well my encouragement meant nothing if I wasn't on the promotion committee.

At the end of the day, with my task list complete, I cut out of work at six on the dot. Parisa and I had a dinner date at her favorite Thai place. I arrived at the restaurant with my listening ears firmly attached and at the ready, because even though she'd made the choice to pull the plug on the wedding, I was sure she had conflicting emotions. Maybe she was regretting it now. Maybe her mother and sisters were guilting her. Whatever she needed to talk about, I was here to be her sounding board. To fulfill my duty as maid of honor, one last time.

She was sitting in the back of the dining room, sipping a mug of tea and grinning from ear to ear. Her grin widened even farther when she saw me. "Hi!"

We hugged, and I sat down across from her. "How are you?"

"I'm great. The best I've been in months."

From the sparkle in her eyes, I agreed. She hadn't looked this happy and satisfied since the night we'd met at Vespa, the night she'd shown me her engagement ring and asked me to be her maid of honor.

"It's like this huge weight has been lifted off my shoulders," she said. "I hadn't realized exactly how much time and energy I'd been squandering on this thing that was totally meaningless to me. I thought I could let the wedding planning happen around me without actively participating in it, but it turns out that's not so easy when you're the bride."

"How's your family dealing? I hope they're not harassing you."

She shrugged a shoulder, unfazed. "Mom's been leaving me teary voice mails, and Roxy's been texting me, telling me how heartless and selfish I am, but whatever. That's their problem, not mine."

"It is. And I'm glad to hear you say that."

"It took me long enough to figure it out. Plus, I had an emergency therapy session with Naomi this morning. That helped a lot. And you helped, too." She extended her left hand across the table, squeezing mine, her diamond ring glittering in the low light. "Thank you so much for everything, Nicole. For spending so much time on the wedding and listening to me as I worked through my feelings. And especially for standing up to my mom yesterday."

"I didn't really do much. All I did was admit the truth. That I tore up the envelope, not you."

"You did a lot. More than my own sisters would do. You're my real family, Nicole. I hope you know that."

I swallowed hard, straining to find my voice against the lump forming in my throat. "You're my real family, too."

At that moment, a server came by, asking if we'd made up our minds. As Parisa ordered for us (without even looking at the menu—she knew what I liked), my phone dinged with a text from Charles: Where are you?

Why the hell did he care where I was? He wasn't my manager, not yet anyway, and tonight I wanted to focus on Parisa. Besides, if this were a real emergency, Jon would be calling me.

Just then, Jon called.

"Oh shit," I said. "I'm sorry, Parisa, I have to take this; it's my boss."

I excused myself from the table, grabbing my phone and hurrying to the exit as I accepted the call. "Hey, Jon, what's up?"

"Didn't you get my text?" That wasn't Jon's voice. It was Charles, calling from Jon's office number.

"What's wrong? Did something happen with Krueger?"

"No."

"Well, why are you calling me?"

"I wanted to see if you could swing by and discuss a few things. In the wake of Jon's departure, we'll be reprioritizing, shifting around a few projects. I need your input."

"Is Jon there with you?"

"He's gone for the day."

Charles was already claiming the director's chair, even though it was technically still occupied. "Let's discuss this in the morning. I'm out to dinner at the moment."

"But your calendar says you're free right now."

"It's almost seven o'clock at night."

The silence on the other end of the phone told me everything I needed to know. Charles never left the office, and he expected me to do the same. I might've felt sorry for him if he weren't holding the future of my career in his hands.

"I'll talk to you tomorrow, Charles."

My shoulders slumped as I dragged myself back to the table, weighed down by uncertainty. Maybe Charles's tenure as director of product design would be temporary. But what if Vimi was right? What if this became a permanent arrangement? I couldn't work for this asshole forever, ducking bullets and dodging missiles every hour of every day.

As I collapsed into my chair, Parisa asked, "What's wrong?"

"Work has become my worst nightmare. My old boss quit, my interim boss is an asshole, and there's a good chance I won't get this promotion I've been gunning for." I squeezed my eyes shut and rubbed my fingertips along my forehead. "You were right, by the way."

"About what?"

"About me." I opened my eyes, blinking hard so the tears wouldn't fall. "That I was hiding behind my work because I was afraid of getting too close to Brandon."

"Does that mean you changed your mind about going to his grand opening?"

My throat tightened. I'd give anything to go to his grand opening, to see the culmination of all his hard work, to go back to my happy place. Instead, I had a feeling I was going to wake up a few years from now to the stark realization that I'd wasted my entire twenties.

Hot tears fell from the corners of my eyes, dripping onto the linen napkin in my lap. Parisa lunged for my hand and gripped it tightly. "What is it?"

I took a deep breath, my whole body shuddering on the exhale. Then I told her everything. How I'd shown up in Idyllwild and surprised Brandon at his cabin. How happy he'd been to see me and how welcoming his brother and Kelsey had been. How much space he'd made in his life for me. And how I'd messed it up by stomping all over his heart.

"So it's over," I said. "He was the greatest guy I've ever dated, and I totally blew it."

"It's not too late," she said. "I'm sure if you talk to him, you can apologize and set things right."

"I don't know about that." I looked down at the napkin in my lap, twisting it in my trembling hands. "There's a lot I need to work on, you know? I've got issues, and he doesn't need that in his life. He's such an amazing guy. I don't really deserve him."

"We've all got issues, Nicole. That doesn't mean we don't deserve to be loved." She pulled her phone from her purse and tapped at the screen. "I'm texting you Naomi's information right now. You should set up an appointment to talk to her about everything. She's incredible. Tell her I referred you, and I'm sure she'll find an opening for you soon."

My phone dinged with her text. "Thanks."

"You'd better call her. I mean it."

"I will. I promise."

The server arrived with our food, steaming bowls of red curry and rad na. We ate without speaking, the only sounds coming from the din of chatter around us and the clinking of our chopsticks against our dinnerware. Crumbling mess of my life aside, I was happy to be here with Parisa. I might have tanked my career and destroyed my love life, but at least I still had her. And I knew I always would. My sister at heart, if not in name.

It also felt nice to spend time together without the nagging feeling that we should be doing something more productive. There were no invitations to assemble, no favors to order. No wedding to plan.

"So what's gonna happen now?" I asked. "Have you and Mike made any plans for your elopement or . . . ?" I trailed off when I saw her grimace.

"God, no. I can't even think about that right now. My brain needs a break from all things bridal."

"I totally get it. But when you're ready, I'm here to help. If you want me to, that is."

"Of course I want your help. I *always* want your help."

"Well, not always." I bit back a laugh as she pursed her lips. She knew exactly what I was referring to.

"For your information," she said, "Mike thinks that Tinker Bell tattoo is cute."

"Does he, really?"

"Yes." Her lips unfurled into a slow, dreamy smile as she thought about the love of her life. I smiled right along with her, because I was thrilled to see her so happy. She deserved it.

And maybe I deserved it, too.

CHAPTER THIRTY

Naomi didn't have any openings on her schedule until late August. She did, however, refer me to her colleague, Dr. Krishna, who could fit me in that very same week. I made an appointment for Thursday at 6:30 p.m., then immediately regretted it. Therapy was a huge step, one I didn't know if I was ready for. Then again, if I waited until I felt "ready," I'd probably never go.

So even though I thought about canceling several (dozen) times, I didn't. When Thursday rolled around, I left the office at six on the dot— but not before putting a vague-looking time block on my calendar titled *UNAVAILABLE*. That way, Charles wouldn't try to call me in the middle of my session.

As requested, I arrived ten minutes early and sat in the small, pristine waiting room filling out form after form after form. Medical history, insurance information, consent to treatment. Perhaps my least favorite document was the intake questionnaire, which was four pages long and awfully prying. Why did Dr. Krishna need to know what my religious or spiritual background was? Plus, some of these questions seemed impossible to answer.

Do you have a history of trauma? Who didn't?

What stresses you out? Everything!

Are you feeling down, depressed, or hopeless? Kind of. But was I really depressed, or was I just in a funk? And how could I tell the difference, anyway?

I rapped my pen against the clipboard and eyed the door. It wasn't too late to get out of here. Sure, I'd probably get stuck paying the cost of the visit, but that was better than being stuck in a tiny room with this random therapist, spilling my guts out about private—

"Nicole?"

At the sound of my name, the clipboard slipped from my hands, and my paperwork scattered to the floor. "Shit," I hissed, bending over to pick it up. This was already off to a great start.

"Here, let me help." Dr. Krishna crouched beside me, calmly gathering papers into a neat stack. We stood up at the same time, and as she took the clipboard from my hand, she smiled at me. It was a warm, comforting smile, like a cup of chamomile tea or a fuzzy fleece blanket. It made me feel like maybe this whole experience wasn't going to be so bad.

Her office was cozy and calming, yet professionally styled. Neutral colors, soft lighting. A philodendron in the corner and a framed print of Santa Monica Pier hanging on the wall. A box of tissues sat on an end table, taunting me with the promise of forthcoming tears.

Dr. Krishna sat down in a bright-green wingback chair and gestured for me to sit across from her, on a tufted gray couch. "So," she said, crossing one slender leg over another, "what brings you here today?"

There were so many ways to answer that question. Perhaps, *I hide behind work because I'm afraid of my feelings.* Or maybe, *I sabotaged a perfectly good relationship because I don't think I deserve to be happy.* Ultimately, I kept it short and simple: "I've been having panic attacks. At least, I think they're panic attacks."

She nodded and jotted something down on the yellow legal pad resting on her lap. "What were these panic attacks like? What were your symptoms?"

"My heart was beating really fast, and I felt like I couldn't get enough air. And I had this overwhelming sense of doom. Like the world was about to end."

"How many times has that happened to you?"

"Twice."

"And what was going on before you experienced these attacks? Were you under a lot of stress?"

"That's an understatement."

She cocked her head, waiting for me to elaborate, but I found I couldn't speak. The part of my brain that formed words into sentences was suddenly suffering a malfunction. I knew what was stressing me out—everything!—yet for some reason, I couldn't explain it. My mind had turned to mush.

I stammered, wringing my hands, until she smiled that fleecy chamomile smile. "It's normal to be nervous, but I assure you I'm here to help you and to listen without judgment. We'll only discuss topics you feel comfortable discussing, and everything you say in this room is completely confidential."

Her silken voice set me at ease. Or as at ease as I could be in that moment. Truthfully, I wasn't comfortable with this, and I wasn't sure I ever would be, but I desperately wanted my life to be different. I wanted balance, to make space for everything and everyone that brought meaning to my world. I wanted to embrace my emotions instead of running from them. Most of all, I wanted to radiate joy.

And I couldn't do that unless I did this. Otherwise, I'd probably keep making the same stupid mistakes over and over again.

So I opened my mouth, and I spoke. Somehow, the malfunction in my brain had righted itself, and the words began to pour out of me, describing everything I'd been through in the past few months. The pressure of striving for a promotion. Parisa's wedding and all it entailed. My ill-fated relationship with Brandon. How I wanted it all to work—how I'd *tried* to make it all work—but had failed miserably.

Talking to Dr. Krishna was surprisingly easy, and once the words started flowing, they didn't stop. It was cathartic, just like talking to the chatbot therapist. But it was also so much better, because this therapist wasn't a computer. There were emotions behind her responses. I could hear the inflection in her voice and see the expression on her face. When she said, "That must have been hard for you," I knew it was coming from a human heart and not an AI engine.

This was a real-life connection. I couldn't believe I'd been avoiding it for so long.

I left feeling hopeful, with an appointment set for the following week. Same day, same time: Thursday at six thirty.

The intervening seven days were a blur of stress and change. Jon finished his last day at Virtuality to little fanfare. He sent a nice, if impersonal, email to the entire design team, wishing us the best in our future endeavors, then strolled out the door at five o'clock on the dot—possibly the earliest he'd ever left this office.

First thing Monday morning, Charles moved into Jon's old desk, and the transfer of power was complete. Like Ursula claiming King Triton's trident, he seemed to quadruple in size, terrorizing the rest of the team, his slimy tentacles slithering into our business and smashing our morale. Every hour, he sent out another bossy message, telling us what to do or where to be. He piled so much work onto our plates that Vimi, Ben, and I couldn't take a lunch break all week.

By the time Thursday rolled around, I was so happy to slap that *UNAVAILABLE* up on my calendar and escape to the solace of Dr. Krishna's office. When I walked in, I collapsed on the tufted gray couch and let out a sigh of relief.

"Tough day at work?" she asked.

"Yeah. And it's so much worse now that Jon is gone and Charles is in charge."

"How so?"

"He's on a total power trip and expects everyone to be at his beck and call. And I don't have a problem with working long hours, believe me, but when Jon was my manager, he at least gave me some degree of independence. He assigned me my tasks and trusted me to get the work done. Charles is always peeking over my shoulder, trying to control every little thing I do."

"That sounds frustrating. You said this is only a temporary situation, right?"

"It's supposed to be, but there's always a possibility he'll get brought on as director permanently." I fought back a sudden intense wave of nausea. "So this might just be the way things are from here on out."

"Have you considered looking for another job?"

I snorted. "No. I can't leave Virtuality."

"Why not?"

Another question with so many possible answers. *Because I can't imagine my life without this company. Because it makes me feel safe to stay here. Because it's where I belong.* But really, those were three different ways of saying, "I'm afraid."

She nodded, like she understood. "Searching for a new job can be daunting."

"It's more than just a job, though. It's my whole world. Aside from Parisa, my entire social life is wrapped up in Virtuality."

"Why do you think that is—that your social life and your work life are so intertwined?"

"I don't know." Except I did. "Parisa always says it's strange, that I hide behind my work so I don't have to face my emotions. She says I'm a workaholic and keeps threatening to stage an intervention."

I rolled my eyes and scoffed to show her how ridiculous this sounded, but she nodded again, like I'd revealed a key insight. "There's more than one way to numb our feelings. Some people choose alcohol or drugs, some choose sex, some choose work. Addiction comes in many forms."

My gaze passed beyond Dr. Krishna to the wall behind her, where the framed print of the Santa Monica Pier hung above her head. The picture was all out of focus now, the Ferris wheel blurring into the Pacific Ocean. A chill took hold of my body as I slowly realized the truth.

I was turning out just like my mom.

There were no drunken breakdowns in the pantry, no hidden bottles of wine in the back of the bedroom closet. But like my mother, I'd been avoiding reality, hiding from my uncomfortable emotions, alienating the people who cared about me. And instead of using alcohol, I was using work.

No. It was more than that. It had to be. Because going to work was productive. Yes, I put in a lot of hours, but I was also doing good things. Making positive contributions to this world.

"I really *do* like my job, though." My voice sounded desperate, like I *had* to convince Dr. Krishna that I wasn't just repeating my mother's behaviors. "Not the politics but the day-to-day stuff. The tasks I'm assigned and the projects I work on. They're meaningful."

"Tell me about that. What's a project that means a lot to you?"

"Well, right now, I'm helping to build a chatbot that's going to revolutionize the health care industry. It's nearing completion. We're going live in a couple of weeks."

She paged back through her notes. "What's the name of your company again?"

"Virtuality. They specialize in artificial intelligence software."

"And you said it's a chatbot?"

"Yes. It can be used to help people with limited access to health care, like those in remote rural regions or with limited mobility."

She stood up and crossed the room, then plucked a trifold brochure from a stack of papers on her desk. "Is this what you're talking about?"

There was a graphic on the cover, a cartoon hand holding a smartphone with the Krueger-Middleton logo centered on the screen. Above it, a bold headline declared: *Introducing ChatTherapy, brought to you by Virtuality.*

"Yes!" I smiled, my chest swelling with a sense of pride and purpose. For months, I'd been holed up in the office, devoting hours and hours to building this software. Now, it was no longer an abstract idea but a real-world product, and soon it would be used by real people, changing the world for the better.

As she set the brochure back down on her desk, I noticed the faintest change in her facial expression. Her mouth curved into a grimace, and her brows drew together, causing frown lines to form along her normally smooth forehead. It lasted a fraction of a second, but long enough to make me wonder why.

"Do you not like the idea of ChatTherapy?"

She took a long, deep breath, her nostrils flaring and her lips pressed into a fine line. I could almost hear her inner voice counting slowly to four as she inhaled and exhaled. Finally, she said, "I don't think it's an adequate replacement for a human therapist."

"Oh, it's not meant to be a replacement. Just a supplement." I chuckled uncomfortably, thinking back to my own ChatTherapy experiences. "It definitely has its limitations."

Dr. Krishna didn't say anything. She simply nodded—one sharp dip of her chin—before steering the conversation in another direction.

We spent the rest of my session talking about compulsive work, setting boundaries, and establishing balance. I left her office feeling hopeful, even though I was shaken by the revelation that I had more in common with my mother than I'd ever thought possible.

I also couldn't stop envisioning those frown lines on Dr. Krishna's forehead. Did the Krueger-Middleton brochure imply that Virtuality was trying to replace humans with chatbots? Thoughts of it plagued me all night, and I was still ruminating on it the next morning when Anna called the daily stand-up meeting.

"On Monday," she said, "Krueger will be entering the final stages of user acceptance testing. I expect everyone to be available at all times to address questions and concerns as they arise."

She shot a pointed look my way, the kind of steely-eyed glare that used to make me shrink down into my chair. But this time I didn't shrink, because I knew I had no reason to doubt myself. I wasn't some slack-off. I was a loyal employee with a strong work ethic, and I'd done a kick-ass job on this project. She didn't intimidate me, not anymore. So I stared her down until she was forced to look away.

"In addition," she continued, "Krueger's marketing team has already started sending mailers to patients and providers, so we can expect chatbot activity to pick up quite quickly after product launch."

"I saw one of those," I said, prompting questioning glances from the rest of the team. "The mailer, I mean."

"Yes, I've seen them, too." Anna's voice was impatient.

"It seems like they're trying to sell our chatbot as a replacement for humans. Are they?"

Someone snickered, though I couldn't tell if it was one of the software engineers or the guy from networking. Meanwhile, Anna scrunched up her face, like I'd caused her physical pain. "What kind of question is that?"

My confidence wavered. "Well, I'm just wondering. At our kickoff meeting, you said this project had the potential to revolutionize the health care industry. But you were talking about helping people who didn't have access to medical care, right?"

Silence reigned as reality settled over me like a lead blanket. I'd been naive. Supremely, unbelievably naive. And any lingering doubt over my ignorant foolishness was squashed the moment Anna said, "Krueger-Middleton is spending hundreds of thousands of dollars on this chatbot. They're not doing it out of the goodness of their hearts."

This project wasn't about changing the world for the better. It never had been. It was simply about helping a corporation that was worth billions of dollars save a little extra cash. This chatbot had the potential to put independent health care providers out of business. And, worst of all, it could put people's health and safety at risk.

I returned to my desk with a sick, sinking feeling in my stomach. It was too much to bear, knowing I'd been working around the clock, devoting my life to a project that could actively cause people harm. I began to question everything about myself. My career path. My core values. My identity.

As I sat there contemplating my very existence, Charles popped his head up over my cubicle wall like a beady-eyed, bearded groundhog. "Nicole, what're you doing?"

He squinted, suspicious, like he'd caught me watching porn or playing solitaire. In actuality, I was staring off into space, lost in despair, but I told him, "Reviewing some requirements."

"Where were you last night?"

Instinctively, I pulled up my calendar, afraid I'd missed some last-minute meeting. All I saw, though, was the block of time from six to seven thirty labeled *UNAVAILABLE*. The time in which I'd seen Dr. Krishna.

"I had an appointment."

"What kind of appointment?"

Was it even legal for him to ask that? Rather than argue, I said, "A *personal* appointment."

He came around the side of the cubicle to stand beside my desk with his arms folded across his chest. "You know, Nicole, just because Jon is gone now doesn't mean you can start slacking off."

"I'm not slacking off. I had one personal appointment I had to keep."

"You should've cleared it with me first. Jon may have been okay with you doing personal business without checking with the rest of the team, but that's not gonna fly on my watch."

Was he serious with this shit? "It was six o'clock at night, and there was nothing else on my schedule. I didn't think I needed to clear it with you."

"Well, you did. And going forward, please do."

I watched him walk away, dragging with him the last shred of my faith in this company. This wasn't a family. They didn't care about me. And any meaning I'd found in the day-to-day work had disintegrated the moment I'd realized what this chatbot was really meant for.

Remember when I said I didn't believe in the concept of burnout? I was wrong. Being productive wasn't the same as being in control, and right now, I wasn't in control. I was overwhelmed, undervalued, and emotionally exhausted. In other words, I was burned out. And this was a problem that was far too big for my meticulously organized schedule to solve.

I didn't know what the future would hold. But now I knew for certain that I had no future at Virtuality.

CHAPTER
THIRTY-ONE

My last day of work at Virtuality was Friday, June 18. Vimi and Ben threw me a small going-away party in the dining hall. Dwayne baked a sheet cake and piped the words *WE'LL MISS YOU, NICOLE* across the top in white icing. Everyone from the design team came to see me off. Everyone except for Charles.

Not that I wanted him there. Nobody did. Ever since Jon had left, there'd been a rising sense of mutiny among my team members, which had intensified after I'd announced my resignation. Now there was a collective swell of support for Ben, who'd made no secret of his desire to unseat Charles and claim the director position for himself.

"I've got a meeting with HR tomorrow morning," he now said.

"Are you sure you want all that responsibility?" Vimi said. "You know, once you're a director, you'll never be able to leave the office."

"I'm fine with that."

"But I thought you and Cass vowed to take more time off together," I said. "No distractions, just the two of you."

He shrugged and stared down at his plate, mashing his fork into a thick lump of frosting. "I don't think Cass is really committed to the idea."

Poor Ben. His shoulders drooped, and it made me wonder if he really wanted to lead the design team or if he was simply chasing this promotion as a way to distract himself from other things. Like the emotional minefield that was a relationship. "At least you guys still have your treadmill dates," I said.

"Yeah," he said, his voice flat. "There's that."

I shot a glance at Vimi, but she was looking over my shoulder at the entrance to the dining hall. Her face was the embodiment of a heart-eyes emoji, all gaping smile and rosy cheeks. When I turned around, I wasn't surprised to see Abram striding toward our table.

"I hope you don't mind that I invited him," she whispered.

"Of course not." While Vimi and Abram weren't officially an item, she'd told me they were secretly hooking up in empty conference rooms from time to time. I'd have been lying if I said I wasn't the tiniest bit jealous. After all, I knew what it was like to have that burst-into-flames feeling just watching someone walk into the room. But it wasn't Vimi's fault I'd sabotaged my relationship with Brandon, and I would never begrudge her happiness. "There's plenty of cake to go around."

When the party was over, I packed my personal belongings into a box, left my access card on my desktop, and walked away from Virtuality forever.

Then I went straight to Dr. Krishna's office.

"How are you feeling?" she asked.

"Anxious. Free. Scared. Relieved. Mostly anxious."

"That's perfectly normal. Transitions are hard. How do you feel about the plan you've developed?"

Dr. Krishna had given me an assignment: to create a plan for moving forward without Virtuality in my life, including a self-care regimen and a budget. For the time being, I would be okay financially; I had enough in savings to tide me over until I found another source of income. I'd also signed up for some decent chatbot-free health coverage for a not entirely unreasonable monthly cost. This meant I could take my time with my job search and hold out for a position at a company that wouldn't require me to sleep in the office. My life would no longer be ruled by my work schedule. I wouldn't allow it.

"Okay," I said. "As comfortable as I'll ever feel, anyway."

"And what about Brandon?"

The sound of his name was so jarring I actually flinched. "What about him?"

"Well, you quit your job to make space in your life for things besides work. Could there be any space for Brandon?"

"I don't know." That was a lie. I did know, but one question kept me from telling the truth. One big, haunting question: "What if he doesn't want me back?"

"You'll never know unless you ask him."

She was right, of course, but that didn't mean I had the courage to actually do it.

That night, I lay in bed, holding my phone in my hand, trying to work up the nerve to send him a text. First, I typed: Hey.

Too brief.

I added: How's it going?

Too casual.

I deleted it all and frantically tapped out: Brandon, you are the greatest guy I've ever known. The only man I've ever sparked with. I'm sorry I didn't treat you like a priority. Will you give me one more chance?

Could I sound any more desperate?

I scrapped the whole thing and pulled up the website for Mountain Air instead. There were still so many things missing—menus, photos, links to social media—and the bold *Coming Soon!* messages made me cringe. I never left a job half-finished. The grand opening was tomorrow, and no matter what happened between Brandon and me romantically, I had an obligation to him—and his brother—to see this project through to completion.

Immediately, I texted him:

Hi.

I wanted to talk to you about the Mountain Air website.

> There are some loose ends that need to be tied up.

> Menus, photos, social media.

> If you send the information to me now, I can update the site, so it'll be ready for tomorrow.

There. That wasn't so bad. I'd kept it light and professional. No mention of the angst and yearning that were tearing me up inside.

Five minutes later, I got his response:

> Hi.

> Thanks for this.

> I can send you the menu but I don't have time to take photos.

> Been running around like crazy doing last minute stuff for opening.

> I have time.

> I quit my job.

> What if I came to Idyllwild and helped you out?

My phone buzzed in my hand, the word *Brandon* lighting up my screen. The sight of it quickened my pulse.

"You seriously quit your job?" His voice was a balm for my bruised heart.

"I seriously quit my job."

"But why?"

There were so many possible answers to that question. *The work held no meaning. I didn't feel valued. I needed more balance in my life.* But they were all different ways of saying the same thing: "It wasn't making me happy."

"What are you going to do now? Do you have another job lined up?"

"No. I'm gonna take a little time to figure out my next move. Which means my weekend is free. And I'd really like to come to the grand opening. If you still want me there."

He answered without missing a beat. "I absolutely want you here. And I'd love your help updating the website. It completely fell off my radar with everything else going on. Starting a business . . . it's a lot more work than I thought it would be."

His voice sounded strained. I almost made a comment about burnout before I realized that wasn't what he needed to hear right now. What he needed to hear was, "I'll be there first thing tomorrow morning."

I'll admit it: on the drive out there, I was so nervous I considered calling the whole thing off. But once I got to the base of the mountain and saw the sign that read STEEP GRADES AHEAD, I knew there was no turning back. And I knew I was making the right choice. At the end of this winding road, I'd find my happy place.

I reached Brandon's cabin shortly before nine o'clock. He answered the door with his hair still damp from the shower, and a familiar warmth settled in the center of my chest. I wanted to wrap my arms around him, bury my face in the crook of his neck, inhale his woodsy scent.

My lips tingled, longing to kiss him, but I held back. Maybe he didn't want my affection anymore. After all, he wasn't opening his arms to give me a hug, and his gray eyes still looked awfully stony.

A moment later, a brown-and-white bundle of fluff came whirring my way. Barking and panting, Hops jumped up on my leg, his dangling tongue dripping drool all over my jeans.

"Hey there, good boy!" I crouched down to scratch his head, relieved by the distraction.

When I stood up, Brandon's eyes were on the floor as he asked, "How are you?"

Suddenly, I was overcome with the urge to run back to my car, to drive down the mountain and flee from these uncomfortable emotions. But if I left now, I knew I'd regret it. I needed to face this conflict head-on.

Somehow, I summoned the courage to say, "I've missed you."

I was hoping he'd missed me, too. But I wasn't sure if he had, because all he said was, "Come in."

The moving boxes were gone. His books were on the shelves, his throw pillows on the couch. The landscape painting—the one Kelsey had painted, the one that used to hang above his fireplace at his apartment—was now hanging in the foyer. This was officially a lived-in house.

"It looks so good in here," I said.

"Thanks. I've still got some work to do. Gotta get some patio furniture and get the loft set up and—"

"I'm sorry." The words fell out of my mouth before I could stop them. It was an emotional outburst, a surge of sorrow and regret that had bubbled up uncontrollably from somewhere in the depths of my heart. And now there was no stemming the flow. "I should have made you a priority. I should have showed you that I cared."

He rubbed his hand along the back of his neck, eyes still aimed at the floor. "I'm sorry, too. I shouldn't have pressured you."

"You didn't pressure me. And if you did, it was a pressure I needed."

"But I told you I would never make you choose between me and your job, and that's exactly what I did. I made all these plans—out here, in this house—expecting you to change things for me, to rearrange your schedule and adjust your whole life."

"I'm happy you did that. Because it forced me to acknowledge some really hard truths about myself. I thought I had my life under control, but really I was flailing and totally lost. I have been hiding behind my work for so long I didn't know who I was without it. I'm still not sure I do. So that's why I'm taking some time off now. To find out who I am. To make space for myself and my feelings. To make space for other people in my life."

With my heartbeat roaring in my ears, I took a step toward him. Then I opened my hand, an invitation for Brandon to take it. He didn't. Instead, he just stared at my palm, studying each line and crease like he was trying to foretell the future.

"I don't know what the future holds," I said. "But I know I want you in it. I want all of you, Brandon, all the time. Even when it's complicated and inconvenient."

Slowly, hesitantly, he lifted his gaze to meet mine, and I let out a sigh of relief. The hardened, impenetrable stones were gone, replaced by a blazing fire. The warmth in my chest spread through my limbs, fast and fierce, like a back draft.

"I want you in my future, too," he said. "I know we both want to carve out the best lives for ourselves that we possibly can. We'll make mistakes, and we'll fumble. We don't have an example to follow, no map to tell us how to get there. But I want us to pave this path together."

He reached out to grab my hand and linked his fingers through mine. Then he pulled me toward him, closing the space between us. Our bodies melted together, and when our mouths met, any lingering tension evaporated, replaced with an unwavering feeling of certainty. That at this moment, there was nowhere else I was supposed to be than right here, in this cabin, with this man.

I drank him in with all my senses, relishing every tiny moan he released as his tongue danced with mine. Struck with an urgent need to strip him down, my hands grasped at his shirt, but he pulled back abruptly.

Oh no. He'd changed his mind.

"Listen," he said, breathless. "It's not that I don't want this. I do. Want this. Very much."

"Then, what is it?"

He shook his head, his eyes darting around the room. "I think I'm just nervous. It's a big day today."

Oh, right. The grand opening.

"It is a very big day." I gave his hands a reassuring squeeze. "So let's get to it."

Mountain Air Brewpub was located just off the main drag of the village, set back among the cedar trees, overlooking Strawberry Creek. An outdoor staircase led to the main entrance, which opened up onto the wraparound deck I'd seen in the photos. Inside, there was a long wooden bar and an open kitchen, already bustling with cooks and waitstaff. The brewery itself was in the back of the restaurant, visible through a wall of windows, kegs stacked beside big silver tanks.

As soon as we arrived, Brandon got to work. "Eric's waiting for me. Do you need anything?"

"I've got everything squared away," I said, holding up my phone. "Lemme take some pictures, and then I'll connect to your Wi-Fi to update the website."

"Thanks." He kissed me, but it was fleeting. A nervous kiss.

"Hey." I grabbed his hand before he turned away. "You're gonna kick ass today."

His mouth curled into a smile. "I'm glad you're here."

"Me, too."

Brandon kissed me again, and this time, his lips lingered.

After he ran off to huddle with his brother, I bounced around the brewpub taking photos from all angles. The outdoor seating with the forest in the background. The row of beer taps lining the bar. The mural on the side of the building, hand painted by Kelsey.

I took a photo of Kelsey, too, as she sliced lemons and limes for her garnish tray. As I snapped her in action, she asked, "How've you been?"

She smiled, but there was a tightness to her voice. Like she wanted me to know she had her eye on me. Which made sense. Kelsey was protective of Brandon. A sister at heart, if not in name.

"To be honest," I said, "I was struggling for a bit. But I'm doing much better now."

Her face softened, and I clicked the shutter.

Once I filled my camera roll with photos, I headed back to the office, where Eric hooked me up with the Wi-Fi password. "Thanks," I said, frantically tapping away. "The doors are gonna open any minute now, huh?"

"T minus fifteen minutes," he said.

"How are you feeling?"

"Ready to do this." He was confident and calm, not a hint of the edginess Brandon displayed. "How are *you* feeling? Brandon told me you quit your job."

"I feel good. It's weird not working for Virtuality anymore. But it's a good kind of weird."

"Have you given any thought to what's next?"

I stopped tapping and shrugged. "I'm still trying to figure that out."

"Well, those small business owners I was telling you about, the ones who asked for your info? A lot of them'll be here tonight. If you're interested in picking up some freelance work, I can make some introductions. Seeing as you're no longer strangled by that moonlighting clause."

Oh, right. I could do whatever I wanted now. I was free to control my work schedule, rather than the other way around. This sudden realization had me smiling from ear to ear. "I'd love that, Eric. Thank you."

"No problem." He whirled around, nearly colliding with Brandon, who'd rushed into the room. "You doing okay, bro?"

"Yeah." He didn't look like he was doing okay. He actually looked a little pale. "There's someone out there asking for you, though. Says he's a reporter from the *Idyllwild Weekly*."

"Damn, I forgot he was coming early." He rushed out the door, leaving Brandon and me alone.

"How're you doing?" I asked, but he didn't answer. He just stared straight ahead, totally zoned out. "Brandon, are you okay?"

He shook his head, like he was clearing away a patch of fog. Then he looked at me, fear flashing in his gray eyes. "What if this is all a massive failure?"

I hurried toward him and pressed a comforting hand to his bicep. "It won't be. This place is beautiful, and it's going to be amazing."

"What if it's not?" Beads of sweat formed on his hairline. He swallowed once, twice, then said, "I've worked so hard. Put so much time and effort into building this. What if I made a mistake?"

His hands hung limp at his sides. I picked them up and said, "Close your eyes."

"What?"

"Close your eyes. Let's take some deep breaths together." He did what I said, following along with my slow counts of four. Inhale, exhale, again and again. "Now picture yourself in your happy place. The most relaxing place you can think of. Where it's calm and quiet and peaceful. No stress, no worries."

His eyelids began to flutter. I had a feeling I knew where he was thinking of—if not the exact location, then the general atmosphere—but ultimately I didn't need to know. Because wherever he was dreaming about, I was still standing right alongside him. Here, in my happy place.

Eric popped his head into the office. "Brandon? You okay?"

He opened his eyes and exhaled. His cheeks were pink. The moment had passed. "Yeah," he said. "I'm good now."

"We're about to unlock the door."

That look of panic dashed across his face again, but I squeezed his hands and whispered, "You've got this. It's going to be amazing. And I'm here for you, however you need me to be."

In an instant, the panic was gone. He pressed his body to mine and kissed me, and I savored every sensation. The soft, sweet taste of his lips. The warm, woodsy scent of his skin. The gentle thudding of his heartbeat. This was everything. This was mine.

Moments later, Mountain Air Brewpub was officially open for business.

Once the guests arrived, Brandon was in his element, all traces of nervousness gone. For the most part, I hung off to the side, drinking water and mocktails, exchanging quick kisses with him whenever he walked by. This was his show. I was simply his support system.

But every so often, Eric would call me over and introduce me to someone from town. The woman who owned the pottery shop, the couple who owned the toy store. I pitched ideas for their websites, which were met with enthusiastic grins. We exchanged contact information, and I made a mental note to order business cards as soon as I got home. *Happy Place Web Design* had a nice ring to it. Maybe I'd text Vimi and Ben to see what they thought of my new business name.

When I pulled out my phone, though, a text from Parisa stopped me in my tracks:

> I think we're gonna do it.

> City Hall. Next week.

> Wanna be our witness?

Wow. They were doing it. They were having the wedding they wanted, their way.

But as I gazed out into the treetops, inhaling the scent of pine and fresh mountain air, I realized I had a better idea.

> Why don't you get married in a happy place?

CHAPTER
THIRTY-TWO

It was a beautiful day for a wedding in Idyllwild.

The sun shimmered in the clear blue sky. Off in the distance, the San Jacinto Mountains peeked above the tops of the pine trees. There was a steady, soothing burble from the nearby brook, and the scent of cedar floated through the air.

Parisa and Mike got married on Saturday, June 26, the same date that had been printed on their expensive, elaborate wedding invitations. But the venue was no longer the Grand Palace Banquet Hall. Instead, we were standing in Brandon's backyard.

The bride was a sight to behold, a goddess descended from the clouds in her off-white, open-back gown, its chiffon train flowing along the green grass. There was no veil or headpiece, just a cascade of long dark curls falling freely over her shoulders. In her hands, she held a bouquet of wildflowers; Mike had picked them for her earlier that morning. She'd picked a wildflower for his boutonniere, too, which he'd pinned to his untucked linen shirt, right above his heart.

There were only three guests at this wedding: Abigail served as Mike's witness, I served as Parisa's, and Brandon was my date. Actually, there were four guests if you counted Hops, who lay at Brandon's feet and chased the occasional squirrel. The ceremony was performed by the managing director of the Idyllwild community theater—who just so happened to be an ordained minister.

She was also one of my new clients. She'd told me all about her side gig as a wedding officiant when we'd had our kickoff call to discuss the redesign of the theater's website. This past week, it seemed like half the town had contacted me to help them overhaul their web presence. Don't get me wrong; I was thrilled for the new business opportunities, but I hadn't said yes to everyone. Not just yet. I didn't want my schedule to fill up too quickly.

I needed some space for myself and for my feelings. For other people. And especially for Brandon.

"Parisa and Michael," the officiant declared, her hands swooping in a dramatic flourish, "you are officially married. You may now seal this union with a kiss."

The bouquet of flowers scattered to the ground as Parisa threw her arms around Mike—her husband!—and pressed her lips to his. I clapped softly, tears rolling freely down my cheeks. Because my best friend had found someone to spend the rest of her life with, someone who made her radiate joy. She was truly embarking on the adventure of a lifetime.

I felt the gentle pressure of Brandon's hands on my hips as he turned me around and brought me in close, his gray eyes burning into mine. When our mouths met, it was flint striking steel. And I thought maybe I'd finally made enough time on my schedule to have an adventure of my own.

ACKNOWLEDGMENTS

Writing a book is never easy (for me, at least), but writing a book during a pandemic has been unfathomably difficult. I never would've been able to do this without a lot of help from the following amazing people.

My editorial team: Maria Gomez and Angela James. Thank you both for seeing the potential in this story, for helping me to bring out the best in it, for respecting my voice, for inspiring me to connect with my emotions, and for being so understanding in a time when I felt like I was flailing.

My agent: Jessica Watterson. Thank you for your professional guidance, your emotional support, your industry insight, your authentic kindness, and your general badassery. Thanks for always believing in me, even when I'm not so sure I believe in myself.

I'm grateful for all my friends, who listen to my gripes and help me stay grounded. In particular, I'm thankful to my neighborhood friends who've kept me sane through months of homeschooling and existential dread: Cathy, Maren, Hollie, Stephanie, and Susanne.

My best friends love me for who I am and always want what's best for me. Marci and Jessica, you are my chosen family—my sisters at heart, if not in name. Thank you for everything.

Thanks to my rescue dog, Diffy, for being the best writing companion I could ever ask for.

Finally, thank you to the two guys who make my life complete: Andrew and Emilio. This book wouldn't exist without your unwavering love and support. I'm forever grateful for you.

ABOUT THE AUTHOR

Photo © 2016 Holly Rone

Kristin Rockaway is a native New Yorker and recovering corporate software engineer. After working in the IT industry for far too many years, she finally traded the city for the surf and chased her dreams out to Southern California, where she spends her days happily writing stories instead of code. You can find her on Instagram at @kristinrockaway and on her website at http://kristinrockaway.com.